The Secretive Wife

~

More Than a Wife Series

JENNIFER PEEL

*To those who have felt the pain of secrets,
whether they were yours to keep or to be kept from.*

*May you heal from
the crosses you've had to bear.*

*A special thanks to Kathryn Biel.
Your insight was invaluable. Thank you for sharing
your faith with me and helping me accurately and
respectfully portray it.*

Prologue

New York Times Best Sellers list in the eBook and paperback category—*Black Day Dawning.*

I rested my head on my hand and stared at the screen where my book cover was displayed next to the number two spot. Autumn Moone glared back at me. She had taken over my life. Sometimes it seemed like a battle raged within me and I wasn't sure who was calling the shots anymore. Now, more than ever, I was glad Peter and I had made the decision to keep Autumn Moone's real identity a secret when I was approached by my publishing house. Even so, I felt that I was slowly losing Delanie because of her.

Autumn even had me living in Barbie's dream house in a gated community. If the secret ever got out, we would need the security and privacy it would provide. The house was ironic, considering I wasn't allowed to have a Barbie growing up. My parental figures, Cat and Ron, believed they objectified women and gave girls eating disorders. To complete the ensemble, I now had a Ken doll to go with the perfect house. Though there was nothing plastic about Peter; he was as genuine as they came.

1

My grounding force, lover, best friend, and the reason I was in this mess, though I could hardly blame him.

It wasn't his fault a foul-mouthed, opinionated redhead fell deeply in love with him. Did I mention he had been a priest at the time? If there was a hell, I was probably going there. In my defense, I tried desperately to despise him for at least a few seconds. I had been taught growing up to always question people who looked to a higher power. Then Peter crashed my world.

I was volunteering at an impoverished school supported by his parish in Phoenix where many of the children spoke English as a second language, if at all. Being bilingual, I taught them English and helped with homework. The children spoke often of *el dulce padre*, the sweet father. Never once did they say, *sacerdote*, priest. Though I should have guessed, considering the type of school it was. That would have better prepared me. Those children were spot on, though. There was no one as sweet as him.

On the other hand, the first time we met, I was not sweet at all. I was emphatically expressing myself while assaulting one of the few paid teachers at the school, using all the swear words I knew in English and Spanish. She had embarrassed one of the teen girls in front of her peers by drawing attention to her mismatched shoes. Like the young woman had any choice in the matter. Poor thing spent the day crying in the bathroom. Once it came to my attention, I couldn't let it go. I found the teacher alone in her classroom and lectured her. My voice could carry if I needed it to, and carry it did. Peter, or Father Peter, walked in to see what the commotion was all about.

From the moment our eyes locked, he rendered me speechless. His green-as-a-painted-landscape eyes drew me in, making me want to color myself right into the portrait staring back at me. He couldn't speak either, but I think it was more out of fear. Think Anne of Green Gables letting Gilbert Blythe have it after slighting her.

"Can I be of some help?" Peter had asked.

My first thought was that I doubted a priest could be of much help; my second thought was how I wanted to help myself to the achingly beautiful man. Everything about him was perfect, from his angular cheeks to his golden-brown hair. But the clerical collar around his neck said he was already taken by his god. Peter was still hoping someday I'd become acquainted with his first love, but he had yet to introduce himself to me. Sometimes I worried that Peter would leave me for him, but I tried to push those thoughts out of my mind.

I had answered Peter's question that day with a profanity-laced tirade about hypocrites before I marched out of the room and straight to the shoe store to buy the humiliated teen girl matching shoes. When Peter found out what I had done for the girl, he came to find me. It was then that my love affair with him began. He never mentioned my vulgarity from the previous day, or the vine tattoo that ran the length of my arm, or even the shiny nose ring that seemed to distract him by how he stared at it. No, it was much worse, he asked my name and thanked me for my kindness. From that moment on, he and I began working together to provide all the children there with new shoes. We must have talked to every shoe manufacturer in the U.S. and every shoe store in the Phoenix area.

I began to crave our time together talking about Shakespeare and world affairs while acquiring one pair of shoes at a time. I was happy to have finally found someone who agreed with me that there was nothing romantic about the story of Romeo and Juliet. At the time, I was against most fictionalized romance stories. I found them cliché and nothing like the hard-hitting pieces I wrote for the different online news outlets I worked for, trying to scrape out a living. I used to ask myself why people cared *When Harry Met Sally*? They should have been worried that an enormous part of the world's population didn't have clean drinking water and that there were children with no shoes.

But then...then...Peter got to me in a way I never knew existed. He made me question everything Cat and Ron, even my professors, had taught me about people of faith. Peter not only lived what he taught, he embodied it. *El dulce padre* spread goodness wherever he went. In the months we spent there together, I watched the children at the school follow him around everywhere, and it wasn't only because of the candy he kept in his pockets. He dried eyes full of tears, helped solve math problems, played football with them in the field of dirt behind the school, sang songs, and pushed swings. Mostly, he gave those children hope that they could change their circumstances and that someone cared for them.

I was in awe of him. I wanted to be like him.

Teachers at the school began to talk, saying we spent too much time together and perhaps I was a bad influence on the good father. They thought his eyes lingered too long, or he stood too close. He began to distance himself from me. And I let him. I may have been a lot of things, but I never wanted to rob Peter of his innocence, or what—or should I say who—he loved the most. That was when Hunter Black came to life.

I stared at the end of my newly finished desk where my old red typewriter sat. I had poured my soul into it trying to purge myself of the priest, the man in black. Cat and Ron bought me the old red relic on my tenth birthday. I'd asked for a computer, but that was too commercial and normal. I was one big social experiment for them, and the gift of the ancient typewriter played right into another chapter of the book they were writing about parenting at the time. They patted themselves on the back when I was twelve and handed them my first manuscript titled, *My Life on the Moon.* I was always fascinated with the celestial orb. At times I wanted to live on the moon because I felt like I didn't belong where I was. Just like in my story, I thought for sure I had been misplaced and my real family lived on the moon.

Cat and Ron were decent people. I was always sheltered, fed, and clothed. But they never gave much affection. I once asked Cat if she loved me and she said she had every wish that I would grow up happy and well adjusted. Occasionally I got a side-hug from Ron. They were more worried about how many PhDs they could accumulate than paying attention to me. They believed in free-range parenting, and that it was better for me to learn from my mistakes and experiences than to be given guidance or to be spoiled by any of the wealth they had accumulated. While they took trips around the world, I took trips all over Portland, where I grew up. Cat and Ron generously, or so they thought, provided me with a bus pass and memberships to several museums. When I was older, I started finding myself more at the homeless shelters helping out. The people I served food to there were warmer to me than my own parents.

Was it any wonder Peter captured my heart?

I wanted the love I felt when I was near him. I wanted the love of the family he spoke of so much. To have a real mom and dad. Since then I've had to rethink that, well, at least with his mother, Sarah. I've been pretty sure Joseph, his father, was fond of me, but was too afraid to show it in front of the b—, I mean, my mother-in-law. I was trying to stop using the words that made my husband do his best not to cringe when they came flying out of my mouth on a semi-regular basis. He'd never once asked me not to, but he always smiled when I substituted something else mid-profanity. I loved his smile.

I'd enjoyed the occasions when only Joseph had come to visit us. Once he held my hand while we watched the mind-numbing sports all the Deckers seemed to love. My relationship with Joseph was another secret I'd had to keep. I was good at keeping them. Just ask the Barbie under my bed I had growing up that was never discovered.

My husband even began as a secret, one-sided love affair, or so I thought. *A Black Heart*, my first published novel, was pounded out key by key as I tried to get over him. The sound of the typebars hitting the ribbon and paper soothed my heart while it bled out on the paper. Hunter Black embodied every good quality Peter had, except his physical appearance. Not that I expected the book to go anywhere, but how he looked I kept to myself. Instead, I gave him Peter's best friend Reed's physical attributes. Peter had spoken of him so often, I looked him up on social media. It was awkward now that he would soon be marrying my sister-in-law, Sam. How was I supposed to know that Sam would get divorced and marry the younger man? Not even she saw that coming. And I never thought I would know any of them. Peter loved to tease me about it now. One of our inside jokes.

Hunter Black's best friend, Laine, represented me. Hunter and Laine were meant to be together, but the timing never worked out for them, except for once, briefly. Even now, six books later, their timing hadn't quite gotten there. Family issues and secrets were now keeping them apart. Laine, like me, was a good secret keeper and, like me, she had her reasons. In the end, though, I knew when Hunter discovered all the reasons why Laine kept her secrets, he'd be understanding. It would all work out. After all, Peter was the most understanding of men.

But like I said, I could blame Peter for this secret life I led in our attic. The attic he had finished especially for me in our new home. I had no idea publishing *A Black Heart* under my pen name, Autumn Moone, would lead to this. I stared back at my screen again and the accolade that shouted back at me. I had only hoped for some extra income, being a starving writer who had frequently given every extra bit of money I had to the children both Peter and I loved. I got more than I ever bargained or hoped for out of the deal. More money than I ever imagined, and now a foundation called Sweet Feet that bought children's shoes for those in need all over the country. Most importantly, I got my man in black.

Apparently, the distance we had placed between us wasn't enough. Peter asked to be reassigned to another diocese months earlier, unbeknownst to me. In what we both thought was the last time we would ever see each other, he admitted why he was leaving. He had come to have feelings for me. He apologized for his transgression. I begged him to never be sorry for it and confessed to being in love with him. I'll never forget the shock in his green eyes, like he never fathomed the possibility. That was before he fled, sprinting down the hall. I thought it was the last time I would ever see him. I went home to my apartment and mourned like I had only one other time. There was no pain that compared to losing someone you loved, no matter the relation.

My first loss, years earlier, would be lasting. Losing Peter, though painful, was short-lived, even though at the time it seemed like forever. From the way he tells it, once he left me for what we both thought was the final time, he talked to God all night, first asking Him for forgiveness for allowing himself to fall in love with me. Yes, he had fallen in love with me too. Then he asked for guidance. He wanted a sign to know whether he had chosen the right path for himself. When he arose in the morning he had not received any answer until he walked by the office in the church. The women who worked there were discussing a shoe sale. One of the women was particularly excited about a red pair for her daughter. He said, for him, it was like divine inspiration. His calling was to be with me, the redhead who was passionate about children having shoes.

According to my husband, he had never received such a clear answer. It was then he sought permission from his superiors to be officially laicized. Meanwhile, I quit volunteering at the school. I couldn't bear being there knowing he left because of me. Instead, I poured all my energy into finishing my novel and doing my best to forget about him, trying to tell myself it was for the best. Even if Peter hadn't vowed to live a celibate life, he wouldn't have wanted a woman like me, who broke almost all the rules he lived his life by.

But amazingly, he did.

Three months later he found me at the college I attended at night working on my master's degree. I almost dropped my green tea when I saw him walk into the student union building in jeans and a T-shirt. His nervous smiled beamed at me from across the room. I stood frozen, unable to breathe, thinking it couldn't be him. It wasn't until he was inches from me that I let myself believe it was truly him and not my imagination.

"What are you doing here?" I stared into his beautiful eyes, amazed.

When his shaky hand reached up and rested briefly on my cheek I knew then something had changed. "I have a story to tell you," he said.

I took him back to my place, since he had no place of his own, for probably the most awkward first date ever, if you could call it that. I still smiled thinking of how uncomfortable he was and how he sat far away from me on the opposite side of the couch. He kept rubbing his neck where the clerical collar no longer rested as he told me what had transpired during our time apart. I could tell he missed it. Sometimes I wondered if he still did.

"Are you sure about all this?" I had asked.

He gazed at me for the longest time before answering, "You are my choice."

It was then I decided I should probably tell him about my story, the one I had written about him, which was just starting to take off at the time. I spent most of the first night reading it out loud to him. I loved watching Peter blush during the more intimate moments. I didn't know men could blush. Finally, right before we said goodbye for the night, he asked if he could kiss my cheek. It was an easy yes. No man had ever asked that or ever wanted so little of me physically. But the little he asked of me made me realize that he wanted so much more.

It took him several attempts before his lips landed on my cheek, but once they made contact, I knew my life would never be the same. Every tender feeling imaginable was felt in that simple kiss on the cheek. His lips only lingered for seconds, but he left a life-changing impression.

We eloped two short months later. Our honeymoon was spent driving to Chicago in my old compact car. We only had enough money between us to cover our living expenses for a few weeks and the first month's rent and deposit on an apartment. We had tossed aside reason for the dream of being together and being part of a family, like I'd always wanted. The one I thought so long ago waited for me on the moon. It was the best road trip ever, stopping at every point of interest during the day, and at night getting to know each other in every way on our old air mattress that served as our first bed.

I looked around my office now, my secret hiding place Peter had built me. Times had certainly changed for us in the four years since that long drive. We were unsure of what the future held, other than the promise of being together. Four years ago, I couldn't have imagined this office with the counter desk piled high with my current research running alongside one wall, and the built-in bookshelves lining the opposite one. This space was as big as the first apartment we lived in. A lot nicer too. Peter took such care handcrafting each piece of furniture when he finished the room. He took such great care of me. No one worked harder than him, even though he didn't have to anymore. Yet five to six days a week he was working for his dad's landscaping business, coming home tired and dirty. He did it for more than just keeping our secret safe. He did it because he wanted to be a contributor, a provider. That, and I don't think he enjoyed the profanity-laced rap music that at times blared from my office while I worked. Rap was my preferred inspirational music. On occasion the Beatles or Elton John made it on my playlist. They were Peter's preference.

I gave the screen one more glance before looking above my computer at the framed posters of each one of my books to hit number one on the *New York Times* Best Sellers list. Peter would get an actual copy of the *New York Times Book Review*, blow it up, and frame it. Until our recent move, they had been hidden under our bed. Now all five were proudly displayed on the wall. Soon, I knew there would be six, if my latest climbed one more spot as my publisher, LH Ink, predicted it would.

For now, I had to protect the life Peter and I had made. I didn't want the fame or baggage that came with it. But sometimes the secrets that we kept felt heavier than the consequences we might reap if they were ever discovered. The frightening part was never knowing what those consequences might be. Which was a good incentive to stay quiet.

Chapter One

I HAVE SOME NEWS, I texted, just in case Peter was with his brother, dad, or even at the office.

Did you take the test?

I didn't need to see him or hear his voice to know the hope and excitement that went into those words. I ran my hand across my smooth abdomen. I was afraid it would forever remain flat. It's why I hadn't taken the pregnancy test yet even though my period was two days late. I'd been late before, and disappointed.

Not yet.

My phone buzzed. I turned down the music before answering. "Hey, there."

"I'm sorry."

"What are you sorry for?"

"I realized you wouldn't text me with that kind of news and I remembered you always look on Monday." For some reason I couldn't look on Sunday when *The New York Times Book Review* came out. I felt like it would jinx it somehow, or perhaps I was proving to myself that I was more than Autumn Moone.

"How did *Black Day Dawning* fare?" the most considerate husband asked.

"Are you alone?"

He chuckled. "I'm in my truck waiting for James, but even if I wasn't, I've heard more about your book at work the last few weeks than I do at home. Sam and Avery still can't get over it."

I smiled thinking about my sisters-in-law, who might love Hunter Black more than me, and who always got advanced copies from my other self. "She made it to number two."

"Congratulations, baby, next week it will be number one."

"We'll see."

"You sound down, are you okay?"

I sighed audibly. "Just deadlines looming and...I'm nervous."

"Delanie, no matter what the test says, it doesn't change what we have together."

"I know, but I know how much you want that second line to appear." I did too.

"I want you, plain and simple. Though you are neither."

"Are you saying I'm complicated?"

"I'm saying you're worth figuring out."

"Nice way to spin that."

He laughed. "I'm getting pretty good at this husband thing."

"You do okay," I teased. "Why don't you come home for lunch and we can work on our husband and wife skills together?" That I was not teasing about.

"Mmm. I wish I could, but James and I have to finish the Finley job this week. They're hosting a large party for their company this weekend at their home and we're behind schedule because of the rain last week. But how about I take you to dinner tonight to celebrate? Pick any place."

"Even sushi?" I could picture his scrunched face.

"Even sushi." He was doing his best to hold back his disgust. One of my favorites was his least favorite.

"I'll think about it and let you know," I partially acquiesced for his benefit.

"Honestly, pick anywhere." Bravery threaded his statement.

I laughed at my sweet but masochistic husband. "Okay, I'll see you tonight."

"Can't wait."

"Peter, thank you."

"For what?"

"Always being unselfish."

"You're wrong; I'm very selfish when it comes to you. Love you."

He hung up, leaving me breathless. Four years together and he could still get to me. And I do believe Hunter Black had a new line to use on Laine. That was if I could ever get them together for good. Hunter's mother was a bit of a pain. She may or may not resemble a certain someone who wished I'd never married her son. My blood pressure rose thinking about dear Sarah, who swore up and down I was a drug dealer with possible ties to the mob.

She was partially right. I dealt with the most addictive emotion there was—love—and I had mobs of fans who ruled my life. If only Sarah knew the truth. Avery and Sam had convinced her to start reading my books, and though she said they were a little too spicy, she enjoyed them. I think she more than enjoyed them—she read the first five books in three weeks. And I'd noticed her being more affectionate to my father-in-law the last few Sundays during dinner. That was the power of a good romance novel. Now if only they could get her to like me, or at least not scowl at me or make underhanded comments. True, sometimes I provoked her. I could only take so much.

Maybe I laid on the PDA a little too thick around her and I made sure that I wore sleeveless shirts and dresses so the tattoo that was visible to the world was proudly displayed. If only she knew about the tattoo for Peter's eyes only. If she wasn't careful I might let slip where it was. And my diamond nose stud might get an upgrade. I wasn't sure which she hated more, the nose ring or the tattoo. Probably me in general. To her, I would always be the woman who seduced her baby boy and ripped him away from his true calling. It was one thing Sarah and I agreed on. Peter could tell her until he was blue in the face that was false, but it would be a waste of his breath. Except I wanted to believe Peter when he told me I was his calling. Most of the time I did.

I took a deep, cleansing breath. I wasn't writing any evil mother scenes today and needed to get Sarah out of my head. This seventh and final installment of the Hunter Black saga was proving to be difficult. I wanted the series to wrap up in a satisfying yet true-to-the-characters way. Hunter and Laine deserved their happy ending, but it had to be fluid and believable. They were facing what seemed like insurmountable opposition. Not only did Hunter's mother despise Laine, but now she blamed Laine for the death of Hunter's father in the last book, and Hunter was torn about it.

Laine was innocent, even a martyr in the situation, but she was keeping the truth hidden to protect Hunter and his family's reputation. When he was alive, Hunter's father had two sides to him. The world's best father, husband, revered landowner and mayor was the side he portrayed quite cleverly. Then there was his dark side littered with shady business deals, drugs, and a woman or two who wasn't his wife. Laine, or should I say off-duty Officer Laine Cavanaugh, caught him with one of those women on a dark road. She recognized the Jaguar and thought Mr. Black was in some sort of trouble. He was, but it was the kind that ruined not only you, but everyone you loved. The woman he was with fled the scene and left Laine to deal with an inebriated Mr. Black.

Against her better judgment, she decided to take Mr. Black back to her place and sober him up while shaking some sense into him. Mr. Black began confessing all his sins in Laine's car. Forged documents, infidelity, blackmail, and coercion—enough information that an officer of the law should investigate. But Laine's main concern was for Hunter, her best friend and the man she'd loved since she was sixteen. She knew even then she could never have the man born into privilege. Her life had been anything but privileged. Ghosts from her past still haunted her, though she had done her best to leave behind the poverty and terror of her youth.

Laine began to question if Mr. Black's privilege and wealth were only a façade. She knew all too well the damage one rich man who thought he was above the law could do. She still bore the physical and mental scars from one such man. In her anger, she went on a tirade directed toward Mr. Black. He didn't appreciate the lecture Laine gave him about what this would do to Hunter if he ever found out that his hero had fallen well below the pedestal Hunter placed him on. In anger, Mr. Black grabbed Laine's steering wheel, causing them to veer into the other lane of oncoming traffic. Laine wrenched back control before they hit another vehicle, but in her attempt to spare more lives, she hit the median and her car flipped. Mr. Black didn't survive, and Laine inherited more scars.

The sixth book ended with Laine in the hospital, Hunter by her side holding her hand. She was barely conscious enough to hear Hunter confess how much he loved her.

Fans of Hunter and Laine were going crazy online over that final scene. Fan boards had blown up wondering what would happen in the last book. Would Laine tell Hunter about his father? For now, she was letting Mr. Black's secrets die with him as much as she could. She couldn't stand the thought of breaking Hunter's heart, but it was breaking his heart in other ways. Gossip ran wild in their Montana town about what really happened the night of the accident. The release of Mr. Black's toxicology report caused even more rumors to swirl around an innocent Laine. Mrs. Black was doing her best to paint Laine as a liar and going as far as saying she was a cold-blooded killer. Hunter was caught in the middle of it all. But Laine felt if he had any doubts about who she was, then there was no future for them.

It was all so dramatic, but my readers ate it right up. At least most of them. The more popular the series had become, the more detractors I had gained. Some days I dealt with that better than others. Peter had begged me to stop reading reviews. Joan my agent/lawyer, and Fiona my assistant, even tried filtering them for me and only sending good ones, or those that had actual constructive criticism rather than those wishing me a painful death, questioning my moral compass, or if I had even graduated from high school. I had a Master of Fine Arts degree, thank you very much. People took fiction way too seriously, and sometimes I took the bad reviews too personally. As much as any critic or reviewer thought they knew who Autumn Moone was, they had no idea. This I could tell you—she was a living, breathing person with feelings, feelings she felt so deeply at times it scared her.

There was the rumor that Autumn Moone wasn't a real person, only a marketing scheme by my publisher. An actual website had been created and dedicated to proving that each book in the series was written by a different author. They pointed to discrepancies in writing styles between the books and how the voices of the characters changed. That site gave me a lot to laugh about. I wondered if it ever occurred to them that not only had my characters evolved like they should have, but that my skills as a writer had grown. Or at least I'd hoped they had.

I sighed. I supposed I should get back to work. The first draft of *Black Confessions* was due in October and we were already into August.

But first, I needed my Sam fix for the day. I typed thesidelinedwife.com into my browser. Sam was probably one of the most hilarious people I knew, besides Peter's grandma, Mimsy, who thought throwing holy water was a sport. No one appreciated her favorite pastime, per se, but I had to say I hoped I would be that spirited at her age. Like her, I didn't mind making people cringe from time to time. She was another person I thought might appreciate me if it wasn't for her daughter, my mother-in-law.

Oh, well. I knew Sam did and it meant the world to me, even if I couldn't properly articulate it. Keeping such big secrets meant keeping emotions guarded. Even Peter, at times, had to guess at my feelings, though I tried to be open with him. When he said I was complicated, he wasn't exaggerating. I had to unlearn years of emotional neglect from my parents. Toss in a couple of heart-shattering experiences, and now being in a family where I felt like I didn't belong, plus my secret life, and it created the perfect storm that I hid from in my protective shell. Peter had to coax me out of it more often than I wished upon him. I hated feeling like I didn't belong. I had felt that way most of my life. And more than anything, I feared having to give up those who belonged to me.

I shook my insecurities out of my head and focused on Sam, who had inspired me to be better by the way she bravely shared her own insecurities with the world. She had no idea how her heart-wrenching and poignant blog posts had helped me. Today's post was no different. It started with a question.

What do you get the man who has everything for his wedding to his pregnant twenty-year-old nanny? I'm asking for a friend.

Some of the posted answers were off-the-chart crude, even for me, but some were hilarious:

A vasectomy.

A good lawyer.

A prenup.

She and her followers had me belly laughing in my seat. I already knew that her ex-husband, Neil, was apparently hell-bent to be the classic midlife crisis. Sam, Avery, and I had discussed at length this latest development yesterday at Sunday dinner after everyone else left the table. Sam had been suspicious Neil was cheating on Roxie, the woman he cheated on Sam with and had a baby with last year. Honestly, we all saw this coming when he hired Kimmy to be his nanny several months ago. Not only was she young, but she was eager, and I do mean eager. She screamed *I'm looking to be your next mistake.* The entire situation was a mistake and knee jerk reaction, in my opinion. Neil couldn't stand the thought of Sam marrying Reed and moving on. So, in a stomach-churning move, considering he was close to fifty and the girl was barely out of her teens, he sealed his creep status by proposing to Kimmy and pushed his son Cody even further away. My poor nephew was vowing to never see his father again.

More drama than in my books. The saying *truth is stranger than fiction* was alive and well in the lives of the Decker family. You had Sam, who was engaged to a man she once babysat and to her mother's dismay wasn't married yet and a grandma who told scintillating—bordering on titillating—stories about the assisted living home where she stayed. And if that wasn't enough, they were all related to one of the most famous women in America. Now, no one would believe that.

Chapter Two

PLEASE, PLEASE, I begged the white stick of torture—a more accurate description than *pregnancy test*—resting on our bathroom counter. I'd lost track of how many of them I had urinated on. I closed my eyes and breathed deeply, counting the seconds in my head. I had one hundred more to go. Two minutes mixed with a drop of hope and a healthy dose of bargaining, just in case Peter was right about God.

If you are really there, I promise to give up swearing for at least a month. Okay, the entire pregnancy. I meant business.

I promise to try to not be snarky to Father Alan when I attend RCIA classes. Unbeknownst to my husband, I was secretly attending Rites of Christian Initiation for Adults. I didn't want to get his hopes up that I would convert to his faith or have any faith at all, but for him, I wanted to at least try to see what it was all about. Many Wednesday nights saw me driving two towns away to annoy and perhaps amuse my second favorite priest. I had a feeling Father Alan kind of enjoyed my cynicism. He said I kept him on his toes and he hadn't heard such colorful language in a long time.

Please do it for Peter. Even if I don't believe, he does. How many prayers does he have to offer up? Please.

One hundred eighteen, one hundred nineteen...

I opened one eye to peek, zeroing in on the stark white test against the dark granite. The other eye opened, brimming with tears. Negative. Again.

In the worst timing ever, I heard the door from the garage leading into our mudroom close and the voice I loved more than any sound. He was early.

"Hey, baby, I'm home."

I wiped my eyes and quickly disposed of the damn test. Swearing was back on. I took some deep breaths to compose myself. I began twisting my long red hair like that's what my real reason for being in the bathroom was, hoping he wouldn't notice the red blotches my creamy skin broke out in when I was upset.

Peter was quick to find me. He slid open the wood-framed etched glass bathroom door all smiles until he caught my reflection in the mirror above my sink. His eyes darted toward my blotched, bare shoulders and chest.

I faked a smile. "Hi. You're home early."

His eyes narrowed while he approached me in his dirt-stained Decker and Sons Landscaping T-shirt and khaki shorts. "You okay?"

I nodded through the mirror, afraid to meet his actual eyes. The concern they reflected was going to be my undoing.

He pressed a kiss to my neck. "What's wrong?"

I let my hair fall out of the twist. "I'm fine."

He met my eyes again in the mirror. "You only say that when you're not."

I stared into those green eyes that yearned to understand me. They always promised a safe landing. My own eyes betrayed me with a sheen of moisture. "I took the test."

He spun me around and drew me to him.

I buried my head in his chest while he stroked my hair. I soaked in not only his comfort but the smell I had come to associate with him. It was a combination of perspiration, his spicy cologne, and a touch of sod and dirt. For some it might be considered a little gamey, but I couldn't get enough of it. Of him.

I stifled my tears the best I could while clinging to him.

He kissed the top of my head. "We have to quit doing this to ourselves."

I leaned away to meet his warm eyes, still in the comfort of his arms. "You don't want to have a baby?"

Tenderness filled his features while he took a moment before answering. "I do, but not at the expense of you or us."

I tilted my head. "What do you mean?"

"I mean," he leaned down and brushed my lips with his, "no more tracking your cycle and taking ovulation tests. We aren't going to wait on bated breath every month to see if your period starts." He picked me up and set me on the counter.

I wrapped my long legs around his body. My arms fell around his neck.

He pressed his body against mine. "When we make love, from now on it's only going to be about us in the moment. No more *what if this is the time.*" He nuzzled my neck. "You are all I need."

I ran my fingers through his hair and tried to take solace in his words. "Are you sure? Maybe we could get one of those handmaidens your people were fond of in the bible," I teased.

He leaned back with a smile in his eyes. "My people?"

"All those men who talked to God. Didn't they all get handmaidens when their wives couldn't conceive?"

"I don't know where you are getting your information from, my dear wife, but those handmaidens were given to their husbands by their wives, and more often than not, it caused a lot of trouble."

"I know I would want to claw her eyes out and probably maim you if you ever touched another woman like that."

"Like this?" He captured my lips and hungrily parted them, no longer the man who was nervous about kissing my cheek.

My legs tightened around him. All my emotions poured into him.

He groaned and kissed me deeper, taking his time not to leave any territory in my mouth unexplored. It was a frequent travel destination of his and he knew it all by heart. Each prod and taste of him made my heart race.

Still, I couldn't help but wonder. I placed my hand on his cheeks, pushing pause on the passion. "Are you sure?" I peered into his green eyes, so alive with passion.

"I definitely don't want a handmaiden." His semi-wicked grin appeared. It could never be fully wicked. He was too good.

"You were never getting one," I whispered.

"I would never want one." He leaned his forehead against mine. "Delanie, you are my life."

I ran my hand across his stubbled cheek. "We could...*adopt*." I always had trouble saying the word.

"Let's put a pin in that thought until the end of year."

I wondered if his reluctance came from fear of the process or if he sensed my hesitation. I wasn't brave enough to ask.

"Okay. I love you."

"My favorite words." He picked me up off the counter, trailing kisses across my cheek.

"Where are you taking me?" I tried to be coy, but I knew it was probably one of two places.

"I would like your company in the shower."

That was my first guess.

Lying in his arms, I traced circles around his smooth, bare chest, breathing in the clean scent of his bar soap. I still reveled in listening to the strong, steady beat of his heart and the feel of his defined muscles shaped by manual labor. His calloused fingers glided down my arm. A contented sigh escaped his lips.

"Was this your way of getting out of sushi?"

A deep laugh rumbled in his chest. "I should have thought about that. I guess it worked out, though."

I playfully smacked his chest.

"You want to go now?" he offered.

It had been dark for a while and was well past dinnertime. "I think it's another night of cereal." That's how I cooked dinner.

He breathed a sigh of relief.

"We can go tomorrow."

"Of course," he groaned.

It was my turn to laugh. "I look forward to it."

"Me too," he lied.

"Uh-huh." I kissed his chest before I sat up and ran my fingers through my damp, tangled hair.

Peter admired me in the semi-dark room. "My T-shirts have never looked so good."

I rested my head on my pulled-up knees and smiled down at him. "Thanks to you, I haven't bought pajamas in four years."

He turned to his side and rested his head on his propped hand. "It's been entirely my pleasure."

I ruffled his mussed hair. "Do you want Cocoa Pebbles or Frosted Flakes?"

"Probably both, but first I'd like you to think about something."

"What's up?"

He gave me his most charming smile. "I was thinking it would be nice if we had my family over to give them a tour of our new house."

I did my best, which wasn't good at all, to hide the disgust on my face. I knew who he meant by "family." While my mother-in-law tried to be nicer to me in front of Peter after the blow-up last fall, I wasn't buying it for a minute. I don't think my sweet Peter was either, but family was important to him, so he tried to keep the peace whenever he could.

"Avery and Sam have been here. Twice, actually," I responded. They loved it, though I knew they wondered how we afforded our beautiful home, even if it was the smallest in the neighborhood. It's not like Peter and I wanted such a nice place, but we had to think of security and eventualities just in case my worst nightmare happened and our secret got out. I mean, I still drove my crappy seven-year-old sedan. Money meant nothing to me other than we could fund our shoe and water charities.

Avery and Sam were smart enough to question if my job working for the online magazine my publisher owned under a different name paid well enough. It didn't, but it gave me a great platform to bring attention to the causes near and dear to my heart, like clean water for everyone and the mutilation of women and girls around the globe. Plus, it was a legitimate cover. It allowed me to be truthful when I told people I was a writer and content manager, even though doing both jobs was taxing.

The charm in his smile turned strained. "Ma would really like to come see it too."

My face contorted in disbelief while I scoffed. "Your mother, who declared I was selling drugs to pay for it and that she would never step foot inside this house of cards?"

"Did she say that?" He played innocent while reaching up and tucking some hair behind my ear. "I know she's not the easiest person to get along with and she's been unfair to you. But she's trying, and maybe this is a chance to start mending some fences."

My eyebrows shot up. "Unfair?"

"How about awful?"

"You're getting warmer."

"Baby, please?"

He asked so very little of me. I hated to say no, even though his mother was determined to hate me no matter what I did, and the thought of her here gave me metaphorical hives. And I was suspicious as to why she wanted to visit after being so adamant about never coming over. She only came to our apartment once, and thankfully I wasn't home at the time. I closed my eyes and let out heavy breaths.

Peter did his best to coax me by sitting up and brushing kisses along my neck.

"I'm above your powers of persuasion now," I said between shivers.

He didn't believe a word I said and inched up toward my lips where he skillfully skimmed them. "We'll have everyone over at the same time just in case you need a buffer."

"Just in case?"

"Let me rephrase, so you will have a buffer."

"She's going to badger us about how we can afford it and she's going to criticize our lack of furniture. In between that, she'll make underhanded comments about how I don't feed you well enough and how she read that tattoo ink gives you cancer. Though she'll be praying that last part is true." She had said it under the guise of trying to be helpful a couple of weeks ago, but I saw the evil glint her in eye.

"She doesn't wish you dead," he said with no confidence at all. "And I'm a grown man. I don't need my wife to feed me, nor do I expect her to."

"Which is lucky for you."

"I am a lucky man."

I placed my hands on his cheeks and took a deep breath. "Stop being so wonderful."

"So, is that a yes?"

"Peter."

"I know." He took my hands from off his face and kissed them. "It would mean a lot to me." He cinched it right there.

"All right, but it could get ugly if she asks me to submit to a drug test...again."

He chuckled. "She won't, I promise."

I wanted to believe that.

Chapter Three

$\mathcal{I}$F STARING AT a blank screen was a contest, I would be the champion. Scenes filled with dialogue always took longer than I liked, but words had meaning. Saying the wrong word could affect the entire story. Just like in real life, one should always be careful to say what one means and mean what one says. It was important that the conversations between Hunter and Laine be precise and not give too much away too soon. The right amount of tension had to be created, all while making it natural. In real life, fights aren't scripted, which means they're messy. In books, that same feeling needed to come across.

While I thought about how to craft Laine's response to Hunter after he basically accused her of lying about how the car accident happened, I did something against the best interest of my mental health. I pulled up one of my biggest critic's website, blaring Eminem as I went and letting Hunter's words stew in my mind, *You must be remembering wrong. My father would never hurt you.*

Hunter refused to believe his father caused the accident that killed him and severely hurt Laine. He wanted to think it was because Laine had a concussion. Laine wanted to blurt the truth, but that was a risk in and of itself. If he didn't believe her about the accident, he probably wouldn't believe her about the second life Mr. Black led, even though she had proof. But she also wanted to protect Hunter. Mr. Black was dead now. What good would it do to ruin a dead man's reputation other than hurting those who still lived?

I should have been reasonable and not searched Ms.-I-Hate-Books's site. Seriously, I'm not sure why this woman kept reading my books—or any books for that matter. If she ever gave a good review, it was for books everyone else abhorred. Yet she had thousands of followers and at times was quoted by notable sites and other popular critics. Peter and Joan sounded in my head not to torture myself, but I knew sooner or later a nasty quote from her would pop up and slap me in the face. Better to just get it over with. I mean, how much worse could she get than last time when she called *A Black Night* the perfect cure for insomnia?

It didn't take me long to find her review of *Black Day Dawning*. She was reaching new heights of nastiness. The title of her review was, *Reading This Book was Indeed a Black Day.* My sanity begged me to stop there. I should have listened.

In Ms. Moone's latest overpriced excuse for literature, you will find yourself reading a train wreck in slow motion. It ran out of steam on the very first page. The chemistry between the supposed hero and heroine was more like a bad case of puppy love with a side of does-anyone-really-care-about-these-two. But if you are looking for a good doormat, then Laine is your girl and doesn't disappoint. She seems willing at every turn to let Hunter walk all over her without consequence...

The rest of the review was more of the same. I was seething. How dare she call Laine a doormat. She was anything but. She had been through hell and was tough as nails. Sure, Hunter was an idiot around her at times, but that was because she confused him. He loved her, but he feared losing their friendship and losing her.

I got up and paced around my office, breathing heavily as I went. Who did this woman who only went by the name of Grace think she was?

She was neither gracious nor graceful. She wouldn't know a good love story if it bit her in the a—...dammit, I meant butt! Both Avery and Sam thought Laine and Hunter's chemistry was off-the-charts hot, as did at least a million other fans.

My phone buzzed on my desk. I was amazed I heard it over the music and the diatribes coursing through my head. I picked it up to find it was Joan. I grinned. It was fitting she would call now. The first time I talked to her, she was in the same kind of dark mood I was in now. She had answered the phone, "What in the hell do you want?" I knew then she was the lawyer for me. She'd mistaken my number for her ex-boy-friend's. We still laughed about it to this day. She had become a trusted friend and confidant. It was why she was my agent and lawyer. I learned quickly there were many willing to take advantage of you, and Joan could sniff them out in a nanosecond. And could she ever work out a deal.

I turned down my music and put her on speaker. "Hello," I growled, not on purpose. It was a residual effect.

"Let me guess, you're reading reviews again."

I threw myself in my chair. "Guilty."

"Why do you keep doing this to yourself?"

"I think I have impostor syndrome."

She laughed a deep-throated laugh that matched her sultry alto voice perfectly. "What in the hell is that? And please tell me it's not contagious."

I rubbed my hands over my face. "I feel like one day everyone is going to figure out I have no idea what I'm doing, and they will all agree with the Graces of the world."

"You know that's a crock, right? Do you think everyone is given seven-figure advances? Thank you, by the way. My new Porsche loves me."

I rolled my eyes. "You're welcome."

"Oh, don't get all high and mighty on me. I donated a nice sum to Sweet Feet."

"You're a saint," I teased. "But, really, thank you."

"Don't get all sappy on me, kid."

"You're barely old enough to have given birth to me."

"When you're in your late forties, you can start calling everyone kid."

I laughed at her. "Is there a reason for your call?"

"I just thought you would want to know that the first few chapters you sent to me were bloody brilliant."

"Really?"

"I wouldn't lie to you. You're my meal ticket."

"There's that."

"Del, get those haters' voices out of your head. You're the real deal. Those women with bad bangs who obviously have nothing better to do than read all day and criticize people while surrounding themselves with a million cats are lonely and miserable. You should feel sorry for them."

I don't know how she came up with bad bangs, but I appreciated her attempts to cheer me up. "Yeah, I'll work on that."

"Forget them. Way more people love your books than hate them. Don't let the negative reviews outshine the overwhelming positive ones."

"That's what Peter says."

"Listen to him."

"I'll try."

"Now get back to work. I'm looking at a townhome on the Upper East Side today and it's not cheap. Hugs and kisses." She hung up.

I stared at my phone for a moment. Joan sparked a thought. I swiveled my chair so I was facing my computer.

"Hunter, there is a long list of people in this town who've never believed me or in me. I always hoped you would never be one of them. If you can't trust my word by now, then maybe it's time," her voiced cracked, "that we finally prove to everyone they were right about us. We don't belong together."

My heart broke for Laine. A tear leaked down my cheek. Another chapter down. Now off to have lunch with Sam and Avery. At least one meal I ate today wouldn't be cereal.

I stopped by a deli I frequented and picked up salads to take to the office where almost everyone in the Decker family worked. Though I wondered how long Sam would continue to do so. She only worked part time as it was, and now that the Sidelined Wife was so lucrative, it seemed to only be a matter of time before she quit. Not to mention she was planning a wedding. Well, sort of. Her mom was planning it and Sam was doing her best to put it off, which seemed odd. She and Reed were inseparable, and I thought for sure they would both be eager to tie the knot. I knew Reed wanted to sign that NDA, the one she mentioned in her most talked about post about making her next husband sign a non-disclosure agreement before he could see her naked. It was pure gold. Reed was ready to get down to business and was practically groping her at every family function whenever Cody wasn't in their presence. Sam didn't seem to mind one bit. Sometimes I wondered if...well...I wondered if Sam was going against her mother's wishes and...let's just say Sam was glowing a lot more the last few weeks and Reed was over-the-top happy. Peter said it was none of our business when I brought it up, and he didn't want to think about his sister that way.

When I arrived at Decker and Sons Landscaping on the outskirts of Clearfield, the sleepy town we all lived in, my sisters-in-law looked relieved that I had bought lunch. No one, including me, trusted my cooking skills. Peter tried and was lucky I hadn't given him food poisoning yet. It was bound to happen. My good husband and his brother were not there. Too bad. There was something about the way Peter looked when he was sweaty and dirty that was quite inspirational. I supposed I would have to wait until later that night to be inspired. Except he probably wouldn't be home by the time I left to volunteer at the shelter before I headed to my "class."

My cover for attending the RCIA classes with Father Alan was I was helping at a women's shelter. Which was true. I always dropped off bags of food, clothing, and diapers before I headed to my class. Most of the time I also helped with things like writing resumes, organizing donations, playing with the children, even vacuuming if needed.

I guess missing Peter gave me something to look forward to tomorrow. I was going to need something since his family was all coming over to tour our home tomorrow night and have dessert—meaning store-bought ice cream, and if we got real fancy, hot fudge. There was a good chance I would burn that in the microwave, though.

Avery and Sam smiled at me when I arrived, and both got up to hug me. They were both huggers. It took me a while to get used to it, but now I found I looked forward to it, even if I tensed up every time we touched. It wasn't in my nature, or was it that I wasn't nurtured like that? Probably both. Peter was the exception. I melted into him after that awkward first date where he was the stiff one.

They both looked amazing. Sam had gotten a new shorter haircut that really made her dark curls standout. It was sexy and fun, and she had been exercising like crazy. She said she needed to get naked skinny. I would say mission accomplished. I was certain Reed didn't care; he would take her in any shape or form. And by the way she was glowing, I had my aforementioned suspicions. Avery had just finished her third marathon and was looking fierce and fit with her blonde ponytail. She didn't look old enough to have a senior in high school this year. You would never see me running a marathon unless my mother-in-law was chasing me with a sharp object. Maybe I should start training now.

"I'm sorry I'm a little late." I placed the bag of food on Avery's desk where we always ate. Right before I left, my assistant, Fiona, had asked for a teaser from the new book they could post on Autumn Moone's site. She also sent me a mock-up of the cover. I didn't love it and made suggestions.

"No worries." Sam was taking containers out of the bag. "I know how busy you are, but I need your expert advice again."

I took a seat at the desk and grabbed my strawberry avocado salad, trying to remember to smile and relax. I knew I would never be the amazing mom and wife they both were, but they had accepted me even though I was younger, unbridled, and at times prickly. I didn't mean to be. It was a defense mechanism. But despite all of that, they liked me, even loved me and valued my opinions.

"What can I help you with?" I asked Sam.

Sam took the seat next to me while Avery sat across from us.

Sam blew out a heavy sigh. "I've had an interesting offer come my way."

"More interesting than being a pinup girl in *Fabulous over Forty?*" She had even had an offer for a Real Housewives type show based in Chicago.

Avery and Sam both snorted.

"Maybe not that interesting," Sam snickered, "but almost as scary as posing nude."

My interest was piqued.

Sam took another deep breath. "One of the producers for Weekend Musings contacted me. At first, I assumed it was because they said as soon as my cookbook came out they would ask me on again. But," she paused, "they want me to be a regular contributor," she almost squealed.

Avery must have already known, as she didn't react other than to pop some watermelon in her mouth. The news didn't surprise me either. Her first appearance on the Saturday morning show was a smashing success. The hosts, Marla and Manny, ate her up. And like I said, Sam was hilarious and her new cookbook coming out in two weeks, *Glorified Cookie Recipes and More*, was going to be a hit. Sam had given me an advance copy, not because I would use any of the recipes, but because she was excited about it. Her wise words were sprinkled throughout, and the pictures of each recipe were stunning. I was proud to say I had contributed to that. Sam had shown me some initial drafts and they were trying too hard by embellishing each picture of food with plants, ribbons, and other things that didn't belong on food, at least I was pretty sure they didn't belong. I suggested to Sam that clean and simple was always best and it would take away from the message of the book if left as is. She mentioned it to her editors, who my editor may or may not know, and they changed it.

"What did you tell them?" I asked.

She pressed her lips together. "I told them I was flattered, but I would have to think about it."

"And what do you think?" I smiled.

"Tell me what to think," she begged.

No way was I doing that. She was a smart woman, and this was her choice. "What does Reed think?" I asked instead.

"Of course he thinks she should do it," Avery jumped in. "I do too, for that matter."

Sam gave Avery a smile that said you aren't helping me.

"What are your concerns?" I stabbed a strawberry with my fork.

"Looking like a fool in front of everyone about sums it up."

"The odds of that are extremely low based on your last appearance." I tilted my head and studied her for a moment. "What are you really afraid of?"

Sam dropped her plastic fork; her gray eyes bore into my own. "How do you read people so well?"

That was a long answer rooted in being left alone a lot growing up. Other people's lives became my focus. People on the bus, people in the shelter, people at school. I wondered what each of their stories were. Did they, too, wish for a life other than the one they had? Did they have real moms and dads? How did they end up where they were? Couples particularly fascinated me. That should have told me something. I was drawn to their interactions. Small touches and gestures, stolen glances, cold shoulders, and awkward conversations. During high school and college, I excelled at predicting who would hook up and who would break up, except when it came to myself. The one time I was wrong, did it ever cost me. My mind shut down that train of thought, just like I had conditioned it to.

I tucked some of my curls behind my ear. "It's all in your body language."

"Is it screaming how scared I am that I *can* do this?"

I tilted my head with an understanding smile. "The fear of success can be worse than failure."

"Yes," Sam lamented. "I feel like someone hit the fast-forward button on my life this past year and I haven't had time to catch up or process. A year ago, I had a different last name and I was barely showering every day."

"Now you're changing your name again and you're happier than you've ever been."

"Samantha Cassidy does have a ring to it." She blushed while staring down at her sparkling engagement ring. "Sometimes I wonder if this is all a dream."

I could relate to Sam on so many levels. I stared down at my ring finger that was empty by choice. Peter and I had no money for rings when we got married and now that we had more money than we knew what to do with, I found I didn't need the symbol. Peter was woven into my soul. I'd suggested tattoos with each other's names around our wedding fingers, but Peter wasn't too fond of that idea. I still might do it someday. Add it to my Peter collection. His name sat nicely inscribed in a crescent moon on the small of my back already. But there were times I wondered how I'd gotten here and if it would last. Not only did I feel like an impostor in my career, but in my marriage too.

So much of my life wasn't how I imagined it would be. Growing up, I'd never had dreams of getting married and having children. My own mother, Cat, warned me against it on several occasions. She said she was lucky Ron never stole her identity. When I told her Peter and I were trying to have a baby a few months ago, she implored me to wait until I was at least forty. She said I owed it to myself to have a career first because I may not be so fortunate as to have such a self-sufficient child like I had been. I think it was her way of thanking me for not ruining her life. Because of her, I feared what kind of mother I would be. Peter had no doubt I would be a good mother. He said one of the reasons he fell in love with me was because of the way I loved and fiercely protected the students at the school where we met. And he said I never smiled so big as when our foundation received cute little thank-you letters written in crayon thanking us for the new shoes. Maybe, just maybe, my husband was right about me.

But we may never know. I inadvertently held my angry womb that was cramping. Stupid period started this morning.

"You deserve all of this," Avery said to Sam, making me look up and focus back on the present.

I nodded in agreement. We'd all watched her go through hell and back when she found out that Neil was cheating on her and having a baby with another woman.

"Do you want to take this job?" I asked.

Sam bit her lip. "I do, but..."

"No buts," I cut her off, "offers like this don't come every day, and this is perfect for you and your platform."

"But," she wasn't going to let this go, "I'd have to quit my job here," she whispered. My father-in-law was in his office. He was doing more office work now since he'd strained his back a few months ago. He never came out when we got together for lunch. Too much femaleness for him, he said.

"We can hire a payroll service," Avery suggested, "And I can take over invoicing."

Sam still didn't look convinced. "It's early on Saturday and football season will be starting soon, so I'll be up late every Friday night for a few months."

Both Avery and I laughed at her.

Avery tossed a balled-up napkin at her. "You're going to need a better excuse than that."

Sam caught the napkin and shook her head at herself. "I know I'm grasping for straws here, but this is a big deal."

I rested my hand on Sam's shoulder. "It is, but so are you."

Tears filled her eyes. "Where would I be without you two?"

"Probably grocery shopping or making out with Reed all day long," Avery teased.

Sam grinned while a little sigh escaped her.

If only I could use Sam's grocery shopping stories with Reed in my books. My fans would eat that up. I had to hand it to Reed, anybody who could make grocery shopping sound sexy had a gift. And there was no one who deserved that present more than Sam.

I took a bite of my salad and swallowed before asking Sam, "So, what will you be doing on the show?"

Her gray eyes lit up. "It sounds like I'll do a cooking segment using recipes from my cookbook while talking about fun things like perimenopause, coping with life after divorce, raising teenagers, you know, fun stuff like that." She grinned. "Oh, and my favorite books. We all know who's at the top of my list. Speaking of which, I re-read *Black Day Dawning* again. I can't get over how good it is."

"Me too," Avery squealed.

All I could do was pop a strawberry in my mouth.

Chapter Four

$\mathcal{I}$ DID SOMETHING I normally wouldn't. I bought a sugar cookie for my father-in-law when I picked up lunch. I knew they were his favorite. I'd hidden it in my bag in case I chickened out giving it to him or if I decided I really needed it for myself. However, because I ate cereal on a regular basis, I tried not to eat a lot of treats unless Peter brought me my favorite candy, sour cherry jelly beans.

While Avery and Sam went back to work, I braved walking to Joseph's office toward the back. I could feel Avery and Sam stare after me. Everyone knew I was the least favorite Decker and how tenuous my relationship had been with my in-laws. Again, I played a part in it. But in my defense, I tried really hard at the beginning. I moved here expecting to love my in-laws and for them to love me based on Peter's endorsement. It was false advertising at its worst. From the moment Sarah laid eyes on me, I was enemy number one. Not only had I lured her baby away from one of the highest honors as far as she was concerned, I wasn't even worthy to be in his presence.

At first, I tried dressing more conservatively around her and letting her underhanded criticisms go without retaliation, but it only made me more miserable and caused tension in my marriage. If she couldn't love me for who I wasn't, she was never going to love me for who I was. That's when the gloves came off. I never struck first, but I wasn't one to let others walk all over me. If she made a rude comment about me, I hit her where it hurt most, my place in her son's life. I kissed Peter more in front of his family than I'd ever anticipated, but it did the job. More than anything, she hated our united front, but that didn't stop her from checking for chinks in the armor of our relationship on a regular basis. She was desperate to drive a wedge between us.

But the fact of the matter was Peter loved his parents, and Joseph and Sarah might someday be the grandparents of my child. Despite how awful Sarah had been to me, she was an amazing grandma. I would never say that out loud or admit to it under torture, but she was. She was the kind of grandma who went to every track and cross-country meet and football game. Sarah was at every ballet and play Avery's and James's daughter, sweet Hannah, was in before she passed away. Sarah had pictures of her grandkids everywhere, and even the yellowed pictures they had drawn as toddlers were hanging on her refrigerator. She was as proud of those pictures today as I'm sure she was the day they were given to her.

Joseph was right there with her. He was always one to play catch with the boys and he'd even let Hannah put makeup on him.

I wanted them to both love my child the same way. It's why I knocked on Joseph's door.

"Come in," Joseph's deep voice rang.

With trepidation I twisted the knob and slowly opened the door.

Joseph's eyes were green like Peter's and currently wide in surprise. "Delanie," his voice sounded even more astonished. He stood up from behind his messy desk filled with stacks of paper and several old styrofoam coffee cups.

"Hi...Joseph." I was the only one to call him that. Everyone else called him Dad or Grandpa.

I swore he peeked behind me to make sure Sarah wasn't there before he asked, "To what do I owe the pleasure?"

I reached into my bag and walked toward him, pulling out the frosted sugar cookie wrapped in plastic with a blue ribbon. "I brought Avery and Sam lunch and I know how much you like these," I rambled, "so I bought you one." I stretched out my hand over his desk, allowing him to reach for my tiny mend in a fortress of a fence that needed repair.

Before he reached for the cookie, his eyes grabbed ahold of me, so much like Peter's. It was the one physical attribute they shared. James was built more like his father, large and looming, though James was in much better shape, running marathons with his wife and all. Joseph had a beer belly and time showed on his sun-weathered face. But there was something in his countenance that was gentle like Peter's.

Joseph's gaze continued as he gathered his words in the awkward silence. He took the cookie and cleared his throat. "Peter says you need some landscaping done in your backyard."

It wasn't exactly the response I was looking for. Not that I knew what I hoped for. Maybe a, *Hi, honey, the new ruby nose stud really suits you,* or even a, *how are you?* But I could see the fear in his eyes behind the warmth.

I stepped back. "We do."

Peter had felt stuck between a rock and a hard place about how we should proceed to landscape our backyard. He wanted to use the family business, but he didn't want them to see the cost. On the other hand, he didn't want his brother or dad to feel slighted that we hadn't used them. Peter could do it by himself, but it would take forever, and his dad and brother would still feel bad in that scenario.

The house and the money we had made Peter feel more uncomfortable than me. He had promised God at one time to live a simple life with few worldly possessions. Our house had very few possessions, but it was in and of itself very worldly. And obviously a sore point for some in his family. Cough, cough—his mother.

But we only had sixty days after closing to finish the yard per the homeowners' association's guidelines, which meant we would have a very nice backyard when it was all said and done.

Joseph gave me an uneasy smile. "I'll take a look tomorrow night while we're there and see what we can do."

"We appreciate that." Disappointed we had nothing better than landscaping to talk about, I began to turn around. "I'll let you get back to work."

"Delanie."

I had almost made it to the door. I turned back toward him.

He held up the cookie. "Thank you." A disheartened sigh came with the expression of gratitude.

I felt the same way. "You're welcome." I opened the door.

"You can...stop...by anytime."

I smiled to myself at the sentiment but felt a twinge of despair about how much bravery he had to exert to say it. I gave him a wave of acknowledgement while wondering if it would always be this way. And if my real family still lived on the moon.

Spending time with Peter's family was always good for writing. The hope and discouragement that punctuated each visit was the perfect blend of tension. I was able to channel it and pour it into the several pages I wrote before I had to leave for the shelter and my class. My car was already packed with dozens of the biodegradable diapers I purchased online once a week. The UPS driver must have thought we had twenty kids or ran an orphanage. That thought had crossed our minds. Maybe someday when Autumn Moone didn't rule our lives we could do something like that, or even be more hands-on running Sweet Feet. Since Autumn Moone was much more popular than me, she was the founder of the charity. Because of her, fans all over the world donated to the cause through her website.

She also helped me spread the word about clean water. Autumn Moone had partnered with a fantastic organization run by a genius of a man who built sustainable water pumps for poor villages, mainly in third world countries. Anyone who donated could log in to their site and see, through GPS, exactly what their money was being used for.

So maybe Autumn ran my life more than I liked, but I was thankful for her. She allowed Peter and me to do things we only dreamed of when we were first married.

I rushed downstairs to grab my bag before heading out. I was surprised to hear the garage door open. I met my husband in the three-car garage that seemed too large for my small car and the company truck Peter drove. I'm sure our neighbors probably wondered why we weren't driving expensive luxury cars like the rest of them. One of our neighbors we hadn't met yet mistook me for a maid last week and asked what my rates were and if I was available to clean her house. I was so taken aback I said the first smart-aleck thing that came to my mind. "Sorry, I only sleep with the guy who lives here." The spluttering and her red face were still giving me a lot of pleasure. I made sure to wave every time I saw her now. She, on the other hand, pretended she didn't see me.

I smiled from the steps leading into the garage.

Peter exited his truck carrying a bag from a local toy store. He returned my smile. "I'm glad I caught you in time." He rushed up the steps, dirty and sweaty, just the way I liked him, and planted a kiss squarely on my lips. "I missed you today."

"I missed you too."

He held up the bag. "I stopped by Landermans and bought a few things for the shelter."

I placed my hands on both sides of his five o'clock shadowed cheeks. "You are a good man."

"Not as good as you. My dad said you dropped by his office today."

My hands fell to my side, a little embarrassed. "It was no big deal."

Peter tucked a curl behind my ear. "It meant a lot to him. A lot to me."

"I'm trying."

"You amaze me, Delanie Decker."

"Because I bought your dad a cookie?"

His green eyes hit me full force while he shook his head. "No, because you keep trying even though some in my family have given you little incentive to do so."

"You can just say your mom." I smirked. "And I won't be buying her cookies anytime soon." Unless they were laced with laxatives.

"Someday she'll come around and she'll see what the rest of us already know about you."

I laughed and felt his forehead. "I think the summer heat is getting to you."

All that heat manifested in his eyes, causing a hot spell to wash over me. He wrapped his free arm around my waist to draw me closer. "You get to me."

I leaned in and kissed him, soaking in his goodness. "How did a nice boy like you ever end up with a girl like me?"

He smiled against my lips, a masculine laugh playing between us. "I told you I was lucky."

"I'm glad you still think so."

"I know so. Mark my words, my mom will too someday."

I kissed him once more before leaning away. "I want to believe you."

"Trust me."

"That's what you said when we moved here."

A sheepish grin inched up on his handsome face. "It's a work in progress."

"Did you mean retrogression?"

"I know it may seem like that, but I have a feeling tomorrow night will be a step forward."

I didn't disagree with him, though I felt it was a pipe dream. "I better go or I'm going to be late."

Peter handed me the bag of toys. "I'll wait up for you."

"Then I may have to hurry home."

He squeezed my hand. "Don't rush on my account. You are always worth the wait."

He was why I sold millions of romance books.

Chapter Five

OLUNTEERING AT THE shelter had a way of putting life into perspective. The eyes of the women and children who lived there told such stories. Some eyes wore the mark of terror, some of utter exhaustion and last straws. Relief and hope filled those who had been there longest.

Tonight, I was relegated to help in the children's playroom while many of the mothers took a class from an amazing woman who was a victim of domestic abuse herself. She was not the stereotypical victim. Domestic abuse knows no socioeconomic bounds, Jocelyn was living proof. She used her wealth now to provide training on how to dress for success and to provide each woman at the shelter with a new outfit.

The children's playroom, though decorated in bright cheery colors, had a subdued feeling to it. Its little occupants were quieter than you expected children to be. Though their eyes showed more resilience than many of their mothers', they were all cautious, which meant less playing with one another. One particularly sullen girl with corn-silk hair caught my attention while I gave one of the directors the bag of toys, so she could log the donation and make sure each toy met their standards before she put them out to be played with.

The pretty girl sat by herself coloring at a table, hoping to stay invisible. She was practically coiled up into a ball. I could only imagine the horrors she had seen to make her behave in such a way.

I approached her cautiously and sat across from her at the tiny wooden table. My five-foot-nine frame barely fit on the small chair. At first, I didn't say anything to her. I grabbed the nearest coloring book filled with pictures of fairies and began to color my own picture. Every so often the girl would glance my way, but her eyes immediately dropped if she caught me looking at her.

"I'm Delanie," I said nonchalantly after several minutes of our cat and mouse game.

She wasn't biting.

"That's a great picture. Blue dogs are my favorite." I was rewarded with a hint of a smile.

She braved looking at what I was coloring. I noticed her eyes light up.

"Do you like fairies?"

She nodded.

I pushed my coloring book toward the middle of the table. "Do you want to color together?"

I got another nod.

The fragile beauty began coloring on the page next to mine. After a few minutes of silence and small glances, she finally said, quiet as a mouse, "I'm Amber."

"It's nice to meet you, Amber."

Her cheeks pinked.

"How old are you?"

"Nine."

Oh, nine. My heart skipped a beat. "Nine is my favorite."

She looked up and this time met my eyes. "How old are you?"

I refrained from laughing. Children were so without guile. "Twenty-nine."

"My mom is that old every year on her birthday."

I couldn't keep from laughing. I knew a lot of women who had been twenty-nine for a long time. This year I truly was twenty-nine. To be honest, turning thirty next year didn't bother me. Maybe because Peter was already in his mid-thirties. Or perhaps because Cat and Ron never made a big deal about my birthdays. We never celebrated big milestones, at least not mine. Peter, though, had made each of my birthdays since we had been together a special occasion. This year he made it into a scavenger hunt that ended at a cozy out-of-the-way bed-and-breakfast at a Wisconsin nature preserve. Best birthday weekend I'd ever had. I would be using some of the inspiration from that weekend for the end of *Black Confessions*. It involved a lake, a rowboat, and hopefully no witnesses.

"Besides coloring, what else do you like to do?"

She thought for a moment like she didn't want to say before she shrugged her thin shoulders, making my heart break. We both reached for a pink crayon at the same time. I noticed her delicate little hands bore bruises and her fingernails looked like she had chewed them with a vengeance. I hoped whoever was responsible was behind bars.

I made sure she took the crayon while I gazed into her beautiful, frightened blue eyes. I wanted to tell her she was safe here and that no one would ever hurt her again, but I couldn't promise her that. I knew too often victims of abuse were in a terrible cycle of either returning to their abuser or ending up in another abusive relationship. This child's mother probably came from an abusive home. Too few broke the cycle.

With all that I was, I wanted to take her in my arms and make her believe that she and her mother were worth so much more than the deal life had handed them. That she could break the cycle. If Peter were here, he would know the right words to say. I had seen him do it so many times with the children at the school in Phoenix. Many came from these types of situations. He would tell them God loved them and was watching over them. I wasn't sure I believed that. What god would allow this to happen? I had asked Peter that many times. His response, "We live in a fallen world. Bad exists so we may know the good. Beautiful hearts like yours are made not despite the bad, but because of it. Think about that." I had thought about it so often.

At times I could almost see his point, but when I looked at Amber, so timid and bruised physically and emotionally, all I could see was the injustice of life. And if I were God, I would fix it all. I would make every child safe and happy. All I could do now was offer her a smile and sit in the silence with her, hoping she knew that she was safe with me now.

I left the shelter thinking I had no right to complain about my life. Life hadn't always treated me fairly, but I had never known the horrors in Amber's young life. I would try to remember that when my mother-in-law came to visit tomorrow night.

❧

Peter was propped up in bed with the lights still on, book on his chest, sleeping. Poor guy. I felt bad I was returning so late; it looked like he had done his best to stay awake. After my time at the shelter, I stayed after my class and talked to Father Alan, who noticed I was unusually quiet. I couldn't get Amber out of my mind. There were too many nine-year-olds who were in her situation or worse in the world. I had a hard time reconciling that and told Father Alan I might not return. That did not deter him. Instead, his kind brown eyes dared me. He said I was looking at it all wrong.

"Who are you to say that God isn't involved in Amber's life? For all you know God had a hand in bringing her to the shelter and making sure someone kind was there to color with her." His eyes twinkled when he said it.

The man reminded me so much of Peter. It was exactly the kind of thing he would say.

I told Father Alan I might return. He grinned and challenged me, "Why don't you start looking for God in all the good you see?"

I stared at my sleeping husband. He was good. And if God had a hand in giving him to me, I would convert to Peter's faith in a second.

But why would God give me so much and others so little? Thoughts to keep me up at night.

I quietly changed into one of Peter's T-shirts before I slid into bed next to him. I removed the C.S. Lewis book from his bare chest and replaced it with my head.

"Hey, baby." He woke and began stroking my hair. "What time is it?"

"Ten-thirty. Sorry I'm late."

He kissed my head. "You're doing good things. Don't apologize."

I felt a tad guilty he didn't know everything I was doing, but I had good intentions for attending those RCIA classes. But I couldn't get Peter's hopes up. I needed to figure this one out on my own. If Peter was involved, it would cloud my judgment. Someday when I came to my conclusion I would tell him.

I snuggled closer. "How was your night?"

"Good. I went to the store and picked up the ice cream and cookies for tomorrow night."

I stopped myself from saying something negative about his family's impending visit. "Maybe one of us should learn how to cook."

He laughed. "Hey. I can make oatmeal."

"Hopefully, our children will...," I choked on my words before I thought about what I was saying.

Peter's arms tightened around me.

"I know we agreed not to think about it."

"Baby, of course we're going to think about it. I just don't want it to overshadow what we already have together."

"Life has been good to us."

"Very good."

I knew that tone. I looked up to see a pair of longing green eyes gazing at me.

"I love you," he said barely above a whisper before he pulled me to him. His lips magnetically locked with mine. I melted into him, ready to be consumed by him. But far too quickly he leaned away. "I should probably mention Mimsy is coming tomorrow."

Normally, I would have groaned or sighed, but in light of the night, I gave him a strained smile. "Just keep her away from any water sources."

"Deal." He leaned in, but I interrupted him.

"Any other surprises I should know about?"

He gave me a seductive grin. "I might have a few more."

"You don't say."

"I don't plan on saying anything."

Those were my favorite kinds of surprises.

Now if only his mom would surprise me tomorrow night and do a good job pretending she could stand to be in my presence.

I wasn't going to hold my breath. Maybe catch it a few times, though, while my husband showed me just how surprising he could be.

Chapter Six

I LOCKED MY OFFICE and doubled checked it before I headed downstairs to wait with Peter for our guests to arrive. It was nice to have a space for Autumn. In our apartment, we were constantly in fear of having someone drop by and accidentally see Autumn Moone evidence. There were a few times we had to hastily shove papers and laptops under our bed. Now it was always behind lock and key, disguised as a walk-in attic. The entrance was within one of the bedrooms. And by looking at our almost bare home, no one would think we kept anything in our attic. We also had a decoy desk and laptop in the "real" office across from our dining room downstairs.

It was going to be a short tour tonight. Mostly, look at this empty room and oh hey, here's our couch and small TV. I wanted to get Peter a larger one because I knew he would enjoy it. He seemed to ogle the big screens his dad and James owned, but he wouldn't allow the luxury. It was as if he had to prove to himself and God he didn't need those things or even want them. He justified the house because it might have to protect me someday—I hoped with all that I had, that would never happen, but with technology, it was getting harder and harder to keep secrets. My publisher had to constantly be on guard. Communications to me went through a virtual private network my publisher set up especially for me. There were several tabloids willing to pay a lot of money to anyone who could prove who I truly was.

We laughed at how many people swore they knew who Autumn Moone really was. There were sightings of me all over Montana, where I was apparently a recluse living in a small mountain town. I supposed since my novels took place in Montana that was a good guess. Some had even surmised that Sam was Autumn Moone since her posts frequently ended up on my website. That had delighted Sam to no end. One of my favorite rumors, though, came from a man named Hunter Black from Rhode Island. He swore up and down he was me. His interviews were priceless. Peter and I laughed when he made up all sorts of nonsense about how he came up with the storyline. It was based on him and his high school sweetheart, Laine, of course. She died and came to him in a dream and told him to write their love story. Funny how he never knew the plot of the next books or even the titles. He would get flustered in interviews, but he would keep on telling lies.

My publishers loved it. It was marketing gold for them. It was so lucrative I had a clause in my contract saying I could only tell my spouse and authorized personnel who I was. They were also contractually bound to keep my identity a secret. It helped me sleep at night. At least when I could. My characters were Chatty Cathys and loved to talk to me and each other all night long sometimes. It was why we kept a bed in the spare bedroom leading into the walk-in attic. Many nights saw me getting out of bed and heading to my computer to relieve the noise banging around in my head. At times, I was so exhausted after my midnight writing sessions I would crash-land on the spare bed. Often, I would find Peter there sleeping soundly. I always loved to come out and see him there waiting for me to curl up beside him.

Beside him is where I planned to stay tonight. I wouldn't say his mother scared me, but I didn't underestimate her either. I didn't expect her to come over here and be all sunshine and daisies. I did hope, though, that if I was near Peter, she would keep her comments to herself or at least to a low-grade insult. This way I would not have any reason to retaliate. She was lucky my period had already started, and PMS had subsided. That, and I still couldn't stop thinking about that nine-year-old girl. There were bigger worries in my world than why my mother-in-law continued to hate me. All little girls should be safe and loved. I hoped... *No. No. No. Not now. You did what you had to do*, my heart whispered. I wasn't sure if I would ever believe it. Or forgive myself.

"Delanie." Peter shook me out of my thoughts in the nick of time.

"I'm sorry, did you say something?" I met him by the ecofriendly bamboo butcher block island in our large kitchen that would probably remain underutilized.

He reached for my hand, then with his free one he brushed my long hair back. His eyes gave me a good look over. "Are you okay? All the color drained from your face there."

I felt that blood returning as heat rushed to my cheeks. My emotions were too transparent sometimes. "Just a lot on my mind."

"Are your characters giving you trouble? Should I talk to them?" He could always get me to smile.

"They are mostly cooperating, except for the *mother*."

He gave me a knowing grin. "I told Ma to be on her best behavior tonight." Peter knew exactly whom I'd based Mrs. Black on.

"And I will do the same."

He drew me closer and nuzzled my neck. "Only until they leave, right?"

I ran my fingers through his hair and reveled in his touch and words. "Are you suggesting I should be—"

A windchime sound filled the house. Whoever rang that doorbell was not getting any cookies or ice cream tonight.

Peter groaned and released me, but not before giving me a sly grin. "Don't lose that thought; it was exactly what I was suggesting."

Something to look forward to when this bad idea was over with. I smoothed out my long, patterned gypsy skirt, my favorite thing to wear, along with a tank top that my mother-in-law would consider too revealing.

"You look beautiful." Peter took my hand and led us to the reclaimed wood double front doors in rustic gray. The thing I loved about this house was that we used repurposed or environmentally friendly materials wherever we could.

The sound of my bracelets jangling echoed throughout the mostly empty, largely open home with high wood beamed ceilings. Those were reclaimed too, as were the wood floors my feet padded against trying to slow down my husband. He laughed and tugged me along.

Before we opened the door, I could hear them all on the other side. You don't know how much I appreciated that. Sam and Avery promised me they wouldn't leave me alone with the woman who birthed some of my favorite people. I could hear Sarah's shrill tones now wondering very loudly why our doors looked so old. "If you're going to buy a house in this fancy neighborhood, you should have a nice door. And can you believe we had to use a code to get into this place? Who does she think she is, a Kennedy?"

Peter kissed me before some choice four-letter words came flying out of my mouth. I breathed him in. He was my sanity.

"You owe me," I whispered against his lips.

"Big time." He pecked my lips once more before opening the door.

The whole motley crew stood there on our covered porch. Dear, dear, dear, Sarah was front and center. Maybe if I called her dear enough times I might believe she was marginally not evil.

Sarah squinted at me before throwing her arms around Peter, making sure Peter's and my hands broke apart. "Peter, your home is beautiful." She proceeded to pat him down. "You're so thin." I got some more narrowed eyes.

I wanted to tell her this was no longer the Brady Bunch era. Peter was a big boy who could feed himself. And he wasn't thin, he was lean and muscular.

Sam and Avery barged in wearing invisible superhero capes. They were ready to save the day, or at least keep another rift from happening. Both women embraced me and whispered, "Don't pay attention to her."

Easier said than done. But I would try my best for my husband, who was doing his best to untangle himself from his mother.

The rest of the crew filed in, including all my teenage nephews. Cody was first, he belonged to Sam and I could safely say Reed too. Reed was more of a father to Cody than his biological one. Jimmy and Matt belonged to Avery and James. The boys were laughing loudly about some prank they had seen on YouTube. Each boy bore the Decker jawline and nose. It was a good nose. They should be thankful for it.

Joseph followed, giving his mother-in-law, Mimsy, a steady arm to hold. I believed she was well into her eighties, but her eyes said she was still twenty and kicking. She wore a light blue jogging suit and looked ready to take on the world. Joseph looked around the entry and into the large empty space that was our great room. He nodded, impressed. Last came James. He seemed reluctant to enter. Normally confident and booming, he seemed reticent. His gray eyes were darting all over the place.

Once everyone was gathered into the foyer, Peter made it out of the clutches of his mother and back to me. He took my hand and gave it a good squeeze. "Welcome to our home."

"Where's all the furniture?" Sarah wasted no time with her criticisms.

I took a deep breath and focused on Sam and Avery who were already staring my way giving me encouraging smiles. Or perhaps Sam was smiling because Reed had his arms wrapped around her from behind, whispering in her ear. He was probably saying something like, "Thank God for Delanie; your ma hates her so much she doesn't even realize I've signed your NDA." Or something along those lines. Lines Peter said we shouldn't be thinking about.

"We are taking our time," Peter responded to his mother.

"Probably can't afford it after buying this house," Sarah said under her breath.

I was about ready to accost my husband and give Reed and Sam a run for their money in the groping department, but Joseph came to the rescue. "It's good to live in a home for a while and get a feel for it before you start filling it with a bunch of crap."

We all stood surprised at not only his wise words but his bravery in contradicting Sarah. But no one was more surprised than his wife, by the way her eyes pulsed. She might break a blood vessel if they throbbed any harder.

I, on the other hand, was going to buy Joseph all the cookies in the world and maybe kiss his cheek. Though I was afraid that might cost him his life.

"Well, let's head to the kitchen." Peter tried to smooth it all over.

"Ooh, I love the kitchen." Avery grabbed James's hand. "I want you to see their double oven. It's just like the one I want."

James's face turned a shade of red before he sullenly followed his wife. What was wrong with him? Normally he was the loudest of the bunch and life of the party. I didn't have time to focus on him, though. Mimsy had caught her breath after walking up the porch stairs and was now ready to jump into the mix.

"I'm thirsty. Do you think they have glasses?" Mimsy asked Joseph.

Peter and I gave each other alarmed looks. Maybe Mimsy was faking being thirsty. My guess was she wanted to throw her brand of holy water all over the house, or maybe she thought Reed and Sam were acting too frisky. But how do you refuse water to an elderly woman when she says she's thirsty?

Peter gave me an apologetic smile before answering his grandmother. "We have glasses, Mimsy. Do you want ice too?"

"Just water."

Did her eyes turn a shade of devious, or was that just me?

We all congregated in the kitchen and everyone looked wary when Peter filled a glass of water and handed it to Mimsy. I noticed everyone took a step away from the little old troublemaker. Except Sarah, who inspected the glass to make sure it was clean. I was no Martha Stewart, but I knew how to run a dishwasher. Not to say my office was spotless; it was in quite a bit of disarray now, but such was the life of an artist. When I was in the middle of a manuscript, cleaning took a back seat.

While all the adults looked warily at Mimsy and the glass of water, I noticed the teenagers were standing around bored. They were looking toward the family room off the kitchen and were unimpressed with our small couch, chair, and thirty-two-inch TV screen.

"No video games," Cody whispered to Jimmy and Matt.

"I don't think they have anything cool here," Matt replied.

Maybe Peter and I needed to up our game. I was hoping we might be the hip aunt and uncle. It's not like we couldn't afford to, but Peter and I were both very reluctant to cross that line. We knew once we did there would probably be no going back. Staring at my nephews made me think of any children we might have. I didn't want to be my parents, withholding luxuries for the sake of research. There was no doubt we wouldn't want spoiled children, but I never wanted them to think of us as lame or like we wouldn't share all that we had with them. I would never make them feel like Cat and Ron had made me feel, like I was only a science experiment.

"We have cookies and ice cream," I offered to the boys.

That got a few appreciative smiles.

"I hope she didn't make the cookies," Mimsy said, not even trying to be quiet about it.

Sarah didn't hold back her smile.

Peter swiped the glass out of his grandmother's hand. "I'm sure you didn't mean to slight my wife like that." He slammed the glass on the island. Mimsy didn't look offended at all. It was almost as if she applauded his spirit with her eyes.

It didn't help break the tension that filled the kitchen while everyone stared around the room at each other, not sure what to say. I knew this was a bad idea.

"I would love some ice cream and cookies." Joseph seemed intent to be the peacemaker tonight.

I smiled at my father-in-law. "We bought your favorite, mint chocolate chip." The smile he gave me in return gave me some courage, and maybe a bit of hope.

Sarah, on the other hand, didn't appreciate her husband's enthusiasm. She gripped the counter she was near so tight I wondered if she was going to leave indentations in the wood. She wanted to say something, but the look Peter gave her said it would be best if she didn't. Her obvious irritation with the situation was replaced with a fake sweet smile. "I'm not ready for dessert yet, I'd rather see the rest of the house."

The nephews all groaned. They knew if grandma wasn't ready, no one was getting any dessert yet.

Peter and I gave each other looks of resignation. His eyes said how sorry he was. My eyes said, if we're going through hell, might as well keep on going. I just wanted it to be over.

"Why don't we go upstairs," Peter suggested before leading the way.

Everyone followed. Avery and Sam both patted my back as they passed me. I was happy to take the rear before I said some things I wouldn't regret, but my husband might. I watched everyone ascend the L-shaped staircase while I took some deep, cleansing breaths.

Peter explained as they walked up the stairs how energy efficient and eco-friendly the house was. "We even used sheep's wool for insulation."

"That had to be expensive," James commented.

Peter shrugged. "In the long run it saves money."

My nephews were helping their great-grandma up the stairs, which she found offensive. She kept smacking away their hands saying, "I don't need your help." But the next second, she was handing out cash to them that, unfortunately, she pulled out from her bra. That was a new one for her. The boys looked warily at the breast-rubbed ten-dollar bills. "You boys aren't afraid of old boobies, are you?" Mimsy cackled.

Everyone stopped where they were, some still on the stairs and some in the loft.

"Mimsy, what a thing to say," Sam said.

Mimsy wasn't having it. "Don't lecture me, little miss sex talker." She was referring to some of Sam's Sidelined Wife posts. There was nothing graphic about them in nature, just Sam lamenting about how hard it was to be in a sexless marriage and how she wished she would have loved her body more through the years.

The boys lost it to fits of laughter. They ditched the cash and ran past me down the stairs.

"Feel free to help yourselves to the ice cream and cookies," I said as they passed by me.

Everyone else decided it was better to move on and not respond. Mimsy shrugged and shoved the money back in her bra. She took the stairs by herself slowly. I stayed close behind in case she fell.

Once we were all situated in the empty loft, Peter obviously wanted to get this over with as soon as possible. He began pointing from where we stood. "Down that hall is the master suite. Over there are some more bedrooms. We aren't sure what to do with this space yet, but we'll figure it out."

I was already heading back downstairs, but it wasn't meant to be.

"I want to see all these rooms." Sarah took charge of the tour. "Did you put wood floors in all of them?"

"Yes, Ma," Peter sighed. "They are easier to clean and make for less toxins in your home."

"It's an awful idea if you ever have children." She narrowed her eyes at Peter as if she was asking him if he planned to breed with me. She was obviously hoping that he didn't want to. We never told her we were trying.

"Ma, children can learn to crawl and walk on wood floors just fine," Peter responded.

Sarah's eyes widened. It was apparently all the clue she needed. The wheels started turning in her eyes and I knew it couldn't be good. Yet we allowed her to nosily inspect every room, starting with our own.

It was a no-frills room, but I loved it. The light gray-blue walls were serene and played well against the hardwood floors. Our bed was simple with no headboard, only ivory covers and lots of pillows in varying shades of white. Other than that, we had a chair and dresser. For me it wasn't what was in it, it was who I shared it with. When his mother tsked at the bareness of it, I almost blurted out that we didn't need much to make love in here and how often that happened, but I bit my tongue.

Avery and Sam oohed and aahed over the wood beamed ceilings and wrought iron chandelier. Those elements were a nice touch, I must confess, but Sam and Avery had already seen the entire house, minus my *other* room.

Mimsy helped herself and sat on our bed. She bounced up and down a few times. "It doesn't squeak, that's good."

We all internally begged she would say no more. She left it at that. It was the one time the night went right.

Sarah looked mildly impressed with the master bathroom. It was beautiful, with a free-standing soaker tub and a stone walk-in shower. After all this I might need a soak in the tub.

"There's no door on this shower." Sarah found something not to like.

Peter wrapped his arm around my waist. "We like it that way."

There were some low chuckles by Sam, Avery, Reed, and James.

That concluded the fun part of the tour. Basically, the rest of it consisted of empty bedrooms and closets, except for the one spare bedroom with a bed. Peter and I both tried not to make a big deal out of any of the rooms. We basically flipped on the light and said, "Here's another bedroom."

Unfortunately, Mimsy was like a child and decided she needed to sit on the bed in the spare bedroom to try it out too. "It's a little lumpy and it squeaks." She bounced some more.

No one really paid attention to her until Sarah decided to join Mimsy. She agreed with her mom's opinion but took it further. "This would make an awful guest bed. Good thing I live in town."

Peter squeezed my hand. It was like he was asking me to hold on. I was sure he knew I wanted to say that she wouldn't be invited to stay even if she lived out of town. If only she did live far away.

"Let's all go have some ice cream." Peter turned off the light.

Most everyone filed out except his mother and grandmother, who for some odd reason became fascinated with the attic door. They tried to open it.

"Is this an extra closet?" Sarah asked.

"It's an attic," Peter responded.

"Why's it locked?"

"No reason." Peter played it cool.

"Is it a walk-in attic?" Sarah wasn't letting it go.

"Yep." Peter turned to leave. I followed.

"Let's see it. It's probably the most interesting thing in the entire house. Why else would it be locked?"

My patience was running thin. I turned back toward her. She dared me with her palest of blue eyes to contradict her.

"Let's go have some ice cream, Sarah," Joseph jumped in before I could say anything.

Sarah stood firm. "Are you hiding something, Peter?" She sounded like she was trying to give him an out, like, just tell Mommy and she will save you from whatever evils your hideous wife is hiding.

"Ma, let it drop. It's an attic," Sam jumped in.

"I didn't hear Peter deny he was hiding anything."

Oh sh . . . I meant crap. I couldn't let Peter lie. He was too pure. Me on the other hand, not so much. I took a breath with an evil gloating smile. "Peter doesn't want to say because he's embarrassed."

Peter's wide eyes looked directly at me and played right into it.

I kissed him once and whispered, "Sorry," against his mouth before I turned and unleashed my fury on my mother-in-law. I gave her the most sardonic grin I could muster up. "We wanted to keep it a secret, but we have nothing to be ashamed of."

Sarah clenched her fists, ready to lash out.

Everyone else had gathered closer to Peter and me at the door, waiting on bated breath.

I paused a bit more for dramatic effect and just when I had Sarah where I wanted her, I let out, "It's where we keep all the boudoir photos of each other."

Sam, Reed, Avery, and James all snickered behind me, knowing it had to be a joke. Anyone who knew Peter would know he wouldn't be down for that sort of thing. Though he did enjoy a sexy pic of me now and then being texted to him. Joseph just shook his head and headed downstairs.

Mimsy clapped her hands together. "Can we see?"

Sarah, dear, dear, dear, Sarah, did not disappoint. Her clenched fists shook while her face turned fifty shades of red. "You're corrupting my child!"

I glared at her. "Your child is a man who can make his own choices." I kept my voice steady.

She turned on Peter. "So, this is what you choose to do? Take naked pictures of yourself? Are you selling yourself online to pay for this house? Is that what it is? I thought it was drugs, but this is worse."

"Ma, we aren't selling ourselves or drugs."

"Then tell me how you afford all this and why you would keep naked pictures of yourself. You were a such a good boy, a man of God, and then this woman," she pointed at me, "she came and—"

"Reed and I eloped last month!" Sam shouted, interrupting Sarah's tirade.

A shockwave went through the house, and for a fraction of a second all was still. But almost like we choreographed it, we all whipped our bodies and heads toward a nervously smiling Sam and Reed.

Reed wrapped his arm around his bride with a wide, almost apologetic smile. "We've been waiting for a good time to tell everyone."

"What? What?" Sarah pushed her way through us, grabbing her chest. "Joseph, Joseph," she yelled. "Are you hearing this?"

Joseph came running up with an ice cream scooper in his hand.

"How could you, Samantha Marie?" Sarah was shaking.

Joseph fell by his wife's side. "What's going on?"

"Tell your father what you did," Sarah demanded.

Meanwhile Avery, James, Peter and I looked at each other. We were all in shock. No one saw this coming.

Reed pulled Sam closer while Sam bit her lip. "We eloped last month."

"Is that true, baby girl?" Joseph asked, disappointed.

Sam nodded with her eyes cast down.

"How could you do this to me?" Sarah leaned into Joseph, distraught. "At least tell me it was at a church."

Sam shook her head.

Sarah tipped her head up and threw her hands in the air. "Two children now married outside the eyes of God. What have I done to deserve this?"

I had a list for her, but I kept it to myself, not wanting to direct the attention back on me. I would be forever grateful to Sam for the beautiful gift she gave me of taking the heat off me for a few minutes.

Sam reached for her Mom's hands. "Ma, we didn't do this to hurt you. Neil is doing everything he can think of to fight the annulment of our marriage. And we felt it was best not to wait any longer."

Sarah yanked her hands away. "Because you wanted him to sign your NDA."

"That's part of it." Sam blushed. "But more than anything we wanted our lives to start together as a family."

That set Sarah off again. "Cody Joseph!" Her loud voice carried through the entire house.

Cody was smart enough to yell, "We're headed outside!" The back door slammed.

I loved that kid.

Sarah turned back to Sam. "Did Cody know about this?"

Sam pressed her lips together and thought about what to say. "Of course he did. It's not something we would have done without him."

"What about the rest of us?" Sarah was on the verge of tears.

I almost felt sorry for Sarah. I knew one of the reasons she hated me was because Peter and I eloped. I understood why that would be painful. From the look in her eyes I think she felt even more betrayed by Sam, her only daughter. If she could only see why her children felt the need to do things behind her back and that her way wasn't the only way.

It was time for me to jump back into the fire. "I think it's terrific. Congratulations!"

Before Sarah tried to set me ablaze with her eyes, Avery and James were congratulating them as well. Even Joseph was hugging Sam, although he didn't look happy at all with Reed.

Mimsy was shuffling toward them, muttering about adultery. Good thing she didn't have any water on her.

And that's when I found myself in Peter's arms. We said not a word, but clung to each other in our private island of safety. As long as I had that tiny slice of paradise, it didn't matter what raged on around us. Peter would always be my refuge.

Chapter Seven

PETER WALKED HIS family out while I cleaned up the kitchen. Only my nephews and father-in-law had any of the treats, but in true teenage fashion they not only left out the ice cream, but they dripped it all over the island. I didn't mind the mess. I was glad to have something constructive to do. The night was more...just more of everything. More surprising, shocking, revealing, you name it. My head buzzed with the night's revelations.

This I knew, I was over-the-moon happy for Sam and I was done with Sunday dinners and Peter's mother. I'd heard her whisper to Mimsy on the way out in between her tears that she was sure we were growing marijuana or cooking meth in the attic. She swore she was never talking to any of us again. If only I could get a guarantee on that. She was crazy, and if ever we had children, they would be better off without her. Not like she would treat them well anyway, because I was their mother.

While I loaded the dishwasher, Peter crept up behind me and brushed my hair away from my neck before his lips rested there.

I took a moment to enjoy the feel of his lips against my skin. "I'm sorry for making you sound like a centerfold."

He spun me around and held me close. "Maybe that was a little over the top, but it was my fault for inviting them over here."

"It was the first thing that popped into my head."

He chuckled against my ear. "Should I be worried about what's in your next book?"

"Maybe," I teased.

He kissed my head and sighed. "Tonight was an unmitigated disaster."

"That is an understatement." I took a deep breath and let it out. "I don't think I can do Sunday dinners anymore."

Peter's shoulders fell.

"Your mother is never going to like me or accept me."

"I'm sorry, Delanie."

"I'm sorry, too. I haven't exactly engendered her goodwill."

"You've at least tried."

I sank further into him, letting my head rest on his shoulder. "What about Reed and Sam?" I needed a change of subject. "I didn't see that coming, though I had my suspicions they were—"

Peter tipped my chin up and kissed me before I could finish my thought. "I'm with James here—Sam is, was, and will always be a virgin."

I rolled my eyes at him. "Does that make Reed one too?"

Peter kissed my nose. "Yep."

"I'll let you live in your fairytale land."

He gazed into my eyes. "I already do."

I ran my hand across his cheek while returning his gaze. "Am I really your happily ever after?"

"You are my happy every day."

"Even when I tell people there are naked pictures of you in our attic?"

"Even then," he groaned.

I sank back against him.

Peter rubbed my back. "I think this moment calls for some MJ."

"Not him."

"Baby, it's our song."

"I don't remember us officially declaring it *our* song."

"It was the first song we ever danced to in your kitchen."

"That I remember."

"Do you also remember," he whispered in my ear, "that I told you I was going to marry you that night?"

My stomach still fluttered over it. It was insane, but for some reason it felt so right even though technically we had only been dating for two weeks. But I already knew I was in love with him. "I do. And I told you, you were the only man I would ever consider marrying."

"It's the magic MJ, I'm telling you."

"Now you're giving credit to Michael Jackson for our union?"

Peter reached into his pocket and pulled out his phone. He must have had it ready to go because he only tapped on a couple of buttons before, "Rock With You" began to play. Peter placed his phone on the counter before wrapping me up and swaying to the disco classic.

I laughed against his chest. "I can't believe this is our song."

"Believe it, baby; I want to rock with you all night long."

He had me laughing hard while I breathed in his spicy clean scent.

"James always told me if I wanted to get the lady, to play this song."

That made a lot of sense. James was a reformed lady's man from the way Avery told it. She wasn't keen on dating him at all. By all accounts she had turned him down several times. As she put it, he was one of those guys who knew he looked good and could get almost anyone he wanted. She didn't want to be another notch on his bedpost. The elder brother was no angel. I don't think Sarah knew, or if she did, she had chosen to ignore it. Even after James finally convinced Avery to go out with him, they broke up a few times. Avery had never said why. I didn't think she liked to talk about it, so I'd left it alone.

"Speaking of your brother, is he okay? He's been a bit moody lately."

Peter stopped swaying for a moment and rested his chin on my head. "I've noticed too, but he's not one to talk about his feelings. Growing up, he'd rather shove me or punch me before opening up. Has Avery said anything?"

"No, but I'm not sure she would. I have a feeling she's the type who wears her game face as much as she can."

"Hmm. I'll try and talk to him tomorrow at work. But for now," he pulled me closer and began swaying off beat to our ridiculous song, "we are going to share the beat of love."

My laugh came out more as a bark. He was so cheesy, but I loved him for it. Only he could get me to laugh after such a night. We danced to several more of Michael Jackson's songs, sharing the beat of love and some heated kisses before Peter whisked me upstairs. There we made our own kind of music.

Peter had this uncanny ability to easily drift off to sleep even when the day was emotion filled. I envied him that talent. Emotionally charged days made my mind race more than usual. With my head resting against my husband's chest, listening to his pure heart, I wrestled with my thoughts. As much as I hated to admit it, Sarah could get to me. She had me thinking about past choices. I was no angel, unlike the man who held me so close and at times spoke my name in his sleep. I didn't sell or make drugs like my mother-in-law implied, but I had stupidly tried a few when I was growing up. Thankfully, I hated the way they made me feel and never had any desire to try them again. Peter knew that. He had grimaced when I told him but tried to make me feel better by saying we all did dumb things when we were younger. I knew, though, that my carelessness way outdid his, and I didn't like the thought of him being disappointed in me. Or questioning his choice—me.

My fingers lightly brushed his smooth chest while I wondered what he would think of his wife if he knew all the things I would go back and change if I could... and most especially the one I wouldn't. A single tear fell on his warm skin, causing him to stir but not wake. At times I ached for him to know all of me, including the parts he might not like. Those parts who made me who I was, the complicated woman he loved in the here and now. The question was, would he still love me? Would he still choose me? Most of me believed he would, but there was enough self-doubt to make me keep pieces of myself in a secret vault. Like the Barbie under my bed when I was younger that I knew couldn't be inherently bad, yet it would have deeply disappointed Cat and Ron to know I had chosen to be like the masses. It wasn't that I wanted to be like everyone else; I only wanted to belong. That Barbie made me feel like I belonged with my classmates at the time. It was "normal."

If I gave Peter the combination to my vault, would he still think I belonged with him after looking inside? Would he see that my choices weren't inherently bad? That we didn't see good and bad in the same way? The unknown answer kept me up at night. In these arms was the first time I knew I belonged somewhere. My family wasn't on the moon, it was with Peter. My past choices shaped me. I would even say they helped me become a better person. Did Peter really need to know everything about me before we met? I didn't need to know every piece of his past. Was I only trying to justify myself? I took in a deep breath and held it, trying to decide. I let it out slowly.

Peter's arms tightened around me. "I love you," he whispered in his sleep.

I squeezed my eyes shut. That was all the answer I needed.

Chapter Eight

"I HOPE I'M NOT calling too early."

I looked at the clock on my computer—7:00 a.m. I had been awake for over two hours. My imaginary friends had decided it was time to play. Peter had been gone for an hour already. He and James had to finish the Finley job today. I rubbed my tired eyes. "You can call anytime."

"I might take you up on that someday," Sam said.

"I hope you do."

"You're sweet. I'm calling to apologize."

"For what?"

"I hope you understand the reason why we didn't tell anyone about getting married wasn't because we didn't want you there, but—"

"Sam," I interrupted, "you don't need to explain yourself or apologize. Believe me, I've been there. There is something to be said for it only being the two of you and Cody."

She sighed happily. "It was perfect."

I thought the same thing when Peter and I eloped. "I'm happy for you all."

"Thank you," she sounded relieved. "It happened so fast. One moment we were joking about it, and the next, we're heading down I-55 to a map dot of a town with the cutest courthouse where no one knew who we were. And it's been kind of nice keeping it to ourselves while we adjust to our new roles."

"What does Cody think?"

"In light of his father's asinine decisions, I think it's been a nice distraction. Reed is the dad I always wanted for him. So much so, I've teased Reed that he only wanted to marry me for Cody."

"I highly doubt that by the smile that's been on his face for the last few weeks."

"You noticed."

"I told Peter that NDA had been signed, sealed, and given a big stamp of approval."

Sam laughed. "You are observant."

"It wasn't hard to tell. Your brothers are just pretending you're an eternal virgin."

"That would be my mother's wish." She paused. "That was the other reason I was calling. I'm so sorry about the way Ma treated you last night."

I shrugged to myself. "It was to be expected."

"No one should expect that. And you certainly don't deserve it, even if you are keeping naked photos of yourself locked in your attic," she teased.

We both laughed.

"By the way, thanks to you, my husband—" she took a moment, "that's still so weird for me to say—is begging me to get some boudoir photos done now. He's going to call Peter this morning to ask him where."

My poor husband. "That should go over well."

"Reed only wants to give him a hard time; he knows you weren't serious."

"It wasn't my finest moment."

"Are you kidding? It was brilliant. Reed and I had a good laugh over it."

"I'm glad someone did. Thank you for your heroics last night."

She playfully scoffed. "Well, I'm not sure I saved anyone's day. I probably did more damage than good. But we'd been waiting for the right moment to disappoint Ma, and—"

"You didn't think anything could be worse than her son posing for nudes?"

She half snorted, half laughed. "Something like that. Unfortunately, I didn't account for how disappointed Dad would be."

"I'm sure he understands."

"Be that as it may, I won't soon forget the moisture in his eyes or when he whispered, 'I was looking forward to walking you down the aisle again.'"

Ouch. I felt that in my gut. "Oh."

"'Oh' is right. And I feel bad that I'm sure he had to put up with Ma ranting to him all night long."

I had no doubt that had happened.

"She's already left me a dozen messages this morning," Sam lamented, "but I haven't been brave enough to listen to them yet."

At least my mother-in-law never called me. I wasn't even sure if she had my number. "I don't envy you."

"I truly am sorry about Ma. She holds tightly to her ideals, as if they are the only ones that exist. It's not you. It was her expectations for Peter."

I was confident it was me but didn't voice it. "I don't think anyone expected me, especially Peter."

"For him, I think you exceeded his expectations. He found his real calling with you."

Sam always knew what to say. She had this mothering quality to her that I wished to have and needed more than she knew. She reminded me of another mother who appeared years ago when I needed her; unfortunately, it wasn't Cat. It certainly was never going to be Sarah. And I wondered if I would ever respond to Sam's mothering the way I wanted to. It meant the world to me, but as much as I craved it I didn't know how to take it, internalize it, and return it without awkwardness.

"I think at this rate he'll be calling for a refund." See? No thanks or warmth.

"Never."

I hoped that was true. "The real question is are you accepting Weekend Musings's offer?" Deflection at its best.

She took a deep breath in and let it out slowly. "Yeah. I think I am. Is that crazy?"

"I think it's terrific."

"I'm going to need your help."

"I don't think so, but regardless, I'm here for you."

"You always have such great tips. Did you take a class in college or something? I need one."

I swallowed down all the lies I could tell and thought carefully about how I could tell the truth. "I did take several journalism classes in college." It was my first love, but it also got me into some trouble; no need to bring that up. "And my work runs workshops on how to ask good questions to net the best answers."

That was all true. I had even attended some via Skype, but where my real knowledge came from were all the endless interviews I had done through my assistant. Obviously, I only answered questions that wouldn't reveal anything about me personally. Autumn Moone, on the other hand, was highly sought after and several news outlets wanted the scoop on her and Hunter Black. The less we gave them, the more they wanted. Just another strategy of my publisher.

For Sam, it was the opposite—the more she gave people access to her thoughts, the more they demanded. She struck a chord with women, whether married, sidelined, or single. We could all relate to trying to figure ourselves out, being looked over at times, or even looked at in the wrong light. Didn't we all feel like we didn't belong in some way? Sam had a talent for making women feel like they weren't alone.

"I need some of those workshops."

"You're going to be great. You're a natural. Just keep it real."

"If I was going to keep it real, I would show up PMSing in yoga pants without my roots done."

"It's not a bad idea." I laughed.

"It would probably make for a short-lived TV career."

"I don't know. I think it might work, actually."

"I'll keep it in mind. I better go. My guys are headed off for practice." She sounded so happy saying that.

"Congratulations again."

"Thank you." There was such heart behind her words. I wanted to be like her when I grew up.

Back to work for me. I turned to my screen. An evil mother moment was on tap. Unfortunately, I had some raw material from the previous night to work with. Laine too was getting a visit from her least favorite person, making her question whether she really wanted a relationship with Hunter or not. In her heart she knew the answer. Like me, I would have married Peter even if I'd met his mother first, though it would have better prepared me. And I would have suggested another place to live. At the time it made sense to move here because he had employment right away with his dad, and Peter longed to be with his family.

I loved Laine's spirit. I could see myself using this line in the future. *How your ovaries ever produced such an amazing person, I will never know.*

How many times had I thought that about Sam, Peter, and on occasion, James. Joseph's gene pool must be strong. Thank goodness.

In an odd turn of events, my phone vibrated, and Joseph's name flashed on my screen. I wasn't sure he had ever called me. The only reason I had his number was because Peter insisted I program it into my phone for emergency purposes. It was sweet on my husband's part, but I'd lived in some mean parts of Phoenix, as he well knew, and there wasn't a street in downtown Portland I hadn't walked. If I had to be tough, I could be. I'd taken down a two-hundred-fifty-pound police officer in a self-defense class back in college. But I appreciated the chivalry Peter exuded on my behalf.

My heart did a hiccup before answering. Maybe Peter was having an emergency. Why else would Joseph call me? I answered in heart-pounding haste. "Hello."

Joseph cleared his throat. That wasn't good. Characters in my novels only cleared their throats when something unpleasant was about to roll off their tongues.

I curled my bare legs under me, waiting for the worst, but then thought I should probably be running to get dressed out of Peter's T-shirt. Showing up half-naked at an accident or hospital would only make the situation worse. This was the way of a writer's brain.

"Delanie, how are you this morning?"

He wouldn't ask me that before wrecking my life, right?

"I'm . . . good." Please let it stay that way.

"Good. Good. Good."

His nervousness, as well as the dead air that occurred after the brief exchange, was making me nervous.

"How are you?" I thought I should ask.

"Good."

I should have guessed his response. If this conversation was being typed out, my editor would have redlined the repetitious use of the word *good*.

It was a shame all our conversations had to be so strained. I didn't know how to have real conversations with my own father. Ron was good at one-sided conversations, and only called once a quarter when an alarm went off in his phone reminding him to call me. It was sad but true. At least Joseph had asked how I was. Ron would have plowed right into all his magnificent accomplishments or a travel log of a recent trip he and Cat had been on. Our last call consisted of a recap of Venice. It sounded like a lovely place to visit.

Joseph cleared his throat again. This time it didn't make me plan out Peter's funeral in my head. That was good, because that scenario mainly consisted of me fighting with his mother after telling her that I was putting *World's Best Lover* on his headstone. But that was only after she tried to hijack the arrangements. I was just going to die first. It would be easier that way.

"I had a brief look at your backyard last night and I have some ideas. I was wondering...I mean, I was hoping you could come to the office today and we could go next door to the nursery to pick out some plants and trees."

My feet dropped back to the floor. This was most unexpected. Was Sarah there waiting? A nursery was a good place to bury a body. Not like I had thought about it. But I made a note just in case—you know, for my book.

I was at a loss for words. "Uh..."

"Are you busy?"

My editor, Chad, was saying, *Del,*—everyone in New York called me that—*don't make me get my butt on a plane to come babysit you. You owed me ten chapters yesterday. You may be the darling of the literary world and of my own world, but don't think I won't slap you upside the head. Love you.*

I was still working on chapter five. You couldn't and shouldn't rush creativity. Besides, I had recently moved. Not to mention I had a crazy mother-in-law. And I wasn't getting pregnant and trying not to think about it. I had more good excuses lined up if needed. Believe me, they would be. I expected a call or an email from Chad any second.

"I would enjoy your company," Joseph added while I bargained with Chad in my head.

Would he really? "What time should I be there?"

"Would nine work?

"Yes..."

"Are you sure?"

"Yes," I repeated firmly, but I wasn't as sure as I sounded. This was a new one for me.

"Great. See you then."

I ended the call and immediately texted Peter. *Did you ask your dad to invite me to the nursery this morning?* I got up and left Laine waiting for a response from her formidable opponent, Mrs. Black. Neither were happy with me. Mrs. Black was anxious to put Laine in her place and Laine was past caring what she thought and ready to fight back. They had been battling in my head for hours now, but they would have to wait. I had my own war to wage and I needed all the allies I could get. Not that Joseph would choose me over Sarah—I would never expect that—but maybe if we could take our "relationship" out in the open, Sarah might back off some. Maybe? Probably not, but one thing Peter had taught me is that there was hope in this world.

While I was brushing my teeth, Peter texted back. *I didn't. Are you going?*

I spit in the sink and rinsed it out before responding. *I'm meeting him at nine. Are you sure you didn't put him up to this?*

I promise. His promises were always sure.

In that case, what should I do? I'm not exactly the right person to be picking out foliage that if left in my incapable black thumbs would die a cruel and unusual death. You've seen what I've done to food.

You're hilarious and gorgeous.

Thank you, but you're not helping.

My phone vibrated.

I put my husband on speaker while I threw my hair up. "Hello."

"Are you getting domesticated on me?"

"I don't think that's possible."

"I don't know, once you start picking plants it's all downhill from there. Before you know it, you'll be throwing dinner parties and baking edible cookies."

"Excuse me." I smiled to myself. "You're not funny."

"I know you're smiling and thinking about the time you mistook corn starch for flour."

"See what you know, I was thinking about the time I tried to make caramel popcorn and the caramel turned out more like molten lava and

I forgot to take the plastic wrapper off the microwave popcorn package before nuking it."

Peter's gut splitting laughter rang loud and clear. "That was epic. We needed a new pot and microwave anyway."

"I think it's safe to say I won't be turning into the domestic goddesses my sisters-in-law are. Now, please help me."

"First of all, you can do anything you set your mind to. And second, you've got this. You know what looks good together. It's no different than giving input on a cover design or website. My dad can guide you on what grows best in our area and what plants do well in the shade or sun."

"Are you sure you don't want to come? This is our home."

"Baby, you make it home for me. That's all I care about."

I paused doing my hair. I never thought I would enjoy a sappy man, but his sincerity got to me. "I love you, Peter Decker."

"I know. Enjoy your time with my dad. And maybe go easy on the black flowers."

"Is that a thing?" I admired my favorite black nail polish on my fingernails.

He chuckled. "Have my dad show you the black pansies and black dahlias."

"I will." Now I was a little excited about this excursion.

"I need to get back to work."

"I'll see you later, and FYI, if Reed calls, don't answer."

"Why?"

"Take my word for it and thank me later."

"Will do. Love you."

I took a deep breath and got ready to do something I never thought I would do. I wasn't talking about buying plants, though that was shocking too.

Chapter Nine

SAM DIDN'T WORK on Fridays, so it was only Avery and Joseph in the office. Avery was looking a bit tired when I arrived. The perkiness seemed to have percolated out of her. She gave me a forced smile when I walked through the office entrance to the jangle of the bell.

"Hey there. Dad said to expect you."

"How are you?"

She straightened up in her chair. Her fake smile grew. "Just dandy."

I tilted my head and studied her for a moment longer. Her blue eyes had storm clouds in them.

"I'm detecting some sarcasm."

Her smile added a hint of genuineness. "Using your Jedi mind tricks again?"

"If I had those powers I would probably use them for something more nefarious."

She laughed. "This is why I like you. I would probably use them to make Jimmy and Matt clean their rooms. James too, for that matter." When she said her husband's name she inadvertently tensed up.

"Everything okay with James?"

Avery tucked some hair behind her ear. "Of course."

"He seemed out of sorts last night."

She waved her hand around. "He was just taken aback by Sam and Reed. I mean, crazy, right?" She was trying to evade personal questions. James was acting off well before we knew about the elopement. I could understand the desire to keep things private, so I backed off.

"I would say more like brave."

Avery gave me a knowing nod. "Right?" She lowered her voice. "Dad looks like he didn't get any sleep last night. No doubt Mom kept him up last night fuming."

wMy brazen long red hair along with the nose ring and tattoo gave me an aura of unbridled passion. It wasn't too far from the truth, though I had learned to mostly tame that unbidden passion of mine. I wasn't as reckless as I used to be unless I was particularly vexed about something, in other words, Sarah.

I didn't long to be anybody but me. I only wanted to be accepted for who I was.

"I can't imagine it was a pleasant night for him." My passion was left out of my response to Avery.

"I can relate," Avery let slip before trying to recover. "I mean everyone has those kinds of nights." She smiled uneasily.

My eyebrow quirked, but I didn't verbally draw attention to her faux pas. "The important thing is Sam is happy."

Avery took a breath of relief and let it out. "No one is more deserving than her."

I was going to agree and add that she fell into that same category, but Joseph emerged from his back office scrubbing his hand over his salt-and-pepper stubble. Indeed, he did look haggard, wearing a wrinkled Decker and Sons Landscaping polo and eyes that said he needed a few more hours of sleep.

Avery said, "Hi, Dad," while I said, "Hi, Joseph."

Joseph stopped not far from us and looked between us with a crinkled brow as if it was the first time he noted we addressed him differently. His narrowed green eyes rested on me as if he was bothered by my greeting. I didn't get the feeling that he was upset with me, but perhaps the situation. Or maybe he needed some coffee.

Joseph shook his head and mustered a smile. "Good morning."

"Good morning," I returned.

Avery smiled between us as if she knew a secret. "I'll hold down the fort here, Dad; you two have fun."

"I appreciate that," he addressed Avery before falling by my side. "Are you ready?"

I wasn't sure about that but nodded anyway. "See you later, Avery."

Some of the twinkle her eyes normally had appeared with the wink she gave me.

I wondered what secrets she was keeping while I walked out into the sultry August air with my father-in-law. Even with a sleeveless sundress on, I wished for some shade. I reminded myself not to complain because soon I would be wishing for warmer days.

We both silently drifted toward the dirt pathway littered with rocks and pebbles between the two businesses. The scenery was pretty with an orchard nearby, though I focused a lot on my sandaled feet, waiting for Joseph to make the first move.

Several paces in he did just that. "Thanks for coming."

I lifted my head to meet his hopeful eyes. "Peter and I appreciate your help."

"I'm happy to help. This is fun for me."

"You should probably know, I have no clue about these types of things."

Joseph chuckled. "I might know a thing or two."

"Peter says you could have been a botanist."

"Maybe there's still time," he teased.

"Are you planning on retiring soon?"

He stopped in his tracks. "That is a good question. Sarah…" he paused as if he felt guilty for mentioning his wife. "She would like me to." He ran his hands through his good mane of hair for a man his age. "I wanted to apologize for last night."

"Is that why you invited me?" I tried to keep any hurt feelings out of my voice.

"Yes and no. I wanted to apologize in person, but…I think…it's well past time that I welcomed you into the family."

I stood blinking at him, not knowing what to say. That was, until visions of an irate Sarah popped into my head. "Are you sure you want to do that?" I was afraid to ask.

Joseph rested his calloused hand on my arm. "You shouldn't have to ask that. I'm sorry, Delanie, and not only for that. I realized last night how my actions or inaction have made me miss out on some of the most important moments of my children's lives."

"You mean Sam and Reed?"

"And you and Peter. We've made our children choose between us and their spouses when there has been no good reason for a choice to exist. I, for one, am not okay with that."

I assumed that meant Sarah was, at least when it came to me.

Joseph rubbed my arm in what I imagined was a fatherly way. It felt nice, whatever it was. "If possible, I would like to start over with you."

I choked back my tears. I wasn't one to show emotion in front of those I wasn't completely comfortable with, so basically anybody besides Peter and occasionally Sam and Avery. On a rare occasion Joan. I recognized the sincerity in his eyes. I had seen it many times reflected in Peter's eyes. I jumped into the pool of the unknown with a smile. "Hi, I'm Delanie, your daughter-in-law."

A wide smile appeared on Joseph's face. "My son's a lucky man."

"That's what he says."

Joseph's hand dropped, and he continued walking forward. "I've always known him to tell the truth, even if it meant he would get into trouble."

"That sounds like my husband." I followed his lead and kept pace with him.

Joseph waved to the owners of the nursery. "We are browsing, if that's okay," he called out to them.

They hollered back that we should take our time.

Joseph led me to the rows and rows of trees they had for sale. It smelled kind of like Peter—earthy, real, with maybe a touch of the holidays. We were suddenly surrounded by pine trees.

"What do you think of these white firs?" Joseph delicately touched the blue-green needles of the tree. "I thought they might look nice along the back part of your yard. They grow to about thirty to fifty feet, so they are good for privacy."

I liked privacy. "They're nice." I wasn't sure what else to say.

"If you don't like them, they have other varieties."

"No. No. I think they'll look great. They kind of remind me of where I grew up."

"Oregon, right?"

I nodded.

"Douglas firs are most common there," Joseph said knowledgably. "I think it's the state tree."

"That sounds right."

"Do you miss Oregon?"

I shrugged. "Not necessarily."

"How about your parents?"

"Not necessarily."

Joseph gave me a thoughtful grin. He had met Cat and Ron once, and like most family gatherings, it was like listening to someone scratch a chalkboard for hours on end.

"Do you enjoy living here?" Joseph asked.

I thought for a moment. "Peter loves it here and I love him."

"You didn't answer the question."

"It hasn't been...what I hoped for."

A pained expression lined his weathered face. "Things can change. People can change."

I nodded. I believed that to be a mostly true statement. Not sure it applied to Sarah.

"You know, Peter called me after he met you."

"He did?" I was half worried. I made quite the first impression.

"He said he was afraid."

"I can be scary."

Joseph laughed good naturedly. "No, no. That's not what he meant. He said, 'I met someone today who I fear could change my life.'"

"I didn't want to," I stammered. "I mean, I never would have—"

"Delanie, I know my son, and know he would have never broken his vows. I wasn't sure he should have taken them in the first place. I fear we pushed him to go to the seminary."

"Peter was happy being a priest."

"I'm not sure I would agree with you. He was content. Now he's happy. I told him when he called that he needed to face his fear. Only then would he know where his heart truly belonged." Joseph gave me a warm smile. "I'm glad he finally figured it out."

"Me too," I whispered.

He tapped my nose. No one but Peter had ever done that before. "I want you to feel like you are a part of this family."

He had no idea how much I longed for that.

Chapter Ten

"Have I ever let you down before?"

My phone call from Chad had finally come. Actually, several phone calls. He'd left message after message, each getting a little testier, while I shopped for trees and plants with Joseph. I ignored them all and was only now calling him back.

The time I spent with my father-in-law getting to know each other better was far more important to me. I had no idea Joseph was a reader. He spoke of being a boy and reading *The Chronicles of Narnia* and *The Lord of the Rings* series. I thought his only hobbies were sports and ice fishing. He was also well versed in world events. He spoke eloquently of his feelings when Rosa Parks refused to give up her bus seat in 1955. He remembered his mother telling him it was a step in the right direction, but so much more needed to be done.

There was a glimmer in his eye when he spoke of going to Disneyland as a child and when he met Sarah for the first time. I knew he hesitated to mention her, but I think he hoped maybe I could see her in a different light. He was seventeen and she was fifteen. It was a storybook meeting. He was visiting a cousin in Chicago while she laughed with her friends across the street. They each caught each other's eye. They wrote to each other when Joseph went back to Indiana. He came to Chicago as soon as he graduated so he could court her.

I had to admit I was intrigued, especially since the way he spoke of Sarah reminded me so much of how I felt for Peter. And apparently Mimsy and her husband weren't sold on him to begin with, yet he persevered. But I wasn't ready to see Sarah as a human yet and I had other pressing matters, like a bossy New Yorker.

"There is a first time for everything. Now where are my first ten chapters?" Chad's heavy New York accent filled my office.

"I can send you five. The other half are safely in my head."

"You better tell your pretty damn little fingers to get to typing."

"You know when you talk to me like that it only impedes my creativity," I taunted him. We've played this game many times before.

"Please, honey, don't play delicate female with me today. I've watched you tell off our CEO and I know you can write better in your sleep than most of the authors we have signed here, so go sell your sob story somewhere else."

"If I didn't know better, I would think you didn't love me anymore."

"Love you, yes, like you is another question."

"I guess you won't be finding yourself on my acknowledgment page."

"You forget I'm the editor. I already have your glowing dedication to me written out."

"This dedication is reserved for Peter."

"My eyeballs are rolling into the back into my head and I'm retching in my wastebasket. How many have you dedicated to him?"

"All of them." No one knew it was Peter. I said things like *thank you for showing me how to love* or *let's play out page 219 again*. It was a good one. I got butterflies thinking about it.

"We all agree he's a beautiful man and obviously inspirational judging by some of the scenes in your books, but listen, I make your work shine. Give a man some credit. And by man, I mean me."

"I'll think about giving you a shout-out on the dedication page…if you will give me another week."

"Dang woman, you're cold. And you drive a tough bargain."

"Does that mean we have a deal?"

He hummed some ridiculous tune while he thought. "You have yourself a deal. But in one-hundred-sixty-eight hours you better be making me cry tears of joy, baby. Got it?"

"I promise it will be worth the wait."

"I know it will be. Love you. Now get to work."

This was good. I needed the motivation. I flexed my fingers before blasting my new favorite artist, Logic. His lyrics evoked the kind of grit I needed for the next few scenes. Mrs. Black wasn't going to be backing down anytime soon and Laine and Hunter's complicated relationship was about to undone, hanging only by a few tattered threads. I hated to inflict the pain on them. But I knew they had to go through it; it was the only way. Out of the pain the truth would be revealed, and then they would be free to choose each other. And I was sure they would, because I got to script it out. Real life was never that easy.

I pulled up my manuscript. I had left off with a zinger from Laine.

Mrs. Black's ice blue eyes narrowed into slits akin to a snake. She was ready to strike back with her weapon of choice, her venomous tongue. Laine, for once, stood her ground where Mrs. Black was concerned. After her last conversation with Hunter, Laine had her epiphany. If she and Hunter were meant to be together, then no one, not even his mother, would be able to come between them. She knew if she didn't take a stand now she would lose everything, including Hunter and herself. Never again would she lose herself to anyone, not even the man she loved.

"Say what you want about me, but this I know, never will a Black come forth from your womb. We don't do recycled material. One man's trash will never be Hunter's treasure."

With great effort, Laine made sure not to react to Mrs. Black's implied meaning behind recycled. The truth behind the rumor was too precious and worth a million times more than her wounded feelings, so she let it slide. Instead, she gave her a sardonic grin. "Tell me, who is of more worth, the woman sought by many or the woman scorned?"

Red engulfed Mrs. Black's botoxed and collagen-filled face like a prairie wildfire. "Exactly what are you accusing my late husband of?"

"I didn't mention him. Funny, though, how you were quick to assume I was speaking of you."

"Don't pretend you know anything about my marriage."

"I don't have to pretend. I know."

I sat back in my chair, pleased. Another chapter down, and what an emotional ride it was. I turned down my music and did some meditation breathing while plotting out the next scene in my head. I knew where I wanted it to go but needed to fine-tune it. Hunter and Laine swirled in my brain. Hunter argued that he was ready to know Laine's secret. Laine countered the argument, and I agreed. I let them go back and forth until we all came to an agreement.

Chapter seven began with Hunter and Laine at their usual place, the Burger Shack, for their standing dinner night that they'd kept for years, no matter who they were dating or where they were in their lives. Even when the tension between them was strung like a tight wire, they each clung to the hope that they could keep their friendship, though they both longed for so much more. Dinners together every night in their own home was their ultimate desire.

The words flowed on the page until I heard the garage door below me open late that evening. I'd lost track of time. My grumbling stomach and full bladder weren't all that pleased with me. I saved my work and headed for Peter. My body could wait a little longer.

Peter came in bearing some of my favorite smells—him and Thai food. Fridays, when it wasn't high school football season, were our take-out movie nights. Tonight was my night to pick the food and his turn to pick the movie, which meant a biography or comedy. I usually chose a documentary or foreign film. No romances here. Why watch it when I could live it?

As soon as Peter set the food on the island, I threw my arms around him and my lips told his how much they had missed them. "Thanks for picking up dinner. How was your day?" I asked when we took a breath.

He tilted his head and studied me for a moment. "Interesting."

"How so?"

He took my hand and led me upstairs. "I'll tell you while I clean up."

I sat on the bathroom counter anxious to hear what Peter had to say. He was acting so mysterious, like he wasn't sure how to tell me. He didn't say much of anything until he was in the shower.

"Are you going to keep me in suspense?" I had to raise my voice to be heard above the running water.

He peeked his gorgeous head out. His hair was already wet and slicked back. He rubbed his lips together. "My mom..."

I may have groaned at the mention of you-know-who. But knowing his mother was involved, it explained why he was hesitant to talk about his day.

He gave me a sympathetic grin. "I know, I know, but believe me, this was unexpected." His head popped back into the shower.

"What? Did she decide I was the best thing that ever happened to you?" I laughed to myself at the preposterous statement.

He didn't answer right away, making my laughter die off quickly. His head poked back out and with it came a shrug. "Well, I wouldn't go that far, but—"

"But what?"

He shook his head.

It was then I noticed the deer-in-the-headlight look he had.

"She brought James and me lunch and said she'd been thinking."

I rested my hands on my legs and leaned forward, waiting for the punchline.

"More like my dad got her to thinking. He warned her they were on the brink of losing their children if they didn't change how they approached us."

"You mean her approach?"

"I'm sure that's what he meant, but he's a smart man."

I nodded. I believed that about his father. "So, what does this all mean?"

Peter rinsed off and grabbed his towel to dry off. He exited with the towel wrapped around his lower half. His farmer's tan had become more pronounced each day this past summer. His muscles too. He met me at the counter with a tentative smile.

I mussed his wet hair.

He took my left hand and kissed the palm of it before lingering on my bare ring finger. "I should buy you a wedding ring."

"We've already had that discussion. I don't need a ring and you're avoiding the question."

"No. I'm admiring my wife and thinking I'd like to revisit the ring discussion."

"All right." My fingertips brushed his stubbled, sun-kissed cheek. "But after you answer my question."

"Honestly, baby, I'm not sure what it means. All I know is she was crying and saying all she's ever wanted was the best for her children."

"So not me."

"She didn't say that. She said . . . that maybe she hadn't given you a fair chance." Peter could hardly believe it himself by how hesitant he was to say it.

I jostled my head, stunned. "Are you sure it was your mother?"

"Positive."

"Was she coming from the hospital where she had been treated for an aneurysm? Perhaps a stroke or amnesia?"

He laughed. "She seemed of sound mind."

"I don't think we should rule out alien abduction."

He kissed me once. "It was her, I promise. Though I admit I was as surprised as you."

"I'm more suspicious than anything."

He let out a heavy sigh. "I can understand that, but she seemed sincere. And when I told her you didn't feel comfortable coming to Sunday dinner anymore, she said she hoped you would reconsider."

I felt Peter's forehead. It felt a tad warm. "Maybe you have sun sickness and you hallucinated all of this."

"I swear on our love, I've been lucid all day. James can back me up."

I pursed my lips together. "Hmm."

"I know it seems like an unlikely one-eighty, but I think Dad really put his foot down this time."

"I got that feeling too when we talked today, but when has your mom ever listened to your dad, or anyone for that matter?"

"He still has his ice boat." Peter grinned. "And there were times growing up when Dad took a stand. I remember once when James wanted a dog and Ma absolutely refused because she would be the one who ended up taking care of it. James begged and begged, even saved his own money mowing lawns. Ma still said no. Dad bought him a golden retriever puppy for Christmas that year."

"What?" I leaned away, shocked and impressed at Joseph's bold move.

"We had Cooper for five years until he got sick. I think Ma cried the most when we had to put him down, though she did it in private to save face."

That sounded more like her. "I'm pretty sure if you had to 'put me down' she would throw a party and stomp on my grave. She'd probably even bring a swarm of nice single women from church to my funeral to comfort you."

Peter stood between my legs and cupped my face in his hands. "She could bring ten thousand women and I wouldn't notice one of them."

"That's good, because I would haunt you if you hooked up with someone at my funeral."

"You already haunt my soul." He kissed my forehead. His lips lingered.

I closed my eyes, wondering how I ever deserved someone like him.

"Do you think you have it in you to give Ma one more chance?" he whispered. "If you say no, I would completely understand."

I breathed him in while I thought. How many times did you give someone a chance? Before Peter, my answer would have been zero. Cat and Ron taught me that attachments made you weak and self was most important. Look how easily they had forgotten their own daughter. They didn't even call me daughter. I was a unit to them. Single and complete unless they were speaking to their esteemed colleagues, then I was a component of their lives. An achievement of theirs. Something to throw in the face of traditional and antiquated parenting.

Little did they know how incomplete I'd felt most of my life. How difficult it was to make and keep connections. How unprepared I was for love and loss. The struggle it had been to let Peter love me so fully and not fear it, but return it.

"My dad really enjoyed your time together today, by the way," Peter interrupted my thoughts with more to think about. "He said you have a good eye. And that I have one too."

"Are you trying to coax your wife?"

"No. I'm not even sure I want you to give her another chance."

I leaned back. "You're not?"

He brushed my hair back. "I don't like the way she's treated you. I know she's better than that. She was the best mom growing up. I wish you could know the woman I know. And I wish she could see you the way I see you."

I took a deep breath. "I'm probably going to regret this, but," I held up one finger, "I will give Sunday dinner one more chance. But if one insult, even an underhanded one, rolls off her tongue, I'm leaving."

"If that happens, I'll be right behind you."

I leaned my forehead against his. "I must love you."

"I thank God for that every day."

If there really was a God, I would thank him for Peter too.

Chapter Eleven

*P*ETER HELD MY hand as we drove to his parents' home. I held tighter than I normally would. It was never fun to face someone who thought you could be selling drugs or your body. Okay, so I may have given her some fuel for the latter. Again, not my proudest moment, even if I got some pleasure out of it. Tonight was a test. Did Joseph have real influence over Sarah? And did having a relationship with her children mean more to her than being right? I was leaning toward no to both questions, but I hoped for Peter's sake I was wrong.

To fill the nervous silence in the truck, Peter decided to share his day with me. He was always a bit hesitant to talk about church. "Today's homily about grace was excellent. Father McKinley's insights always inspire me to want to be a better person. He can take any scripture and relate it to the here and now. Maybe I should ask him to lunch. I'd love to talk to him about some of my own studies."

I swallowed down my fears. "Do you miss it?"

Peter turned my way with a furrowed brow. "Miss what?"

"Your former occupation."

He raised our clasped hands and kissed mine. "There are some aspects of it I will always miss, but the perks of my new gig make up for it."

"Is that what I am?"

"Yes, and I've booked you for life."

I squeezed his hand a little harder, hoping he always felt the tradeoff was worth it, trying not to worry that he missed his former calling. He tended to be more reflective on Sunday mornings before he left for Mass. His bible was his constant companion and he wrote page after page in a journal he kept while studying. I never read what he wrote, but I had a feeling he had several entries that would have made for beautiful homilies. I had seen him in action, having sneaked into Mass a few times while he was still a priest. I had no idea what he was talking about half the time, but he spoke with such eloquence and passion that it made me want to believe what he said was true.

"I'm glad you enjoyed it." I tried to be supportive.

"You know you're always welcome to come with me." He gave me a hopeful grin. He hadn't asked me in a while. I was grateful for that. I hated disappointing him when I said no.

"Chad is having heartburn and breathing down my neck right now, but when I'm done with this first draft…I will." I had worked all day, staring a lot at my screen. I knew what I wanted to happen, but some days I couldn't get it out of my brain. I barely got a page in.

Peter's eyes grew wide. "You will?"

I had promised Father Alan I would give Mass another shot, but this time I would go into it with a better attitude. In a rare moment of being open, I happened to privately mention to him that attending Mass exacerbated my fears and guilt about Peter's choice. He counseled that I look at it as an opportunity to grow with my husband, not as something that would tear us apart. There was some wisdom there, but religion was so foreign to me. And the concept of an all-powerful being was honestly frightening. But how would I ever really know unless I gave it my all?

I nodded reluctantly.

Peter's smile filled his truck. "I would love that."

I gave him an uneasy smile in return.

Before I knew it, we had arrived at what I liked to refer to as the yellow house of perpetual torment. Normally I was expected to bring a dish to share, but Peter always ended up eating most of it so I didn't feel bad, which made me feel worse because I knew how awful it was. Avery and Sam always had some too because they were good people, but that made me feel horrible. So, this week I decided to stop the cycle of torture and show up empty-handed. I wondered what Sarah would have to say about that.

Sam, Reed, and Cody pulled up the same time we did. They looked about as tentative as us. But Reed was going the brown-nosing route with an extra-large bouquet of pale pink roses he held in one hand. He held Sam tight with the other. Cody was a smart kid and yelled, "Good luck," while laughing before he ran in ahead of all of us. His cousins waited inside. Avery and James were always the first to arrive. Maybe that's why Sarah loved Avery. Avery was eager to please and help in any way she could. I wasn't unwilling to help in the kitchen; my help would be a hindrance. And I avoided Sarah like pop music.

Reed and Sam gave us commiserating smiles once we all landed on the sidewalk.

For a moment, I saw Hunter and Laine in Reed and Sam. After all, I did base Hunter's physical characteristics on Reed, and Sam had the tenacity of Laine. I imagined a tense scene where Hunter and Laine visited Mrs. Black after finally figuring out how to be together. I could see Hunter bringing flowers to his mother and Laine wearing a grin of dread with a hint of I-don't-care-what-anyone-thinks-I'm-happy-dammit. Sam did look thoroughly happy in Reed's grasp.

"After you," Reed ungraciously offered.

"Oh, no, please, we'll follow you." Peter waved his arm toward the house.

Sam and I both laughed, yet we all remained firmly planted as if our shoes had melted into the concrete.

From the house we heard Sarah yell, "Samantha Marie are you here?"

Peter smirked at his sister. "We're right behind you."

She rolled her eyes. "Fine. Let's get this over with."

Reed didn't look too sure, but he led the way, flowers out in front as if he were storming a castle and the roses were his shield. Peter and I did follow, but at a leisurely, almost non-existent pace. The August sun that would burn my fair skin in a matter of minutes had nothing on the heat I was sure we would experience once we entered Dante's Inferno. A line from the poem came to mind. "*Lasciate ogne speranza, voi ch'intrate,*" which meant, "Abandon all hope, ye who enter here." It was much more accurate than the welcome mat that greeted us at the door.

We stopped at the gate of hell where Peter kissed my nose ring and ran his hand down the length of my tattoo, as if he were reminding me how much he loved those aspects of me and it didn't matter what anyone else thought about them. I grabbed his butt because I loved that aspect of him and we both needed a reason to smile before we entered. It did the trick.

We walked in to hear the normal level of chaos going on in the kitchen, but this time Joseph emerged and met us in the entryway. He patted Peter on the shoulder. "It's good to see you, son." Then he turned his sights on me and before I knew it I was dislodged from my husband and wrapped in Joseph's embrace. This was a new one for me, so much so it took me a minute to respond properly and revel in what my father-in-law was offering. I forced myself to relax and return the hug.

"I'm glad you came, honey." He had never used that term of endearment when addressing me. I wasn't sure anyone had in such a way. It sounded fatherly. I felt the genuineness of it in his embrace and in the kiss on the head that followed. This is what it must feel like to have a father. Like a safe harbor.

I wanted to stay docked in that harbor when Sarah appeared, sure to bring a category five storm to beat upon me. She stood stunned in the hall, dark clouds starting to swirl in her blue eyes, but by some miracle they dissipated. I stepped away from Joseph, but father and son flanked me as if they had rehearsed the move in battle preparation. I was no wilting flower, but I appreciated the gesture all the same. I stood tall between my self-appointed protectors, waiting for Sarah to say something about my bare midriff and bohemian skirt her eyes darted toward. Instead, she steadied herself and tiptoed toward us. Very unlike her normal march. It made more sense when I glanced up and noticed the warning in Joseph's eyes. For half a second, Sarah's eyes resented the warning, but before we knew it, she began to channel June Cleaver. Well, sort of.

"I'm…glad you…both," she choked on her words while squarely focusing on Peter, "made it." She exhaled dramatically as if that was the toughest performance of her life. Yes, it all came off as an act, but I gave her credit for trying to play the part and gave her a hint of a close-lipped smile.

Peter must have been wary too as he took my hand and nodded.

Joseph broke the tension by clapping his hands together. "Dinner is almost done. Come on back." He went to his wife's side and put an arm around her. Sarah at first stiffened but must have decided it was a good offer. She leaned into him as if she was gathering strength. How sad it was that we all needed it to tolerate being in each other's presence.

The entire Decker clan awaited us in the kitchen, even our nephews, who were trying to help themselves to the overabundant food that filled the counters. Avery was doing her best to smack hands away, but it was a losing battle. The boys had outgrown their mothers and they were quick and moved in a pack, which made them more successful. Avery gave up, knowing it was better to pick her battles. Besides, our entrance into the foray was much more interesting.

James walked in from the back porch with a large tray of steaks. With the amount of red meat this family ate, it was a wonder no one had had a heart attack. I typically only ate salad and fruit during our adventures here, occasionally having a bite of Peter's steak. That didn't help engender any fuzzy feelings with my mother-in-law. She took it as a slight that I didn't partake in the weekly consuming-of-the-fatted-calf ritual. Cat and Ron were vegetarian, but like everything in my life, they left my palate choices up to me. I don't know if it was nature or nurture, probably the first because nurture was not a strong suit of Cat's and Ron's, but I leaned toward a more plant-based diet with fish for protein. And cereal, but I used almond milk instead of cow juice like Peter. Occasionally I would eat a hamburger or something, but nothing to the extent of Peter's family.

James's grin said he was ready for the fireworks to ensue. Mimsy stood with a bottle of water, itching to sprinkle it on someone. Reed was poised in front of Samantha, ready to take any direct hits from Mimsy.

Joseph looked around at his pensive clan with a resolve to bring us together if it was the last thing he did. He did linger on Reed for a bit longer with squinted eyes that said *you aren't off the hook yet for stealing my baby girl away.* Joseph was about to speak until Mimsy stole the spotlight.

Mimsy looked between James and Avery. "Do you two have any skeletons in your closet or your attic?" She bounced on the balls of her feet, eager. "I promised Giovanni I would return to prison with a juicy story." She frequently referred to the assisted living home as a prison.

Did James give Avery a guilty look? If he did, it got lost in translation when Sarah asked, "Who is Giovanni?"

"My lover." Mimsy bared her teeth in an evil grin as if she had been waiting for the perfect moment to spring this latest bit of the soap opera that seemed to always play out at the assisted living home.

"Lover!?" Sarah exclaimed while the rest of us, by the shocked and squeamish faces that erupted around the room, were trying not to imagine what that entailed.

"Don't look at me like that, young lady, I told him I don't do the horizontal mambo until he buys the cow. No free milk for him."

That was it; I lost any appetite I may have had. Though I must say I enjoyed the angst Mimsy was causing her daughter. Sarah spluttered for words.

"It's your own fault," Mimsy continued. "You're the one who imprisoned me there looking like this." She waved a hand over her tiny body like she was a beauty queen. "They can't keep their hands off me. You don't know what a turn on it is that I still have my own teeth and that my tuckus only takes up one cushion of the couch."

Bursts of laughter erupted first from the boys, spreading to the rest of us, minus Sarah.

"Mom, what about Dad?" Sarah cried.

"What about him? He'd want me to have some fun. And you know what they say about Italians. It's all true."

Sarah crossed herself and looked up to heaven.

Joseph let out a defeated breath. "Let's eat."

Chapter Twelve

T WAS THE first time I had ever felt the slightest bit at ease at the enormous custom-made dining room table. For once, I wasn't the one who made Sarah distraught. We may have all been a bit overwrought. The only sounds were the clinks of utensils against the china and chewing while we all tried to digest Mimsy's news and the graphic details she gave us about the STD video they made all the residents at her home watch after a massive rash of herpes and gonorrhea spread through its residents. She informed us it was another reason she was refusing her Italian lover's advances. She would not be a statistic or a sinner, she assured us. Afterward she handed out cash to her great-grandsons, thankfully not from her bra this time. Apparently, the wad of cash she had stashed there previously caused some irritation, so it was back to her pockets.

I couldn't make this stuff up. If only I could put it to good use and base a character off her, but it would be too obvious to Sam and Avery.

The reprieve of Sarah, as I was calling it in my head, was too good to last very long. After she took a long sip of her wine, she set her sights on the newlyweds. "I see you announced to the world today that you eloped." Sarah's voice at first was sharp, but unnaturally lightened by the end.

I had read Sam's post earlier in the day too. It was titled "Full Disclosure." It was a play on how Reed had signed her NDA, which allowed him full access to her, and how she was fully disclosing her secret elopement to her fans. She got real about how hard it was to love herself again after her divorce, maybe love herself for the first time ever. How much courage it took to let Reed love her. She didn't go into too much detail, unlike her grandma. She bravely spoke about being scared to be intimate with Reed, but how grateful she was that he took his time, not only waiting for her to be comfortable in her own skin, but in the actual act itself and how that made all the difference for her. How it gave her confidence in a way she had never experienced with her ex-husband. She basically said if you aren't with the kind of man who instills that in you, something needs to change, and it may even mean finding a new relationship. It was a post I would be sure to have my assistant put on my website. It was something every woman needed to hear.

I glanced at my husband, who was enjoying a decent home cooked meal. He was the kind of man Sam spoke of. I rested my hand on his thigh under the table and squeezed. He smiled at me as if he knew I was trying to nonverbally say I loved him.

Sam paused before responding, as if she too couldn't believe her mother's change in trajectory. The entire table seemed to be perplexed except for Joseph, who smiled at his wife. He must have had some talk with her.

Sam reached out to touch her mom's forehead. "Are you okay?"

Sarah batted away Sam's hand, but gave her a strained smile. Or was that trained? "I feel fine. I'm just... It's just that I was thinking since you've announced your *marriage,* it would be nice if we still had a celebration."

Sam and Reed looked at each other, grimacing.

"We appreciate the thought, but football games start in less than two weeks and my book is coming out around the same time. The next little while will be crazy for us."

Sarah's face reddened, but she took a breath and plastered on a faker smile than before. "What if we did something this coming weekend?"

Sam shook her head. "There's not enough time to put a party like that together, not to mention book a venue."

A cat-like grin replaced the fake one. "Honey," Sarah said, sickly sweet. "You know I was already in the process of planning your reception with Bethany Vargas. Remember, I introduced you two at church last month? She runs a party planning business out of her home and she said she could squeeze us in this weekend. Not to mention Janice Kilroy, who owes me a huge favor, is willing to cater all the food."

Sam leaned back in her chair, obviously not interested. "Are you talking about the woman who thought chartreuse would be a good color for bridesmaid's dresses?"

Did anyone look good in yellow-green?

Sarah patted Sam's hand. "She likes to think outside the box, but don't worry, I already told her I wanted...I mean, *we* wanted pale green, black, and white."

"Ma. I said I was thinking about those colors, but it doesn't matter now because—"

"It matters to me. I'm your mother and I wanted to share in this time with you."

Was she going to cry? We all looked alarmed.

"I was looking forward to celebrating your special day, and so were all the people who love you and watched you grow up, including those around this table." Sarah knew how to lay it on thick. Some tears did appear.

"Amen," said Mimsy.

Even Joseph was nodding.

Sam looked to Reed for a lifeline. Before Reed could respond, Sarah plunged the shovel of shame deeper into the pit of guilt. "How did your parents feel about it, Reed? You're their only child."

Reed rubbed his neck. "They weren't exactly happy—I mean, they are thrilled Samantha is my wife, but—" He stopped himself before he went down the rabbit hole.

It was too late, though, Sarah's shovel just lengthened. "See how important this is? This could bring us all together."

Reed's expression said he had nothing after that.

"Ma," Sam sighed, "maybe we can do something over Christmas break."

"The holidays are a terrible time; everyone will be busy with company and family parties. Let's just do it now. I promise you will hardly have to lift a finger."

"This coming weekend is in six days. That's insane." Sam wasn't giving in. "We can't even get invitations out that fast, and where would we have it?"

"Oh, honey, get with the times. We'll use Headnovel."

The nephews busted into gut-splitting laughter.

"You mean Facebook?" Jimmy could hardly breathe that out, he was laughing so hard.

"Don't laugh at your grandma." Sarah sat up dignified. "Yes, that's what I meant."

"Even if we could get the word out and Reed's parents are available to come, we still don't have a place."

"We could host." Avery wagged her eyebrows at Sam. Avery loved a good party.

Sam wasn't pleased with the suggestion. She returned Avery's offer with an I-thought-you-were-on-my-side glare.

Sarah turned toward Avery with a bright smile for her favorite daughter-in-law. "That's sweet of you, honey, but your place isn't big enough."

Avery's face fell while James forcibly pushed back his chair. "I think I might have left the grill on," he grumbled on his way out of the dining room.

Peter and I shared a concerned look. James's reaction was only validating our suspicions that something wasn't right. But there Avery sat with a brave smile like nothing was off. Except her smooth skin—which looked like it belonged on a twenty-year-old, not someone in her forties—was blotched and she was blinking as if she was staving off tears.

Peter started to whisper in my ear, "I'm going to go check on—"

He didn't get to finish because somehow we had made it through the first circle of hell only to find ourselves at the cusp of not the second, but more like the tenth. Dante's nine circles had nothing on us.

I vaguely heard Sarah say, "I already have a place in mind," when a loud ringing in my ear occurred. Or was that the loud collective gasp that escaped every person at the table? The most unexpected words came spewing out of Sarah's mouth, albeit stilted, as if even she couldn't believe what she was suggesting.

"I think it would be...love...ly if we had it at Peter's house...and Delanie's." I was an afterthought she obviously was hoping to forget. Honestly, I can't remember the last time she said my name. She usually only used pronouns or unflattering adjectives when referring to me. But none of that mattered now because I was reeling in shock. Peter's dazed eyes said he was too. For a moment, all we could do was stare at each other in disbelief, but Sarah interrupted us.

"What do you think?" she asked, batting her eyes.

What did I think? I thought she was out of her mind. It was only a few days ago that she was disparaging our home and accusing me of selling drugs and my body to pay for it.

Thankfully Peter spoke before I broke my new no swearing on Sunday rule in honor of my husband.

"Ma, as much as we would like to help celebrate Sam and Reed," he gave the newlyweds a pressed smiled, they in return looked at a loss for what to say. Everyone seemed entranced by the undiscovered tenth circle of hell we'd found ourselves in. "I don't think that's a good idea," he continued. "We haven't furnished it yet and our backyard is going in this week, so—"

"That's what makes it perfect." Sarah was giving us that unnatural, or was that unholy, smile? "We can rent cocktail tables and chairs." She had obviously thought this through. "Bethany said that receptions at homes are all the rage now."

"Ma." Sam came out of the fog we all seemed to be in. "If that's the case, we can have it at our home or not at all. We don't want to put anyone out."

"Honey, you can't host your own reception; that would be tacky. Besides, your brother's house is bigger, and we wouldn't have to move any furniture out since they don't have any." That sounded like a slight there at the end.

"Ma, Delanie works from home, so—"

"We would only need to come in and take a few measurements during the week and set up on Friday," Sarah interrupted Peter again. "Besides, it would give us the opportunity," she made herself look at me, "to get to know each other better." She immediately reached for her wine and downed the remainder of the glass. I swore she swished a little of it in her mouth like she was rinsing out dirty words.

If only I was still drinking—ever since we started trying to have a baby I'd given it up. What I wouldn't do for a margarita right now.

Before I could string two words together, Joseph changed the game entirely. "I like it. It's exactly what this family needs."

We needed it like blunt force trauma to the head.

Chapter Thirteen

"CRAZY DAY, HUH?" Peter stroked my hair.

I pulled the sheet around us and sighed against his bare chest. "What did we agree to?" The better question was how did I get talked into it? The man who I shared my bed with and his father were the main culprits. Two good men full of unrealistic ideals and a desire to keep their family together.

"I told you once you started picking out plants you would be throwing house parties."

I groaned at the lunacy of it all. "Don't expect edible cookies anytime soon." Except Sam had specifically marked a recipe in her new cookbook for me. It was one of Peter's favorite breakfasts, blueberry bake. Sam promised me it was Delanie-proof. I meant to prove her wrong someday and burn down my house while attempting it. Maybe I should do that tomorrow, then we couldn't have Sam's and Reed's reception here.

Peter laughed while continuing to stroke my hair. "I think Dad's right; this is a good thing."

I lifted my head to meet his eyes, which I could barely make out in the dark. "You really think so?"

He nodded. "Don't you?"

I thought for a moment. "I can't shake the feeling that..."

Peter brushed my hair back. "That what?"

"Something doesn't feel right about it. I'm sorry, I'm just having a hard time believing that all of a sudden your mom wants to be my friend."

Even in the dark I could see the warmth emanating from his eyes. No judgment or disappointment.

"I understand that, but I think Sam eloping has shaken her up."

"Maybe."

"Delanie, thank you."

"For what?"

"For allowing the small glimmer of hope a chance to grow."

I wasn't sure how hopeful I was, but I didn't want to dash Peter's hope. My head fell back on his chest. "The timing of this could have been better. I have to get those chapters to Chad this week."

"Dad said he would come and oversee the backyard, so you shouldn't have to worry about that. The house should be pretty quiet until Friday." Peter wanted to take care of our backyard, but he needed to help James this week with their biggest client, the town of Clearfield.

"I won't be able to work in my office."

"That's probably a good idea. You can work in bed like you used to."

It was my favorite spot, but it wasn't all that great for my neck and back. My new setup was much more ergonomic. "Don't say that out loud or your mom will start telling everyone I make all my money in bed."

He chuckled. "Not many people can say they've made millions from bed." He got me to laugh.

"True. Maybe someday I'll write a book titled, *How to Make Millions on Your Serta Mattress.*"

"Sounds like a best seller. Speaking of which, I checked the *New York Times* today."

I froze. "You're not supposed to."

"So, you don't want to know?"

I thought about it for all of two seconds. "Tell me." I squeezed my eyes shut.

He hugged me tight. "Congratulations, baby. Number one."

For some reason I felt guilty for being happy about it or relieved that it was doing as well as my previous books. It made me feel like I wasn't an impostor. Was it ridiculous I felt almost ashamed that I was successful and liked it? I kissed Peter's chest. "Thank you."

"I'm proud of you."

"You give me my best material."

"I do enjoy that, but that's not the only reason I'm proud of you. You quietly do so much good, including putting up with my crazy family."

"I like most of them. I'm even looking forward to meeting Mimsy's lover," I teased.

"Do you think she'll bring him to the reception?" He sounded alarmed.

"I forgot to tell you—when you went out to talk to James, she called him. They have a hot date for Saturday night, but your parents will have to drive them. Giovanni had his licensed revoked in 2002 for drag racing, so he says."

Peter groaned.

"How's James?" Sam and I had both noticed Avery's reaction and we tried to get her to talk, but she played it off.

"He's troubled."

"About what?"

"He wouldn't say. Told me to mind my own business."

Ouch. That was harsh. "I'm sorry."

"That's James for you. We ended up tossing around a football, talking about the Cubs' chances for going to the World Series this year."

I didn't know much about baseball, but from all the yelling they did during the games, I was going to assume their chances were low this year. "Do you think they are having a rough patch in their marriage?"

Peter thought for a moment. "I don't think so. Avery's his world. She has been from day one."

"Hopefully whatever it is will get better soon." I yawned, exhausted from the day.

Peter kissed the top of my head. "Sleep well. We have a big week ahead of us."

I had a feeling big wasn't going to be an adequate adjective.

Monday started out good with congratulatory emails from Chad, Joan, and Fiona. Chad's email wasn't entirely friendly, more like snarky on steroids.

You don't want to see me become a thirstbucket. That isn't going to be pretty for anyone, especially for you when I crash your love nest and make good on my earlier threat of babysitting your butt all day long. So get me those chapters. By the way, congratulations. You make me proud. Love you.

The love really oozed off the screen there. It was a good thing I had learned to speak New Yorker and knew that *thirstbucket* meant desperate or I would have been wasting more time looking up New York slang words like I had had to a few years ago. Sometimes I honestly felt like I lived in a different country than my New York friends.

I took a deep breath, flexed my fingers, ready to start shaking things up with the appearance of Mr. Black's mistress, who felt that discretion had gone out the window with his passing. With her would come the unraveling of the secrets Laine desperately wanted to protect Hunter from. I had barely gotten a few lines in when our doorbell rang. I wasn't expecting Joseph until 9:00 a.m. and it was 8:30. I climbed out of my bed, my office for the week, and hurried downstairs.

Joseph beamed brightly at my door. "Sorry, I'm early." He held up a bakery bag and a drink carrier with two steaming, lidded cups. "I thought we could have breakfast together. Peter mentioned you loved kolaches."

What was there not to love about puffy warm bread filled with fruit? I smiled at Joseph. He wore a look reminiscent of a teen boy who on a hope and a dare knocked on the girl of his dream's door. It was very sweet. Any annoyance I had from being interrupted evaporated.

I hardly knew how to respond. I wanted to tell him how touched I was and that I'd dreamt of a moment like this with a father. All I managed to get out was, "Thank you. I do love kolaches."

Joseph didn't seem to care or notice my greeting wasn't as heartfelt as I wished it to be. He came right in and I led him to our couch. We hadn't invested in a table yet. We should at least get some stools to go around the island. Sarah had not so subtlety suggested that, which made me not want to do it, but perhaps she had a point. Peter and I would probably still eat on the couch, at least until we had . . . Were we ever going to have a baby? Maybe the universe was punishing me for . . . *her.*

I shook myself out of my thoughts and sat next to Joseph, who handed me a warm cup. "You like green tea, right?" He'd obviously talked to my husband.

"It's my favorite. Thank you." The warmth from the cup had nothing on how I felt toward Joseph at this moment. "I hope you didn't have to go out of your way for all this."

The twinkle in his eyes said he did, but his curled lips said he wasn't going to own it. "It's been a while since I've had a good kolache." That was a nice way to spin it.

"I've never had a bad one." I grinned.

Joseph laughed while handing me my favorite—raspberry filled. Peter was definitely behind this.

We silently indulged in bliss for a moment. No need to talk when you could eat a kolache. That could be the motto of the bakery.

"How's work?" Joseph attempted small talk. I liked it. It was a good place to begin.

I tossed my head from side to side. "Busy. Lots of deadlines, but I can't complain."

"You write for some internet company, right?"

I nodded, thankful that was true. Well, it wasn't really an internet company, but I knew what he meant. Besides, less specifics were better for me. "I'm working on a piece now about human trafficking in the U.S."

It was another thing I was behind on. I made a mental note to ask Fiona if she could get me an interview with a group out of Utah that was waging a war on child trafficking. I'd run across them in the minimal research I'd been able to do.

Joseph's eyes widened. It wasn't normal small talk, or even pleasant. "Is that a big problem?"

"Unfortunately, and you would be surprised how much of it happens in our own backyards."

Joseph swallowed hard. "That's got to be tough to write about."

"It's frightening, but it's the only way to bring it to light so we can hopefully end it."

He tilted his head and studied me as if he were taking inventory, maybe reevaluating. "You sound like you wouldn't mind leading that charge."

"I hate to see any child suffer. I try to do what I can, where I can, but it seems so insignificant."

Joseph took a swig of his coffee and downed his kolache in two bites. "You're a good woman."

"I try to be. But I have a lot to work on."

"Don't we all?"

"The exception could be Peter."

Joseph laughed a booming laugh. "I hope you haven't placed my son on a pedestal, because believe me, in marriage it isn't pretty when the pedestal crumbles. And it will. Peter has his faults like everyone else."

"Well, he doesn't like sushi."

Joseph's laughter continued to fill my family room. "Can't say I blame him there." He turned more thoughtful and rested his large hand on my bare knee. Today was one of those rare days I wore shorts instead of a skirt. "Delanie, can I give you some advice?"

I nodded.

"Don't do Peter or yourself the disservice of believing he is better than you."

My eyebrows shot up.

Joseph gave a knowing smile. "I've noticed the way you look at my son. The way you both look at each other with those blinding stars in your eyes. I'm grateful he's found someone who loves him as much as you do, but don't forget he's a man. Speaking from experience, we tend to do and say stupid things from time to time. And sometimes the better we are, the bigger our mistakes tend to be."

I leaned back against the cushions of the couch, letting that ominous piece of advice bounce around in my head. There was some truth there. I could even see it in my imaginary friends I'd been writing for the last few years. But it was hard to imagine Peter doing more than leaving the toilet seat up or forgetting my birthday, which I wasn't all that sentimental about anyway.

Joseph patted my knee. "I didn't mean to worry you. Peter is a good man. I know. I raised him, and sometimes I thought he was abnormally good. Kind of wish Reed got him into more trouble on occasion. But from what I've observed, you're good for him. And if you don't mind me saying, I hope you both get into a little trouble together. Every relationship needs its ups and downs." He stood up and stretched his back. "Now it's time for this old man to get to work."

I stood up too, still trying to process our conversation. "Thank you for breakfast."

"It was my pleasure. Thank you for being willing to invite some trouble into your life this week." He gave me a wink.

"Yeah," I sighed.

"Sometimes the only way to fix things is to shake all the pieces together and see what new configuration you get out of it. If that doesn't work, you keep trying until you get the right one."

"Sounds painful."

"Yes. Always."

Chapter Fourteen

OSEPH WAS RIGHT. My week was painful, but not because of him. I could honestly say I was beginning to adore him. He brought me breakfast every morning and was transforming my backyard along with the day workers Peter had contracted with, and it was turning out beautiful. He truly behaved as if he wanted to get to know me. He even kissed my cheek when he said goodbye yesterday. He was becoming the father-in-law I had hoped for when we moved here. His wife, on the other hand... The one who said she only needed to take a few measurements? She didn't mention that was going to be an every-freaking-day thing. She even dragged Sam into the mix after telling her she didn't need to lift a finger.

Most of the time Sam and I stood there watching and hoping it would all go away, but no. My house was filled with tulle—I wasn't even sure what that was or what they were using it for, but there were rolls of it everywhere. On top of that colored net stuff there were tubs and tubs of who knows what, but I was sure to find out soon.

That wasn't the worst of it. Sarah had lots of friends that came too. Who knew she had friends? Okay, that was petty. I was in the process of trying to retrain my brain, but it was hard when Sarah was turning my life into a sequel of *The Wedding Planner*. This movie, though, was going to be more along the lines of a horror film. I was calling it *Chucky's Bridezilla Mother*. And heads were going to roll at the end of it if I didn't get some writing done. Chad was now frequently sending me texts laced with friendly threats and four-letter words. My responses were not all that friendly. I upped his four-letter words with some trashy mash-ups of those vile words and accompanied those responses with pictures of the Little Shop of Horrors Bridal Boutique that had thrown up in my house. Soon I would be begging Seymour to feed me to his overgrown Venus fly trap, or better yet, that's where I would dispose of the heads that were going to roll.

Maybe I needed to lay off the sadistic pop culture references.

The scariest thing, though, was how nice Sarah was being to me. I'm not kidding when I say I had taken major precautions before she set foot in our house again. I had not only locked the attic, but every bedroom door. I even took down all the framed *New York Times* posters and any other incriminating evidence and placed them in boxes just in case. But Sarah and her minions never went upstairs, except to measure the staircase for that tulle stuff.

I watched them like a hawk, but Sarah didn't so much as look in the direction of the bedroom that led to the attic. Instead, when Bethany surveyed the bottom floor from above and said, "Whoever designed this house deserves a medal. It's stunning," Sarah smiled and nodded. Sarah also greeted me every day and introduced me as Peter's wife without once choking on her words. That was more alarming than anything. What was she playing at? Or was I being paranoid?

While Sarah invaded my home, Sam and I caught up on her life in between Sarah asking for Sam's opinion on everything and begging her to invest in a wedding dress—a white one, preferably. Sam rolled her eyes so many times I was getting motion sickness from it. I could hardly blame her though. She didn't want this shindig and, like me, she had better things to do than watch grown women get excited over paper flowers, several of which were placed above my fireplace.

Poor Sam was also dealing with the first day of school blues. She sat tearing up on my couch while we faced each other with our feet tucked beneath us. "I can't believe Cody is a junior. I wanted to hold onto his legs this morning and beg him not to leave like he used to do to me when he was two. Reed talked me out of it."

I laughed at her. "That was a good call on his part."

"No one warns you about this part in life. They always tell you to hold on tight to them when they're little. They don't prepare you for the gut-wrenching ache when they can walk out your door and drive off without a second thought about you."

"Cody loves you; he's just a typical teen boy."

"I think he loves Reed more."

"I doubt it, but that's not a bad thing."

Sam let out a heavy enough breath she ruffled some of her hair. "You're right, especially since Neil has decided to father a child with every woman under twenty-five he meets. Can you believe he had the audacity to tell me that eloping was immature?" She gave me an evil grin. "I may have responded that at least Reed didn't need to have his parents' permission."

"How did that go over?"

"He mumbled something about this still being all my fault and we could have worked it out."

"Someone's delusional."

"I suggested medication."

"How's his mother dealing with all this?" Gelaire was like a second mother to Sam. Sam still took her grocery shopping once a week. I could never picture Sarah and I alone like that, especially if Peter and I were no longer together.

"Gelaire, while unhappy about her son's poor choices, is happy for me. She's coming Saturday, along with everyone else Ma invited, unfortunately," she tried to say quietly.

"I heard that," Sarah called from the dining room. "You should be grateful so many people love you."

Sam rolled her eyes. "They don't love me. They all want to say they went to the Sidelined Wife's reception."

Not that I didn't think people loved Sam, but I had a feeling she was right. It was bizarre how many people RSVP'd on such short notice. A woman with a small cake decorating business had even volunteered to make a massive four-tiered cake and cupcakes for the soiree, free of charge I might add, unless you counted that she wanted to be able to post pictures of her creations on her website. I had no doubt the benevolent baker would make sure to have Sam and Reed in some of them.

All the attention Sam was receiving made me even more thankful no one knew who Autumn Moone was.

"Speaking of your alter ego, did you sign on the dotted line for Weekend Musings?"

Sam clasped her hands together. "Yes. I'm so nervous. I start in a few weeks."

"Congratulations. You're going to be fantastic."

She took my hands and squeezed them. "I hope so. I also have two book signings next week. Can you believe it?"

"I can."

"How do you think I should sign my name? These are the things that are keeping me up at night now."

"Not Reed?" I teased.

Sam blushed. "Yeah, well, him too. He's already planning a big honeymoon for us over Christmas break."

"That sounds like fun."

"Being married to Reed is fun, and not just because of the S-E-X," Sam whispered.

"I heard that too, Samantha Marie," Sarah yelled. She must have cat ears. Good to know.

Sam shook her head at her mother. "Don't get me wrong, that part is good. More than good." Her cheeks glowed.

"So I read on your blog."

Sam waved me off with a cat-like grin. "Seriously though, he's my partner in every sense of the word."

I knew exactly how she felt. Peter was my best friend.

"Enough talk about men. Please tell me you will come to my book signings. If you and Avery come, at least I know two people will be there."

"Of course I'll come." Though Chad was in my head telling me not to. "I predict a line out the door."

"I doubt it."

"Mark my words."

She let out a huge breath. "How did I ever get here? I guess I can thank Autumn Moone." She laughed.

I could only nod with a pressed-lipped smile. What did I say? What I wanted to say was we could both blame Autumn Moone for the lives we were leading. "Do you ever wish she wouldn't have posted your blog?"

Sam rubbed her lips together and thought, making me more nervous of her answer. She let out a meaningful sigh. "When I receive negative comments or people I don't know think they have every right to judge me, at those times I wish for my quiet life back. But...in a weird way, she gave me confidence to be who I am. To give Reed a chance. For that I can't thank her enough."

Internally I breathed a sigh of relief. Outwardly I squeezed her hand. "I'm glad she did."

Amid all the chaos and me staying up way too late trying to make my deadline, an interesting thing happened. *Perspective.* Wednesday night before I left to help at the shelter and then attend my "class," Peter was giving me a much-needed long kiss goodbye in the kitchen. We were hiding from the women who were now perpetual fixtures in our home.

Peter had me backed up against the counter, his arms employed to hold me as tightly against his body as they could. His warm mouth crushed my own while his tongue teased my lips to part. I was in the middle of enjoying the taste of Peter and his hands all over my curves when we heard a cleared throat. I told you, cleared throats were never good. We reluctantly pulled apart, not really caring we had been caught kissing in our own home.

Peter groaned and turned around. That was about as annoyed as he ever behaved. He took my hand and we faced his mom together. It was the first time all week she scowled, but she made sure to recover from it quickly, raising my suspicions yet again. But then she made me doubt my doubts about her.

"We're leaving," Sarah informed us.

"Do you need help taking anything out?" Peter asked.

Sarah gave her precious boy a big smile. "As a matter of fact, I do."

"Okay, let me finish saying goodbye to Delanie before she leaves for the shelter."

"Shelter?" Sarah's face scrunched with the question.

"Delanie volunteers at a women and children's shelter every week."

A wash of astonishment fell over Sarah's face. She stared at me as if she had never seen me before. "What do you do there?" Her tone bordered on skeptical.

"A little of everything—playing with the children, helping women with resumes, cleaning. It depends on the week."

Red appeared in Sarah's cheeks as if she was embarrassed. What did she have to be embarrassed about?

"I had no idea," Sarah stuttered.

That's when it hit me. We didn't know each other at all. I had watched her for three days interact with what seemed like nice women, and guess what? They all liked her a lot. She laughed with them and gave advice, even comfort when one lady mentioned that her dad was diagnosed with dementia. She was nothing like the woman who had no issue showing me how much she didn't like me. I also caught a glimpse of how much she really wanted to do this for her daughter. To show Sam and Reed off.

She spoke several times of how proud she was of Sam and all she had accomplished, and what a fine catch Reed was.

There Sarah stood looking at me with the same bewilderment I felt toward her. For the first time, I think she was truly questioning if she knew who I was. And for the first time, I saw her as more than my enemy.

Chapter Fifteen

THE CHAOS WAS finally coming to an end, but it was culminating in my house with me wearing a ridiculous pale green dress. Sarah had gotten it in her head that this was a real reception and Avery and I were acting as the bridesmaids, plus we all needed to match because Sarah and Joseph wanted family pictures.

I stood in front of the mirror in our bathroom, appalled at the silk gown that draped my body. I'd never worn silk or an evening gown before. It didn't really go with the nose ring or tattoo. Sarah may have politely asked that I not wear my diamond stud; I more than politely refused. Sarah tsked before Joseph elbowed her, making a forced smile appear on her face.

Peter walked up from behind me, looking handsome in a dark suit with a silly floral tie to match my dress. All the Decker men were up in arms over the choice of tie, but Sarah wasn't backing down. I swore she purchased all this stuff as soon as she had heard that Sam was engaged back in June. There was no way she pulled this all together in a week's time.

Peter smiled with delight while he perused me.

"I know. I look absurd."

Peter ran his fingers down my arm. "Your skin is always so soft."

"You're saying I do look ridiculous?"

He laughed and turned me around to face him. "I never said or thought such a thing." He played with one of the curls that outlined my face. "You're stunning."

"I look like someone played dress up with me."

He leaned in and brushed my lips. "Can we play dress *down* later?"

"Are you trying to seduce your wife?"

"Yes." He nuzzled my neck. "Is it working?"

"If you keep doing that, we're going to be late, if that answers your question."

"Mmm," he groaned against my skin. "Tempting." He planted a few more kisses on my neck before meeting my eyes. "I suppose we should go downstairs."

I grabbed a hold of the lapels on his jacket and pulled him to me with a sultry smile. "I'm not opposed to being late."

I barely saw the passion flare in his gorgeous green eyes before his mouth crashed into mine.

"Peter!" Sarah yelled from downstairs. Wow, could her voice carry.

Peter stopped mid-kiss, not sure what to do. "Sexy wife," he whispered against my lips, "or Ma's wrath?"

I skimmed his lips, running my fingers through his styled hair.

"Sexy wife it is," he whispered with pleasure.

"Peter!" Sarah screeched again.

We both sighed in defeat, knowing we better get down there before she came up here.

Peter took my hand and led me downstairs. I smoothed his hair as we went. Did I also mention I was wearing heels? My feet were in shock and questioning whether we should traverse the stairs. I was a barefoot kind of woman, and if I had to wear shoes I preferred sandals. Winters were rough when I had to wear boots. I stopped Peter at the top of the steps. We both stared down at the sparkly gold heels I had been forced to wear. It was there I reminded myself I was still me. I may have given up my home for the week, making my manuscript late—I gave Chad nine chapters, not ten last night before the stroke of midnight. He wasn't happy about it until this afternoon when I received a text, saying, *Best damn thing you've ever written. Now quit acting like Colin Cowie; I need to know what happens between Laine and Hunter.* I had to ask who Colin Cowie was. Apparently, he was Oprah's event planner. Why Chad thought I would know that I had no idea. But despite all my acquiescing for the week, I had to draw the line.

I stepped out of the heels that were holding my feet hostage and making me as tall as my six-foot-tall husband. Peter laughed when I ditched them by the stairs but didn't say a word about it as we walked down together amongst the tulle. Lots and lots of ivory tulle entwined with twinkle lights lit up our staircase. As I looked out, our entire downstairs seemed to be twinkling. And somehow a flower garden had sprouted amongst a café. There were several tables and chairs filling our great room. Bryan Adams music drifted in the background, per Sam's request. He was her favorite artist and Reed had proposed to her in the grocery store while Bryan Adams played.

Peter squeezed my hand. "Do you regret we never had a reception?"

My face crinkled at the thought. "I'm counting my lucky stars we didn't."

"Hmm," Peter responded.

"Did you want one?"

He shrugged. "It would have been nice to show off my new bride. Maybe it could have eased tensions back then."

I never knew he felt that way. And it wasn't like his parents offered to throw one. Cat and Ron certainly would have never thought about it. They believed marriage was now a dead institution. They claimed the only reason they got married was because society many years ago forced them to if they wanted any credibility. I never found that reason credible. For many years I agreed marriage was a pointless endeavor, but I had obviously been proven wrong.

"You never said anything."

He pulled up my hand and kissed it.

We didn't get to say more on the subject because his mother appeared at the bottom of the stairs wearing a typical mother of the bride suit in beige. Her gray hair was in an updo. "There you are. Dad wants you to see the backyard before everyone arrives." Sarah's eyes dropped to my bare feet that barely peeked out under the long gown. "Where are your shoes, Delanie?" She said my name without cringing. She was getting better at it.

"Heels aren't my thing." I kept my voice light.

Sarah's left eye started to twitch, but she reigned it in along with her frown. "Well, maybe you can put them on when we do pictures."

"Maybe." I smiled while we walked past her.

She didn't say another word on the subject as we headed toward the back door. We had to weave in and out of several people dressed in white shirts and black pants prepping and setting out food that I knew I didn't make; it smelled incredible and looked pretty on all the crystal platters. There was a table set up in our breakfast nook that held the large cream-frosted cake with black roses trailing along one side. I had to admit, if I ever had a wedding cake, that would be it. Black roses? Yes, please. The cake was striking amongst all the cupcakes placed around it as if they were worshipping the mighty frosted god that towered above them all.

The three of us walked out the back door to find Joseph waiting for us in a suit and tie that matched Peter's, except Joseph's white shirt was barely holding in his gut. Joseph could hardly contain his excitement. He took my hand and pulled me out onto our natural stone patio that had been transformed. A charcoal gray rattan patio furniture set had been added and several pots of green plants in all sizes made it look like a magazine layout. Around the patio, Joseph had planted black dahlias that looked like hundreds of dark starbursts. Forget the black roses, the dahlias that were the deepest shade of burgundy were beyond beautiful. The yard was also fully landscaped with full moon maples, picked especially for their name, and the white firs, not to mention other flowering shrubbery that Joseph thought would look good. He was right.

"What do you think?" Joseph stood next to me, admiring his handiwork.

"It's gorgeous." I hugged him without thinking. Something I had never initiated before with him.

He wasn't awkward like me and reciprocated instantly.

"Thank you," I whispered against him.

"My pleasure." He kissed my cheek.

Peter and Sarah joined us. Sarah gave me an appraising sort of look as if she was holding off judgment. I could live with that. Peter patted his dad on the back. "Did you rent the furniture?"

Joseph's ears pinked while giving Sarah a glance. "*We* thought since we never bought you a wedding gift, we should."

Sarah stood stoic with a blank expression, making me wonder if it was a mutual gift.

Peter hugged his mother and she clung to him as if he was going off to college and she wouldn't see him for months. Peter held onto her just as tight. Guilt wriggled in my stomach. They weren't going to miss each other, they *had* been missing each other, all because of me.

"Thank you," I said to everyone and no one, really. "I better get back in and…" And what? I wasn't in charge of this party and the only thing I wanted to do at that moment was lock myself in my office and bleed my feelings out onto my computer, but that wasn't an option. It didn't matter; I turned around anyway and let my bare feet take me across the cool stone back into the chaos ensuing in the home I didn't even recognize as my own.

I was so glad the first people I ran into were Sam and Avery, who had arrived in all their glory. And they *were* glorious. Sam was in an ivory lace gown that showed off how hard she had been working out. It wasn't a wedding dress, per se, but she fit the part of blushing bride. Avery wore the same dress as me but did it more justice —the pale green suited her more and she had glammed up for the night with her hair swept to one side in a classic twist. Her all-American-girl look was made for the evening gown.

"Are you okay?" Avery asked.

I looked down at what I was wearing and put on a game face. "As good as I'm going to get in this," I lied. But I didn't know how to explain how I was really feeling at the moment.

They both laughed.

"Says the gorgeous, ethereal creature every woman wished she looked like," Sam said. She always paid me compliments like that. I was never sure how to respond. Growing up, Cat told me it was a shame I was so pretty; no one would ever take me seriously. I meant to prove her wrong and always downplayed how I looked. I even got a pair of nonprescription glasses in high school so I looked more studious. Do you know how many guys found that attractive? More than I imagined.

"I look like I lost a dare."

"We all did," Sam lamented. "Where's the alcohol, by the way?"

We didn't get a chance to find out. All the Decker men descended upon us, along with the matriarch who was still clinging to my husband when they walked in the back door. She only let go of him because he gravitated toward me and she was distracted by how handsome all her grandsons looked. She doted over them the way a grandma should, kissing their cheeks and hugging them. I still wondered how she would treat a child of Peter's and mine. Were we really on the path to make things right between us? Would Peter no longer have to choose between the women in his life?

We were also joined by the Cassidys, Reed's parents who I had to say were the "it" couple. They had both maintained their figures and had unusually smooth skin for their ages and fabulous jawlines. No sagging necks, not even a trace of loose skin. They were retired and lived in

Wisconsin. Oddly, they resembled the Mr. and Mrs. Black in my books. I suppose that was fitting since Hunter's looks were based on Reed. The parents of the groom looked happy to be there and gushed over how lovely their new daughter-in-law was. I envied the easy relationship Sam automatically had with her in-laws.

"As soon as Linda arrives with Mimsy, we're going to take pictures," Sarah announced.

I wasn't sure who Linda was, but I hoped she knew what she was getting into picking up Mimsy and her lover, Giovanni. By the several snickers in the group, I wasn't the only one thinking along those lines.

I took note that James was behaving like his normal self. He held Avery close to him and only had eyes for her. They truly were a stunning couple. The kind that made people envious, that showed that age was only a number and the forties could be fabulous.

It wasn't long before Mimsy arrived like the ushering in of the apocalypse. We all knew we were in for a show, but none of us were prepared for figurative carnage, and by that I meant how we all were dying inside, some of us with laughter and others—like Sarah—with mortification, when Mimsy and her *lover* arrived. What could I say? They were, um…well…furry. And I had to think very hot. It was August, after all, and though the evenings were getting cooler, it was still very warm.

Mimsy and Giovanni came strolling in through the entryway and great room like a geriatric knockoff of Kanye West and Kim Kardashian. They were draped in black fur and dripping in what I could only think were fake diamonds. If they were real, they should have had an armed escort with them. Mimsy's coat was too big for her tiny frame and she had a harder time than normal walking, making it look like she was carrying a dead animal on her back. Giovanni, on the other hand, was tall and walked with authority for someone of his age. And though his face was wrinkled, his bald head was unnaturally shiny. It had to be from some type of oil, or maybe it was the reflection of all the bling around his neck.

I looked up at Peter who was in as much shock as me. No words passed between us because there hadn't been any invented to fully articulate the sight before us. For a moment no one spoke. Even the catering employees all froze in wonder, perhaps terror. And poor Linda, who had had the displeasure of picking them up, wandered in looking like the dryer in a carwash had hit her and scared her witless.

It was a horrifying sight, especially for Sarah, who found some words to say.

"Mom, why aren't you wearing the dress we picked out for you?"

The better questions would have been, do you know how many animals had to give their lives for that coat? And what tween girl's jewelry box did you raid? Or probably most important, did you overdose on your medication? But this wasn't my circus. I was only providing the space for all the flying monkeys to land.

Giovanni looked affronted that no one greeted him first. He took matters into his own hands, which were covered in gigantic ice rocks, and didn't let Mimsy answer. He ran his hand over his bald head like he had forgotten he no longer had hair and flashed us a smile full of dentures. "I'm Giovanni Smith." *Smith?* Why did I think her Latin lover was more like a Midwestern liar? His accent was all Chicago. Not a trace of Italian. "My girl," he wrapped his arm around Mimsy's waist, "she ain't going to wear nothing but the best."

"What he said." Mimsy stood a little taller, well, she tried—that coat had to weigh as much as her. Mimsy dared us all with her beady eyes to contradict her. And did I detect a hint of *Jersey Shore* in her tone? What was she watching besides STD videos in that assisted living place?

I had to hand it to Joseph, he was becoming an excellent mediator. The world could use more people like him. He reached out his hand and introduced himself to Giovanni, as well as going around the room introducing each one of us while we all stood there transfixed, except for the nephews, who were shaking due to the laughter they were suppressing. After introductions, he offered to take their coats and hang them up. I never thought I would say this, but it would have been better if they kept the coats on. Think Saturday Night Fever. Giovanni was in a white suit and Mimsy was wearing a red off-the-shoulder dress that was barely being held up by her less-than-voluptuous chest. I was going to guess those old boobies she talked about didn't have the perk they needed to pull off such a dress.

Once Mimsy was free of the coat and our jaws were all properly dropped, she announced, "What are you all standing around for? Let the party begin."

I had a feeling it was one we were never going to forget.

Chapter Sixteen

*T*HE ONLY GOOD thing that could be said about family pictures in the backyard was that Sarah was so preoccupied trying to keep Giovanni out of them and Mimsy's dress from taking a plunge, she'd forgotten I wasn't wearing shoes and didn't keep me out of most of the photos like she had done in years past. I didn't even bother to show up last year when they took family pictures. Maybe Sarah would photoshop me out like she had in the past and say it was by accident. We would have to see.

Oddly though, the photographer, Deann, an old friend of Sarah's, was over-the-top nice to me. She couldn't keep her hands off my hair and kept commenting how she had never seen my unique color of smoky red. "Do you color it?" she asked me.

I shook my head and shied away, not comfortable with strangers petting me or asking personal questions. I also had to rescue my nephews from Giovanni, who was saying something about how he knew a guy who knows guy and getting something off a truck. Whatever it was, it didn't sound good, and my nephews' wide eyes were swimming with possibilities that I was sure their parents wouldn't appreciate.

I never thought I would say this, but I was happy when guests started to arrive. My neighbors and homeowners' association probably didn't appreciate it since we had to get a special onetime use code for the guests to enter our community, and several cars were parked in front of neighbors' houses. I didn't think we were going to win any popularity contests amongst our stuffy neighbors, but they already thought I was a call girl. There was an increasing amount of people who could be added to that list. I should probably be more bothered by that than I was.

There were plenty of things to be bothered by tonight, though. Giovanni was on top of the list. I didn't like the way he treated Mimsy—like a misogynistic Neanderthal who believed that women were only put on the earth to please their men and look pretty for them. I was more put off and surprised that Mimsy put up with it. During the last four years, I had never seen her let anyone push her around. Well, I wasn't one to put up with it, so after the second time I saw him order her to get him a drink, I'd had enough. I was all for couples serving each other, but the way Giovanni spoke to her was a clear indication he wouldn't return the favor.

I met Mimsy at the table covered in crystal champagne glasses filled with their namesake. The table was one big, sparkly, bubbly magnet. I'd hoped parents were watching their children, aka the parents of my nephews. Not that I hadn't done my own share of underage drinking when I was growing up, but like many before me, I was becoming a hypocritical adult, not by choice, per se, but having the police show up with my neighbors already under the impression I was a call girl wouldn't be in my best interest. Though it would be a good story to tell and use for a future book. One worry at a time.

I pulled up Mimsy's dress before removing the champagne glass from her hand. Her beady eyes bore into me like a drill. Sarah had the same look down and had used it on me many times, so I didn't flinch once.

"I'll take that." I was tempted to down the drink myself, but instead reminded myself there could be more important things than a brief happy buzz at stake. *Was I ever going to get pregnant?*

"What do you think you're doing?" Mimsy shook her gnarled finger at me.

"I could ask you the same question." I stood firm.

"I don't answer to you."

"You're right, you don't. And you shouldn't be answering to Giovanni either." I made sure to say that loud enough for the nearby jerk to hear.

And hear he did. He'd been bragging about how well connected he was to Deann, who was still following me around and snapping candids of me and the other guests. He stopped mid-sentence and marched right over to us—more like shuffled with purpose. His arm immediately went around Mimsy, making her fall into him. "Do you have a problem, young lady?"

I hadn't been spoken to like that since I told off my principal in high school. Oddly, I had the same type of problem with him as I did with Giovanni. I gave him my politest sneer. "I think you're capable enough to get your own drinks, don't you?"

"I don't care what you think," he threw back at me. That caught the attention of my husband and his mother, who both hurried over.

Peter placed his hand on the small of my back. "What's going on?" he asked more me than anyone, but Giovanni was quick on the draw.

"Your wife needs to mind her own business."

Peter stiffened next to me as if ready to pounce. I wasn't sure I had ever seen Peter behave in such a way, but he didn't jump in right away like a knight in shining armor; instead, he let the woman he treated like a queen fight her own battles like she wished.

"Mimsy is our business and we expect her to be treated with respect." I dared Giovanni with my tone to bring it on.

Sarah's clenched fists and red face that had been directed toward me for causing a mini-scene now didn't know what to do. Her hands, which had been in motion, dropped on her hips. She was spluttering incoherently.

Giovanni yanked Mimsy tighter against him. "Let me tell you something—ain't no one going to talk to me like that. Mimsy doesn't even like you."

Mimsy owned the statement with her eyes that hit mine directly and said *what of it?*

The admission didn't surprise me, and I was far past being hurt by the knowledge. "Mimsy, I know you don't like me, but I hope you like yourself enough to know that you deserve a real man, not this cheap imitation who probably can't even spell *respect* much less show you any."

Mimsy continued to stare at me, but disbelief now flooded her features and maybe gave her some pause.

I set my sights on the con man next to her. "Now excuse me while I go see how much cash you managed to steal from my nephews."

His dentures came falling out.

"Yes, I saw that too. Keep your hands out of their pockets and Mimsy's. And if every cent isn't returned, you'll be dealing with more than me tonight." I turned to leave but not before Sarah caught my eye. The same look of wonder she'd been giving me the past several days filled her pale blue eyes. But she shook it off quickly to rescue her mom.

With my head held high, I walked away with my knight ever by my side holding my hand, reminding me that humanity and decency existed despite the Giovannis of the world. I bet Giovanni wasn't even his real name.

By now our house was full. I didn't think many witnessed the scene that had played out in our kitchen. Most everyone was congregating around Sam and Reed in the great room.

Peter stopped me and wrapped me in his arms before I could find our nephews in the sea of people. "I love you," he whispered in my ear. "Are—"

"You are the cutest couple." Deann interrupted by snapping picture after picture of us while she gushed. Not only that, she blinded us with her flash. If only Sarah and I had a better relationship, I could have gotten a real photographer for the event, the same guy who had done Sam's photos for her website. He was amazing. I'd hired him to do some work for my *other* job when I'd done a piece about the homeless in Chicago. His lens was able to capture not only physical destitution, but the poverty of the soul in those people's eyes. It was haunting.

While Peter and I were recovering from having our corneas burned, Deann, with her camera hanging around her neck, placed her arms around us. Her jovial, aged face poked right between our own. Her gray hairs tickled my nose. "I saw what you did back there." Her voice was conspiratorially low. "You have some balls, sister. I love it."

Peter cracked a smile. I admit my lip twitched.

"I'm going to go upstairs if that's okay with you and take some shots from up there so I can capture the crowd, and while I'm up there I'll keep my eyes on you know who." She winked ten times in a row.

"Sure," Peter answered. "That would be great."

She stepped back all smiles. "Don't worry, I've got you've covered."

That didn't make me feel any better, but I was happy to have her be wherever I wasn't. Peter and I needed a moment to figure out what to do about Giovanni.

Peter led me outside where several people had gathered to drink and mingle. A few people looked familiar, and they waved and greeted Peter. Most stared at me like I was an aberration. Must be friends of Sarah. I gave them my best smile, making them turn their sour faces away.

Our new patio loveseat was available, so we tried it out. It was comfortable, but the company was even better. Peter sat close to me, held my hands in his lap, and gazed at me. "Are you okay?"

"Why wouldn't I be?"

Peter's thumb stroked my hand. "You're incredible. Only you would ask that after my grandmother insulted you."

"I'm used to it."

He let out a heavy breath. "You shouldn't be. If we were in a different setting I would have said something. I'm so sorry."

"Don't be. We've got bigger problems to worry about. You or your parents need to contact the assisted living center. And if your parents are on Mimsy's bank accounts, they should probably check to see if any large or unusual withdrawals have been made."

Peter's eyes doubled in size. "You don't think he's..."

"I hope not, but swindlers like Giovanni know who to target and how to lure them to get what they want."

"We should call the police."

"I agree, but maybe we should wait until after the party."

Peter looked around at all the nicely dressed people swirling around us, laughing as if they didn't have a care in the world. "You're right, but we can't leave him alone. I'll talk to James and Dad. We can all keep an eye on him."

"That's a good idea."

Peter's warm hand rested on my cheek. Tenderness burned in his eyes. "If I haven't said it lately, thank you for putting up with my family. They don't deserve you."

"Maybe it's a good thing we never met each other's parents before we tied the knot."

He leaned in and kissed me once. "Another thing to thank God for."

I grabbed his tie, not ready for him to leave. "Peter."

"Yeah."

"I still would have married you." I pulled him to me for one more kiss. "Now go kick Giovanni's a— I mean..." No, that was exactly what I meant.

Peter's eyes and face lit up. "I love—"

"There you are," both Avery and James loudly interrupted our moment. There was a lot of that going on tonight and I wasn't happy about it.

They were practically jogging over wearing smiles that hovered between shock and amusement. This couldn't be good. My first guess was Mimsy's dress had finally taken the plunge, but no. More flying monkeys had landed.

James and Avery stood in front of us bursting to blurt out their unwelcome news. But first they had to take a moment. Peter and I sat warily waiting for the bomb to explode.

Avery was finally composed enough to say, "You will never believe who just walked in."

"The cops?" was my first guess and at this point maybe a wish, even if it did lend to my neighbors' theory that I was a call girl.

Avery and James both shook their heads.

"Why would you guess that?" Avery asked. "Never mind, tell me later."

"The cops may need to break up a fight," James interjected.

"What?" Both Peter and I stood, ready to act.

"Not yet." Avery waved us down, but we both stayed on our feet.

"Who's here?" Peter asked, losing patience.

"Neil," they said in unison.

I shook my head. I hoped I'd heard them wrong. "As in Sam's ex-husband?"

"The very one," Avery answered.

James cracked his knuckles. "Looks like I may need to call in some favors after all." James was always joking, or at least I hoped he was, that he had friends who knew how and where to bury bodies.

Peter placed a hand on James's shoulder. "Hold that thought." Surprisingly, his tone wasn't against it.

"How's Sam taking it?" I asked.

"She's flustered, but so far seems to be handling it with grace. Reed on the other hand..." Avery gave a mischievous smile. "He's all for calling in James's favor."

James gave an appreciative smile.

Peter, on the other hand, was more alarmed. "We better get in there and see what we can do."

"Grab a shovel, brother," James teased.

"Why don't you two go check on Reed," I suggested to Peter and James. "But don't forget to talk to your dad and keep your eye on Giovanni."

"What? Why?" Avery was more than curious.

"I'll explain as we walk."

Avery looped arms with me. I was happy to see she had ditched her shoes too. She was such a tiny thing. I probably looked like the jolly pale green giant next to her. Scratch that, make that unjolly bordering on ready to snap some wings off some flying monkeys. Regardless, I never imagined myself being friends with the cheerleaders of the world. In high school, I fashioned myself as part of the anti-popular crowd, though I'd been popular in my own right, or more like infamous. It probably served me right to marry into a family that bred popular kids for a living. Good thing they were some of the most wonderful people on the planet. It still didn't make me sorry for writing that exposé in my high school newspaper about the head cheerleader who believed hazing was a right. I was still proud to have stripped the mean girl of her pom poms.

Avery and Sam, though both cheerleaders, were anything but mean.

I was able to tell Avery most of the story as we traversed the crowded house, making our way to Sam, where she'd last been seen near the entryway greeting Gelaire, her ex-mother-in-law, though Sam would never call her that. According to Avery, Neil brought his mother, Gelaire, along with his infant daughter, Farrah. Not sure how that all came about. The only bright spot was that he didn't bring his pubescent pregnant fiancée. Or, at least, she hadn't been seen. With the way things were going, I wouldn't be surprised if she showed up.

Before we made it to Sam, Deann called my name and waved to me from my loft. She had two other women with her I recognized as Sarah's friends who had been in and out of my house all week. "I'm getting some great shots up here!" she yelled down.

Great. Like we needed this crazy-town parade to be immortalized in pictures. I had no time to pay her any attention or tell her I would be more comfortable if people weren't up there. There were more pressing matters at hand.

Peter and James had made it to Reed in the nick of time. Reed was about ready to throw a punch if his icy glares directed at Neil from the fireplace said anything. Sam's grace was expiring quickly as she stood with Gelaire, who was holding her hand and fretting.

"Darling, I'm so sorry. He insisted he drive me instead of taking a cab and I thought perhaps this could heal some wounds." Gelaire scowled at Neil, the cause of each and every one of Sam's scars. "I never meant to upset you."

Sam took a breath and squeezed the elegant Gelaire's hand. Sam had the best luck with mothers-in-law—even after she was no longer married to their sons, they still loved her. I had to keep my envy at bay.

"Gelaire, I could never be upset with you." Sam whipped her head toward Neil. "But how dare *you*," she kept her voice low, "come here after everything you've put Cody and me through and tell me I should rethink this. There is nothing to rethink. Reed is the best man I've ever known, and you should be thanking him for the dad he's been to our son."

Neil's face exploded in green waves of jealousy. His hair plugs looked about ready to pop. "It will be a cold day in hell before I thank him for breaking up our family."

Was he delusional? Avery gave me a look that said she was thinking along the same lines as me.

"Son, enough," Gelaire demanded.

Neil didn't acknowledge Gelaire. He continued to stare at Sam with cold eyes. "I think I'll help myself to a drink. I'll see you at Cody's home opener next week."

Sam didn't let him shake her. "Make sure you're there for the right reasons—the only reason. Cody."

Neil sneered at her before stomping off.

Sam nodded at both Avery and me to tell us she was okay before she led Gelaire back with her to be with Reed.

"Well, that was exciting," Avery commented. "I better go find Jimmy and Matt and make sure Mimsy's sugar daddy isn't taking any candy from my kids."

I had a feeling it was Mimsy who was the sugar momma. Which was why I was happy to turn around and see that Sarah and Joseph were glued to the pale, wrinkled Kanye and Kim wannabes. Giovanni was trying to stare me down, but all he got in return was a smirk. Mimsy, I noticed, was pouting like a child, and Sarah kept grabbing her and pulling her back like she was a toddler. Joseph smiled warmly at me and mouthed, "Thank you."

I wasn't sure why he was thanking me, but I would take a kind word from him any day. And hoped to give him many in return in the future.

First, though, my new fan Deann with her two sidekicks accosted me when I made it to the stairs as if they were waiting for me to pass by. Deann reached for me and they circled around, making me feel like I was the sacrifice for the weird ritual they looked ready to perform. They were all staring at me in what could only be described as bewilderment. I began to back away, more than uncomfortable, but Deann pulled me back into their unholy circle. Where was Mimsy's holy water when you needed it?

"We were just saying how lovely your home was and how Peter hit the jackpot." Deann petted my arm. The women all smiled at some inside joke I'd apparently missed.

I wasn't even sure how to respond, but didn't need to. The perky dyed brunette to my right who was wearing a puffy dress as if she was going to prom in the 1980s spoke before I could.

"You know, Peter dated my daughter in high school."

"I didn't know that." Nor did I care to. Not like I was jealous, but what difference did it make now?

"They were such a cute couple. I thought maybe he might change his mind about entering the seminary then. He broke Eva's heart, but I guess he was . . . well, I guess he wanted *bigger* things." That sounded like sour grapes with a topping of BS.

I suppose you could consider God *bigger* things, but I was sure they were slighting me somehow. I should have kept my mouth shut, but I wasn't going to be insulted one more time tonight in my own home. "You know what they say—good things come to those who wait." I got too much pleasure at the taken-aback, wide eyes of each woman. "Excuse me ladies, I'm sure *my husband* is looking for me."

Like startled mice, they all scurried over to Sarah and instead of acting affronted they seemed excited. Why it was such a thrill for them to tell Sarah what an awful human being I was, I would never know. Newsflash—she already knew. Or at least she thought she knew. To add to the oddity of it all, Sarah hushed them. She didn't seem happy to have others confirm what she already knew. She looked up from her circle of friends and locked eyes with me. In hers, I saw a look that teetered on perplexed and ashamed. What that was all about, I had no idea. I expected gloating.

No time to think about it. The party gods got their final revenge on me for the evening. Cody appeared with his baby sister wailing in his arms. I assumed he was looking for his dad, or maybe not since he wasn't exactly on speaking terms with him, but the kid was looking for help and I was it.

Cody thrust ten-month-old Farrah into my arms without a second thought. "I don't know what I did. One second she was laughing, the next...this happened. And she won't stop."

I rarely had the opportunity to hold a baby. I was as unprepared for it now as I was the first time. And just like the first time, I instinctively held her close to me, not sure where those inclinations came from. "Shhh." I bounced Farrah, trying not to get emotional myself. So many memories flooded my mind and I ached desperately for *her*. The baby with no name. I smoothed Farrah's blond, wispy hair while she calmed down, wishing for the red hair I had only touched once. Farrah looked up at me with her big brown eyes full of wonder. A smile filled her cherubic face. Tears filled my own eyes. I never knew the color of *her* eyes.

Peter surprised me and wrapped his arms around me from behind, bringing Farrah closer to me. It was both ecstasy and agony. Farrah calmed and snuggled against me. I held onto her with all that I had.

"You've never been more beautiful to me," Peter whispered in my ear.

Would he feel the same way about me if he knew about *her*?

Chapter Seventeen

$\mathscr{I}$ STRETCHED IN BED, careful not to wake up Peter. I knew how exhausted I still felt and was sure he felt the same. He had helped with more of the cleanup last night than I did, and on top of that, he had to calm his mom down when Mimsy basically declared she thought we all were liars and Giovanni was the only person who really cared about her. Joseph and Sarah were supposedly going into the assisted living facility today to have an emergency meeting with the executive director. James said he would call in a favor and get a background check done on Giovanni.

I lay there and watched Peter's chest steadily rise and fall. I had to stop myself from touching him. I knew he wouldn't mind. He said I was his favorite wakeup call. For today, though, I only admired and wondered. I was still amazed that we ended up together. It was as if black and white got married and decided to live in gray. For the most part I think it worked for us. I didn't believe life was black and white, but sometimes, like last night, I was reminded of the stark contrast between our two worlds. I was not an Eva, who had five children and was married to an oncologist as her mother had told me. Not only that, but she was PTA president, a terrific cook, taught Sunday school, and from the sounds of it, would be canonized immediately upon her death. But she was sure to live forever because she was a nutritionist and taught spin classes regularly. Eva's mom, whose name I couldn't remember, wanted to make sure to drive that home as if it were a competition.

I could write a kissing scene that would make toes curl. Did that compare? Probably not. That said, Peter did like to be my test subject.

"I never saw you coming," I whispered. Maybe if I had, I would have made different choices. I didn't even know someone like him was an option. As much as I wished we'd met ten years ago, I wasn't ready for him then. I wouldn't have chosen him, a thought that made me shudder. However, I did make choices—hard ones, stupid ones, life-altering ones.

I lay back on my pillow, trying to decide if I should try and go back to sleep. My phone said it was only 6:05. Early for Sunday. I was surprised I didn't have any texts from Chad demanding more pages. I supposed I could get up and work. I looked at my slumbering husband. I could wake Peter up and we could spend our morning under the covers. Yes, I liked that thought very much, but we hadn't gotten to bed until well after midnight, and he wasn't stirring at all, which spoke of how tired he was. Normally when I moved away from him in the morning he always reached for me.

What to do? Working didn't sound appealing at all. A weird thought popped into my head. What if I made breakfast? I internally laughed at the thought. That would be quite the wakeup call when our smoke detector went off or I blew up our microwave again. Sam did promise me the blueberry bake Peter was so fond of was easy enough for me, but she didn't know about the microwave popcorn incident.

This was ridiculous. I was a competent, capable woman. I could master cooking. I didn't need to become Betty Crocker, nor did I want to. But dang it, I wanted to be able to make something not only edible, but good. Challenge accepted. I threw off the covers.

I crept out of our room, not feeling guilty at all passing the door leading to my office. I would work once Peter left for church. Besides, maybe the mayhem I was bound to make in the kitchen would make for a good scene. Laine, like me, was an awful cook.

It was so nice to come downstairs to a quiet, empty, tulle-free home. The only evidence that a party had occurred was the large bouquet of black roses Sam had given me displayed beautifully in a glass vase on the island. The thoughtful thank you card still sat next to it. I picked up the sweet card and read the sentiments again.

Dear Delanie, my sister, my friend,
Thank you for enduring a week of hell. I love you.
Sam

It still choked me up and almost made having the party worth it. I think, overall, Sam and Reed had an enjoyable evening. Or they put on a good show. They laughed and talked to everyone while hardly letting go of one another. There were the few hiccups, but I don't think most guests had a clue we were harboring what I was guessing to be a felon, and then there was Neil who, thankfully, left early. Sam and Reed took Gelaire home.

I couldn't forget Sarah's weird friends who may or may not be part of a cult or coven. They watched me all night with interest. Every time I walked by them, their heads went together. My guess was they were talking about how to boil me in their cauldron or how to kill me with their knitting needles and make it look like an accident. Then there was Sarah, who seemed to want to say something to me, but she tried and failed on more than one occasion. It was probably the nicest thing she'd ever done for me.

I was only glad it was done and over with and I banked on never having to deal with Sarah's friends again. I was ready to enjoy a relaxing Sunday with my husband. Family dinner was even canceled. The vulgarities going through my mind celebrating that fact were making me smile. Life for the moment felt good.

I got out Sam's cookbook and flipped to the page she marked for me. She had even made little notes for me, like what each dry and wet ingredient was. That should have been self-explanatory, but when it came to recipes, no one would know that I had a master's degree or that I wrote books for a living. Sam also suggested that I get every ingredient I needed out and set them on the counter before I started, so I didn't get flustered during the process. And she put a star next to the note reminding me to preheat the oven. *I got this.* Maybe.

I went about following Sam's instructions line by line and double checking as I went. I was more impressed that we had all the ingredients. I wasn't sure how we had baking powder, but I rolled with it. I'm sure I bought it for some disaster I had taken to his parents at one time. I probably should have checked the expiration date, but I was living on the wild side this morning.

I laughed at Sam's notes telling me exactly how to wash the fresh blueberries that Peter always bought—he loved those things and popped them like candy. After reading Sam's note about vinegar and baking soda, I was sure we had never eaten clean fruit in this house. Oops.

By some miracle I was able to get everything mixed properly, as far as I knew, and get it into the prepared baking dish. And by some freak of nature it looked like the picture in the cookbook. It looked so pretty I was afraid to drop it on the way to the preheated oven. I should have brought my phone down so I could have taken a picture. If I didn't burn it, it was getting its own photo shoot. But I was getting way ahead of myself.

It made it in the oven without a hitch. I even remembered to set the timer and, not to brag, but I set it for the right time this time. I swore I stood there for forty-five minutes watching it bake, waiting for the explosion or for the house to smell acrid from accidentally using a cleaning chemical in place of a real ingredient. But no. It smelled not only edible, but good. I had this feeling I was about to become the best freaking wife in the history of wives. A feeling I had never felt before swelled in me. I felt giddy. I didn't think that was a thing for me. I would probably never admit to it out loud, but, dang, I felt it.

Sam's note of *don't forget the hot pads* rang in my head as soon as the timer went off. That was a good call on her part. In all my excitement, I had honestly forgotten. And no one had time for third-degree burns. The anticipation was more than it should have been, but this was a first for me and I was going to enjoy it. Even more, Peter was going to. I couldn't wait to show him. We were having breakfast in bed!

The smell was even more incredible when I opened the oven. Peter must have caught a whiff of it, because I heard him coming down the stairs while I was pulling out my masterpiece. So there went my surprise of breakfast in bed, but that was okay; I was so excited to show him, this worked out better.

He came flying into the kitchen just as I pulled out his favorite breakfast. My first thought was *wow, he must be hungry.* It didn't click that he was harried and holding up his phone. I was too enamored with what I had created.

I held out the dish like it was our first-born child. "Get ready to be impressed and want to rip my T-shirt off." To my irritation and dismay, he didn't even look at it or respond to my sexy wife routine.

"Delanie, baby, your secret's out." He sounded out of breath.

"That I can cook?" That made no sense at all. Then in a rush it dawned on me what he meant. "No." I shook my head.

Peter carefully inched closer holding out his phone. "There's pictures."

In my tunnel vision, all I could see on the screen was a box in my office filled with awards Autumn had won. I couldn't breathe. I went numb. My masterpiece slipped from my hands and crashed down around me, just like my life. The glass dish slammed into the wood with a loud clang. Food splattered, and Peter jumped back. A part of me knew my bare legs had been burned, but it didn't fully register. I leapt over what I could of the damn breakfast I had spent so much time on and ran up our stairs. Peter chased after me, asking me if I was okay, but I had no time to answer. And the obvious answer was *no.*

I flew to the bedroom door. Unlocked. Who had come in here? I raced to the closed door to my office. I had almost reached my destination when searing pain shot through my foot all the way up my leg. "Aargh!!! What the hell?" I hopped on one foot and fell onto the spare bed.

Peter was to me in no time, patting me all over. "Where are you hurt? What happened?"

"My foot, my foot," I cried.

"You're dripping blood everywhere." Without a thought, he ripped off his shirt and pressed it against my foot.

In another place and time, I would have thought that was sexy, but I was in the middle of a nervous breakdown, so his beautiful chest didn't get even a glance.

Peter was visibly shaken and began giving me a more thorough examination. "Your legs, baby, they're burned." He slowly pulled back his bloody T-shirt. "I didn't think the pan broke downstairs."

"I don't think it's glass. It's something in here." Or maybe it was glass. So much adrenaline was coursing me through me, I might have run up here with glass in my foot.

Peter looked down around him. "Hold on." He bent down and came back up holding a silver hairpin with my blood on it.

"Is that what I think it is?"

Peter walked to my office door and opened it. Without a key. I hopped off the bed, not caring that I was dripping blood all over the wood floor. I leaned against Peter and scanned the inside of my office. To my horror, I saw opened boxes and my framed *New York Times* posters lined up against the wall like they had been posed for a picture.

"Who? How?" I begged to know.

Peter scooped me up. "Let me take care of you first."

I refused to relax in his strong arms. "No. Tell me what you know."

Peter hung his head and sat down with me on the bed, holding me against him as if he was trying to brace me for the worst. The pain from the pin and burns hit me. I took deep breaths and let them out in heavy sighs to try and stave it off.

"Delanie, you're hurt."

"Just tell me."

He reached over for his phone he'd left on the bed. He pulled up the pictures again. This time he swiped through them. "James sent me these asking if it was true that you were Autumn Moone."

There were several pictures, everything from the awards to the framed *New York Times* lists. There were even pictures of my red typewriter.

"Where did James get these?"

Peter's chest filled with air. He held it for several seconds, all while a dozen notifications popped up on his phone. So many I couldn't keep up with them or comprehend them, but knew they all had to do with the pictures and me.

"Peter, please."

He exhaled in a loud whoosh. "Baby, I'm so sorry, it looks like Deann took the pictures."

I sat up straight. "Your mom's friend?"

Peter nodded. "That's not the worst of it."

My heart dropped before he said more.

"She's posted them on Facebook."

Then there was no keeping it quiet. "That b—"

Peter kissed me mid swear, but I still got it out against his lips. He stroked my hair. "Ma is so sorry."

I jerked back away from him.

"She didn't know—"

"Didn't know what?" My tone was so icy even I felt the temperature drop.

"According to James, she asked Deann to break into the attic last night to see what we were hiding."

I jumped off his lap and landed on my bloodied foot. I crumpled onto the floor from the pain and pure shock of the situation. "What did I ever do to her?"

THE SECRETIVE WIFE

Peter dropped down next to me.
My head fell on his shoulder. "Peter."
He took my hand. "I know, baby."
"Our lives will never be the same again."

Chapter Eighteen

"WHAT IN THE hell is going on over there?" Joan's voice made my pounding head throb even more. "I have ten messages from that rat bastard, Lucas, from LH Ink."

Joan and Lucas Hirsch III, the CEO and the current LH in LH Ink, kind of had a romantic history but they despised each other now.

I sat on the hardwood floor of my office leaning against the wall in a state of shock. I didn't want to move or talk to anyone. All I wanted to do was stare at my things. *My things.* Things that someone touched and photographed without my consent. I couldn't muster the energy to cry or rage, though a hurricane stirred inside me. All I could allow myself to feel in that moment were the burns on my legs and my punctured foot that had been carefully wrapped by my husband, whose raised voice I could hear in the other room. Never once had I heard him raise his voice. It didn't even sound like him. Nothing in that moment felt real.

"Delanie, are you there?"

"No."

"Shake out of it, kid, we've got a mess to deal with. I need you to focus."

My eyes drifted toward my red, angry legs. Peter had missed some of the blueberries when he cleaned them off. I thought of the perfect blueberry bake splattered all over my floor. Of course, the one time I made anything worth eating, the universe was thrown into disarray. A nonsensical laugh bubbled up and escaped.

"Del, are you okay?"

No, I wasn't, but if I could bake, I could get through this. My laughter allowed for the tears to flow.

"Don't crack up on me."

"What's a rat bastard?" I sniffled.

"There's my girl. You keep that sense of humor; you're going to need it. Now tell me what happened."

I guess I would have to look up later what made the "rat" variety different from a run of the mill kind. "Here's some advice you can take to the bank. Don't ever tell your mother-in-law that you keep nude photos of yourself and her son locked in the attic. She might have sneaky little wenches for friends who've watched one too many episodes of *Murder She Wrote* and can pick locks with their hairpins."

"They broke into your office?"

"Yes, and rifled through all my boxes and took pictures of everything Autumn Moone. Then posted them publicly and now they're going viral."

Joan was deathly quiet, which meant she was seething and probably formulating our strategy.

"Is LH Ink going to sue me for breach of contract?" Besides my privacy being obliterated, this was my biggest fear.

"Not if I have anything to say about it. You let me handle Lucas. Don't talk to anyone from LH Ink. Not Fiona or Chad. Actually, don't talk to anyone until we get a handle on this."

"Okay, but the texts and messages have already been nonstop." I'd heard at least thirty buzzes while I was on the phone.

"I'm afraid that's going to be your life for the foreseeable future. We need to get you a new phone and make sure it's unlisted."

"Joan..."

"I know, kid, but we always knew this was a possibility."

"I didn't see myself being taken down by the Nancy Drew club."

"I need their names."

"Why?"

"Because we're suing them for invasion of privacy."

"Can we?"

"We can, and we will."

"Money won't replace what they've taken from me."

"It's not about the money. You can sue them for a dollar; I don't care. It's going to cost them a fortune and their good names to face me in court. What they did was wrong and illegal."

"I'm going to have to think about it. As much as I hate my mother-in-law and her friends, I don't need the headlines, and they are sure to come."

"More than you know. Sorry, Del, this is going to be a whole new world for you. That's why I need those names. At the very least we need to send them an order to cease and desist sharing those photos. With it will come a nasty letter from me telling them if they profit monetarily or otherwise from those photos they will wish they would have stuck to knitting."

Tears streamed down my face.

"I can fly to Chicago this week if you need me to," she offered.

"I appreciate that, but I need you in New York putting out the flames there."

"Don't worry your gorgeous head. It's going to be nothing more than an ember by the time I'm done with that weasel, Lucas. I've been saving some dirt I have on him for a time like this. But, kid, you better write the best book of your life."

Easier said than done. I'd never written well under pressure, and I had a feeling the pressure to come was going to be enough to squeeze all the creative juices out of me.

"Thanks, Joan."

"Don't thank me—do you know how much I charge when I work on the weekends?" She laughed.

"Go take a drive in your new Porsche."

"You needed to put a little more edge into that, honey."

"It's all I have right now." I let out a heavy breath.

"Del, I'm not going to lie to you and tell you this is going to be a cakewalk. It's going to be more like a hell hole with no cake, not even a finger lick of frosting, but if anyone can get through it, it's you and Peter."

We did make a good team.

"Just remember, don't do anything until you hear from me except send me those Mata Haris' names."

"You know Mata Hari was more than likely innocent?"

"You watch too many documentaries."

That was probably true.

"Hang in there, kid, and tell your husband to say some prayers."

If Joan thought God needed to be involved, it wasn't good. She was more skeptical than me about his existence.

I hung up, not feeling any better, and with even more of a desire to stay in the attic away from what awaited me. I couldn't bring myself to look online or to respond to Sam and Avery, who had each left several messages and texts. Hopefully they didn't hate me for keeping this from them. I turned off my phone and set it next to me, clinging to the small vestiges I had left of my privacy.

Peter was still on the phone, and by his curt tone, it wasn't hard to guess that he was still talking to his mother. Hate bubbled up in me.

"Do you have any idea what you've done?" Peter asked her exactly what I wanted to except I would have used some not so nice words. "We opened our home to you out of the kindness of our hearts, but for you it was a ploy."

Did she ever play us for fools. She was a world class actress, making us believe she wanted to get to know me. All she cared about was getting into our attic. And for what? Did she really believe Peter would be married to someone involved in illegal activity? Maybe we should have lied and told them I had a trust fund from my deceased grandparents. Or maybe I shouldn't have taunted her with the fake boudoir photos. But who could have guessed she would have gone this far to get what she wanted? I hoped she was satisfied now that she'd gotten what she wanted. Now that Peter and I were left to deal with the aftermath.

"I can't say that I blame Dad for not speaking to you."

That made me feel better. I was worried Joseph was in on it too.

"No, I won't talk to him for you."

She had a lot of nerve, but I already knew that.

"You will have to deal with the Mimsy situation on your own then. Ma, there are consequences to your actions. I should have been a better husband and not subjected my wife to you."

Those were some bold words.

"Your apologies won't repair the damage that you've done. Not only have you exposed my wife to the world, but there will probably be legal ramifications."

My stomach twisted at the thought. Was it awful for me to hope that Joan had some persuasive dirt on Lucas?

"That's because all you thought about was yourself." His voice was getting testier. "Don't go there. Did I look like I was unhappy? I've never been happier. Why couldn't you accept that? Accept Delanie?"

That was the million-dollar question.

"Ma, what you've done has changed the course of this family, of *my* family. Now I need to go and check on my wife." His voice cracked. There he was again, choosing between his mom and wife. This time, though, Sarah made it easy for him, and I think he hated that more than anything. If I wasn't mistaken, I heard his phone hit the wall. I'd never seen him behave this way. I didn't even know he had it in him.

Peter strode through the attic door looking for me, confused and maybe alarmed when he didn't see me.

"Down here," I eked out.

He turned to see me close to the door on the floor. His face was tight and red. His hair was more than disheveled. He must have run his hand through it dozens of times. His eyes gave me a once over. I must have looked pathetic sitting there in his T-shirt, bandaged, with red and blue marks running up and down my legs. His features immediately softened. "Baby."

I patted the floor next to me.

He wasted no time taking the invitation and sat right next to me. His arm snaked around me. My head dropped on his shoulder. He kissed my head and lingered. Nothing was said for minutes. What could we say?

"You know this means I'm never cooking again," I tossed out into the heavy air that hung between us, trying to lighten the moment.

Peter chuckled, albeit subdued. "Delanie, I'm—"

I placed my finger on his lips. "Don't say it. This isn't your fault. We always knew this day might come. Just tell me you'll be by my side through it all."

He kissed my finger before removing it. His hands cupped my face. His gaze penetrated my own. "Forever."

That's all I needed to hear.

Chapter Nineteen

$\mathcal{I}$T DIDN'T TAKE long before the siege began. By Sunday afternoon, there were news crews not only outside the gates of our community, but Peter's parents' and siblings' places as well. Those we were still talking to came seeking refuge behind our gates, though getting them through was no easy task. The security service our community employed was called in to deal with the situation. Which we were told we would personally be paying for. My neighbors were really going to love us. For now, no one was allowed into the community unless they could verify they lived there. If someone was visiting a resident, that resident had to come out and visually identify them before they were allowed in.

Peter took it upon himself to go out and get our relatives.

When Peter entered with Sam's and Avery's families, the adults all looked like Linda had the previous night after bringing Mimsy and Giovanni—harried and a tad frightened. My nephews, on the other hand, thought it was the coolest thing ever to be chased by reporters.

Like the rest of the adults, I was scared too, but for other reasons. Were they going to hate me for lying to them all this time and thrusting them into a spotlight as bright as the noonday sun? My worries were quickly put to rest when I saw Reed and James bearing food I was sure their wives made. You didn't bring food to people you hated unless you were Snow White's stepmother or my mother-in-law.

As soon as Avery and Sam saw me, they rushed to me squealing and throwing their arms around me. For a minute I thought they might start jumping up and down too, but they refrained. My legs, foot, and dignity would have refused. However, I was so happy they didn't hate me I might have joined in.

"I can't believe it." Avery squeezed me tight with her toned arms. "We thought maybe you were an heiress or even a princess in hiding. We even thought witness protection program and Cat and Ron were your 'handlers,' not really your parents. But this is the best secret ever!"

I had to laugh at the first two preposterous guesses. Unfortunately, I could see why they would have thought that about my parents.

Sam leaned away from us and stared at me for a moment. "I can't believe it's been you this entire time."

I swallowed hard and nodded. "Are you still glad *Autumn Moone* posted your blogs?"

"I'm happy *you* did," she choked out.

I fell back into them both. "I'm sorry I couldn't tell you. I wanted to."

"Judging by all the craziness, I can see why you kept it to yourself," Avery was first to respond.

"My Facebook page and blog have exploded. Everyone wants to know if it's true and if I knew."

I knew this would affect Sam the most. "I've been too afraid to look yet. And my lawyer told me to stay off social media until things get worked out with my publisher."

They both stepped back with looks of concern.

Sam's brows crinkled. "That sounds serious."

I blew out a large amount of air. "Millions of dollars serious."

Both sets of eyes popped out.

"Let's eat," James interrupted us. "You ladies can chitchat all you want over food."

"James," Avery scolded her husband, "Delanie could be sued for millions over this, and all you can think about is your stomach?"

James walked past us with food in one hand, and with the other he smacked Avery's butt. "You women worry too much. Delanie's their cash cow, and judging by the circus out there, she's more valuable to them now than ever. Mark my words," he grinned directly at me, "you've got nothing to worry about. So, let's eat."

I wish I had his confidence, though his words made me feel slightly better, and I hadn't eaten all day due to the stress and the trauma over my masterpiece hitting the floor.

Peter took my hand. "Some food would do you good."

Reed joined the mix with a devious smile on his face. "No one's eating until everyone admits I look like Hunter Black."

Peter and I looked at each other before we both busted out laughing.

"Don't I?" Reed struck a stately pose.

"Well . . ." I bit my lip, "Hunter is technically based on Peter—"

"You didn't need to tell us that." Sam sounded ill. "Hunter will never be my brother. I'm wiping that thought out of my memory now."

Avery cringed at the thought too.

"This should make you feel better then. You see, Peter always talked about Reed, so when I started writing I looked him up on Facebook—"

"I knew it!" Reed shouted.

Sam playfully smacked his chest. "What did you know? You didn't know Delanie was Autumn Moone."

He pulled Sam closer to him. "Didn't I say the first time I read to you that Hunter looked exactly like me?"

James responded before Sam could. "Men, and I use the term lightly, you can't keep reading this crap with your wives. No offense, Delanie." He flashed me a smile. "It's not natural. We are not metro-males in this family."

Reed gave Sam a seductive look. "Natural or not, it works."

Sam pecked Reed's lips for the thought.

The nephews were sick of the conversation and made retching noises while grabbing the food from their respective parents and darting toward the kitchen.

"Just do me a favor," Avery pleaded. "Don't write anymore dedications indicating which page numbers you are acting out with Peter."

The laughter that filled our home soothed my heart.

The men and boys settled outside with the Italian feast Sam and Avery brought while the three of us took my couch. Once on the couch, Sam and Avery gave me a good look over. They had already made a big deal over my physical state in the kitchen when they noticed my legs. I got to regale them with my tale of making the perfect dish only to have it end up on the floor. While we all laughed, we seemed to understand it was quite the metaphor for how the day had gone and how our lives would be in the coming future. Their once-over now was more of a mental state check.

Sam touched my knee, careful to avoid the burned spots that, thankfully, hadn't blistered. "So, tell us how you are. Really."

How was I? I stared down at the lasagna sitting on the coffee table waiting for me. I wanted to eat it, but my stomach twisted, reminding me of how I really was. I held my stomach and faced my sisters-in-law, who were each anxiously waiting for my reply, but also wore the faces of concerned friends I could trust.

"I don't even know where to begin. Violated, betrayed, scared. That's a good start."

Sounds of disgust escaped from both Avery and Sam.

"Ma has done it this time," Sam lamented. "Dad isn't coming to her rescue, either. He got so angry, he left."

My hand slammed against my chest. "He left?" As much as I hated my mother-in-law, I never wanted that.

"Don't worry," Sam ripped off a piece of French bread, "he's only gone for a long drive. He'll cool off and come home. Well, maybe. He won't be happy to see the vultures still surrounding their place when he returns."

"He left her there with all that?" I asked.

"Oh, yeah." Avery's grin bordered on evil. "Mom called and begged James to come over. He kindly reminded her that she brought this on herself—and the rest of us. Besides, James was preoccupied. He had to go out to the office because the security alarm went off. A reporter ambushed him there."

"Nooo." I couldn't believe it.

Avery waved me off. "Don't worry. James handled it in his colorful fashion and our friend at the police department said they would patrol the area and our homes."

I put my face in my hands. I didn't even want to ask what James told the reporter. "I'm so sorry about all of this. What a mess."

"It's not your fault." Sam chewed her bread with a vengeance. "Ma and her friends should have minded their own business. I mean, the rest of us were happy thinking you had some huge trust fund that someday you would share with us." She gave me a sly grin.

Avery gave an appreciative smile as well. "But word is those busy bees are getting theirs," Avery sing-songed while swirling her glass of spiked lemonade.

"How?" I was more than curious.

"Don't you know?" Avery looked surprised.

I shook my head, more surprised by her surprise.

"Well." Avery's gorgeous blue eyes lit up. "You have a scary lawyer, from the sounds of it."

"Joan?"

"Is that her name? I like her. We should all be friends." Avery spoke with anticipation. She loved making new friends. I was sure she hardly met a person she didn't try to befriend.

"I'll let her know." I laughed, knowing how much Joan would find that hilarious and perhaps unwelcome. Joan, like me, didn't have a lot of girlfriends. She had colleagues, clients, and opponents, just the way she preferred it.

Avery took a sip of her drink. "Make sure you tell her that it's a good thing Deann wears bladder control underwear. According to the grapevine, she wet herself when Joan called her and ripped her a new one and threatened to sue her."

Now that, Joan would be happy to hear.

Sam set down her plate. "Are you going to sue them?"

"Joan thinks we should sue them for invasion of privacy, but I'm not sure yet. I need the dust to settle first."

"All I know is it's scared her enough to take the pictures down."

I sank back against the cushions. "Too bad the damage has already been done."

Sam leaned back next to me and rested her head on mine. "I don't think those women or Ma had any idea what they were dealing with. Now they are all at each other's throats."

"Why?" I asked.

"Ma's mad because she asked them to delete the photos and the other women are upset because Ma asked them to break into your attic in the first place."

"No one made them," Avery commented.

"You know how it goes," Sam said. "It's always easier to place the blame on someone else."

"Like Neil?" I responded.

"Exactly like him. I can't believe he showed up last night." Sam was still seething over it.

"The night was full of surprises." Avery set her glass down and leaned back to join us. "What about Mimsy and her looovver?"

Laughter erupted from us, but it was the kind born of trying not to cry over the entire situation.

"Let's just hope no one gets Mimsy in front of a camera," said Sam.

We groaned at the thought. There we were, the three of us sitting head-to-head and heart-to-heart, all wondering what kind of mess I had gotten us into.

Avery giggled. "At least tell us Hunter and Laine end up together."

"I love you guys." It felt good to say the sentiment I'd wanted to a hundred times. Even better was how is easy it came out.

"We love you, too," Sam responded. "But seriously, we need to know about Hunter and Laine."

Chapter Twenty

"ARE YOU WATCHING this?" Joan's tone bordered on amused and snarling pit bull.

I curled against Peter on the couch, watching the TV with one eye open and my phone close to my ear so Joan didn't burn a hole in Peter's brain with her marvelous—teetering on scary—proficiency of the mother of all swear words. Our second worst fear happened. A local news station snagged an exclusive interview with the bling twins, otherwise known as Mimsy and Giovanni.

Giovanni looked straight into the camera and flashed his dentures. "So, like I was saying, me and Autumn Moone go way back. I was just at a party last night at her house." He wrapped his arm around Mimsy like a boa constrictor.

I feared I gave Giovanni more reasons to lure Mimsy deeper into his web of deceit. His eyes were flashing dollar signs.

"Is it true your grandson is married to Autumn Moone?" Serena Lively from Channel 4 asked.

Mimsy adjusted herself so she sat taller. She looked ridiculous wearing a fake diamond necklace and a Cubs hat. I guessed I should be grateful she wasn't wearing that red dress that made us all wish for a lobotomy.

"Are you talking about Delanie?"

The reporter looked at her notes. "Delanie Decker, yes."

Mimsy pressed her thin lips together—lips, I might add, that were covered in some awful shade of orange lipstick. "She's the one all right. That Delilah used her ways and led my Peter astray from his true calling as a priest."

I dropped my phone and sprung up.

"Oh, hell," Joan yelled loud enough for both Peter and me to hear. "It's going to really hit the fan now."

"Your grandson was a priest?" The reporter couldn't have sounded more pleased, as if someone had given her the juiciest apple and she got to bite first. The figurative juice was dripping down her chin.

"Such a good boy until that tattooed girl used her feminine ways on him. Now they are taking naked pictures of each other and selling drugs."

Joan spat out a laugh while Peter and I cringed.

I put Joan on speaker. After Mimsy, I didn't think anything she was going to say was going to be worse.

Peter gripped my hand like a vice.

"Now, now, Mims," Giovanni cut in, "you must be confused. Peter and Delanie are our favorites."

Mimsy elbowed him. "Speak for yourself. I like Reed. He has a nice butt."

I covered my face with my hands. "I can't take it anymore."

"Who's Reed?" Serena asked, wanting another juicy bite.

We didn't get to hear the answer. Peter, in an act of mercy, turned off the TV and threw himself back against the couch cushion, scrubbing his hand over his face.

I took his hand back, trying to lend him some comfort while I talked to Joan, who had also turned off the Looney Tunes.

"Well, Peter, you have quite the family." Joan wasn't helping the situation any.

Peter gripped my hand tighter without saying a word.

"Tell us what Lucas said." I held my breath.

"Pack your bags, kid."

Peter sat up while I tried swallowing my heart back down. "They're releasing me?"

"Releasing you?" she cackled. "No, honey, they're pulling you in and wrapping every tentacle around you they can."

"What does that mean?"

"It means you're coming to New York tomorrow and you're going to find out what it's like to be a real celebrity."

"No. Not happening." I shook my head.

"Listen, Del, interviews like your supposed family members just gave and the press knocking down your door and the doors of everyone you know isn't going to stop until you give them what they want. You."

She was not exaggerating. Here's another rule of life to live by: don't taunt your neighbors about being a call girl. They will let reporters through the gates and tell those reporters that you aren't all that friendly. I really needed to think of some new comebacks that didn't paint me as a hooker or a centerfold. It's caused me nothing but trouble and long lenses and people hiding behind our trees and bushes.

"Besides, kid," Joan continued, "if you want to save those millions for all your charities, LH Ink is demanding it. So, come to New York, smile pretty for the camera, be your charming yet smart-aleck self for interviews, and take advantage of all the free press. The world wants you, and LH Ink is going to take advantage of that and kindly forget you had an anonymity clause in your contract. You're welcome."

Peter and I stared at one another, dazed and confused. A million unanswered thoughts reflected in our eyes.

"Peter can come too," Joan added in.

Peter let out a breath that said it all. This sucked. "I can't right now."

He rested his warm hand on my cheek. "I want to, but I need to stay here and help my family with our business. Our voice mail is full because of all the new inquiries we received today alone."

If even ten percent of them were legit calls, Decker and Sons Landscaping was going to have to hire a lot of new people to keep up. James was excited by the prospect.

I placed my hand on top of Peter's, never wavering my gaze from his. "What time tomorrow is my flight?" I resigned myself to my fate.

"You should have an email, but I think mid-morning. You fly into JFK, and I like you so much I'll even come pick you up. As an added bonus, you can stay with me."

"Okay," I said without thinking.

"Del, this is going to be okay. The vultures will quit circling after you feed them your carcass."

"Are you trying to cheer me up, Joan?"

"I'm just giving it to you straight. Get some rest, make some love, because you're going to need it. I'll see you tomorrow." Joan believed sex was the answer for everything. I wasn't sure I could agree with her. Sometimes it caused more problems than it solved. She hung up without letting us say goodbye.

Peter and I kept our staring contest up. It was a source of strength and comfort.

A thought hit me while I peered into his deep green eyes. "We've never spent the night away from each other since we've been married."

"Do you want me to go? I'll go."

"Of course I want you to go, but you need to stay here to help James and your dad. I'll slumber party it up with Joan."

Peter cracked a small smile. "I know how Joan parties, so don't have too much fun."

"We could take her advice before I start packing, minus the getting rest part." In this case sex couldn't hurt.

"I like the way you think."

"Peter."

"Yeah, baby."

"I like you."

He kissed my nose and let his forehead rest against mine. "I like you too."

"After all this, are you still happy you chased after me?"

"Uh-huh." He skimmed my lips.

I breathed him in, trying to forget even for a second that I'd just been humiliated on TV or how much our lives had changed today. "I'm going to miss you."

"Not yet you aren't." He crushed his lips against mine, leaving no doubt how he felt about me or that we were a team.

We could do this.

Chapter Twenty-One

THE THING I loved about big cities was that you could be as invisible as you wanted to be in them. It was one of the reasons I loved taking the bus into Portland so often growing up. It was the one place I felt like I belonged. Those streets owned me and protected me. They made me feel wanted and free. My parents had thought they were making me free, but I could always tell when my choices displeased them. When I didn't give them the data points they were hoping for. It made me second-guess my choices or choose what I knew they wanted me to. Anything to make them happy. Anything to make them see me, claim me, and belong to me. Now the cities had turned their backs on me just like my parents. There was no more safety in the crowd. I became the bullseye in the middle of the target. I had become the reason for a crowd.

It all started by being followed to the airport by two persistent men with cameras, giving Peter more concern for sending me to New York alone. I kept my hand on his tense thigh all the way to O'Hare as he weaved in and out of traffic trying to lose the men in the black car with tinted windows. For a moment, I thought he was going to swear. I always thought I would be happy to hear him be a normal human, but the man driving well over the speed limit, gripping the steering wheel, breathing heavily, was not Peter. It didn't help when those two men rushed me as soon as I was out of the car. Peter placed himself and my luggage between me and the rather large men taking picture after picture. Thank goodness for airport cops. They don't take kindly to people leaving their vehicles unattended. If they hadn't intervened, I was afraid Peter was going to throw a punch.

"I should go with you," he breathed out, upset once the men were shown back to their car.

I placed my hand on his warm red cheek. "I'll be fine."

His right brow raised. "There's that word 'fine' again."

I mustered a smile for him. "I meant to say fantastic."

His lip twitched. "I might have believed you, but you never use words like that."

"How about, I'll survive? And I'll bring you back a cheesy *My Wife Went to NYC and All I Got Was This T-shirt* shirt."

His genuine smile appeared. "Only if you promise to be the one who wears it."

I pressed a kiss to his lips. "Now you sound like my husband."

"Do you really think that's her?" A voice caught our attention. We turned to find several cell phones pointed at us.

"I hate this," Peter whispered.

I did too. More for him than me. Peter didn't use words like hate. But I was determined to be me and not Autumn. And Delanie wouldn't miss the opportunity to kiss her husband goodbye. I pulled on Peter's shirt and yanked him toward me. "Let's give them what they want."

His eyes widened before my lips collided with his. This was no peck on the lips. This was a, I'm going to miss you, soul reaching, lips parted, I'm going to taste what you ate last week kind of kiss. Peter had stage fright at first, but it didn't take him long to wrap me up tight and let his emotions bleed into my lips. His kiss bordered on hungry and angry, the kind of emotions that normally would have led to the shedding of clothes, but not even I was that risqué.

He pulled away too soon only to smile down at me and shake his head. "You know how to get to me."

I had to take a breath. "That was a kiss for the books and probably going on several social media pages. Good job." I winked.

Peter cringed.

"I love you."

"I love you more. Please be careful." His eyes roved over the cluster of people staring and taking pictures of us.

I grabbed my suitcase and slung my laptop case across my shoulder. "I will. Joan is tougher than ten bodyguards."

"Call me when you land."

I nodded while we gave all the lookie-loos a picture-perfect departure with Peter grasping my hand until only our fingertips touched as I walked away.

A group of women shouted, "We love you, Autumn!"

I put on another show and smiled and waved at them. It was the first time someone had called me Autumn. I wasn't sure how to feel about it.

Not everyone was as pleasant. While I was checking in, some women behind me hadn't learned the art of whispering. "OMG. Did you see her husband? He's freaking hot. I heard he was a priest. If my priest looked like that I would go to church more."

Ignore them.

"I heard last night on the news that she's not even catholic and he had to leave the church because they were caught together in the rectory."

What the hell? I'd never been in a rectory. Did Mimsy say that? Maybe I should have watched the entire interview. If everyone thought we were like that novel *The Thorn Birds*, they were sorely mistaken. We had nothing to be ashamed of. No vows were broken. We didn't even consummate our relationship until we were married. Admittedly, that was hard, but I knew Peter would have regretted it any other way. It took everything I had not to lash out at those women who should really learn to whisper properly.

It didn't get any better once I was on the plane. In first class, of all places. I'd never flown first class. All that meant, besides more comfortable and roomier seating, was that everyone who boarded the plane who recognized me, which was more than I would have guessed by this point, had a chance to gawk at me or ask me for an autograph. The flight attendants didn't appreciate it and ushered people along, to my relief. Signing autographs was weird. I'd never done it in person. I'd signed stacks and stacks of books, but never in person. I had to remember to write Autumn Moone, not Delanie Decker.

I quickly realized no one was interested in Delanie, except for the sordid, untrue details of my life. And maybe the slick businessman who became my seatmate. He didn't have a clue who I was but stared at my empty ring finger and tried to engage me in conversation. Not even my earbuds deterred him from talking to me, and he asked me for my number after I told him I was married.

The only good thing to come out of the two-hour flight was when we landed, a savvy flight attendant took mercy on me by personally retrieving me and letting me deplane before anyone else. For her kindness, I gave her Fiona's email and told her to contact her. I would be sure she got a signed copy of each one of my books in hardback. For that I received a genuine hug.

I hustled through the airport, well, as much as you can hustle through JFK. Like the city where it resided, it was wall-to-wall people. I only had a carry-on, so I was calling Joan as I walked, letting her know to come pick me up. She promised she would be on time and waiting in the cell phone lot when I arrived. She lied.

"Ten minutes. Traffic is hell."

"You don't know what hell is. People are staring and pointing at me," I whispered into the phone.

"That's because you look like a Calvin Klein model and FYI, you're all over social media and the news. Go hide in the bathroom or something. On second thought, don't use the bathrooms there."

"Just drive fast."

"Kid, you've been to New York; there's no such thing."

"Fine. Call me when you get here."

"Will do, *darling*," she mocked me.

I tried to blend in and headed toward Starbucks, but my phone rang. I assumed it was Peter. I was planning on calling him from the car so it would be somewhat private, but I guessed he was anxious to know if I landed. And I was eager to find out how it was going there.

More surprises were on the horizon. It was Cat. We'd already had our quarterly call. It hit me that maybe I should have told her about my big secret, but she never knew any of my other secrets, even the biggest one of them all. A sudden pang hit my heart. I had to catch my breath. No one would find out about *her*. I'd made sure. I tried to calm myself. I answered the phone as a distraction, not because I wanted to talk.

"Hi, Cat."

"Hello, *Autumn*." She didn't sound pleased. What did she expect?

"Funny," I brushed off the slight.

"I wasn't trying to be humorous. Our phones have been ringing non-stop thanks to you."

"Sorry about that."

"A heads-up would have been nice; we are your parents after all. Ron says hello, by the way." How did they call themselves my parents when they didn't want me to call them Mom and Dad?

"Tell Ron hello for me."

"The rumors are true then."

I maneuvered around a crowd and tried to find a corner to hide in. All I could find was a sparsely populated gate. "It depends on what you've heard."

"You're a romance author?" She didn't even try to hide her distaste.

"I have written a few romance books."

"You're the biggest name in romance right now." She wasn't taking kindly to my attempts to keep it light. "You do realize you're perpetuating unrealistic fantasies that hurt the general population? Books like yours only fuel unmet expectations. Ron and I see this all the time in our practice. I never thought our daughter would be part of the problem."

Resentment boiled inside of me. I tried hard to keep it to a simmer, but my mouth was burning. "Daughter? Since when have you called me your daughter, or better yet treated me like one?"

"I have no idea what you are talking about. Ron and I did our best to raise you."

I scoffed. "On more than one occasion among your friends you referred to me as your *subject*."

"You heard that?" she whispered.

I gave her some credit for not denying it, but it still hurt, maybe even more now that she gave it validation. "Yes, Cat. And for once, I wish you would be proud of me. Me. Not the experiment you had already written your desired conclusion about before the test was even conducted or concluded."

She stayed silent for a moment, but she came back swinging. "Judging by how successful you are, you should be thanking us for giving you the tools to accomplish your goals."

This was never one of my goals, but she wouldn't have known that because she didn't know me. And she would never be proud of me.

I sighed. "I'm sorry for any inconvenience this is causing you. I'm in New York now to do some promotion and interviews, so hopefully the calls will die down soon."

"You're in New York?" her voiced perked up.

"My publisher is here."

"You know Ron and I have written several books and have been published in the most prestigious scientific journals in the world. We would be happy to explore some new ideas we have with one of your contacts there."

I had no words. My own mother wanted to use me. "My publisher only takes works of fiction." I bit back my retort that I had read some of their works and some of it bordered on fiction. "I have to go."

"I'm sure you will be thrown in the path of those who might be interested in what we have to offer. I'll email you our latest outline."

That was going to be deleted.

"Goodbye, Cat."

"Delanie."

"Yes?"

"I'm...well...I...well...goodbye."

I think she hurt herself there at the end, but nowhere near as much as she hurt her *daughter*.

Chapter Twenty-Two

$\mathcal{J}$OAN LIVED IN an upscale neighborhood in Chelsea where it cost over $6,500 a month for a two-bedroom apartment with a view of the Hudson River. I was never sure why that view was worth so much. Maybe it was a lovely river further downstream. Her apartment building was nice and had every amenity imaginable, from a workout center to concierge service, but for the money she paid she should have had catered meals every night and maid service. That said, the neighborhood was charming, straight out of a classic Cary Grant movie, and the nearby Chelsea Market had some of the best places to eat. However, under the current circumstances, I would keep any public outings to a minimum. Which was why I was more than grateful Joan was letting me crash with her. Besides, it never hurt to stick with a native when traversing the Big Apple.

Joan watched me unpack from the bedroom door. She loomed like a formidable yet arresting figure. Tall and straight, with medium-length hair cut to precision that had grayed early but worked with her pale skin and dark lipstick. She always wore a dark business suit and stilettos that she could use as a weapon if needed. I'd wondered if she had used them on Lucas yesterday. I could picture his neck under her sharp heel—while she was still wearing it, mind you.

"I think we should go shopping before our dinner meeting with *Lucas*," she spewed his name.

I pulled out Peter's *Whose Pete's Sake?* shirt. It was kind of our thing. I bought him cheesy shirts for myself to wear to bed. I smiled at the shirt while addressing Joan. "Shopping? For what?"

She stepped closer while giving me a shrewd once over. "Here's the thing, Del. The bohemian goddess thing you have going on, with your flowing skirts and shirts that are ready to fall right off you, no doubt makes your husband and most men want to worship the very ground you walk on. But tonight, kid, we need a no-nonsense look."

I tilted my head, not sure if I should be offended or curious. "Why? I've met with Lucas before in similar attire."

"But you weren't renegotiating your contract those times."

I shook my head, not sure I heard her right. "Why would we do that?"

Her violet eyes electrified. "The question is, why wouldn't we? Everything changed yesterday. You are no longer lurking in the shadows. Believe me, Lucas plans to use that to his full advantage. And what have I always told you?"

"Never pass on the opportunity to give someone a piece of your mind."

"The other thing." She grinned.

"Never drink tequila on an empty stomach."

"No. But don't do that." She held up her hands. "What are these for?"

I stared at her sleek hands with nails that looked more like razors dripped in deep red blood. "One is to keep the upper hand, the other is to squeeze them where it hurts."

"Exactly. We are going to squeeze that weasel Lucas until his bloody azure eyes pop."

"I see he's making his way up the rodent chain from rat to weasel." I smirked.

"You keep that smart-aleck attitude; you're going to need it."

The T-shirt, along with my heart, dropped. "What more do they want from me?"

She took my hand. "Everything, if we let them, but you know I'd never let that happen to you."

I squeezed her hand. "Let's go shopping."

"My favorite words."

❧

"You should see me." I held on for dear life in Joan's Porsche trying to have a conversation with my husband while she drove like she was starring in the *Italian Job*.

"She looks killer," Joan yelled so Peter would hear.

I looked down at the black business suit with ankle pants and a snug jacket that showed off all my lines. Joan, too, wore a black suit. We were dressed for a mob hit. Which may very well have been her intent.

I shifted in my seat. I didn't like being so restricted by fashion.

"Send me a picture."

"I will, but later and in less."

"Miaow," Joan purred.

"I can't wait." Peter sounded tired.

"How's everything there?" We hadn't been able to talk much when I called him earlier.

He let out a meaningful sigh before pausing.

"Peter?" He had me worried.

"It's been a long day is all, and I miss you."

"I miss you too, but what are you not telling me?"

"You worry about what you have going on there."

That wasn't going to happen no matter how nervous I was about the morning and late shows I would be doing the next few days, not to mention a photo shoot. "I worry about you. You didn't exactly sign up for this when we got married."

173

"I signed up for exactly what I wanted." His sweet sentiment was laced with agitation.

"Peter, what's wrong?"

"Baby, it's just been a day."

"I can call Sam and Avery to find out what's really going on."

His small chuckle made me feel a little better.

"You win." He took a breath. "Besides being under a microscope, things aren't good with my parents. They aren't talking to each other at all. To make matters worse, they found out Mimsy withdrew a few thousand dollars from her account and gave it to Giovanni. Now they are moving Mimsy in with them, and you can guess that isn't going over well with anyone. And that interview with Mimsy—"

"I know. I heard some women talking about it. I'm sorry that anyone would question your integrity. But we know the truth."

He took a moment to respond. "It was the hardest decision I've ever made and…"

I waited on bated breath for him to finish. All my fears about him wishing that he'd stayed a priest bubbled up to the surface. Even Joan noticed me squirming and mouthed, "Are you okay?" I couldn't respond to her.

"… it's a personal one between God and me. I never expected to have to answer to anyone for that choice besides Him and my superiors." I'd never heard him so melancholy. And was that regret in his tone?

"I am sorry." I had to choke down the emotion.

"Please stop apologizing to me. This isn't your fault. I love you. You're going to be great tomorrow. How many guys get to say their wife is on national TV?" His fake enthusiasm didn't do anything to quell my worry because this *was* all my fault. If it wasn't for me, his family would probably be happy, and no one would have ever questioned Peter's reputation.

Joan came to a screeching halt in front of the restaurant near Rockefeller Center where my publisher was located. There was a large crowd of photogs already gathered waiting anxiously. My first thought was it couldn't possibly be for me. The upscale restaurant had plenty of famous patrons from what Joan had said, but when Joan began ranting in four-letter words all my hopes sank.

My attention was split between the cameras pointing in my direction and Peter. I was torn on what to do. Joan took it out of my hands. "Bye Peter, lover will call you later, we have a situation here."

"Delanie," he panicked, "is everything okay?"

"My corneas may be irreparably damaged from all the flashing lights, but other than that everything is great," I lied. "I'll call you later. Love you." I dropped my phone in my lap. "What is all this?"

"Lucas is going to pay for this. Guaranteed he tipped them off."

"Why would he do that?"

"Kid, it's all about the game, and right now, you are the hottest ticket in this town. So smile pretty and don't say a word."

It was so much easier when I was telling Sam what to do with all the attention and interviews she had thrown her way. Again, thanks to me. What had I done to Peter's family? *My* family?

Two valet attendants opened our doors casually as if they were no longer impressed by celebrities pulling up in cars that probably cost more than they made in four years. I had to practically launch myself out of the low-riding car. More like Joan had to push me. It was only two days ago that I was cloaked under a veil of anonymity and my biggest worry was how ridiculous I looked in a silk gown. This pantsuit was even less my style. I mean, who was I? The loud voices wielding cameras told me I was Autumn Moone. My heart said otherwise.

Joan walked toward me with an air of confidence as if she were merely walking into work. She linked arms with me and reminded me to smile. I felt so numb I wasn't sure if I was smiling or not. The only reason I knew I was walking was because my heeled feet were screaming how much they hated me at the moment. The press was shouting all sorts of questions behind a rope line. *When will your next book come out? Is it true your husband was a priest when you got married? People are saying this is all an elaborate scheme put on by your publisher! What do you say to that? Are you really the author?*

Joan kept us moving forward.

Once we were safely in the low-lit restaurant, I let out the breath I'd been holding.

Joan laughed. "You did good, Del. Not quite as good as the pictures circulating around of you sucking the face off your husband this morning, but you get an A in my book."

Joan and Fiona were checking social media for me, per usual, though there was a lot more to see. I was still doing my best not to get pulled into what everyone was saying online. It was going to stifle my creativity; not that I was getting a chance to write.

A voice I adored most of the time caught our attention. Chad came running toward us with his arms wide open, laughing, and shaking his head. "We can finally take our love out into the open, girl." He was to me in seconds, wrapping me up in his strong, well-dressed arms. He was what James would call a metro male, in his tailored cranberry suit and dark hair styled to perfection. His teeth gleamed bright against his cocoa skin. He was a beautiful man. Not Peter beautiful, but to me, no one was as beautiful as my husband.

I tried to take comfort in his embrace, but my thoughts were still on Peter. "Chad, what are you doing here?"

"Protecting you from the big bad wolf, though I know you can handle him on your own." He released me. "And who needs me when you brought his weakness?"

I gave Joan a sly smile. "Anything you want to say about that?"

She shot daggers aimed at Chad with her eyes. A lesser man would have turned and run from her deadly gaze. Chad only stared back, daring her to contradict him. Her answer was to brush past him. "Where's our table?"

A look passed between Chad and me that said he'd hit the nail on the head. Very interesting.

The restaurant was exclusive, which gave way to a reprieve of onlookers. That and we were seated in a private room upstairs. The room, with brick-lined walls, was illuminated mostly by candles of all shapes and sizes. It could have very well been in someone's home, except for the obscene amount of alcohol that filled one wall and the bartender that came with it. Now I saw why business was transacted here. Good thing I wasn't drinking.

When we entered, Lucas stood up and, like Joan, he came off as a fearsome creature. He and Joan had more than one thing in common—he was also a lawyer by trade but took over the family publishing business about ten years ago. His previous occupation served him well as CEO and it had introduced him to Joan, if I wasn't mistaken. I believe once upon a time they worked for the same law firm.

Lucas was dashing in his own right in a dark suit and red power tie. It went well with his cappuccino hair with hints of gray and his electric blue eyes that landed first on Joan. He directed both longing and frustration toward his opponent for the evening. I'd wondered what had happened since Thanksgiving. The last time I saw them together, the overriding emotion was loathing. Now it was more I loathe you, but I would love you if you'd let me.

Joan squared her shoulders and met his gaze. For a fraction of a second, I swore I saw a hint of vulnerability, as if he had hurt her, but she recovered quickly and sneered at him, causing him to breathe out in disappointment. Whatever their story was, it no doubt had the makings of a delicious tale. But we were not here to play out their love affair. This was business.

"Delanie," Lucas's baritone voice filled the room. "It's good to see you again." He was playing the nice guy angle up front.

"You as well." I played along. I didn't dislike Lucas, but we didn't exactly see eye to eye. He was all about the business, which was understandable, but if he had it his way, I would be pumping out a new book every quarter and dragging Hunter's and Laine's saga out three more books. That wasn't happening. It was either now or never for them.

"We could have done without your welcoming committee down-stairs." Joan took the first shot.

"You think I called the press?" Lucas acted affronted.

"I know you did."

Lucas gave her a Cheshire cat grin. He liked to play the game, espe-cially with her. He held out the chair to his right. "Join me, Joan." There was a double, maybe even triple meaning to that invite.

While Joan debated, Chad placed his hand on the small of my back and led me toward the table. "We'll be the fun side of the table." Chad held out a chair for me across from Lucas.

Lucas and Joan were still standing, arguing with their eyes about what should be done. There were only four seats at the round table, so Joan had to take that one. But I could tell she was debating whether or not she should stand for the night.

"Jo, come on." Lucas's disarming smile appeared.

Jo? I had never heard anyone call her that. Hmm. I was beginning to think that their relationship had more meat to it than Joan had let on. I knew one of the reasons she took me as a client was because she knew how cunning Lucas could be and she felt a need to protect me from him, but now I wondered if she hadn't hoped to cross paths with him more.

Joan glowered at him, eventually taking the seat he offered to her, but she refused to let him push her in.

Chad and I smiled at each other as if we had a front row seat to the best show in town.

Once we were all seated, a waiter appeared and filled the crystal gob-lets in front of us with water and asked if we would like anything from the bar.

Lucas once again acted boldly. "A dry martini with several olives for the lady." He smirked at Joan. "And I'll take a scotch, neat." Lucas winced suddenly while Joan smiled with satisfaction. I had a feeling her stilettos made direct contact with his foot.

The waiter handed us each a small menu printed with gold leafing. Was that really necessary? Who needed to print anything in gold?

Before I could even look at the menu, Lucas was happy to tell us what was good. "They have an excellent sea bream with zucchini or chilled corn soup and peaches. Or," his attention landed once again on Joan, "we could always order dessert first. Blackberry sorbet, perhaps?"

What was going on? Was he only trying to throw Joan off her game or was he declaring his feelings? Either way, I could go for that blackberry sorbet.

Joan gripped the white linen covered table and swung right back at him. "That's the problem with you, you always go straight for dessert instead of recognizing how important the three courses before it are."

Ouch.

Lucas recoiled, any playfulness in his features erased, only a red tint in his high-boned cheeks remained.

The gloves had come off. It was time for the games to begin.

Chapter Twenty-Three

THEY WANT ME to do a book tour and be the keynote speaker in Atlanta at one of the major romance conferences in the country in a few weeks," I whispered into my new phone—courtesy of Joan—from bed. The calls I was getting with my old number were insane. Was nothing private anymore?

"What did you say?" Peter yawned.

I felt terrible for waking him up, but there was so much to tell him, from the undeniable chemistry between Joan and Lucas to the lucrative extension of my contract if I agreed to write another series with them. Lucas was even willing to donate twenty percent of the proceeds of the new series to Sweet Feet if I signed on. I had notebooks full of new ideas, but the thought of writing a new series terrified me. What if it wasn't as well loved as the Hunter Black series? What if it had all been a fluke? Was I truly an impostor? A second series would answer all that and so much more.

I rested my head on my pulled-up knees. My head had yet to touch the pillow even though I was mentally and physically exhausted. "I told them I would think about it. I wanted to talk to you first. Though…"

"Though what?"

"I'm not sure I really have a choice about the tour and romance conference. Lucas is holding the breach of contract over my head even though sales have skyrocketed, and we are renegotiating. I suppose it's still the ace in his pocket, so I can't blame him for using it."

"Hmm," Peter was mulling it over or maybe he was sleeping.

"You could come with me. We could make it an adventure in a fish bowl."

His laugh sounded more tired than ever. "How long would we be gone?"

"Around three weeks. That includes the five days at the conference."

"That's a long time. This is a busy time of year for the business. Busier now with all the inquiries we've received by phone and online."

"I know, and I hate taking you away from helping your family but... maybe it's time to make a change."

"What do you mean?"

"Do you love your job?" I realized how we never really talked about that. Probably because he was a happy person in general and working for his dad made sense. But we didn't need the income.

"It's a good job."

"That's not the same as loving your job. And we have different options now. You could... run our foundation. Expand it to other countries like we've wanted to."

He didn't answer right away.

"Could you at least come for part of the trip?"

"Delanie, you know I want to be with you. If that were the only consideration I would say yes in a second. I don't want to leave James and Dad high and dry."

"I completely understand that." I tried to hide my disappointment. This change was hard on all of us. I didn't want to make it any harder, but I wanted to experience this with Peter. We were a team.

"We'll work something out."

"Will you think about the other thing too?"

"Yes." He blew out a large breath. "I have a feeling we will be making a lot of changes in the near future."

My head popped up. "Did something else happen since we talked?"

"I'm just tired, baby."

"I know this is a lot to take in."

"Just come home soon. I miss you in my arms."

"I miss you too. My last taping is on Friday evening. I'll catch a flight that night."

"If I haven't said it yet, I'm proud of you."

I wasn't sure for what. "I feel like I've made a mess of everything."

"You've certainly livened things up, but you have from the first moment I met you. Sometimes it just takes me a while to catch up. Wait for me."

"I'm not going anywhere, you know, except all over the country."

He paused. "I'll be there with you."

"You will?"

"Yeah. I wouldn't miss it."

Suddenly the tightness in my chest since my secret had been exposed loosened. "I'll tell Fiona to make travel plans for two, and alert Joan and all the other company reps." There was no hiding the smile in my voice.

"As long as they aren't staying in our room."

His lighthearted tone made me feel even better. "I love you."

"I love you. Good night."

I threw myself back against the pillow and took a deep breath. Maybe this all wouldn't be so bad. Except I had to be up in four hours to be on one of the most popular morning shows in the country and I couldn't go anywhere anymore without being recognized. Then there were all the lies already being circulated. And let's not forget I had turned my family's life upside down. Sam had texted me earlier to ask if I minded if she granted an interview to the *Chicago Tribune*. She more than anyone had the press beating down her doors to talk to her. She had attention before, but thanks to me, again, it had exponentially increased. She tried to make me feel better and tell me that her publishers were over the moon about the free marketing and the bookstores where she had her signings were expecting huge crowds. I was sorry I was going to miss being there for her.

I just hoped Joan was right. The attention would taper off when a shiny new story stole the glaring spotlight. I would gladly step out of it. Was it awful for me to wish for Kim and Kanye, the real ones, to break up? I mean, what were the odds of them staying together forever anyway? Okay. That was awful. I didn't wish for any couples to break up unless they really should. Maybe Brittany Spears could shave her head again. Hair grows back. And it would be bigger news than me.

Like Joan said, at least I had Peter.

I'd asked her about Lucas after dinner when we were going over the list of talking points she had given the morning show team. Not that they would stick to it. She was preparing me to answer the uncomfortable questions about Peter. I knew why everyone wanted to sensationalize that aspect of our lives, but there wasn't anything there other than Hunter was born out of the angst of being in love with someone you thought you could never be with. That I would never share in any interview. It was one thing to tell Peter's siblings and best friend Hunter was based on him, it was another to go into detail and tell the world how Hunter was born. That would be my secret. The world didn't need to know every-thing about me. Just like Joan didn't think I needed to know about Lucas. She did let slip that maybe in a different time and place it would have worked out between them.

I wanted to know why not in the here and now, but her look said if I asked she was going to stab me with the pen she was using at the time. I needed my hands, so I kept my mouth shut.

That was another worry. When in this circus was I going to find time to write? Chad and Lucas were very interested in when I would be turning in my manuscript. I respectfully reminded them if they wanted me to do a book tour it would delay the process. Lucas wasn't thrilled about it and tried to say something until Joan got him with her stiletto again. How he walked after that meeting, I had no idea. Pride, probably. Chad was more dramatic about it, begging me to at least give him details. Unlike some authors, I refused to turn in an outline or synopsis because I almost never stuck to them. My characters led the story. Sometimes they even surprised me.

I curled up in Joan's guest bed willing sleep to come. Like a lot of things in my life lately, it didn't seem to be in my control. I hoped they had a good makeup artist at the studio tomorrow to cover up the bags under my eyes that were sure to be there.

❦

Joan, while not what some would call a nurturer, put on a good act when needed. She smoothed some of my curls in the green room. "America is going to eat you up in this floral split dress. Can you get any more gorgeous?"

I rolled my eyes. I was only thankful the small red marks on my legs were fading from my one and probably only baking achievement. Makeup hid what was still there. "My mother would be abhorred you are objectifying me."

"From what little you have told me of your mother, she doesn't deserve the title, and there's nothing wrong with being smart and beautiful as long as you remember to never let your beauty supersede your brains." She gently swiped my hair. She was being uncharacteristically warm this morning, which I was grateful for. "I don't believe that has ever been a problem for you."

"Thank you, Joan."

"Don't get sappy on me, kid." She gave me a pat on the cheek.

I took deep breaths and paced around. Now I knew why Sam was always so nervous before an interview. It felt like one of those dreams where you were naked in front of everyone at school. It was much easier doing this by email or being on the other end asking the questions.

Which I wouldn't be doing anymore. I was going to miss writing for the online magazine, but that was part of the negotiations last night. Lucas easily gave into that. He wanted me focused on Autumn Moone more than anyone, except Joan, who was ready to put a down payment on that Upper East Side townhome. I didn't even want to know how much that was going to cost her.

A smartly dressed production assistant popped her head in. "Ms. Moone, you're up next."

I didn't like being called Ms. Moone but didn't correct her. It was better the world know her than Delanie, I supposed.

Joan walked out with me, to my relief. Her presence was more comforting than she knew. I signed a few autographs on my way to the set. I wasn't sure I would get used to the starstruck looks on people's faces when they met me. I did love hearing they loved my books, even if I wondered how genuine their compliments were or if they'd even read them.

This morning show crew was made up of two women, Isla and Rachael, and the token male, David. I met them all earlier during a commercial break. They were too effervescent for this early in the morning, but I supposed if they were dull no one would watch them.

The studio was open, and you could see a large crowd gathered outside behind where the hosts of the show sat. A high, semi-circle glass table almost made it look as if they were all at a coffee shop chatting at the counter. Except they had screaming fans with signs behind them and a camera crew capturing their every move. I shouldn't have been shocked to see so many of those posters were declaring their love for Hunter Black and Autumn Moone, but I was.

I held my stomach, glad I hadn't eaten. Not sure I could have if I tried, even though there was plenty of food to be had.

I had a surreal moment when Isla began to introduce me. "The big breaking news over the weekend is the identity of Autumn Moone, the author of our favorite guilty pleasure, Hunter Black, has been revealed, and we have her exclusive first interview this morning. For those of you who aren't familiar with Autumn Moone, she currently has the number one bestselling book, *Black Day Dawning*, and her Hunter Black series has sold over seventy-five million copies worldwide."

Those numbers still boggled my mind.

"Until now," Isla continued, "she's been shrouded in mystery ever since she appeared on the scene four years ago. Today, though, we are going to get to know the woman behind one of the most popular series in the last ten years."

That was my cue.

Joan squeezed my hand right before I went out. "Don't trip, and smile like you mean it."

That got me to smile as I walked out, acting as if this was no big deal and I was meeting friends for coffee. At least, that was what I hoped it looked like I was doing.

Isla, Rachael, and David, the super polished hosts, stood to greet me with hugs and handshakes. They were all perfectly molded with capped teeth and designer clothes, without a hair out of place. And they all must have trainers; their bodies were solid as rocks.

Now that I was close to the window wall behind the interview desk, the crowd went nuts. The jumping up and down and screaming was off-putting. I waved at the crowd before I had the pleasure of sitting in the middle chair. More like nerve-racking honor.

All the hosts flashed their dazzling smiles at me. Rachael, with tresses of gold, was first to speak her rehearsed opening question. "So, is it really you?"

They all laughed.

I had to join in and play my part. "You tell me," I teased.

That made them laugh more.

"The question is, how and why did you keep it all a secret?" David asked.

I remembered to smile. "Well, the *how* I obviously didn't do so well. As for the why, as much as I love hanging out with you, I'm much more comfortable behind a laptop screen." I hoped they didn't hear the fabrication in my voice.

They all gave sympathetic nods; Isla even patted my hand. "I imagine all this attention must be difficult for you."

"It's been interesting." I tried to keep it light.

Rachael's velvet brown eyes lit up as if we were at a slumber party and we were getting ready to play truth or dare. I supposed that's exactly what we were playing. "But tell us, is it true that your secret was discovered by some partygoers at your home?"

I had to keep my composure thinking about those sneaky women. Honestly, what they did didn't bother me as much as who was behind it all. I had to push down my feelings of betrayal. I had to remember to keep the smile on. "All I can say is it ended up being quite the party."

"I heard it was more than a party." Isla wasn't going to let me off the hook. "Rumor is that it was a reception for the Sidelined Wife, Samantha Decker, who happens to be your sister-in-law." She looked directly into the camera. "For those of you that don't know the Sidelined Wife, she is a popular blogger and author in her own right of a cookbook out this week." She had a copy of Sam's book and held it up. "The world got to know her through Autumn Moone." Isla turned back to me. "And you kept your identity secret even from her and your family, is that right?"

"Everyone except my husband, yes."

"I suppose that would have been difficult." David laughed. "Even though as husbands we can be clueless. I would hope, though, I would have noticed all the extra typing and, I imagine, larger bank account."

They all waited for me to respond.

"Peter is very attentive and supportive of my *hobby*."

"Hobby, she says." Isla snickered. "That is quite the hobby. Seventy-five million books."

Rachael leaned in. "Speaking of your husband. We have to know. Is it true you met while he was a priest?"

Her cohosts faked being shocked at such a notion.

Keep it cool, I reminded myself. I was here to get the truth out. I placed my hands in my lap and sat up tall. "We first became acquainted while he was a priest, but we didn't start dating until he was laicized." I hoped with everything I had they would move on. Maybe ask me some questions about my current release or what I was working on, but that was too much to ask.

Their faces all said they were skeptical, but they smiled right through it.

"What do you say to all the reports that he was forced to leave the priesthood because of your relationship?"

I say they are all garbage. "There is no truth behind them. People love a good story, which, frankly, I'm thankful for given my line of work. But honestly, we live boring lives. Peter works for his dad as a landscaper and I write. A lot of nights you can find us eating takeout and going for a walk or watching a movie on TV."

"Boring." David guffawed. "She writes *New York Times* bestsellers and she considers that boring."

What I wouldn't have done to have kept my life boring.

"How is the rest of your family responding to this revelation?" Rachael made sure she sounded like she was only asking because she was concerned about their welfare instead of being nosy. And like she didn't know my husband's grandma and her felon lover were giving half-cocked interviews.

I decided not to play into it. I knew they wanted me to. They wanted me to open Pandora's Box. I flashed another fake smile. "My nephews' Christmas lists have suddenly gotten longer." That was partially true. They mentioned Sunday that they hoped we would finally get some good stuff at our house, and a pool.

The hosts all faux laughed, disappointed I didn't give them a good segue to delve further into my personal life. I think they got the hint and finally got to some questions about my books. Everyone always wanted spoilers; none were given. Then they asked the question I knew was coming.

"Where did you get your inspiration for Hunter Black?"

In the moment, a thought came to me. All truthful but it revealed nothing. "When I write, I take a moment that impacted my life somehow in a profound way. It could be from my own experience or from someone close to me. It could even be an article or a blog. Anything that touches my soul. I use all those emotions and breathe them into my characters."

Each set of eyes said, that's it? Yes, that was all they would have of me, of Peter.

Once the interview was over, they surprised the audience outside with copies of my new book. I went out and helped distribute them, all in front of the camera. I posed for so many selfies with fans that my mouth hurt from smiling so much and my hand began to cramp from signing so many autographs. But I'd done my part for my publisher.

Autumn now had a life of her own. The question was, where would Delanie fit into it?

Chapter Twenty-Four

*M*Y WIFE IS *a babe on TV. Good job, honey. Call me later.*

I can't believe they showed my book! Now my publisher isn't sure they ordered enough for my signing today. Wish me luck.

Did you get David's autograph? He's so cute. You should see the line for Sam.

I read all the texts from my family and smiled, but found myself missing all of them, especially Peter. I hoped he wasn't too freaked about all the questions regarding him, but I didn't have time to ask him. We were on our way to apparently one of the most prized photographers in all of New York, Simon Webb. LH Ink was completely redoing their web and social sites now. I was to be front and center. And *IN TREND* magazine had contacted Joan about me being on their November cover. It was a big deal since a magazine's editorial calendar is pretty much set for the year, and exceptions were rare.

Simon Webb's studio was in Greenwich Village, not far from Chelsea, where Joan lived. Chad and Fiona were meeting us there, as well as the VP of marketing, Shaylee. Everyone wanted to be where I was, like

I was a new shiny toy to play with. I wondered if Lucas would come too. He was reluctant to say goodbye to Joan last night. I decided I wasn't going to press Joan for any more information. I respected other people's secrets, even if everyone seemed determined to know all of mine.

The studio had sent a car and driver for us early that morning and they were at our disposal for the day. This felt like someone else's life. More so now when we pulled up in front of the trendy loft with a simple black and white sign on the door that read Simon's. I was out of the fish bowl for a moment, but now I felt like a fish out of water. More and more I could relate to Sam. And more and more I felt guilty for pushing this life upon her. She did seem to handle it with grace, though. I wanted to emulate her. She would cope by writing a hilarious blog about how she was sorry she didn't bring enough protein balls to hand out, or perhaps she would be more poignant and wax poetic about how inadequate she felt, but she would do it in a self-deprecating way that made you love her even more.

Hunter and Laine both screamed in my head that the only thing I better write was their story. Believe me, I wanted to. But I needed an undisturbed place with only me and my music. I looked over to Joan, who was telling off a lawyer regarding a production contract for another one of her clients. She was like that during all waking hours. I think she even fought with people in her sleep. I was pretty sure I heard her say in the middle of the night, "We are past mediation. I'll see you in court!" Or perhaps she was still awake. She drank caffeine like she breathed air. She was still on me about filing a lawsuit against the Nancy Drew Club. I wasn't sure that was a can of worms that needed to be opened. My mother-in-law would be an accomplice, and no matter how angry Peter was at his mom, I was pretty sure he didn't want me to embroil her in a legal battle. Besides, that would mean I would have to talk to Sarah again, which I wasn't ever planning on doing.

And I would say she was getting her just desserts. Sarah dear was at odds with everyone in her life now, including Mimsy. Though Mimsy should be thanking her lucky stars. We now knew that swindler, Giovanni, was actually named Jerry Brown. His little TV interview bit him in the butt. Someone he had stolen money from recognized him and tipped off the police. Avery couldn't tell me a lot over text that morning, but it appeared that he'd been playing this angle for some time and had bilked thousands from vulnerable widows. "Giovanni" was currently on the run as of the previous night. He'd caught wind the game was up and fled. Mimsy was still in denial about it all. Peter feared she was losing her faculties. I wondered if she had only been lonely. The kind of lonely only a partner could fill. I felt sorry for her, even if she'd added to the hell in my life.

Joan finally realized we had arrived and ended her call with a snappy, "Have that new contract to me by the end of day, and this time get someone who passed the second grade to write it."

I shook my head at her and smiled. "Way to be a motivator."

She threw her phone in her bag. "Whatever it takes to get the job done."

Our driver opened Joan's door since she was curbside and we both exited into the warm beginning of a September day. Fall wasn't quite in the air, but the trees growing amid the sidewalks spoke of how it wouldn't be long. The green leaves weren't quite as vibrant as they had been in the spring. They looked tired and almost glad their job would be over for a season. I could relate. I needed a nap myself. But there was no time.

Fiona popped out of the studio door. "Oh good, you're here. We're all waiting for you." Her voice had a nasal quality with a hint of Bronx.

It was always fun to see Fiona. She never failed to have a new hair color or tattoo. Today her pixie hair was a deep red bordering on purple, and she had shaved one side. It went perfect with her frilly black skirt and Converses. I would have to ask her later where the new tattoo was.

We walked in to find several people waiting for us. The expected were there, Chad, Shaylee, and Lucas, which didn't surprise me at all. Nor did the longing look he gave Joan. However, she basically gave him the finger with her eyes. That only made her more desirable by the seductive smile he flashed her. There was also a group from the magazine. I wasn't expecting them. I had been told that they let Simon have reign—that's how good he was. But everyone seemed to want to get a piece of me. To see my flesh and blood. Then there was Simon himself. He was not what I imagined. He didn't seem to take himself too seriously. He was dressed in faded blue jeans and a white T-shirt that matched his almost completely white studio. Even the wood floors were white. His blonde hair was mussed, and he walked around barefoot.

Everyone around him seemed to revere him. They parted in reverence as he approached me. All eyes followed until he landed right in front of me. He didn't introduce himself before he started walking around me, touching my hair. He stood back and gazed at me from different angles. His piercing blue eyes seemed to be x-raying me. I suddenly felt like I was having that dream again where I was naked in front of everyone.

Simon didn't mind getting up close and personal. He was in my face before I knew it, making direct eye contact. "Autumn Moone." He paused. "You don't like to be called that do you?" He was perceptive. I would give him that.

I shook my head.

"Delanie then. You are a woman with secrets. Let's see if we can discover a few with my lens, shall we?"

I swallowed hard, afraid of what he might see.

Before I could answer or run away, he walked off. In his place was a swarm of women in black smocks leading me to a dressing room. My entourage of Fiona and Joan followed. Chad gave me an evil grin as we walked by. He knew I wasn't enjoying this and delighted himself with my discomfort.

A woman from the magazine was calling out that she wanted to come and had ideas for the cover. Simon ignored her request.

One of the smocked lanky model creatures handed me a black silk robe without so much as introducing herself. "Change out of your clothes and put this on." She pointed to a curtain I could stand behind.

I stood defiant. I wasn't used to being bossed around.

The stern woman cracked a smile. "It's only to do your hair and makeup. We don't bite, I promise."

That I wasn't so sure about, but I took the robe and marched toward the curtain.

"Give them hell, kid," Joan whispered as I passed her. Fiona gave me an appreciative nod. I didn't mind that the curtain meant nothing to them. They both came with and while I undressed, Fiona ticked off items on her tablet.

"The hotel in Atlanta wants to know if you require anything special they will need to have on hand?"

"Like what?" I stepped out of my dress after Joan unzipped it for me.

"A certain food or flowers?"

"No. If I need something, I'll get it myself."

Joan scoffed. "Right. Because it will be so easy for you to stroll on over to the local grocery store while you're there."

Ugh. I hadn't thought about that. "Regardless, Peter and I are pretty simple. We eat cereal for dinner at least two times a week."

Both women laughed.

"Are you sure Peter wants to come?" Fiona asked.

I looked up, only in my bra and underwear, puzzled by her question. "Why wouldn't he?"

Fiona and Joan looked at each other as if they had already had this discussion.

"He's getting a lot of scrutiny in the press. This can't be easy for him, and it might make him more of target if he's with you," Joan said.

I hastily threw on my robe, needing some comfort, and not because of the lack of clothing. "It's been difficult, but it should get better, right? They'll see we're a regular couple." Even saying it, I knew it wasn't true. We never had been. I think we wanted to be, but we knew our relationship was much more than opposites attracting.

"I hope so, kid," Joan tried to placate me. "But you're not a regular couple anymore." That, at least, gave me hope that we came off as one. Maybe.

"Who cares what people think?" Fiona ran her fingers through her purplish hair. "So, you married a priest. You're not the first. Or the last." She marked off an item on her list. "No food requests. Is it all right if some of the flights are business class instead of first?"

I waved her off. "We're happy flying coach."

"These do-gooders." Joan rolled her eyes. "Don't book me anything less than business."

Fiona looked up uneasy. "Lucas...thinks...um...Delanie should pay for your expenses since technically you work for her, not us."

That made sense to me. Joan was only coming to the Atlanta portion with me anyway. It's not like I was her only client and she could follow me around the country, though I always appreciated when I came into town she treated me that way. I saw her more as a friend and confidant than someone I paid. And she was only going to Atlanta because they'd asked her to be on a panel about entertainment law and what authors should know. It was a good opportunity for her. Not that she wouldn't be highly sought after now.

The searing fire in Joan's violet eyes said she didn't agree with my or Lucas's assessment of the situation. "Is that right? Excuse me, I need to give your boss a little reminder about our deal." She spun so violently on her stilettos I was surprised she didn't leave a hole in the wood floor.

I wondered what deal she was talking about.

Fiona's cheeks matched her hair, but she gave me a devious grin. "Hmm. He was right."

I reached for her. "Who was right?"

Fiona bit her lip. "Lucas," she whispered. "He's been calling her all morning, but she won't answer. He thought this might do the trick."

My eyes widened. "She's going to do more than talk to him."

She wagged her eyebrows. "I think that's what he hopes for."

The curtain was unceremoniously removed without warning, interrupting us. "We're ready for you," Smock One said. I gave them my own names since no one was polite enough to introduce themselves.

I tied the robe around me quickly before I was ushered to a chair you would see in a salon. A million lights shone down on it. From there I was poked, prodded, tweezed, teased, slathered, powdered, you name it. By the time they were done, I didn't recognize myself in the mirror. I hardly ever wore makeup, so to see myself in a smoky eye and teased hair was unnerving. It got even more so when Simon walked in and behind him trailed more Smock Things carrying what looked like brown tulle and an ivory sheet.

I didn't hide my grimace. I never wanted to see tulle again. In fact, I might have had tulle-induced PTSD.

Simon didn't give any credence to my obvious distaste.

Smock Four held up the pile of tulle, and to my surprise it was a dress. A tiered, puffy mess of a skirt with an off the shoulder top. It had a medieval feel to it, except it was more revealing than was thought proper for that period. Regardless, it was nothing I would choose to wear.

"We'll do some shots of you in the dress first and then the sheet."

Hold up. "Sheet?" I didn't sign up for *that* kind of photoshoot. I joked about doing them, hence the reason I was here. And sure, I'd done some risqué things a long time ago, but those days were behind me and I wasn't wrapping myself up in a sheet for anyone but my husband.

He shrugged his shoulders as if it was no big deal. "Yes, a sheet. Trust me."

I was going to pass.

Or so I thought.

"The Secret Life of Autumn Moone."

"Perfect."

"There is a haunting quality to her. Too bad it's too late to get her on our October cover."

"We are getting some head shots of her, right?"

"The sheet is so symbolic of her uncovering herself. Simon is a genius."

"Keep staring at her like that and I will throw bleach in your eyes." If you hadn't guessed, that was Joan.

Everyone around me was discussing me like I wasn't there lying on the floor against a stark white backdrop, lights zeroed in on me, in a sheet, no less. I had a nude body suit on that covered everything but my shoulders and legs. I refused to do the shoot unless I was dressed underneath. I didn't care how tasteful Simon promised he would be. Or how much I thought the body was a beautiful thing and you should never be ashamed of it. But it was my body and my rules.

Simon had taken too many shots of me in the ballgown against several hand painted backgrounds and seemed pleased, but now something was frustrating him. I think it was me. "Everyone out!" he shouted. "You are inhibiting my work by disrupting Delanie's vulnerabilities with your chatter."

I couldn't get much more vulnerable than being on the ground in a sheet.

It was odd how everyone scattered, even his assistants. Everyone but Joan and Fiona that is. They stood firm.

Simon did not appreciate their stubbornness. "I said out."

I sat up, defiant. "They stay, or I go." There was no way I was being left alone with him. I didn't know him, and the fact the guy wanted me naked under a sheet didn't give me any reason to trust him.

Simon's blue eyes glared at me. "You are risking what we could create here if they stay."

"If you are as good as everyone says you are, you'll make it work." This was nonnegotiable to me.

The corners of his lips ticked up. "This is why you are an amazing subject. You are an enigma. You talk a tough game, but you are probably the most vulnerable specimen I've had the pleasure to shoot."

I rankled at being called a subject and specimen. Growing up that's all I had been, and I resented it.

Simon's smile grew as he drew closer. His camera was off the tripod and in his hands, ready to make use of it. "Yes. I've hit a nerve. This is good. What makes you so vulnerable?" He lifted his camera and took a few shots while my eyes were narrowed at him.

"What makes you think you know me?"

He didn't lower his camera, he only switched angles. "Your body language is screaming it from the way you place your hand on your neck to how you're holding on to that sheet for dear life."

I was about to say I was in a sheet what did he expect, but he wasn't done.

"I know from the way you carry yourself you are physically comfortable in your body. I would say you even celebrate it."

He was right. I dropped my hand from my neck and inadvertently curled my legs.

"Very good. I like that. It speaks exactly to what I'm saying."

"Just take your pictures," I growled before catching a glimpse of Joan and Fiona who, for once, seemed to have nothing to say. They stood there, mesmerized by us.

"I will. You keep pretending it doesn't bother you. This is fantastic. I see now what makes you such a beautiful storyteller. All the good ones carry pain." He took shot after shot without giving me any direction. When I was in the dress, he had told me how to hold my head, what to do with my hands, when to smile, when not to. Now he wanted *me*, and I didn't like it at all. I almost got up and left, but I think that's exactly what he wanted, and I refused to give in.

I'm not sure how many shots he took, but when he was done he sank to the ground as if he had given his all. He lowered his camera with a satisfied smile. "You are a magnificent creature." His eyes penetrated mine. "Do you want to know how to overcome your vulnerabilities?"

I nodded without thinking.

He leaned in and whispered, "Tell someone your secrets." His voice begged that it would be him.

That honor belonged to one man only, and I wasn't even sure I could tell him.

Chapter Twenty-Five

AFTER THE PHOTOSHOOT, I wanted to lock myself in a room and regurgitate all my feelings into my manuscript. It was as if Simon had unleashed all my vulnerabilities and they were taunting me, almost daring me to get rid of them, but they knew how I clung to them, almost needed them now. They knew how afraid I was to be completely vulnerable, even around Peter. How I feared he might react to some of my choices. They knew my secrets. They knew about *her*.

To add to the assault, I had an email from Father Alan. I had sent him a note yesterday to tell him I wouldn't be attending RCIA classes anymore for obvious reasons. I was already afraid that someone else from the class would blab that I had been taking them if they realized who I was, and it would circulate in this digital age. I was hoping, though, that the few people there including the mentor I had been assigned to would keep it private and remember this was a personal journey. I wanted to know for sure before I got Peter's hopes up like that. In that vein, I was hoping for a simple response from Father Alan like *it was nice to get to know you and good luck.* But no, it added to the complexities of the emotions coursing through me.

My hands shook as I read his message.

I'm certainly sad you won't be attending class anymore. Though I would like you to know we can make accommodations if you would be interested. And I would still be happy to answer any questions you may have by email. Perhaps it is time to let your husband join you in this endeavor. From all that you have said about him, I think he would be understanding even if the outcome is not what he had hoped for. For, as he knows, faith is a journey that can only be known to one's self, but it is not a path that need be walked alone. Why not walk it with the man you have chosen as your partner? Open up to him about your doubts and fears; it will only draw you closer together.

Was that true?

I didn't have time to answer that or even hope for how much I wanted it to be true.

We were all on our way to a late lunch where we were going to discuss marketing campaigns for my series as well as the conference in Atlanta, which LH Ink had already been heavily involved with. Now that I was available, they wanted to use me to their fullest advantage.

Fiona was throwing things at me and checking more things off her list as she went.

"Shaylee wants you to approve the copy for the press release regarding the conference. I emailed it to you."

I nodded, halfheartedly paying attention.

"Also, the designer has some questions about the changes you want made on the *Black Confessions* cover. Would you like to call him or email him?"

My brain took a second to comprehend what she was saying. "Um...I'll call him."

Fiona tipped her head. "Are you okay? Ever since we left Simon's, you seem out of it."

"I hope you didn't let that idiot into your head." Joan looked up from her phone. "He was only trying to get a rise out of you. All that crap about secrets and vulnerabilities. You're a tough cookie and he only wanted to taste you. The pig. Did you notice how much he balked at photographing you in the sweater and jeans? And did you see that he picked a sweater that showed off your shoulders from his 'prop' room. I'd like to go in there and see what else he has. Where did he get all those clothes?"

I had wondered that too.

"Total perv," Joan snarled. "I will be steering clients away from him in the future. I don't care if everyone in this town thinks he's a god."

I agreed with Joan that he was a pervert, but it was unnerving how right he was about me. No one knew all the secrets I kept or how much I wanted to share them with someone. To share the pain I'd tried to forget but couldn't because it would mean forgetting her. She was a part of me. I wanted to share it all with Peter, but how could I tell him after all this time? Would he understand why I couldn't bring myself to tell him when we were first together? Why being with someone like him was so intimidating and almost daunting? I didn't want to rock the boat that had taken so much effort to set sail in the first place. Peter changed his entire life for me. For a woman who had grown up vastly different than him, with opinions about love and sex that didn't exactly match his.

His silence was noted when he had asked about my previous relationships and I revealed my less than innocent sexual past, at least most of it. I knew he was trying not to react negatively, but I saw the surprise in his eyes. How he'd left early that night. How he came back the next morning as if he thought about it all and determined we were still meant to be together, but he never brought it up again. Even now he skirted the topic of old love interests.

I continued to examine the situation in my head over lunch while I should have been engaged in the conversation surrounding marketing strategies and weird things like the different types of balls and events they had at this romance conference. I heard something about me having to attend the Sweet and Sexy Ball, and something about the model who portrayed Hunter Black on my book covers being there for women to take pictures with. That was bizarre to me. Besides, I would be bringing the real man behind Hunter as my date. That was, if he didn't leave me after I told him about *her*, the *baby*—I could hardly say it.

Baby X, I called her. I knew she would never be mine, so I never gave her a name and refused to know what it would be. As hard as I tried not to love her, I couldn't help myself. I hated to admit that I wanted to hate her at first for what she had done to me. She made me a statistic. And at the time, I blamed her for taking away the first person I ever thought I belonged with. My stomach roiled at the thought now. Despite all that, a fierce need to protect her overcame me. From there, love swelled as she grew. Then with every kick and move, my heart shattered knowing I couldn't keep her.

I had to stop thinking about her. I hadn't allowed myself to go this far in a long time. Tears were on the cusp of falling. "Excuse me." I pushed back my chair and briskly walked toward the ladies' room. I had to pause to sign an autograph and fake a smile on my way.

Once in the restroom, I realized I was no longer in Kansas. I was in the Taj Mahal of bathrooms, with actual gold sinks. I half expected gold thrones in the stalls. Once safely behind the stall door, I leaned against it, hoping it was as clean as it looked. I took deep breaths in and out, in and out. I held onto my bare abdomen. It felt emptier than ever.

Peter would understand why, wouldn't he? Did I even understand why? My head did, but I don't think my heart ever had. The tears wanted to flow, but they couldn't. All that ridiculous makeup from the photoshoot weighed heavy on my face. There would have been no hiding the evidence, and I was good at hiding the evidence. Too good. But I had no other choice. I had to protect her. But what if I couldn't now? What if Autumn exposed her?

My heart raced.

I began weighing the pros and cons of telling Peter. The overwhelming pro was being able to share the burden I'd carried by myself for so long. To allow myself the opportunity to share everything with my husband. For him to tell me it was okay. And maybe he could help me get over the shame I'd felt for the choices I had to make. The thought filled me with imaginable relief and felicity.

On the opposite end of the spectrum, there was anxiety and despair. What if he hated me for keeping *her* from him? What if he thought I'd brought it upon myself because I chose to be with Blair? I could hardly think his name. I had never hated someone so much in my life. Sarah's betrayal had nothing on his. His name hissed in my head. I shut my eyes. If the press really wanted a sensationalized story from my past, they chose the wrong man. Yes, I had a story for them, filled with power, money, deceit, intimidation, and fear. Fear I still felt. I grabbed my heart. I didn't want to think about this anymore. I couldn't. I was supposed to be in the middle of a meeting.

Deep breaths in and out.

What should I do?

I had no other choice for now but to walk back out and join my colleagues and pretend as if I wasn't having a crisis the size of the Empire State Building.

They hardly even took note when I returned. Most of them were in deep discussion about if they should have some new Autumn Moone bookmarks made with my face plastered on them. Lucas was arguing against the added expense and Shaylee countered that the readers at the conference would be more willing to seek out LH Ink's booth if the swag was more personalized. Joan, on the other hand, was intently reading something on her phone, either bored by the ridiculous conversation or working per her usual.

After some contemptuous debate, Shaylee turned my way. "What do you think?" she asked.

What did I think? I think there were children with no shoes or clean water and nine-year-old girls that were far more important than a bookmark that someone was probably going to throw away. And there were women with painful secrets and choices to make that would alter their lives dramatically who didn't care, not even for a second, if her photo was on a piece of paper.

I didn't say any of those things. I hid behind a faux smile and replied, "Bookmarks seem frivolous nowadays since most people buy digital books."

Everyone paused as if what I said was profound before they went right back to arguing.

I was happy yet terrified to let them. It gave me time with my own thoughts. Thoughts that frightened me. Could I really keep hiding the truth from Peter? Should I? I had rationalized for so many years that I wasn't lying to him. He'd never asked me if I'd had a baby. And the situation was both embarrassing and terrifying. That and I didn't like talking to Peter about previous sexual relationships. I was Peter's first and only. I wished I could say the same. No one had ever loved me so tenderly and deeply, both physically and emotionally. But what if I told him and it all went away? My heart kept telling me that Peter would understand if he knew why. He'd never expected me to live up to his standards or to ascribe to his way of living. He loved me for who I was, tattoos, piercings, swearing, and all. Not once had he asked me to change.

I took a silent deep breath. *I should tell him.*

"Oh, hell," Joan groaned.

Talking ceased and all heads turned toward her, but Joan only gave me the time of day. Which wasn't all that surprising since she'd been ignoring Lucas all through lunch, though he sat next to her and had tried to engage her in conversation on several occasions.

"What?" I asked her.

She sighed in resignation before holding up her phone for me to see. I was beginning to learn this always spelled bad news.

With trepidation, I took her phone that was more like a tablet and tried to casually glance down at it, but it quickly turned into a wide-eyed

gawking session when I saw that the site was from a local Portland channel where I had grown up. My parents were clearly in the paused video
frame. Above it read, *Autumn Moone's Parents and Classmates Tell All.* Tell
all what? My head tipped up to meet Joan's eyes that said she was sorry.
That couldn't be good.

Joan slid her chair back and stood up. "Come with me."

She practically hoisted me up and dragged me over to the bar where
we grabbed two chairs at the end, away from the lunchtime crowd. Lots
of eyes were on us and I noticed a couple of women acted as if they
wanted to come say hi. I could only hope they read the signals right and
stayed away. I didn't need Joan snapping at fans who would probably
write all about it on social media.

Only the bartender approached and asked what he could get us once
we were settled. It was hard not to tell him to bring me a mango margarita and keep them coming. Joan had no problem ordering a double shot
of whiskey.

We put our heads together and I scrolled down to read the story
below the video. I digested print better and wanted to keep it private.
Private? I was beginning to think there was no such thing. Guaranteed
national news channels would be picking up this story. I would be all
over CNN, MSN, and everything in between before the night was
through.

While taking shallow breaths I read first about my parents. They basically took credit for all my success and touted their books as often as they
could. They even talked about the red manual typewriter they bought me
and how I wrote my first story with it. When asked if they had a copy of
that story they regretfully said no. What a joke. I had the story. You know
why? Because after they patted themselves on the back for my achievement, I later found it in the trash. They only cared that I had written it. I
doubt they even read it. If they had, maybe they would have known how
lonely I was. The kicker came at the end of their portion of the interview
when the reporter remarked that they must be proud. Cat is quoted as

saying, "We are pleased to see that our childrearing methods not only work but produce successful human beings."

That was touching. I supposed I should be happy that I had been upgraded from a subject to a human being.

Next up were my high school classmates. Where they dug them up, I didn't want to know. It seemed like anyone connected to me wanted their fifteen minutes of fame.

A few said I was nice. One woman remembered I helped her pass Spanish. But that was boring, so they were buried in the article.

Joan squeezed my arm as if she knew I was getting to the "good" part and wanted to brace me. In bold letters it read, *Juvenile Delinquent or Social Justice Warrior?*

I had an inkling about what might come next, but I had no idea how blown out of proportion it would be or the outright lies that would be told.

It seems as if Autumn Moone, or Delanie Monfort now Decker, was quite the troublemaker at Fordham High School. As editor of the school's newspaper, she did more than write the headlines, she made them. Her former classmate Eli Guthrie remembers her as the girl who wasn't afraid to speak her mind and made sure she was listened to.

What he said was true, even if I had no idea who Eli was.

One of her more memorable stunts was placing a toilet filled with human feces in the principal's office with a vulgar note telling him he was full of ####.

My lip may have twitched remembering my well-coordinated plan of attack protesting the unfair dress code that in essence gave boys a free pass. While I'm not a dress code kind of person, I could understand the need for some guidelines, but they'd better be fair for all sexes. I had to spend two days in in-house suspension because I wore boys' tennis shorts to school. The same shorts boys were wearing every day at the time, but when I wore them I was told they were too short. When I refused to change I was punished, even though I had a signed petition with over a thousand signatures from parents and community leaders who agreed a more balanced approach should have been taken. When the principal refused to back down, I made a statement. A big, smelly one.

She was never formally charged since they could never prove it was her, but it is widely believed that she was the perpetrator.

You're darn right I was.

As editor, she also published an unauthorized copy of the failing grades of athletes, questioning why the school was going against its athletic code by allowing these players to continue to play while ineligible. She and her fellow newspaper staff members also prevented the hiring of a vice principal by discovering inconsistencies in her resume. Both incidents were highly embarrassing to the school and were cause to expel Ms. Decker, though she was never punished for either event. Which is still a mystery to some of those we spoke with who would like to remain anonymous.

Who were those anonymous cowards telling lies? I was punished by being let go as editor even though I was telling the truth.

But perhaps her most outrageous stunt, according to Selah Woods, was when she ran across the football field in the middle of the state championship game while naked and wearing only a sign that complained about the disparity in funding between arts and athletics. We couldn't find a record of her being arrested for public indecency, which makes us question how she skirted charges for such an offense. Which leads us to ask, who is Autumn Moone really? Juvenile Delinquent or Social Justice Warrior? We will let you decide.

I looked up, my face flushed and heart pounding. I never did such a thing, at least not at a game. My friends and I may have streaked through the woods on a dare once, but that was innocent. And what was this crap about letting the reader decide? The article in no way offered an unbiased approach. They obviously didn't interview anyone who could have discounted the stupidity of some of those accusations, and if they had, they didn't report it.

Joan squeezed my hand. "You okay, kid?"

No. I wasn't okay. This wasn't okay. "So much of this isn't even true." I handed her phone back to her before I threw it across the bar.

"Del, I don't care if it's all true. I'd be proud if it was." She smirked. "I only care about how it affects you and if we need to sue anyone for libel."

Ugh. I rubbed my temples. "I don't want to go down that road. I have a feeling it would never end."

"Buckle up, kid, this is going to be a long, bumpy road."

Chapter Twenty-Six

I FINALLY HAD MORE than a minute alone outside of a bathroom stall. Joan was meeting someone who she wouldn't mention for drinks. I had a pretty good guess who. Lucas cornered her after lunch and leaned in close to whisper in her ear. I swore she blushed right before she pushed him away, leaving him to admire her backside. I wanted to know what he'd said to her, but I figured if she wanted to tell me, she would.

I sank into Joan's couch, exhausted. It had been a nonstop day. After lunch I was ushered to an interview with *IN TREND*, where more of the same uncomfortable questions came. Then to a dinner appointment with an exec from a national chain of shoe stores who was interested in partnering with Sweet Feet. It felt good to be able to openly work with our foundation. It was the highlight of my day and helped me forget for a moment my entire life was being played out online without my consent.

After I took a breath and kicked off my shoes, I grabbed my phone. I needed to hear my husband's voice.

He picked up after two rings. I expected to hear his voice, but all I could hear was James laughing and yelling, "DE-LAN-IE, you are my new hero! Please tell me how you got that toilet in the principal's office."

My head dropped. I'd been hoping Peter hadn't seen that yet. I wanted to give him some warning. "Hi, honey," was all I could say, which was weird because I don't think I'd ever called Peter that, but it seemed apropos.

"Hey," he sounded more tired than I was, which was saying something.

"Are you still working?" It was nine there and had been dark for a while now.

James was still spouting off nonsense in the background. "Saintly Peter got himself a wild woman while I ended up with the good girl. God definitely has a sense of humor." He was not helping any.

"Let me walk back to Dad's office." No doubt James was irritating him.

I heard a door close.

"That's better," Peter sighed.

"Why are you at the office?"

"It's been crazy here, and without Sam to help, and with Avery supporting her today at the signing. And…it's just been busy, so we are playing catch up."

I rested my head against the couch cushion. "I'm sor—"

"Don't say it."

"At least tell me how Sam's signing went." Anything to not talk about the elephant that not only filled the room but every corner of our lives.

"According to Avery, they sold every copy and they were there for hours."

"That's great. I'm happy for her."

Uncomfortable silence crept in between us, a kind of quiet that had never happened before.

The elephant needed to be addressed. "I take it you saw the piece done about me back in Portland."

"Yeah," he breathed out.

"And?"

"I'm just surprised, is all. You've never really told me a lot about that time in your life."

"You've never asked, and I didn't think it was important. Besides, half of that article was lies."

"Which half?"

I was stunned by his question. "Does it really matter?" Because if it did, how could I ever tell him about her?

"No," he sighed.

My heart felt as if it had stopped. "Peter."

"I'm just tired, baby." He'd been saying that a lot lately.

"I know you are. I am too. And I wish I could make this easier on you. Try to stay offline for now."

"It doesn't matter if I do or don't. Everywhere I go, people are happy to fill me in and are hoping I will return the favor." His voice teetered on anger and anguish. I'd only heard him sound like this one other time. The day he came to tell me he had been reassigned because of his feelings for me. Now, once again, it was me causing his angst.

What could I say? Sorry wouldn't come close to making it better. "I . . ." my voice quivered.

"Delanie." He blew out a large breath. "I'm sorry for lashing out. This isn't your fault."

I choked back my tears. "I beg to differ."

"Please don't. I'm trying to adjust."

"Me too," my voice betrayed me and cracked.

"Baby, I didn't mean to upset you."

The tears came whether I wanted them to or not. I was so tired I let them fall without restraint. With them came silence. There was no lying and saying I was fine. I wasn't. And worse, I had no idea how to comfort him. How had we gotten to this place?

"Delanie, let's talk in the morning after we've both had some sleep."

He wanted to hang up?

"Okay," I choked, but I couldn't let him go quite yet. "Peter?"

"Yeah?"

"You know I'm still me, right?"

"I know. Good night."

That was it? My phone fell in my lap, heavy and cold. Nothing had prepared me for that call. Though I suppose it was unfair for me to think he would make it all better when he was going through as much turmoil as me. Words Avery had spoken after the death of their daughter, Hannah, came to mind. *The hardest part is that we are both in so much pain we can't comfort each other,* she had said about James and herself.

This situation didn't come close to the loss of a child—I knew from experience—but Peter and I had lost something. It was more than privacy. It was the oasis we had forged when we needed peace from the storms, usually his mother. That oasis had now been invaded by something much more invasive, and we were retreating instead of clinging to each other like we had before. The worst part was I didn't know when the storms would end, and I myself carried a tidal wave large enough to drown us both. How could I tell him now? I would have to wait until the sun rose again. When we had time to catch our breath. I could only hope that it didn't come to light on its own.

I wasn't sure any of my secrets were safe anymore.

I curled up on Joan's hard-as-a-rock wool couch wishing for sleep to take away the hurt if only for a little while. I was too tired to get up and go to bed and the thought of being alone in bed made it even less inviting. My head had barely landed on a throw pillow when my phone vibrated. I barely had the physical or mental energy to look at it. I wasn't sure I could handle one more blow today. I turned over the phone to find my favorite words from my favorite person. *I love you.*

His message was better than any stimulant. I immediately texted back. *I love you more.*

Impossible.

The stranglehold on my heart eased. It gave me hope we could weather the storms together. That we would find our way to each other in this blinding rain that was beating upon us now. I held the phone tight to my chest as if it were a talisman, only to have it ring. I didn't bother looking at it; I answered right away knowing it had to be Peter but ended up confused when the voice on the other end sounded similar but not quite like him.

"Delanie, I hope you don't mind that Peter gave me your new number. I know you may not want to hear from me."

It finally clicked who it was, and I sat up. "Hello, Joseph."

He let out a deep sigh. "I was hoping one day we could dispense with my first name and you would call me Dad."

The tears returned. No one had ever wanted me to call them Dad. I was so touched, I had no idea what to say. I didn't even care that the timing wasn't perfect, or maybe this was perfect timing. A light in the storm.

"That's probably wishful thinking at this point," he said while I tried to sort through my feelings and formulate a response.

"No. It's just..." What did I say? I was terrible at this. I paused and listened to my heart. "That would be an honor, but I fear it may result in bodily harm for you."

"The honor would be all mine and I'm willing to endure any pain for it, but I don't think that will be an issue."

"I wouldn't be too sure." I did a terrible job of keeping the snark out of my reply. I knew very well how Sarah would feel about me calling Joseph *Dad*. It seemed unnatural to think it. How was I going to say it?

"Honey," he sighed. "I'm sorry I let things get this far. I want you to know that I genuinely thought last weekend would bring us all together. Now I fear there are rifts that will never be mended."

"This isn't your fault."

"But it is. I should have spoken up a long time ago and especially over the weekend. On Saturday I knew something was off with..." I wasn't the only one refusing to say her name. "But I didn't question it because over the years I've learned to stay out of my *wife's* way, and because I didn't want to believe it. Now we are all paying for it."

"It was bound to come out eventually," I tried to make him feel better, even though what I really wanted to do was tell him that his wife was an evil witch, and this was all her fault. And what did he ever see in her anyway? But I couldn't do that to Joseph.

"Well it damn sure shouldn't have been from your family."

I couldn't have agreed more, but the problem was that Sarah never saw me as her family. "What's done is done."

"I'm sorry it had to be this way, but I want you to know that I'm proud of the way you're handling it."

"You're proud of me?" My voice squeaked.

"Very. You held your own during that interview and from what I've heard for the last few years, my daughter-in-law is one heck of a writer."

The fact he even watched the interview meant so much to me, but to be proud of me? That was a whole new level. A parent that was proud of me. I had to let that sink in while I wiped away my tears. "Thank you."

"Honey, I should thank you for sticking it out with my son despite what some of us have put you through."

"I love Peter."

"I know you do."

"I'm worried about him," I admitted quietly.

"He doesn't seem to be handling the pressure well," Joseph agreed with me, "but I'm not surprised."

I didn't expect that response. "You're not?" I had to say that I was. Peter had been a rock our entire relationship.

"Most of Peter's life, he has lived a sheltered existence. It's one of the reasons I was happy when he brought you home. He's needed to see that life isn't the straight line he's always imagined."

"Are you saying I'm the squiggle marks?"

He laughed, albeit subdued. "You are the woman who's given him permission to look at life through another lens and see that there are multiple perspectives for every situation or circumstance and realize that things may not be as cut and dry as he used to think."

"I don't think I can take the credit for that. I think his former profession taught him more about that than I ever have."

"You don't like saying 'priest,' do you?"

"You are perceptive."

"That's what happens when you get old. It's okay, you know? Neither of you have anything to be ashamed about."

"I just know how hard that choice was for him and I..." I couldn't admit it out loud to him.

"You worry he regrets it?"

I'd needed someone like him. A father or father figure to know what I was thinking even if I couldn't say it. I knew I had missed out on something by the way my friends growing up would talk about their dads, but until this moment, I had never known how deep that loss was. Joseph was making me question how differently my life would have turned out had I had a father to turn to. Maybe I could have avoided some of my mistakes if there had been someone there willing to guide me instead of the man I felt like I had to hide everything from, lest he be disappointed or dismissive. Joseph made me feel free to share my fears.

"More so now than ever," I breathed out.

"Honey, you have no reason to worry. My son loves you. He's been a bear to be around these last couple of days since you've been gone, if that tells you anything."

"It could have more to do with our names being dragged through the mud."

"I agree that he's taking that hard, but your absence is harder. I know what it's like to miss your wife." Emotion crept into his voice.

I hesitated to ask, "Are you missing her now?"

"More than you know. I better let you get some rest," he hastily moved on.

"I hope you can work things out."

"We always manage to somehow. Good night, honey."

"Good night, Jo—I mean, D...Dad."

Chapter Twenty-Seven

THE THING ABOUT New York is when you first arrive you are ready to leave. All you notice is how crowded it is and how it smells like cigarette smoke, but after a day or two, you could picture your life there. An artistic vibe flowed through the streets. I so badly wanted to take my laptop to the park or a café and absorb it. Use it to my full advantage. Write beautiful words with it.

But the city that never sleeps had other plans for me, like making sure I too had no sleep for the next few days as I was ushered from interview to interview, appointment to appointment, store to store shopping for a new wardrobe. Apparently, my thrift store boho look was fine for Delanie, but not Autumn. To add insult to injury, I had to buy an evening gown for the Sweet and Sexy Ball. My entire life, I had gone without wearing such nonsense, and within a week I was shoved into more ball and evening gowns than the Queen of England owned. I decided if had to dress up, I was going to do it my way. I was going to look more like the queen of the dead than the queen of romance. Joan called the long, snug black trumpet gown vampy. That worked for me.

What didn't work for me, besides being dressed up, were answering the same questions repeatedly. Added into the mix now was my scandalous past as a high school newspaper editor. It was sad how many people wanted it to be true that I was an exhibitionist and how disappointed they were when they couldn't find footage of my escapade. Perhaps because it never happened. No one wanted to hear that, or how Peter's superiors in Phoenix wished us all the happiness in the world. That was glossed over in every interview. No. They were more interested in that awful teacher who made fun of the girl with unmatched shoes. She was happy to dish about us and how it was apparent there was something going on between us. Yes, there was. We were falling in love with each other, but that was a beautiful thing. And we loved each other so much that we did the right thing by unselfishly not acting on it. Couldn't anyone see that?

A bright spot did come in the form of a podcast. The hostess was extremely laid back and interested in me as a person. She didn't ask me one thing about Peter. She wanted to know which writers inspired me and was intrigued to learn they weren't romance writers. I was a Roald Dahl, Stephen King, Leo Tolstoy kind of woman. Sure, I loved Austen and the Brontë sisters, but it had more to do with their wit and commentary on life than the romance. She even read some excerpts of my book and praised them for having poetic beauty. After the week I'd had, I was going to crown her my best friend.

All I wanted to do was be home with Peter and my laptop, mostly Peter, though; he was warmer and kissed a lot better. I hoped he was planning on showering me in kisses when I got home. I wondered, though, since our phone calls hadn't been the normal flirty *I can't wait until I'm home so I can make all your fantasies come true* kind of calls. The kind we used to have every day. Now they were more like support helpline chats and breaking development announcements.

The latest twist in this ever-evolving new way of life was that Sarah was coming into the office every day to help answer phones and do some of the accounting in Sam's absence. I guess she used to do the books when

Joseph, I meant Dad, was just starting his business. I was still getting used to that one. I took more pleasure in saying Dad than was probably normal, but it was a tiny ray of light in the looming clouds that followed me right now. And it made Peter happy too, so that was a bonus. But what wasn't making him happy, besides the obvious, was having his mother in the office every day, which meant Mimsy had to come too. No one could trust her to be on her own. Who knew who she would talk to, or if she might try and contact Giovanni, aka Jerry the felon.

Peter was still furious with his mother and grandmother for bringing this all upon us, and according to Avery, was not his normal forgiving self around them. He was being short with them and Sarah wasn't fighting back, so much so, Avery mentioned being worried about her. She was even more worried about Dad and Sarah's relationship. They weren't talking at all unless they had to. But feisty Mimsy was her usual self. She wasn't making any apologies for her behavior and had the gall to ask Peter how much money I made. And sadly, she was pining for Giovanni. I heard about women being taken advantage of like this all the time, but I never thought it would be Mimsy. She was too independent, or so I thought.

Amid the chaos, the company was trying to hire more employees or contract with smaller companies for the interim to help with all the new business they were getting and to cover Peter while he toured the country with me. All the new business seemed to make James happy, as he was to inherit the company when Dad retired. I supposed that was another silver lining. James was no longer brooding for the time being. From the sounds of it, he found this all rather comical. The bad news was his brother had picked up brooding right where he left off.

I didn't blame my husband. Maybe it was easier for me because my writing had been criticized online by various perpetrators for the last four years. Grace had just written another scathing piece about me since I'd been shoved out of the closet, or attic as it may be. The gist of her post was that I was a laughingstock and no better than a politician who never answered the question asked in interviews because I either couldn't or didn't want the embarrassing truth to come out. Which she couldn't understand since I was an obvious embarrassment. Joan was now on the warpath and vowed to take Grace down. I halfheartedly told her not to waste her time, but deep down, well not even that deep down, more like every cell of my body wanted to see Grace get a taste of Joan.

All I wanted was a taste of my husband and to fly home. It's why I was catching a red-eye Friday night even though I was exhausted, and Joan had asked me to stay for a girl's weekend. I think she wanted an excuse not to see Lucas. I never thought Joan would be afraid of anything or anybody, but I stood corrected. Lucas terrified her. She wouldn't admit to it and told me where I could go when I gave her my opinion. All I knew was she was out getting drinks late almost every night I was there, and she was wearing a turtle neck today even though it was seventy-five degrees out. And she was happy to report negotiations for my new contract were going very well. I bet they were. At this rate I would own half the stock in the company, or maybe Joan would if they decided to merge.

Joan was good enough to drive me to the airport at midnight and do her best to try and kill me one more time in her Porsche. She really needed to lay off the caffeine... and the car horn.

Before I exited the vehicle to retrieve my luggage that had multiplied during my week-long visit, she grabbed my hand and gave it a good crush. "Do not, I repeat, do not get sucked into googling yourself and scouring the web to see what's being said about you. Let Fiona and me be your filters. If anything comes up you should be worried about, we will let you know."

I nodded, knowing that would be easier said than done.

"And," her lips curled up in a sinister grin, "that witch Grace just happens to be an author."

"What?"

"All those horrible books she gives glowing reviews to are her own under different pen names."

"Nooo."

"Oh yes, and I may or may not have called her out on it, not only on her site, but every popular public forum I could think of. All anonymously, of course. My paralegals have been busy."

I shook my head at her with a big grin. "I love you more than my Eminem collection."

"I know, darling, and you're going to love me more when you see that wench take down her site, and when you see your new contract."

I would love to see Grace's site die. I had no respect for other authors, especially women authors, not supporting each other. There was room for everybody at the table. Not so sure about the contract though.

"You know I might not sign that new contract." Peter and I had plenty of money, and I would make money off the Hunter Black series for years to come, hopefully. All this attention had me wanting to ride off into the sunset never to be heard from again. And my fears about living up to Hunter Black's success were almost paralyzing, if I was being honest.

Joan rolled her eyes. "I know you're scared, but you're too talented to walk away from this. And whether you want to admit it or not, at your core you are a writer, and writers must write. It's like breathing for you. Don't think I haven't noticed how twitchy you've been this week not being able to write or all the notes you've jotted down. That isn't going away."

She was right, but… "You know I don't have to get paid for it." I'd written most of my life without getting paid or paid very little for it.

"Yes, but think of all the good you can do with the money you'll make."

"Like paying you?" I teased.

"Among other things." She was not teasing.

"I better go." I had too many things to think about right now other than facing that particular fear.

"Think about it, kid." She wagged her eyebrows. "I hope you have a firework filled reunion with the hubs."

"Thank you," my reply oozed with sarcasm. Believe me, I was hoping for the same, but didn't feel the need to discuss it with her. I hugged her and whispered, "Thank you for everything and maybe I'm not the only one who is scared."

"Ugh," she scoffed before pushing me away. "I don't do second chances."

I opened the car door, securely holding onto the bag with Peter's T-shirt in it. I hoped to be wearing it for him soon. "That's too bad. I think *Lucas* knows exactly what he's been missing out on and would make sure to do whatever he could not to lose you again."

"Don't make me hurt you, Del."

I laughed at her. "I'm not too worried, being your cash cow and all."

"You're much cuter than a cow. Now go home." I started to shut the door, but she got in, "And finish that first draft!"

I didn't need the reminder. Hunter and Laine had been screaming at me all week, along with Chad.

One advantage of flying so late was the airport wasn't as crowded and people were too sleepy to chase after me. There were some stares and some pictures snapped with phones, but after the week I'd had, it was mild in comparison and I was too tired to care.

My seatmate on the way home was better too. A sweet grandma who loved all my books, and if this wasn't fate, I don't know what was. She was married to a man who had been a priest. She told me all about how they had been childhood friends and she'd loved him for all her life, but he kept her in the friend zone. It was his family's wish for him to become a priest, so he did. She married another man, but he died in an industrial accident. By chance, her old *friend* was assigned to her parish and he could no longer fight his feelings for her.

"It was quite the scandal," she said with a twinkle in her eye. "Eventually, everyone moved on from it and we've been married for over forty years. So don't you listen to the naysayers. For the most part, they are miserable people. You live your life and don't be ashamed of it for a second," she encouraged me.

She was exactly who I needed in that moment. Especially since my homecoming wasn't all I hoped for.

A haggard Peter with messy hair and a few days' worth of scruff waited for me in the pouring rain under the cover of an awning. However, the Windy City was living up to its name, blowing some of the rain in. I didn't care if we got soaked. I only wanted to be in his arms.

I got half a tired smile when I approached with two large suitcases, both new purchases, my laptop case across me, and Peter's gift held tightly to me. He rushed to get my bags and throw them in the trunk of my car while directing me to hurry and get in. There were no hugs, kisses, or I missed yous. Only a frantic husband on a mission.

I did as he asked and got in the car. He wasted not a second taking off as if we were being chased.

I reached over and placed my hand on his thigh. "Is everything all right?"

He kept his focus outside. I could hardly blame him since the rain was coming down in sheets, but he was acting uncharacteristically harried. "I'm fine." He was obviously lying.

My hand moved from his thigh and through his windblown hair. "Peter, I missed you."

Those words and my touch made him slow down and take a deep breath. "Baby, I'm happy you're home. I'm sorry. I feel like I've been followed all week and I'm tired of it."

I continued stroking his hair. "I know, but the good news is I'm home and I don't want to leave our bed until at least Monday morning, unless you are feeling adventurous and want to make love to me in various other locations in the house."

The corners of his mouth couldn't help but tick upward.

"That's better." I ran my hand across his rough cheek.

He slowed down more so he could cautiously take my hand and kiss it. "I did miss you."

My hand landed back on his knee and his went back to steering and keeping us safe in the storm.

"I wondered for a second."

"You don't ever have to worry about that." He took another deep breath.

"For that you still get your cheesy T-shirt, which I will happily try on for you." I looked out to the mostly deserted highway. "Right now, if you want."

"I want nothing more," he groaned, "but you better not. Who knows who could be looking with a lens."

I suppose he had a point.

"Peter." I rubbed his tense neck. "I love you and I don't think it will always be like this."

"You don't sound very confident."

"As soon as you stop this car I have every intention of showing you just how confidently I love you."

His smile came easier this time. "That wasn't the part I was referring to."

"I wish I could tell you it will all be better soon, but I can't. It might even get worse before it gets better. I don't know."

He gave me a quick glance, disbelief and dread appearing in those green eyes I'd been missing all week. There was nothing I could say to make this go away, so I turned and rested my head against the cold window protecting me from the lashing rain. My vulnerabilities began creeping in, taunting and reminding me that they would always be there. That I couldn't possibly risk telling him about her now. I stared out the window the rest of the way home. Peter said nothing except to let out a sigh of relief when we reached the gates to our community and there wasn't a car or camera in sight, other than the security ones.

I found that I didn't want to move when we pulled into the garage. I don't know why I expected everything to be magically the way it was before. I guessed I thought he would be as happy as I was to see him and that would override all the outside forces bearing down on us, even if only for a moment.

As soon as the garage door was down, Peter stroked my cheek. "Baby, I'm sorry."

I was the sorry one, so much so I couldn't turn to look at him. I had broken my solid rock husband in two.

He unclicked his seatbelt and moved in closer, kissing my cheek this time. "Hey." He brushed back my hair and kissed my cheek again. "I missed you." He trailed kisses down my neck.

I couldn't resist him and turned toward him. He immediately captured my lips. All his angst came crashing through, crushing my mouth. The overwhelming emotion and sensation made me gasp. His tongue not only tasted and prodded, but delved as deep as it could, as if it was making sure it was me and not the woman playing out in everyone's stories online and in the press.

Peter's calloused hands did the same as they ran all up and down my body. I wanted to tell him that I was still me and we were still us, but I was drowning in him and couldn't catch my breath. I feared, though, he had come to his own conclusion about who we were when he unclicked my seatbelt and pulled me as close as he could, trembling and searching with all his senses, madly enveloping me. The question was, what was his conclusion?

My body shook as well, too afraid to ask.

Chapter Twenty-Eight

ETER DID HIS best to behave more like his *normal* self the next day. For anyone else, I think he would have had them fooled, but a woman knows her husband. There were subtle differences, like when he held me, he clung. It wasn't as desperate as the kiss in the car that had turned into so much more, but it was a need more than a want. I could understand that. There had been times that I needed the closeness only he could provide, to lose myself in him when I felt like I had no place I belonged except with him. But I was afraid this time it wasn't bringing us closer together. It was more like him holding on to what he could of us before fame blew up our door and pummeled us with softball size hail. As much as I hated it, I knew we had to face it head on. There was no hiding from it now. And if we did it together, we would be less likely to get blown over. Sure, we might lose our footing a time or two, but I knew we could weather the storm together if we tried.

His family and my colleagues were kind enough to give us our space over the weekend. Though I did text Sam and Avery a few times. I was anxious to hear how Sam's other book signing went and how Cody and

Reed fared in their season opener on Friday night since Peter didn't feel comfortable going. I was happy to hear they had won, and Sam had another successful signing with fans lined up around the bookstore. Peter also didn't feel comfortable attending Mass on Sunday, which made him grumpy. He took to studying his bible in the downstairs office a good portion of the day while I worked on my manuscript. Or I should have said, tried to work. My mind was on my husband.

I kept staring at the same sentence for over an hour.

Why would you keep this from me, Laine?

Because she loved him, that's why, but she couldn't say that. I couldn't say it.

Around midday, I gave up and placed my laptop on our coffee table. I couldn't bring myself to work in my office. The vibe in there wasn't conducive to creativity. All I could feel in there was violated and spiteful. I wanted those women to pay for what they had taken from me and my husband—our privacy and equilibrium. I blamed them for the nagging fear that no longer remained under the surface, that all of this might take Peter away from me.

I pushed off the couch and headed Peter's way.

His head was down, poring over his worn bible. His hair was ruffled as if his fingers had worn a path across it. He was still in his pajama pants and, to my disappointment, he had thrown on a T-shirt. He turned my way when I walked through the French doors. I got a small, tired smile. His attempt, I'm sure, to be normal, but that smile nowhere near touched his eyes. He rubbed his eyes and set down the pen he had been using to write in his journal. I caught a glimpse of the word forgiveness written in bold letters.

I knew the divide between him and his mother weighed heavily on him. Peter was a forgiving soul, but I wasn't sure anyone had ever hurt him so deeply, and for the first time in his life, he was struggling with a subject he could so eloquently orate about. Even I knew one day I would have to forgive his mother and those women. And myself. Father Alan's words came to mind, *The hardest person to forgive is yourself.* Maybe someday I would be able to. But not today.

Without invitation, I sat on Peter's lap and curled into him, soaking in the scent of our lavender fabric softener. He didn't waste a moment wrapping me up. Before I spoke, I listened to the strong, steady beat of his heart. That hadn't changed. It gave me some hope.

"Peter, we can't live like this. As much as I love only being with you, we can't lock ourselves in this house. You especially. At least I have imaginary friends to play with."

He gave a small laugh before kissing my head. "You're right," he sighed, resting his chin on my head. "I know I've been a beast to live with."

"I would say more like a snappy Chihuahua."

"Chihuahua?" He playfully nuzzled my neck, making me laugh. "At least let me retain my manhood and say something like Great Dane."

"How about a cuddly Lab with a bark bigger than his bite?"

He pulled me closer against him. "I do love to cuddle with you."

I buried my head in his chest. "I love you, Peter."

"I love you, too. I'm sorry for being a *dog* this past week."

I laughed some more. "It's understandable. But now that you're being a *good boy,* I think we should go on a walk."

"Outside?" He didn't hide the trepidation in his voice.

"Of course. We have to live our lives. Eventually they will see how truly boring we are and leave us alone."

"Baby, you are anything but boring."

"I know I'm taking you on a wild ride right now but . . . just hold on."

He leaned back, concerned, and tipped my chin up. "Delanie, I'm not going anywhere."

I breathed a sigh of relief while peering into his eyes that had some light back in them; they warmed me. "Do you want to go on that walk?"

He thought for a moment. "Later. First, I foolishly passed up on my wife's promise to me of a weekend in bed."

"I was wondering about that." I ran my hands up his chest and around his neck. "I thought I'd lost my touch."

"Never." His lips played above mine.

"The offer is still good for the remainder of the day." I was impatient and took a taste of his teasing lips.

"Mmm," he groaned. "That is the best news I have had all week." He stood up with me in his arms, and for an afternoon, we were us again.

That weekend was like a reset button. It didn't make cameras and prying eyes go away, but it was a reminder of what really mattered. We both needed that as we faced the next two weeks, preparing for our public foray into the spotlight together.

We had twelve days before we left for Atlanta. Fiona sent me our itinerary Monday morning. It was jam packed. We would leave the Saturday after next and fly to Atlanta. Sunday, Monday, and Tuesday before the conference began on Wednesday had me all over Georgia and nearby Chattanooga doing book signings, readings at two colleges, and then there was the conference itself. Since it was a reader's and author's conference, there were several meet-and-greet events on top of the classes and panels. I was on two panels, one regarding self-publishing versus traditional publishing, since I had done both, and another titled Amazing Protagonists. Then there were the balls. Thankfully I didn't have to attend the erotica one. I saw the pictures from last year's event and poor Peter would have had a heart attack from the outfits alone.

The biggest event I was worried about was the luncheon that kicked off the conference on Wednesday. I was supposed to give the keynote address in front of all the authors, industry leaders, and readers who paid the pricey fee to attend. The topic I was given was why romance novels are an important part of literature and modern-day society. Like that wasn't a weighty or debatable topic that required hours of research. They wanted me to weave my journey into it as well.

Lucas had originally been set to give the address, but when they found out I was available, he put his ego to the side and gave me the honor. Though I wished he wouldn't have. At least it gave Joan something to rub in his face a time or two. I will say he was kind enough to give me some of his research notes, but that was probably because he was playing Joan's vampire lover. I hoped she was packing turtlenecks for the trip.

In between all the conference prep, packing, answering the plethora of new emails I was receiving, and keeping my husband from becoming a snappy Chihuahua, I was supposed to be writing a book. It didn't help when we ran into bumps as Autumn Moone continued to invade every aspect of our lives. Nothing was sacred. Even the anniversary of the passing of our niece, Hannah, made not only the news, but Avery and James had pictures taken of them at the cemetery mourning their daughter. Peter stared at the photos off and on for an hour when he got home from work. He kept his laptop on the kitchen island and, like a magnet, he kept being drawn to it.

I finally put my arms around him as he scanned an article about the tragic events surrounding Hannah's death three years ago when she was hit by a car while riding her bike. The article unfortunately made it more about me than her. Peter was thrown in there too since he'd given the eulogy at her funeral. He had written it like a poem. It was so beautiful, copies had been distributed at the time. Obviously, someone close to the family gave up their copy as there it was staring back at us. Anything to sell a story or make a name for the journalist.

My head rested against his muscular back. "Peter."

His hand covered mine as it rested on his chest.

I wasn't sure what to say to him, so I only held him from behind for the longest time. With any luck, Brittany Spears would shave her head soon and the press would forget about us. Maybe Joan could get ahold of her people. I was willing to pay Brittany a hefty sum to say goodbye to her golden locks.

I would have suggested a walk around the lake in our neighborhood, so we could get out of the house, but we'd done that last night and all our neighbors, it seemed, joined us. It wasn't terrible, but I was sure we made several Instagram and Facebook posts. And it was hardly a walk, so many people stopped us to talk. The good news was we would probably never have to cook if we took our neighbors up on all their dinner invitations.

Visitors helped ease us into our new normal for the time being. Especially when his dad came by to check on our backyard. Or so he said. I was sure he was looking for any excuse not to be at home. That was another source of Peter's angst. He was worried about his parents' marriage. I think part of him felt guilty that he was playing a part in it because of the way he was feeling and acting toward his mother. I knew he wanted to forgive her and was trying. Avery mentioned he was giving his mom more than one-word answers now, but every time a new story about us appeared, it opened the wound of what she and her friends had done, making it that much harder to extend the olive branch that I knew he wanted to give.

I was fine not talking to her at all. Not that she cared one way or the other if we spoke. Joseph was another story. I loved talking to him, and the smile it gave Peter when I called him Dad was priceless.

Sam, Avery, and their families were also welcomed guests. Our nephews were happy to see we were upping our aunt and uncle game. We'd ordered the latest and greatest in video game technology for their pleasure. They did mention that we should probably get a bigger TV and they were still angling for the pool.

All in all, it wasn't awful. Sure, James and Peter were receiving more attention on the job and the requests for interviews were still coming steady. And going to the grocery store was a production. Nothing like people watching you buy deodorant and toothpaste and making note of your brand choices.

For a moment, it seemed as if the storm had calmed. I felt like we were able to take a breath after being sucker punched. But what I failed to recognize was that we were only in the eye of the hurricane. The peace we felt was only a temporary reprieve from the perfect storm that had been brewing all around us, waiting to unleash its wrath.

Chapter Twenty-Nine

$\mathcal{D}$o YOU WANT the good news or the bad news?" Joan toyed with me. "Door C, thank you." I didn't have time for any news, good or especially bad. We were leaving for Atlanta in two days and I had to finish packing, writing my keynote address, and you know, a little thing called my first draft, which was due in four weeks. Right now, Hunter and Laine were on the brink of destruction. Every aspect of their relationship was in shambles as more and more truths she'd kept from him about his father came out. Laine was hurt Hunter couldn't see why she did what she felt was best and Mrs. Black was happy to feed Hunter's doubts about her motives.

"Good news first it is," Joan declared over the phone before whispering, "Is Peter there?"

"He's still at work, why?"

"We'll get there."

I closed the lid to my laptop, now worried the bad news was more nefarious than Joan's tone had led me to believe. I was thinking along the lines of a decline in book sales, or I'd slipped to number two on the best sellers' lists.

"What's going on?" My heart began to race.

"Fine, if you want to be that way, but the good news is more like excellent news."

"Joan, please."

She let out a heavy sigh. "First, I have to ask you, did you attend Beaumont in San Diego?"

No. No. No. No. Please no. "For three years." I swallowed hard. "Why?"

"There is a man claiming—"

Dammit, Blair. Why would he? He wanted to keep her more of a secret than me. If it had been up to him, she wouldn't have even existed. I threw my laptop to the side of me on the couch and held my stomach.

"—that you exchanged sex for grades."

I shook my head, not sure I'd heard her right, but overwhelmingly relieved. I'd done my best to keep San Diego off the radar. I transferred colleges after she was born and finished my senior year in Phoenix, where I graduated. "Who is this guy?" I finally had the wherewithal to ask.

Joan tapped on her keyboard. "Uh...Tyler Pen."

I spat out a laugh. "You've got to be kidding me."

"You know him?"

"I suppose you could say that. He started out as a TA in one of my political science classes, but he ended up as a—"

"Lover?"

"Absolutely not." The thought made my already queasy stomach churn more violently. "He was a scumbag, and me and another student journalist were sure he was fixing grades in exchange for sexual favors."

"Well, he's given a list of all the favors you gave him. You were obviously very limber." She cackled.

"What? Where are you reading this?"

"First, I have to ask you if it's true. Lucas is about ready to wet himself over this, which I wouldn't mind seeing."

I fell back against the couch cushion, hurt and stunned. "I can't believe you have to ask."

"Kid, it's not personal. I know it's not true, but as your attorney, I need to ask you and you need to respond."

"No!" I shouted. "I went out with him twice to see if I could get him to talk. And talk he did. I discovered he wasn't the only TA fixing grades for sex. There was a ring of them. When we exposed what they were doing, they were all expelled from the school. You can look it up. It made the local news there."

"Del, calm down. I'll do some research and try and shut this guy down. But for now, LH Ink is going to have to address the press about this. These are serious accusations that could undermine you and them."

I had no words. It was the first time I thought about taking Peter and running away to a third world country where we could truly get lost. We could work in an orphanage or anywhere that didn't have access to the world wide web of destruction and deceit.

Things had been better for Peter this week, but I was afraid of what this news was going to do to his psyche. And there was no keeping it from him. He was of the mindset that we needed to be on the offensive, not the defensive, so he regularly checked what was being said about us. We'd been able to laugh about some of the stories, like that man who called himself Hunter Black and had sworn up and down he was the real Autumn Moone. He was now trying to publish the next book before me, like the impostor could. The synopsis was hilarious; it made Hunter and Laine out to be zombies. Yeah, that's where I was going.

There were even sweet stories, like my fourth-grade teacher who had kept a copy of a short story I had written about my favorite park growing up and how it magically transformed each night into what a child of the park's choosing needed, whether it be a birthday party or a family to love them. The park would pick a special child every day. Mrs. Trout was one of my favorite teachers and had encouraged me to be a writer. She said I had a gift.

It was more like a curse now. Were people really that desperate to have their fifteen minutes? And what happened to journalistic integrity? Did no one check sources and facts anymore?

"Are you still with me, kid?"

"Yeah." I yawned.

"You sound exhausted."

"I am. I've been working all hours trying to get the first draft done and getting ready for this conference and tour."

"It sounds deeper than that. Is everything okay with you and lover boy?"

"This hasn't been easy on him and we are having to adjust, but we're okay."

"Good because here's the good news: you are about to be a wealthy woman."

"I'm already wealthy."

"Fine. Wealthier. And before you can say you don't care about the money, read the contract. You'd be a fool to pass this up. I mean, think of the kids."

"You mean you?"

She laughed. "Now that you say it, yes, me. If there were a hall of fame for contracts, this would be the crown jewel of them all. You're going to be thanking me and then paying me."

"I'll keep an open mind, but I want to look over it with Peter, so we probably won't be able to until we are on the plane."

"Perfect mid-flight reading. You will be crying tears of joy in the sky."

I felt like crying now, but if I cried over every headline, it would never stop. "I'll let you know if we have any questions or suggestions."

"Suggestions? I'm going to pretend you didn't say that. Meanwhile, I'll be over here taking care of your little sex for grades scandal. You're welcome, by the way."

"Thank you, Joan."

"Get some sleep kid—you sound like hell."

How could I sleep knowing there were creeps out there like Tyler Pen making up lies? And worse, knowing there were more damaging truths to be discovered. I knew I had to tell Peter about her, but I just needed some time. Time for him to settle into our new life.

I picked my laptop back up and stared at the screen. My life and Laine's life were paralleling each other. Her heart was in the right place. If only Hunter could see that. Would Peter? He would, right? I held my stomach, sick thinking otherwise.

It didn't feel much better when Peter arrived home that night not only haggard, but troubled. He took a moment to stare at me before only saying, "Hi."

I set my laptop down, too tired to get up. "I suppose you saw the new interview." I'd watched it too. I couldn't help myself, and neither could half the country, by how many news sites it was on, prominently displayed, I might add. Unfortunately, the guy sounded credible. If I hadn't known the truth I might have believed him. Sadly, the school was declining to comment, citing confidentiality. Again, there was evidence to dispute his claims if only they'd done a little searching. That's what Google was for.

I'd thought about calling Peter before he got home, but I was hoping he hadn't seen it yet and I didn't want to make work tougher than it had already been since he was trying to get as much done before he left with me for three weeks. But there was no doubt that he had seen it by the question in his eyes.

Peter ran his hands through his hair. "Delanie, is it..."

My eyes widened.

He deliberately changed course. "I mean...Are you okay?"

The answer to that question from here on out was going to be no. I felt as if I'd been electrocuted I was so shocked. "You were going to ask me if it was true."

He shoved his hands in his dirty jean pockets, keeping eye contact with me. "I'm sorry. I hardly know what's up or down anymore. And you—"

"And I what?"

"You've been private about your past."

"So that means I was selling my body to get good grades?" I was doing my best to keep my voice steady, though I couldn't believe I had to say that to him.

He scrubbed his hand over his face. "No. That's not what I meant."

"What did you mean?"

"I don't know." He threw himself in the chair next to the couch. His elbows rested on his knees and his hands ran repeatedly over his face.

I mustered the energy to stand up. I never thought I would think this around him, but I needed to be alone. First, though, I was going to set the record straight. "That man was lying about me. You should Google his name and read the *real* story." I walked off, hurt and in total disbelief.

"Delanie." I heard his work boots stomp across the floor.

"I'm going for a walk *alone*," I called out. I pushed the boxes and boxes of delivered diapers out of the way so I could get to the door—they'd been piling up since I hadn't dared go to the women's shelter. Krista, one of the directors, was supposed to meet Peter at the office tomorrow to pick them up. Once I finally got the front door opened, I set off the stupid alarm. I slammed the door and left Peter to deal with it.

When my cold feet landed on our stone porch, I realized I hadn't really thought this through. The evenings were now turning cooler and I was barefoot and still in one of Peter's T-shirts and some yoga pants. I hadn't even had time to shower today. I was exhausted. In defeat, I took a seat on the cold, hard steps and leaned my head against the wrought iron rail. For a moment, I let the sound of the alarm drown out my senses, but it was gone all too fast. There I was, left alone in the silence of dusk to deal with the screaming in my head and the pangs of a pierced heart.

I was soon reminded that I was never alone. One of our neighbors, who was dressed prim and proper in a taupe pantsuit out walking her Shih Tzu, stopped and waved enthusiastically. "Hi, Autumn." I cringed, but she obviously didn't notice. "Nice night, huh? I love this time of year. Makes me want to bake an apple pie. Do you like pie? I would be happy to bring you one."

I sat up straight and ran my fingers through my rat's nest hair and remembered to play my part to prevent anymore lies being told about me to the media. "That's nice of you to offer, but we'll be out of town for a while."

That didn't deter her. "Well, you just tell me when you're back and I'll pop one over for you."

"Thank you."

"Toodles." She waved after her dog peed on our lawn.

My head fell back against the railing as soon as she pranced out of sight. I rubbed my arms to stave off the chill. I had never felt so alone. The loneliness of my childhood had nothing on this. I knew Cat and Ron never loved me, so their rejection wasn't as acute as Peter's doubts about me.

I breathed in the cool air. It was helping with the nausea caused by my churning stomach.

Before long the door opened, and I felt a jacket draped over my shoulders. Peter landed next to me, but not too close. For a few moments, I didn't bother to look at him. He knew me well enough not to say anything. Or at least I used to think he did. When I finally glanced at him, I noticed he wore a furtive expression.

He reached out and tucked some of my unruly curls behind my ear. "Delanie, what can I say other than I'm sorry?"

I pulled his jean jacket tight around me, unable to utter a word. Everything I thought I knew about us, about life, was being stolen from me. Autumn Moone had become a thief in the night.

We sat there staring at each other for what seemed like minutes. His green eyes that had always been a comfort to me now peered back at me consumed by an intense battle. Love still existed in them, but it now had fierce competition. Part of me wanted to heed the call to fight, but I was exhausted. I was already tired of trying to convince people of who I was or wasn't. More than anything, I was hurt that he didn't already know or had forgotten so easily.

Peter scooted closer to me. "I found the article you wrote for your school's newspaper exposing the sex for grades scandal. I didn't know I had married an investigative journalist." He gave a tentative smile, testing the waters.

I didn't return it or respond.

He inched even closer, this time resting his warm hand on my cool cheek. "Baby." His thumb ran over my skin. "Please say something."

"What do you want me to say?"

"Tell me something else I don't know about you."

I closed my eyes. My heart was aching to tell him about her, but my head was happy to remind me of our vulnerable situation. I hastily stood up and headed back inside. "Not tonight."

Chapter Thirty

THE NEXT MORNING before Peter left for work he came and sat next to me on the couch. I had been up for hours already, unable to sleep even though sheer exhaustion wove through every fiber of my being. My mind had taken charge and was refusing my body the rest it so desperately craved. It was bent on torturing me with not only a lack of sleep, but every fear I had about where I truly belonged in this world. It almost had me convinced I belonged with no one and nowhere. Then Peter wrapped his arms around me.

"I missed waking up to you."

My head fell on his shoulder.

"Baby, I'm sorry about last night. I've decided to stay offline."

I had already scoured the web this morning. Retractions about yesterday's story were being run with pathetic excuses like *after further investigation, we discovered Mr. Pen's claims to be false, in fact, blah, blah, blah.* Why didn't they further investigate before they ran the story? LH Ink had posted a scathing retort on their site and Autumn Moone's site calling out shoddy journalism practices. I noted a hint of Joan's voice in it.

I closed my eyes, too tired to say anything, though I thought it was a good idea for him to say goodbye to Google.

"Maybe it will be good, getting away for a while," he threw out there when I didn't respond.

"You know this isn't going to be like a vacation. Prying eyes and questions will be everywhere."

He rubbed my bare arm. "I know, but we'll be together, and I'll get to see my wife in action. How's your address coming?"

"It's coming."

Peter tipped my chin up. "You don't sound well. Are you coming down with something?"

"Just tired."

"You've been working too hard."

"We both have."

His hand ran through my hair. "I'm trying to do what I can for James before I leave. I'm sorry if I've neglected you in the process, but for the next three weeks all my focus is going to be on you."

I gave him a tired smile.

"There's the smile I love." He skimmed my lips. "Baby, please forgive me for being an idiot."

I nodded and for that I was rewarded with a longer, meaningful kiss. No parting of lips, but I could feel the love he tried to convey as he pressed his lips against mine and held them steady.

"It's going to be all right," he whispered against my mouth. I think more for his benefit than mine. He had no idea, though, how much I wanted to believe him, and perhaps for a foolish second, I did.

In between bouts of nodding off while typing, I managed to get some of my thoughts about the importance of romance novels organized for the address I was supposed to deliver in five days. My bullet points so far:

• It has been widely accepted that romance novels are the ultimate form of escapism, but beyond that, they provide the reader a palatable way to deal with complex issues like divorce, abuse, sexism, forgiveness, etc.

- It could also be argued that they are a form of therapy, as people often explore their own emotions and choices while reading a character's journey through similar circumstances.

- Romance novels also offer hope that even when it might seem impossible, things can work out.

While I managed to get that done, Joan sent me a clip of the infamous Tyler Pen running from his house to his car with a towel over his head trying to avoid reporters. Served him right. I got a much-needed laugh out of it. I was quoted as saying, "I will let the truth speak for itself." And by me, I meant Joan.

I even got a shower in but ended up right back on the couch glued to my laptop until Peter came home. Like him, I too was ready to get away, even though I knew it wasn't going to be easy. But I hoped maybe the time together in new cities sharing this adventure would do us some good. Perhaps we could see the other side of this monster called fame, and hopefully the other side was a big, fat, giant, fuzzy teddy bear. I wasn't holding my breath, but I had to hope things would get better from here.

Peter walked in earlier than he had been as of late. I expected to smell dinner per this being our normal takeout night, but Peter came in empty handed. I didn't mention it because I wasn't all that hungry; the stress had killed my appetite, and Peter was staring at me with a dazed expression. Not only that, but he opened his mouth to speak several times, but nothing came out.

I looked over my laptop. "How was your day?"

He blinked several times. "Fine."

"My kind of fine, or fine, fine?"

"It was fine." His tone bordered on curt.

"Okay." I was confused by his lack of enthusiasm, food, and kisses. Not to mention his tone. "Did something happen today?"

His feet shifted. "The women's shelter director came in and got the donations."

"Krista? She's great, don't you think?"

"Yeah." He exhaled loudly. "I'm going to take a shower."

Something was off. I wondered if he'd already fallen off the wagon and was searching the web for stories about us. I was about to chase after him, but my phone rang. It was Fiona, so I had to answer it. I had been waiting to hear back from her about whether Peter and I should rent a car when we got to Atlanta tomorrow or if LH Ink was taking care of that. There had been some confusion. Either way, we were getting a car. Neither Peter nor I liked the thought of being in Georgia for eight days without a way to get ourselves around. We were hoping we could sneak in some sightseeing here and there.

"Hey, Fiona, what's the verdict?"

"You're all set. I made the reservation and you should be getting the confirmation by email any minute now."

"Perfect. Thank you."

"One more thing." She hesitated. "I was checking your fan mail today and one of the emails I came across was, well, maybe personal; if not, it might be considered stalking in nature. I'm not sure, but I wanted to run it by you before I flagged it and sent it off to be investigated."

I braced myself for another ridiculous made-up scandal or half-truth. Or maybe it was someone claiming to be my long-lost relative in need of money. There had been several of those already. "Lay it on me." I sounded braver than I felt. I was too tired to deal with any more nonsense.

She cleared her throat.

Dearest Delanie,

Weird they used my real name.

We're not sure if this is the correct way to contact you, so we hope you receive this. We've been looking for you for some time now, but weren't exactly sure you would find this welcome, though we would love nothing more than to see you again. There is also someone else who would love to meet you. We know you wanted to cut all ties to ease your pain, but maybe now since some time has passed and you have obviously gone on to do great things in your life, we thought you might have changed your mind.

We will be forever grateful to you for the beautiful gift you bestowed upon us nine years ago and would love to share part of it with you as we had intended. It has come to our attention that you will be touring the country and stopping not far from our new residence in Savannah. We are willing to meet you anywhere—name the time and day. Please feel free to call us at 555-287-9064 or email us at this address.

Most sincerely,

Anna and Henry

I dropped my phone, unable to catch a breath.

"Del, are you there?" Fiona called out.

This couldn't be happening now. I needed more time. Peter needed more time.

"Del."

I picked up my phone, shaking as I never had before. "Fiona, please forward me the email, but don't tell anyone about it."

"No problem. Do you know these people? What gift are they talking about?"

Yeah, I knew them. And they were talking about her. My baby. "Please just send me the email."

I hung up so I could have my nervous breakdown. I got up and paced around the family room feeling like I was going to vomit, possibly pass out. How was I going to go upstairs and tell my husband about her? And how could I meet her after all this time, after giving her away?

I had to tell Peter the truth. He had to hear it from me first. Who knew if Anna and Henry had told anyone who I was. They weren't the type who would, in fact, they were the loveliest of people, but I took nothing and no one for granted anymore. I'd been burned too many times the last few weeks not to be cautious and question everyone's motives.

Peter was reasonable and kind, I tried to comfort myself. When he heard the story, he would understand why I had kept her from him, from everyone I could. But what if he didn't? I grabbed my heart. It didn't matter now. I had no choice.

I gripped the railing up the staircase to keep me steady. My heart was pounding so hard I could hear it in my ears, and on top of the nausea, I thought I was going to pass out. My entire body had to be forced up the stairs as if each limb knew the danger we faced. By the time I made it up the stairs, I was already in tears. I tried to wipe them away to at least not alarm Peter right away, but it was no use.

When I padded into our room, I found that Peter hadn't showered yet. He was sitting on the edge of the bed in the semi-dark with his eyes closed and hands folded as if he'd been praying. I took a long look at him and said a prayer of my own that went something like, "Please don't let me lose him." I had no idea if God was there. He hadn't answered any of my other pleadings, but if I only ever got one prayer answered, this would be the one I would choose.

I walked into the bedroom slowly, knelt in front of my husband, and took his clasped hands.

He opened his eyes and stared hard at me. He didn't ask me why I was crying; it was almost as if he had expected to see the tears. His hands didn't take mine; instead, they were stiff, as if he wasn't sure he wanted me to touch him. Did he already know? How could he? This would be major news if it had already gotten out. Despite his behavior, I had to proceed.

"Peter." I swallowed the lump in my throat. "I have something I need to tell you."

He sat up straighter, pulled his hands away, and waited.

"Please listen to me before you say anything."

His eyes frosted over, and I felt the cold wash over me.

I closed my eyes for a moment and took a breath before I could go on and meet his frigid gaze. "Peter, I . . . I . . . had a baby a little over nine years ago, a daughter. A beautiful daughter," I cried.

The way his eyes popped told me that wasn't what he expected at all, which made me wonder even more why he was behaving so coolly toward me.

He ran his hand through his hair and blew out a large breath. "You had a baby?"

I nodded. "I gave her up for adoption."

He stood up, making me falter to the side. I had to catch myself before I fell over. He paced across our bedroom, rubbing his neck and taking big intakes of breath and forcibly breathing out. "When were you going to tell me about this?"

I stayed on my knees, pleading with him to understand. "I'm not sure. Believe me, I've wanted to."

"You're not sure? You've had over four years to tell me, Delanie," he raised his voice. "That's not a good enough answer for me, but maybe I shouldn't be surprised. You love to keep secrets, don't you?"

"Peter, I didn't want to keep this from you, but I felt like I had to. Will you please listen to me?"

"The only thing I'm going to listen to you tell me right now is what you've been doing on Wednesday nights for the past few months. We'll go from there." Even in the dark I could see his eyes blazing with fury.

I shook my head, unsure. "What are you talking about? And what does that have to do with anything right now?"

He looked at me not only in disbelief, but as if he loathed me. "It has everything to do with what we're talking about. I don't even know who I'm married to anymore," he yelled. "I was trying to give you the benefit of the doubt and think of any other plausible reason you've been lying to me for months—make that years—but you don't deserve it. Tell me, Delanie, where have you been going on Wednesday nights?"

Amid the gut wrenching pain he was inflicting on my soul, I was more and more confused. "You know I've been going to the shelter except for the last couple weeks I've been here."

He narrowed his eyes at me. "Oh, I know you go there. Krista says you are one of her best volunteers." His tone was mocking and cynical. "Imagine my surprise when I agreed with her and told her how proud I was of you even though I missed you because many of those nights you didn't get home until after ten sometimes. She laughed at me and told me she couldn't be to blame because they closed the campus at eight every night. No one goes in or out after that, according to her. Explain that to me," he dared me to contradict him in the most unrelenting manner.

I sank farther to the floor. My head rested against the bed. Tears soaked my cheeks. "What are you accusing me of, Peter?" I looked up at him but saw a stranger instead of the man I loved, from his crimson face to his clenched fists.

"Just tell me the truth. Tell me what you've been doing," he demanded.

In that moment, I realized if he didn't know me well enough to know I would never be unfaithful to him, what did it matter where I was? Or that I was trying to do something for him by taking those damn classes. I lifted my head and, for the seconds it took me to say what I knew spelled our goodbye, my tears stopped. I accepted defeat. "It appears I was wasting my time."

My head fell back against the bed while he shook his head at me in disgust.

"I never thought I would say this, but my mom was right. I should have been careful about a woman who keeps secrets." He stomped off and slammed the door.

I found myself once again not belonging anywhere and wishing I could fly to the moon.

Chapter Thirty-One

M<small>Y HEAD LEANED</small> against the airplane window. I wished I could wake up from this nightmare, but when I looked over at the empty seat next to me I knew this wasn't a bad dream and there was no waking up from this hell.

Peter's words to me this morning kept playing in my head. He'd walked in to find me crumpled on the floor not far from where he'd left me the previous night. For a beautiful second, I hoped maybe cooler heads would have prevailed after a restless night alone to think about what had happened. What we said and didn't say. I was about to tell him about meeting with Father Alan, but when Peter loomed over me, his red, swollen eyes that used to burn bright with his love for me were all but extinguished. Instead, they were charred with no warmth emanating from them.

"I think it's for the best if you go alone on your tour," he'd said with no emotion. Then he left—without another glance or word—to who knows where wearing the same clothes from the day before.

There was nothing left for me to do at that point other than to say goodbye to the house and life we had built together. I packed up what

I could fit in my suitcases, including my old red typewriter, my trusted and true companion that now sat in its own case in the carry-on bin above me.

My hand rested where Peter should have been. Or maybe he never belonged there. Perhaps deep down I always knew we were playing with borrowed time.

I went back to leaning my head against the window, looking at the mass of white clouds and listening to the roar of the engines. There were no tears left to shed. I had left puddles of them on the bedroom floor. I couldn't blame him for walking out on me. I should have told him the truth a long time ago. He deserved that. Now maybe he could go back to his first love and his life of obscurity before I entered the picture and disrupted his life. I wasn't sure if you could go back to being a priest, but for his sake I hoped so.

Now I had to figure out what to do with my own life. Starting with, should I meet my daughter? The thought terrified me. How could I explain to her why I gave her up? And what if she asked about Blair? I was done keeping secrets, but everything I had done was to keep her safe from him.

Simon was right. The figurative sheet had come off, but this time there was no body suit underneath it. I was completely exposed. Every vulnerability, fear, and secret were out in the open. My worst fear had come to life, leaving me with nothing else to lose, not even the vulnerability that was stripped away because of the terrible gift life had handed me. Or I should say the one I had hand wrapped for myself by trying to hide my past.

With the absence of vulnerability came other things, though, like overwhelming doubts about who I was or how I was I going to finish this book. Everything I thought I knew about Peter and me, and Hunter and Laine, was thrown into question. I had always thought Hunter and Laine were meant to be together, but now I wasn't so sure. I mean, how could they be? Hunter, for all intents and purposes, was Peter. I thought

I knew Peter, but my Peter never for a second would have questioned my loyalty to him. And he would have given me the chance to explain why I kept my baby a secret from him. I wasn't blaming him for his reaction. He had every right to be upset at me for keeping something so big from him. But knowing I deserved his anger didn't help with the crater he'd left in my chest when he ripped my heart out last night.

Maybe the answer was to give myself over to Autumn Moone completely. She had taken so much from me, she might as well have it all. It's not like I would be Delanie Decker for much longer. The thought made a tear spring up. I caught it before it had a chance to fall. There were more to shed after all, I guess.

I couldn't believe it was over. His mother's plan had worked. She must be thrilled. Perhaps that's where Peter had gone, and she was saying *I told you so* right at this very moment. Hopefully he would have peace now that he no longer had to choose between his wife and mother, because he had made his choice. No wife. I suspected that the forgiveness he had been longing to extend his mother would be easily given now too.

Would he ever forgive me?

Would I forgive me? Probably not. How could I? *My secrets* had cost me the love of my life. The only love I'd had in my life. When all this came out, I knew I would lose his family too. I shuddered at the thought of Sam and Avery hating me. And what about Joseph? *Dad?* I choked down the tears. For the first time in my life, I'd had a taste of what I'd always wanted, only to have it cruelly taken. I wound my wool wrap tighter around me wishing I could hide from myself beneath it. Not even the warmth it offered gave me any relief.

I felt as if I was back in that delivery room handing my baby and all that I'd loved at the time over to Anna and Henry, wishing they made an epidural for my heart to take away the anguish that consumed me. I had refused one for the pain while I labored hard for five hours before I delivered her because I wanted to experience everything I could with my Baby X before she was no longer mine. I felt like I owed her at least that. For years after, it felt as if I walked around as a shell of a person until I met him. *Peter.*

Now what?

⁓

"Answer your damn phone, Del. What the hell is going on? Fiona says Peter isn't with you and you looked like the walking dead today on camera. If you don't call me, I'm flying out there tonight."

I was too emotionally and physically exhausted to call her back, along with everyone else who had left me messages and texts. Avery and Sam had left their fair share wondering why Peter hadn't come, and what was going on, and if everything was okay. I would think that is was obvious it wasn't. And why hadn't Peter told them? They killed me when each of them said they loved me and they were there for me if I wanted to talk. I didn't think that offer or the warm feelings would stand when they found out the truth.

All I could do was text Joan, *Don't come early,* before turning off my phone and throwing it in my bag. I had a reading to do in thirty minutes and the thought of Joan coming any earlier than planned exhausted me even more. It was bad enough that Fiona hovered. I knew she meant well and was worried, but there was nothing anyone could do. All I could do was play my part during this tour.

Though apparently, I was doing a crappy job. I wasn't sure what to do about the walking dead look. I didn't think they made makeup strong enough to cover the bags under my eyes. I did the fake smiling thing at the signing earlier today, hoping that would help. I even shed some tears with some fans who told me stories of how my books had seen them through some tough times, like their divorces. They were real tears because I felt for them in all too real ways. The toughest part was holding back the tears when well-meaning fans wished me and my husband well.

I was waiting for the moment the media got a whiff that Peter and I had split up. They were going to have a field day. Peter would hate me even more when the press hounded him for answers. Unfortunately, there wasn't anything I could do about that now.

Fiona came bursting through the dressing room door where I was waiting among old, musty smelling costumes to go on stage, carrying a bottle of water and my favorite candy, sour cherry jelly beans. My lips twitched, too tired to smile at the best assistant ever who had orange hair now. She said it was her way to celebrate fall. Not sure what her bright pink tutu and leggings were celebrating today, but I loved she was comfortable with who she was.

She held up the bag of candy. "You haven't eaten today so I thought you might like these."

Normally I would have, but the thought of sugar on my already empty, twisting stomach made me want to heave. "Thank you." I took the candy and water from her and set them next to me on the small, uncomfortable couch I was sitting on.

She tilted her head and pressed her lips together. "You don't look good."

"That seems to be the consensus."

"That's not what I meant. You're one of those women we love to hate who would look good rolling out of bed, but you don't look *well*. Maybe we should hit urgent care. You're worrying me."

I grabbed the bottle of water and twisted off the cap before taking a sip to appease her. Or at least I hoped it would. "All good."

She rolled her eyes hidden behind her faux zebra print glasses. "Oh look, you're magically better. If anything happens to you, Lucas will fire me, and Joan will put a hit out on me, so if you can live with that, just keep drinking your water and lying."

I let out a long sigh. "Fiona, you're doing an exceptional job." Everyone that LH Ink sent or hired locally for this leg of the tour had been great, from the publicist and sales reps to the media escorts and security. It just happened to be the worst time in my life, and as terrific as they had all been, especially Fiona, they couldn't fix the seemingly irreparable.

"That will make me feel so much better when you pass out on stage." She handed me a tube of lip gloss.

I took the lip gloss and applied it to my parched lips. I should be drinking more, if anything. "I'm not going to pass out."

She took the lip gloss back as soon as I was done with it. "Right. And Lucas and Joan aren't sleeping together, and Santa Claus isn't some overweight stalker with a raging case of diabetes."

A laugh bubbled up in me and escaped. "For that, you're going to end up on his naughty list."

She wagged her eyebrows. "I sure hope so. I love me a good jolly fat man. There's more to hold onto."

On that note, I stood up. I may have seen a few stars but didn't mention it. I don't think it went unnoticed, by the concern in Fiona's eyes.

"Del?"

"I'm fine. Do you have the book?"

She sighed and reached into her bag to retrieve *A Black Heart*. The book that started it all. *His* book. I thought trying to get over him the first time was gut wrenching. I had no idea how easy I had it then, never truly having had a taste of him. Now that I knew exactly what I was missing out on, I could hardly breathe, it hurt so bad. If only I could channel some of that pain into bleeding on the page, but I was drained dry. I'd stared at my laptop all night last night in my hotel room, not typing one single thought or word.

She handed me the book as if she regretted doing so. Believe me, no one regretted it more than me. How I was going to get through reading the now infamous first chapter, I had no idea. But I was committed to keeping my word and fulfilling my obligation to LH Ink and the crowd in the packed auditorium. It was the only noble thing I had left to do.

Under the spotlight and in front of the captive audience, I opened the book as if it was sacred text, not knowing why. I had the first chapter engraved on my heart. I held onto the book as if it was my lifeline, the steadying force that saw me through the pain of never having the chance of being loved by him. But the strength I had once felt from it was no longer powerful enough to heal the wounds he left behind where his love had touched me so deeply.

I took a deep breath and relied on my own strength. It was all I had left.

In the beginning, we are told it all began with a man and that he was good. But as good as he was, he could never be great. For the man was without a woman to hone him, test him, and, most importantly, love him. Hunter Black was such a man, as good as any man who had ever lived, and though many women had loved him, there was only one meant to complete him.

That woman wasn't me.

Chapter Thirty-Two

I STARED AT THE picked-through apple pecan salad room service had delivered an hour ago resting on the coffee table, telling myself I should eat more if it, but my stomach begged me not to. The few bites I had gotten down felt ready to make a reappearance. The stress and emotional turmoil were decidedly trying to off me. That, and this story, which I'd also been staring at for what seemed like days in between pretending that life was perfect as I signed book after book and smiled for picture after picture with fans who had taken the time to come and see me. Truly I was honored, but it only reminded me that my life had unalterably changed.

The only thing I had written since I'd been in Atlanta was, *Did he understand what he had done to her?*

The answer was no. I wasn't even sure he cared. It had been three days since his parting words to me. I knew it was foolish to think that he would call, but that's what my Peter would have done. Despite how I'd hurt him, he would have wanted to know I was okay. Hell, he could have even called or texted to say he'd hired a divorce attorney. I knew he still lived because Avery and Sam were relentlessly texting and calling me. They were worried and obviously still in the dark, which surprised me. I didn't shed any light on the situation other than to text them that I loved them, and I was sorry. They desperately wanted to know what I was sorry for. In time, that would all come out without me having to say it.

I gave up on both the salad and the manuscript and pulled up the address I was supposed to give tomorrow to fine tune it. And by that I meant blankly stare at it. When I got bored of that, I stared around the enormous suite I was in. It was too ornate for my taste. Who needed a crystal chandelier above the bed? And the drapes made me feel like I was in the Playboy Mansion. At least the velvet couch was comfortable. I had yet to sleep on the bed or sleep much at all. If I could have, I would have slumbered for days, hopefully without any dreams. When I had managed to sleep, it was restless and filled with visions of Peter, good and bad. I cursed the good. It only made waking up to my nightmare that much harder.

I had dozed off only to be woken up around nine by someone pounding on my door. My first instinct was to reach for the hotel phone and dial security. There had been some incidents already with fans trying to sneak up to my floor, which was only accessible if you had the proper keycard and a code. But I was learning that people were determined and resourceful, and therefore dangerous.

I pressed the first key before I heard, "Del, it's me. Open up." Joan's New York accent could wake the dead.

She was supposed to have called when she landed. I picked up my phone. Oops. It was dead. I pushed myself off the couch and shuffled toward the door. I opened the door and before I knew it, I was accosted by not the woman who knocked, but someone I needed. Sam, though not as tall as me, wrapped me in her arms without a word. My emotions overwhelmed me and the tears I had to carefully fight all day while meeting fans unleashed their wrath, wetting Sam's head. Joan stood by smugly taking in the scene, pleased with the surprise she'd given me.

"What are you doing here?" I cried.

Sam squeezed tighter. "They asked me to come and do your introduction tomorrow. I thought I would surprise you. Surprise. I hope you don't mind."

"Not at all."

She leaned away to judge the truth in my puffy red eyes. Her manicured hand landed on my cheek. "Oh, honey, what's wrong?"

"Everything," I whined like a child.

"Well, you look like hell." Joan pinched my arm. "You're skin and bones, and since when did you start wearing flannel pajamas?"

Since this trip when I realized I had no pajamas and cried all night about it the first night when I had to wear my own T-shirt. I had Fiona go buy me the cream set I was wearing now. I wanted something completely unlike me.

"You know I love flannel." Sam gave me a wink. She had posted about her love for the soft warm fabric many times. I believe Reed loved it too, but probably more when it was on the floor.

"Sit down." I waved toward the living area in the suite, aka my bedroom.

They both eyed the couch where the blanket and pillow I'd been using were crumpled up in the corner.

"Are you sleeping on the couch?" Joan asked.

I nodded and took my place curled up in the corner.

Sam didn't stand on ceremony and sat right next to me and put her arm around me. I felt guilty for indulging in the comfort she offered because I knew it wouldn't be long before she hated me just like her brother, but the affection was more than welcome.

Leave it to Joan to interrupt the warm moment. "Kid, what the hell is going on? And where is your husband?"

That was the worst possible question she could ask. I turned into Sam and lost it, but through my sobs I got out, "He left me. We're over."

For a moment, silence reigned supreme. You knew it was bad when Joan was rendered speechless.

Sam patted my back. "That explains why he's been ripping everyone's head off the last few days, especially Ma's. We've all tried to talk to him, but he's refused. He even told James to go to hell."

That shocked me. I'd never heard Peter swear.

"What happened between the two of you?" Sam gently asked.

I sat up and met Sam's gray, concerned eyes. I supposed I should tell her and get it over with. There was no keeping it secret and frankly, I was tired of hiding it. "I don't even know where to start."

Sam lovingly brushed my hair back with her hand. "Start from the beginning."

My crying had turned to shudders, making me take a few deep breaths before I could begin. "Ten years ago, I was a student journalist for my college paper in San Diego. I was hungry to expose injustices, but naïve and young. I was nineteen, but thought I was so much older since I had graduated from high school early and was already a junior."

Sam gave me an understanding smile. Didn't we all think we knew everything at that age?

"Well," I continued, "a friend of mine on the staff had uncovered some potentially damaging information about one of the school's largest donors, Hugh Kincaid, who was about ready to have the business school there named in honor of him."

Joan gasped.

I whipped my head toward her. "You know him?"

"I've heard of the weasel. He did time for embezzlement. You didn't have anything to do with that, did you?"

I hung my head in shame. "I should have." When I raised my head, both women were intently staring at me, anxious for me to continue, so I did, albeit reluctantly. "Hugh had a son, Blair." I cringed. "He had caught wind that we were investigating his father and he convinced me to hear his family's side of the story. I won't go into all the gory details, but one thing led to another and before I knew it, he had persuaded me that not only was his father innocent, but Blair was more than interested me. We had this fire and ice thing going on, and I admit the older, debonair man charmed me. I don't even know when it began. I seemed to be in the middle of a relationship with him before I could even comprehend we were having one."

For the next part I had to look down in my lap. I wasn't sure I could face Sam's disappointment. "I was stupid enough to believe that he loved me even though we hardly ever went out in public together and he never introduced me to his family. He used our age difference and waiting for the right time as an excuse. But I was so desperate to be loved and feel like I belonged somewhere, I took whatever I could get." The tears began to flow again. "And then I turned up . . . pregnant."

I felt Sam's hand land on her chest. Joan whistled low.

"Yeah. There I was, nineteen, with no clue, no money, and scared out of my mind. When I told Blair, he told me to get rid of it, like it was that simple. I suppose for him it was, but something happened to me. It was like the baby called to me, and I knew with all that I was that I was supposed to protect it. When I refused, he raised his hand to hit me, but I stood defiantly, daring him to. The physical blow never came, but he got his shot in. He said, 'I was about done with you anyway. And if you tell anyone about this, I'll make sure you wish you never lived.'"

Joan jumped up, explicative after explicative came out of her mouth. Meanwhile, Sam took my hand. "What did you do, honey?" I was surprised she was still being so kind to me. She had to have seen where this was going.

"At first I didn't know what to do. I couldn't tell my parents—they would have told me to do the same thing as Blair, all while lecturing me for my poor choice and how this would reflect on them. So, I didn't tell anyone. Until I overheard the conversation of this couple I used to watch all the time at the café I waitressed at. They were lamenting that their recent attempt to adopt a baby had fallen through. There was something about them. It was like I knew I was supposed to talk to them." I smiled, remembering them. "She was a doctor, very conservative in nature, and he was a legal-aid lawyer, her opposite in every way, but such love and respect existed between them even when they disagreed about almost everything except what to order for dessert. Henry was his name and he used to take Anna, his wife, by the hand and say, 'I respect your right to your wrong opinion, now kiss me.' She always did, but not before saying, 'I only state facts, my dear.' They would laugh before tenderly kissing." They were exactly the kind of people I wanted to raise my daughter, open-minded and affectionate. Things I loved about Peter.

Sam smiled. Even unsentimental Joan's lip twitched.

"But they couldn't have children and they so wanted to. And I," my voice cracked, "knew I had no business having one at that time. I never thought I wanted to be a mother for the longest time. And who knows, I probably never will. I'm not sure I deserve to be someone's mother."

"That's not true," Sam contradicted me. "You would be a great mother."

"Well, it doesn't matter because Peter doesn't want me."

Sam shook her head. "I don't believe that for a second. He's miserable without you. Lost."

"Forget Peter for right now," Joan cut in. "What happened to the baby?"

The baby. "I approached Anna and Henry and told them about my situation and asked them if they wanted to adopt her." I remembered how cautious but excited they were and how good they were to me, especially Anna. She mothered me through the pregnancy.

"Her?" Sam asked.

I rested my head on Sam's shoulder. "Yes. I called her Baby X."

"Why?" Joan asked.

"I couldn't bear to know the name Anna and Henry picked out for her or to give her one of my own even though Anna and Henry offered to let me name her. I tried my best to stay detached from her, but she wouldn't let me. It sounds weird, but I felt like she spoke to me in her own way. I had no idea the bond that could exist between a mother and child. Deciding to give her up for adoption was the hardest thing I had to do, but I knew she would be better off with someone else. And I was afraid of what Blair might do if he found out I'd kept her."

Joan growled and bared her teeth. "How did you get around that?" her lawyer side asked.

"Henry tried to help me get a judge to terminate his rights without his consent, but I would have had to prove that he had abused me or intimidated me."

"Sounds to me like he did." Sam stroked my hair ever so gently.

"I couldn't prove that, and no one was going to take my word over his—he came from money and a powerful family. So, I had to approach him and ask him to relinquish his rights."

"No." Sam was horrified.

I nodded. "I surprised him at his office one day when I was seven months along. He had the audacity to think I had come crawling back to him after coming to my senses. I never showed all that much and wore clothes to hide the fact I was pregnant. He was furious when he found out my real reason, but he knew then it was his only option to keep it quiet, so he agreed, but not before threatening me again."

"You poor thing," Sam said.

"Don't say that."

"Why, honey?"

"Because I kept all of this from your brother. Why do you think he left me? That, and he thought I was cheating on him."

"What?!" Both Sam and Joan exclaimed.

I explained the entire story about Anna and Henry contacting me and volunteering at the women's shelter and the secret RCIA classes. How Peter had talked to the shelter director, which led him to believe I was cheating on him. It was the perfect storm.

"Did you explain all this to my brother?"

"He never gave me the chance. I don't blame him for that. I should have told him about my baby to begin with. But how could he believe after everything we've been through I would want anyone else but him?" I buried my face in Sam's shoulder, amazed she didn't hate me.

Sam gave me no answers, but what she gave me was so much more. She held me and wiped away my tears. And most importantly, she loved me despite what I had done.

Joan moved and sat on the coffee table and joined in on the mothering by rubbing my legs. "Del, as your lawyer and your friend, I have to ask if you think these people, Anna and Henry, have ulterior motives in contacting you now?"

I turned my head only enough to see her. I refused to move away from Sam. "I don't think so. They were so good to me. I wouldn't have given my baby to them if I'd thought any different."

She nodded, satisfied. "The question now is, are you going to meet your daughter?"

That was a terrifying question.

Chapter Thirty-Three

*S*AM ENDED UP staying in my room and, I was almost embarrassed to say, she held me on the couch all night long. It was the first night in a long time I got a few hours of uninterrupted sleep. Her presence was medicine for my soul. Too bad it didn't help with the waves of nausea or my appetite, but I would take what I could get at this point. Maybe if I decided on whether I should meet my daughter it would offer some relief. Loosen a few of the knots in my stomach. Both Sam and Joan encouraged me to do it. Sam said I needed to do it because I deserved to know her, and if I wanted to forgive myself, this was the first step. But she said from her point of view, there was no need to forgive myself. I had done the brave thing.

I didn't feel brave. I felt as if I had let my baby down. I remember her crying before they laid her on my chest. For those few precious moments against my skin she was calm, but as soon as they took her away she let out this heart wrenching cry. Anna and Henry tried to soothe her, but they couldn't. I couldn't take her again. I knew if I had, I wouldn't have wanted to let her go. Then I left her and went on to move away to try and forget her and the pain, but I found I couldn't and didn't want to. What kind of person did that make me?

I tried sitting up so as not to disturb Sam. I was feeling more nauseous than ever. I took a few sips of water in the dark morning while staring at my now fully charged phone. I picked it up with the same false hope I'd had the last few days that there would be a message from Peter. Once again, I was disappointed. There was a text from Avery, though.

Good luck today. I wish I could have come too, but things are so busy at the office. I can't wait to hear all about it. Love you.

Those last two words meant more to me than I could express. To know even though I had lost Peter's love, I still had the love of Sam and Avery in my life was something inexpressible.

Thank you. I love you.

No longer was I holding back those words. I realized now they didn't make me vulnerable, they made me stronger. *Huh.* That thought struck me. I opened my email app and pulled up Anna and Henry's message. I read it a hundred times, trying to build up my courage before I hit reply.

Dear Anna and Henry,

I would love to meet her and see you again. Please let me know a convenient time for you.

Delanie

Sam sat up and looked over my shoulder. "Send it."

My thumb hovered over the send button. I took a deep breath and, with one eye open, clicked it. I let out that breath and dropped my phone on the table. "I think I might be sick." I ran to the bathroom and sat in front of the toilet as if I was worshipping it. I would if it would have helped me to feel better. Nothing but dry heaves happened, which gave no relief whatsoever.

Sam knocked on the open door before walking in to witness me in my pathetic state. She sat next to me on the marble floor and smoothed my cheeks with such care, her gray eyes giving me the once over. Her head swayed from side to side as if she was debating to speak. She finally asked, "Is there a chance you're pregnant?"

"No," I blurted without even entertaining the thought because that just couldn't happen right now. Not when my marriage was over.

"Are you sure?"

I thought about the start date of my last period. In all this craziness I had forgotten to keep track. I was late, but I'd been this late before and I was overly stressed, which always affected my periods. "I'm late, but—"

"I think you should take a pregnancy test."

I grabbed onto her arms. "I can't be. Not now. It's the stress."

"Okay, honey," she tried to placate me. "Let's just make sure."

"Sam, I can't go out and buy a test. Do you know how fast the news would get out?"

She thought for a second. "Can you send your assistant for one? Fiona, right? She's the one who initially called me about coming."

I ran my hands through my messy, thick hair. "Sam." I shook uncontrollably.

"I know, honey. The timing isn't great."

"This would be the worst timing ever, except for the last time this happened to me."

"God does have a sense of humor about these things."

"There is nothing funny about this." And if I was pregnant, God was a definite no-go on my list.

"No, there's not, but maybe this was exactly the time this needed to happen for you and Peter. Perhaps a blessing in disguise?"

"Sam, I just can't be," I choked out.

I found myself once again staring at a stick of torture on a bathroom counter. This time I was pleading with every deity I could think of, God, Buddha, Gandhi, Mother Teresa, Brahma, Zeus, Yoda, you name it, that the second line wouldn't appear, all while Sam, Joan, and Fiona waited outside the bathroom door anxiously waiting for the verdict.

Please, please, please, please. I held onto the counter for support, holding my breath. It all came out in a whoosh seconds later when that second line appeared strong and clear. Along with it came tears. I sank back down to the bathroom floor. Why now? How was I going to tell Peter I was having his baby now that he wanted nothing to do with me?

"Del." Joan knocked on the door. "You okay, kid?"

People really needed to stop asking me that.

I didn't respond, which I guess gave them all permission to come in. They had their answer when they saw me on the floor with tear-stained cheeks.

They all sat around me as if we were going to play a game of duck duck goose or have a séance. I focused on Sam, who sat directly across from me. Her smile spoke of understanding and of happiness. "I'm going to be an aunt again." She reached across and took my hands. "This is all going to work out between you and Peter. You'll see."

I shook my head vehemently. "I don't want him to stay with me because I'm pregnant."

"He loves you," she tried to reassure me.

"You didn't see how he looked at me."

She pressed her lips together. "Well, maybe I need to have a talk with him then."

"Please don't talk to him or tell him."

All their eyes went wide.

"I'm not going to keep this a secret from him. I promise." I was done with secrets. "I just need some time to . . . to wrap my head around this."

They all nodded as if they understood.

I'm glad they did because I couldn't understand the timing of this at all, especially when I was supposed to be standing up in front of hundreds of people in a couple of hours. The only thing I did know was that this time I was keeping my baby.

Joan and Sam did their best to make me look presentable and as if I hadn't received life changing news only hours before. I stared in the long, free-standing mirror in my suite. I hardly recognized myself in the chic camel blazer and skinny black pants. Sam had piled my hair high in an updo and Joan had done my makeup darker to give me some color in my already pale skin made more so by the latest development.

My hand kept finding my abdomen. Despite the worst timing in the history of best laid plans of mice and men, I wanted this baby. I tried my best not to think about Peter and what this would all mean to him and us, but I couldn't help it, even though it meant Joan had to reapply my makeup.

I didn't have any clue on how to broach the subject with him. Did I leave a message because I was sure he wasn't going to answer? "Hey, Peter, remember me, your wife? I just wanted to thank you for the parting gift. By the way, you're going to be a father. Congratulations. Should we hash out custody plans now or later? Call me."

I rubbed my face, but not too much. So much makeup. Ugh. That wasn't my only problem. I almost had to take my nose stud out from blowing my nose so much. And I still felt as if I was going to vomit.

Joan was trying to shove crackers in my mouth before we all walked down to the ballroom where the luncheon was being hosted. She meant well, but they were some kind of weird green cracker, and they smelled awful. I pushed her hand away. "I'm fine."

"You're lying." Joan tossed the cracker in the waste bin.

"Yes, I am."

"Can we get you anything?" Fiona asked.

"Not right now. I'll try and eat something after I'm done humiliating myself."

Joan patted my cheeks. "I read your notes and they are as eloquent as ever, so suck it up, buttercup."

"There you go being a motivator again."

She laughed while giving my cheeks one more pat.

Sam had a gentler touch. She smoothed the lapel on my jacket and gave me her signature warm smile. "You look beautiful."

I took her hand. "Thank you for coming."

"I wouldn't miss it."

We all walked down together, and for a moment, it struck me, looking at the three strong beautiful women who surrounded me, that mothers don't necessarily come to you by birth. They are forged in the battle of life and delivered to you through the hands of friendship.

Chapter Thirty-Four

A<small>T THIS POINT</small> in my life I was becoming painfully aware of the many things I didn't know. Some big, like how upset was Peter going to be when he found out that we would be forever linked by a child? Then there were small things, like why did these fancy hotel luncheons always serve dry chicken with lumpy sauce drizzled over it in various colors depending on the venue? Today's could be described as a vomit-inducing yellow. I had to push my chair back as far as I could before I lost it. There were some things I did know, and one of those was when I grew up, I wanted to be like Sam.

Amid the hundreds of people in attendance and the unbelievable schmoozing, Sam laughed and listened. She had this uncanny ability to make people feel like they were the only person in the room. She graciously asked questions about everyone around her, never talking about herself, though people wanted to know everything they could about her. Then, when it was showtime she exuded confidence when she got up to introduce me, even though I knew she was nervous. She looked like a million bucks in a flirty red dress that Gelaire had probably picked out for her.

Sam walked up to the stage that was really a raised platform, smiling, no longer as unsure of herself as she had been last year at this time when I forced her into the limelight. I remembered debating about whether I should post her blog on Autumn Moone's website. But I had watched her and Neil for months at Sunday dinners and I knew something was wrong. I could see her struggle and the defeat in her eyes, but I had no idea what to do or say. I wasn't even sure if she liked me. At the time, I was afraid she felt like her mother, but did a better job of hiding it.

If I could go back, I would have said something to her. Even if it was only that I noticed her. I supposed that was one of the reasons I posted her blog. I wanted her to know she was noticed and how much I admired her, but I didn't know how to tell her in person. Now, watching her, it was amazing to see how noticing a person changed them. And how she did the same for so many women around the world. She gave them a voice. She noticed them. And, wow, did love and self-care look good on her. She was going to look great in all the pictures being snapped, and on the several local news channels that were set up capturing it all. I was informed by the publicist I would be talking to them afterward. One more torturous event to add to the day.

Sam stood tall and proud at the podium. "It's an honor to be here today to introduce one of my favorite people. Everywhere I go, lately, people ask me, 'How is it possible that you didn't know you were related to Autumn Moone?' The answer is easy. I'm not related to Autumn Moone. Although she is amazing, and I must admit I've had to replace my icemaker because of her books—lots of ice-down-the-chest moments, am I right?"

The crowd laughed loud and deeply. Even I joined in.

"All joking aside, the woman I want to introduce today is someone you don't know, but I've been lucky enough to call her not only sister, but friend. I could go on and on and wax poetic about all her accomplishments and awards, but you can read about those. Behind the exquisite words and stories and heart-pounding moments she has weaved for us all to experience, exists a beautiful old soul who is a force to be reckoned with. In my darkest moments, she gave me courage to see myself for who I was, not who the world or my ex-husband saw me for."

I had to wipe my eyes furiously.

"It is a true gift to see somebody for who they are; it is a treasure if you can help them to see it too. In a few moments you will get to see and hear the treasure that is *Delanie Decker*, not the media's tale of who Autumn Moone is."

Sam was brilliant. I never loved her more.

"Ladies and gentlemen, it is my pleasure to introduce to you Delanie Decker."

The crowd was on their feet clapping more for her than me, I was sure. It was my cue to stand. Easier said than done. Nausea was my constant companion and when I stood up, even as slow as it was, stars filled my eyes. I had to hold onto my chair for a few seconds until I could see properly to walk the short distance to the stage. For the first time today, I was glad we were sitting at the VIP table at the head of the room. Flashing lights began to fill my eyes from the hundreds of phones snapping pictures of me.

Sam waited for me by the podium and was quick to hug me when I reached her. "You okay? It looked like you had a moment down there," she whispered in my ear.

"I think I'll survive. Thank you for all the lies you just told about me," I teased.

She laughed and squeezed me tighter. "You got this."

I hoped she was right. I gripped the podium and looked out over the hundreds of eyes and faces staring back at me that filled the entire ballroom. I took shallow breaths, trying to stave off the feeling that I was in a tilt-a-whirl. I think I remembered to smile and thank Sam for the beautiful introduction. I even got as far as looking down at my notes on my phone that told me who else I should thank before I began. On the list were the conference organizers, my publisher, Joan, Peter. No, not

Peter. *Peter. Where was he? He was supposed to be here with me. We were supposed to be doing this all together.*

The room started to spin. I gripped the podium tighter.

"I would also like to thank..."

First the stars came, then the blackness. I didn't feel like I was falling, more like the floor was rising to meet me. I may have heard a scream or two, or perhaps that was the ringing in my ears. All I knew was when I came to, I was surrounded by a dozen people, some I recognized, others I couldn't make out, but they were all worried about me.

I became fully cognizant when someone I didn't know said, "Did you call the paramedics?"

I tried to sit up but thought the better of it when I became aware that my head wasn't feeling all that great. "I don't need an ambulance," I muttered.

Joan, Fiona, Sam, and even Lucas hovered above me and were determined to keep me down.

I caught Joan's eyes, as I knew she would be the most forceful of the bunch. "Please don't let them call the paramedics. Help me stand up."

Joan's violet eyes debated. "Sorry, kid. You should at least get checked out."

"You're fired," I moaned.

Everyone around us laughed.

Joan gently swiped my forehead. "That's my girl. You still have some fight left in you."

Sam knelt closer and whispered for my ears only, "We should call Peter."

I shook my head no as best as I could and begged her with my eyes not to. I would not have him coming here because he felt sorry for me, or worse, have him reject me in this state.

She sighed in resignation.

"Lucas," Joan snapped, "get all these people out of here."

"What are the chances this wasn't caught on camera?" I groaned.

Everyone around me chuckled.

"You're going to be breaking news, kid," Joan didn't sugar coat it.

Ugh.

Sam, Joan, and Fiona formed a barrier around me while I heard all the commotion of everyone leaving. Lucas was heading the expulsion charge with hotel management. While it was just the four of us for a few moments I whispered, "Please not a word about . . . you know."

They all nodded like they knew exactly what I spoke of. I was keeping my baby news out of the media for as long as I could. At the very least, I had to tell Peter first. I still wasn't sure how to do that. A tear leaked down my cheek thinking about it.

Sam wiped it away. "Everything is going to be all right."

I wanted to believe her, but then I heard the unmistakable signs that the paramedics had arrived. All I could wish for at this point was that someday this would make for terrific material in a future book. I was thinking a thriller or murder mystery. I wasn't sure if I could bear to write another romance. I couldn't even finish the one I was working on.

Humiliation ran deep when I saw a stretcher being wheeled toward me.

"If I'm placed on that, someone is going to die, and it won't be me."

The women around me laughed.

"I got you, kid." Joan stood up, finally doing what I wanted her to do. Sam and Fiona stayed with me, each holding a hand and looking at me like I was a pitiable creature. Maybe I was. Who faints while giving a speech? I didn't even want to think about how many times it had been tweeted, posted, chopped, sliced, diced, and regurgitated. Before I could think about it too much, two male paramedics took the place of Sam and Fiona.

The paramedics didn't waste any time after introducing themselves and asking for my name. One immediately started checking my vitals while the other did an oral assessment.

"Has this ever happened before?"

"No."

"Are you in pain anywhere?"

"No." I may have lied. I knew how this would all turnout if I didn't, and there was no way I was being transported to the hospital. So I had a bump on my head.

The paramedic gave me a scrutinizing look but continued. "Are you taking any medications?"

"No."

"Do you have any current or previous medical conditions?"

I had to tell another lie but justified it as I didn't consider pregnancy a medical condition.

"When was the last time you ate?"

"Dinner last night." If you could call a few bites of salad *dinner*.

"Have there been any stressors in your life?"

"Where do I begin?"

"Do you have a preferred physician and hospital?"

"None."

The paramedics laughed. They had probably heard that one before.

Though they were itching to get me on that stretcher and to a hospital to be checked out, I made them reconsider and signed their paperwork refusing treatment. They concluded that I mostly likely fainted due to stress and low blood sugar, as my vitals were fine and I was coherent and obstinate. They gave me a sheet about signs of a concussion and recommended I see my regular doctor when I got home.

Little did they know that home no longer existed.

Chapter Thirty-Five

THE BAD NEWS was my little fainting spell was being played out over all forms of media, and Joan watched it repeatedly on several outlets in my presence to make sure it was being reported correctly. It was so embarrassing to hear the gasps and even screams from the audience when I went down. LH Ink had responded by saying it was due to exhaustion and low blood sugar. They added in that I was resting comfortably and would be back on my feet to finish out the remainder of the conference.

The good news was I was resting semi-comfortably on the couch and Sam knew some tricks to beat morning sickness, or all-day sickness, as it was. Peppermint tea, chicken noodle soup, and saltines were on the menu. She also sent Fiona out for lemon and ginger drops.

It was Sam's presence that helped more than anything. She held me like a child on the couch for a good portion of the day. We hardly spoke a word. I took comfort in knowing she was there, and I was loved and noticed for me, not Autumn, who was unfortunately infamously noticed. I wished Sam could stay with me for the entire conference, but she had to get back to her own life the next day.

I was so exhausted, I slept on and off through the afternoon and evening. I was in pajamas and back on the couch by eight. I did myself a favor and allowed myself to fall into a deep sleep instead of staring at my manuscript all night long, banging my head against a figurative wall. I couldn't afford anymore fainting episodes.

I wasn't sure what time it was when I woke up in the middle of the night, but someone was sitting on the coffee table watching me. In my grogginess, I first assumed it was Sam or maybe Joan who had come to check on me. Or perhaps they hadn't ever left, but I could have sworn they had. I lifted my head off the pillow and blinked a few times, trying to make my eyes adjust in the dark. It didn't take long to realize the figure and outline was not that of a woman. I sat up, alarmed.

A hand I recognized more than my own reached out and touched my leg. "It's me. Sam let me in. I didn't mean to wake you." That voice. I knew that voice. I loved it.

My eyes came into focus and there he sat in his clothes like he'd just come home from work. I made out his suitcases nearby. The smell of grass and earth filled my senses. His eyes were no longer cold, they were warm instead, but unsure.

I pulled my blanket up around me, suddenly feeling vulnerable, though I had thought I was past that particular feeling. "What are you doing here?"

"Hating myself for not being here with you." He scooted toward the edge of the coffee table, drawing closer to me. "How are you feeling?"

Oh, of course, I understood now. There was a traitor in my midst who told him I was pregnant. No wonder it looked like he rushed here straight from work.

He reached out to touch my cheek.

I turned from his touch. "Go home." I didn't want his disingenuous concern.

"Delanie, I'm so sorry," he choked out.

"All I want to know is who told you?"

"Told me? No one had to tell me. It's all over the news."

I threw my blanket off in a panic, looking for my phone. Why didn't anyone tell me? "They know about the baby already?"

Peter took my hands, trying to calm me. "No, baby, that's not what I meant. No one knows about the daughter you gave up for adoption. At least I haven't heard anything. And I haven't said anything to anyone about her." He paused and peered into my eyes. The wheels were spinning behind his. "Wait...you said baby. Your daughter isn't a baby."

I pulled my hands away from him and leaned back against the couch. There was no keeping it from him. I never imagined telling him this way. I was never going to be cute about it even when we were together, but for a long time I'd dreamt of how excited I would be when I finally got to tell him he was going to be a father. Now all I felt was sorrow.

"I'm pregnant, Peter."

His eyes widened, and he took a moment to let it sink in. Tears welled up in his eyes. "You're pregnant?"

"I just found out, so I wasn't keeping it a secret from you. And the baby is yours, in case you're wondering." I grabbed a pillow to hold onto for comfort.

"Delanie, I would never think—"

"Didn't you, though?"

His entire body sagged. "I shouldn't have. I'm ashamed that I did."

I shrugged. "I suppose it doesn't matter now."

"That's not true. It matters to me. You matter to me more than anyone. I had no right to treat you the way I did. These last few days without you have been the worst of my life."

I closed my eyes. "You had every right to be upset with me. I should have told you about my daughter."

He took my hands again and gripped more firmly. "Don't excuse my behavior. I don't deserve it."

I opened my eyes to see his staring right back at me, pleading.

He pulled my hands to his lips and kissed them. His tears fell on them. "I love you."

"I used to think so, but I don't think you want someone like me. You're only here because you saw me faint on TV."

He shook his head, refusing to let go of my hands. "I know that's what it looks like, but that's not true. Delanie." He caressed my hands between his. "I needed to get my head on straight for both our sakes. I'm sorry it took me so long."

I took my hands back, though I longed for his touch. "You don't want this life."

"I want the one where you and I and...our baby," he said it like he could hardly believe it was true, "are in it together. Beyond that, I don't care what it looks like."

I leaned my head back against the couch cushion and let out a heavy breath. "I'm tired," is all I could say.

He stood up and leaned down to kiss my head. He lingered, breathing me in. "I'm sorry I woke you. I can carry you to the bed."

I shook my head. "You can take the bed. I've been sleeping here."

He looked down at me and tilted his head. "Why?"

"Because you weren't there."

The downcast look he gave me said I had never said anything more hurtful. That was not my intent. I was only being honest.

"I'm here now," his voice cracked.

"For how long? Until the next story about me appears?"

I take back my previous assessment. This was the most hurt he had ever looked, like I had knocked the wind right out of him. And maybe this time I meant for it to.

His eyes drilled into mine. "I'm not going anywhere."

I wasn't so sure about that.

Peter took one of the chairs and propped his legs up on the table, determined not to leave my side. I curled back up on the couch, now wide awake. I didn't think I could take much more of this bumpy road Joan warned me about. She had forgotten to mention the man-sized potholes and that the car had no brakes. I felt like I was careening down a hill, waiting to crash and burn at the end. I had been trying to wrap my head around a life without Peter and being a single mother, and now here he was. Did I love him? With all I was I did, but I couldn't stay on the yo-yo, worried about the next salacious story to come out. I felt like he was in denial about where we were headed, and he was only feeling guilty. Probably even more so now that he knew I was pregnant with our child.

I held my abdomen and tried to go back to sleep, knowing both the baby and me needed the rest, but I found it difficult. I felt Peter watching over me. It brought both comfort and confusion.

I managed a few winks of sleep here and there, but by 6:00 a.m. my bladder was calling the shots. This baby was making itself known and it had been, but I'd been too stressed to notice. I grabbed my phone and turned it back on as I tiptoed past Peter to the bathroom that was connected to the bedroom. A notification popped up on my screen that I had an email from Anna and Henry. I wasted no time pulling it up.

Name the time and place. We can't wait.

With shaky hands and a full bladder, I responded, *How about today? I can meet you in Savannah, preferably somewhere private.* I wasn't trying to hide her, but no kid deserved the kind of crazy that would come down on her if the press found out about her now. And today would be the perfect cover as everyone thought I was resting. But how could I rest knowing she was so near? If I left soon, I could be back for the meet and greet I was supposed to attend tonight. First though, I needed to pee.

Though it was early, I called Joan, Sam, and Fiona and asked them to meet me in my suite. They must have been really worried about me, because they were all there within minutes, dressed in various articles of nighttime apparel. Sam matched me in flannel, Fiona was wearing Wonder Woman pajamas, and Joan was wearing someone-who-shall-go-unnamed's button up. The only reason we didn't name him was because we all valued our lives and Joan hadn't had any caffeine yet.

Their arrival made Peter jump up.

Everyone looked between him and me, waiting and hoping for some insight, but I had none to offer.

"I'm going to meet my daughter today and I need your help."

Everyone stood stunned, including Peter.

I headed to the bedroom to pick out some clothes. Delanie clothes, not Autumn's. My daughter was going to know me.

They all followed me.

"Do you even know where they live?" Joan asked.

"In Savannah. I'm waiting to hear where we should meet."

Four sets of eyebrows raised.

Joan shut my suitcase lid. "Del, you can't run off by yourself half-cocked and meet old acquaintances in strange places."

"I'm not. I've given this plenty of thought and they are more than acquaintances." They were raising my flesh and blood.

"Still," Joan wasn't giving in, "you shouldn't go by yourself."

Peter stepped by my side. "She's not. I'm going with her."

I looked up at his disheveled figure. "No, you're not. You're going back to Chicago."

He moved closer to me. "Only when you do."

I glared at him. "I'm not going back."

The room and everyone in it seemed to hold their breath after my announcement.

"Um…I think we better leave them alone." Sam grabbed the other two women and backed out of the room, closing the double doors on their way out.

Peter shook his head out of the daze I'd put him in. "What do you mean you're not coming home?"

I threw open my suitcase and started rifling through it. "Peter, I can't get into this right now with you. I need to get ready."

He gently took my arm. "I'm going with you."

I met his eyes. "I don't need you to protect me."

His eyes narrowed. "You think that's why I'm going?"

"What other reason do you have?"

He pulled me closer to him and leaned in as if he were going to kiss me, but he stopped an inch from my lips. "The second biggest mistake I ever made was letting you leave without me. I'm not doing that again."

I had to catch my breath from his touch and intensity. "What was your first?"

"Letting my pride get in the way of what I've always known about you...us." He brushed my lips before letting me go. "I love you and I want to meet your daughter," he said it with absolute finality.

He had my senses buzzing and emotions swirling. I stood frozen, not sure what to say or do.

He took off his shirt and headed toward the bathroom. "You should get ready."

"Okay," I whispered.

Chapter Thirty-Six

AFTER A MAJOR production of sneaking out of the hotel, which included hotel staff making sure no one got on the elevator while Peter and I were using it and allowing us access to the parking garage instead of bringing the rental car around by valet, we were headed southeast toward the Atlantic and my daughter. Anna and Henry had gotten back to me and we were meeting them at their home.

I still felt like I was careening down that hill with no brakes, accelerating as I went. Not only was Peter refusing to leave my side, which was causing all sorts of emotional turmoil, but I was getting car sick. Thankfully, Sam was ever so wise and sent me with a plastic bag and crackers. It was no more than dry heaves, but unpleasant all the same.

Peter kept reaching over and stroking my hair. "Were you this sick last time?"

I shook my head. "No." My unnamed daughter was much easier on me. Anna and Henry still hadn't mentioned her name. It almost seemed as if they hadn't on purpose, so I didn't ask. All they said was they would take her out of school for half the day and rearrange their work schedules. I felt bad for the short notice, but they seemed delighted to do it when I spoke to Anna by phone to get their address and finalize plans. It was surreal to talk to her again. She had the same soothing voice and refined manners.

"Delanie?"

"Yeah." I rested my head against the window.

"We're having a baby." His tone was filled with excitement, but mostly trepidation. "Do you want to talk about that?"

I let out a long, slow breath. "I do, but not now." I could only handle so many emotions at once.

He squeezed my leg. "How about what I did to make you feel like you couldn't tell me about your daughter...or that you were taking RCIA classes?" He seemed reluctant to admit he knew about the classes through the pain that was apparent in his voice.

I wondered what else Sam had told him while I slept and how to answer that many layered and complicated question. One I feared might end it all when I finally made him acknowledge I wasn't the woman for him. I couldn't face it now. First her, then us. "Peter, I can't right now."

He removed his hand from my leg. "Of course. Just know I want to be the man you can confide in."

That's what I'd always wanted, but how could I trust that now? And did he even fully comprehend how uncomfortable that might make him at times? Is that what he truly wanted?

From there, our trip was mainly a silent affair, except the ridiculous escapades we had to go through so I could use a bathroom and not be seen. I'd never had to pee so much on a road trip in my life.

Peter played his part admirably and stopped at a small-town Walmart to buy us each a hat and sunglasses. I had to laugh at his *I'm the Life of the Party* hat. That was false advertising, but he said he grabbed the first thing he saw that didn't have a deer or beer on it. He was even sweet enough to make sure that each gas station we stopped at had clean bathrooms before I bothered going in. He reminded me of the Peter before this all blew up in our faces. But I worried now more than ever it was him putting on a brave face since he knew I was pregnant.

One worry at a time, I reminded myself. First, I had to meet my daughter. I wondered what she looked like. Was she happy? More than anything, I wanted her to be happy and loved. I wanted her to know that I loved her. That had never changed. I patted the gift I brought her in my pocket, so happy I thought of it before we'd left the hotel. It was the one good thing to come out of packing all my belongings—if not, I wouldn't have had it.

I focused on the beautiful Georgia scenery to help stave off the nausea. So many trees in an array of fall colors. Though the weather felt more like summer here in the South. The closer we got to the coast, the happier it made me. I loved sea air and I loved to know that my daughter was growing up in such a picturesque setting filled with such history.

It was no surprise that they lived in the historic district. It was perfectly charming with homes dating back to the Revolutionary War. Moss-covered trees and cobblestoned streets added to the ambience, making me feel as though I had stepped back in time. Peter and I both smiled at the horse-drawn carriages we passed by.

Perhaps I should come here to write. Though I wasn't sure even the magic of this place could inspire me. Hunter had quit speaking to me and Laine was devastated. I wanted to ease her pain. She called for me to make it better, though she wasn't sure what would help at this point. Neither was I. Not for me. Not for them. We both ached for the loves of our lives, but we both knew the reality was they might be better off without us. They could have their mothers and the quiet, obscure lives they both longed for.

Peter pulled up in front of a small but quaint two-story brick home with not one, but two verandas. The yard was neatly manicured with a swing in one of the trees and lots of bright colored flowers. Perfect for a little girl. I choked back my tears.

Peter took my hand. "Are you ready for this?"

I took a deep breath and held it for a moment. "What if she hates me?"

"Look at me."

My head obeyed. It loved nothing better than looking at him. It was painful now, not knowing what our future held.

He cupped my face in his hands. "She's going to love you."

Could he be right? I smoothed out my gypsy skirt, making my bracelets jangle. It felt so good to be me today. Peter must have liked it too. He ran his finger down the length of my tattoo. "I've missed this, but not as much as your other one."

He knew exactly how to get my pulse to race.

"We better go." My body would betray me in a second for a taste of him.

His smile said he knew. "I'll get your door."

Together we walked up the brick paved path lined with lilies to their home. I wasn't sure if I was feeling more nauseous from being pregnant or the nerves. I gripped Peter's arm to pull me along and steady me. He took the opportunity to hold me tight. He was putting up a good fight. But we had been down this road before, where he seemed to rally, only to go further down the rabbit hole the next time. Again, I would have to deal with it later. Right now, I had to meet a piece of myself.

Peter knocked on the mahogany door. Within seconds we heard footsteps. Henry opened the large door. He hadn't changed much, except his gray hair was thinner and he maybe had a few more wrinkles, but they were deeply etched laugh lines. The kind that said he had lived a good life. He still wore wire-framed glasses. Behind them hid intelligent green eyes.

"Delanie, it is so good to see you." He held out his hand, not to shake, but to hold as if he was welcoming his daughter home.

I rested my hand in his soft hand marked with age spots.

He gently tugged me into the beautiful home that had a more modern flair than the outside suggested. "This must be your husband, Peter."

I looked to Peter, who beamed as always whenever anyone used that title. "I am, sir." Peter stepped in.

"No need for formality here. Please call me Henry."

"Henry, is that them?" Anna called.

"Yes, my love."

"We're ready," she called back.

Henry patted my hand with his free hand. "We told her how much you loved tea, so she wanted to have a tea party with you," he whispered.

I could think of nothing I wanted more at the moment than to have a tea party with my daughter. "That sounds perfect. What is her name?" I asked quietly.

Henry's eyes lit up. "Come meet her and find out."

Henry kept ahold of my hand while Peter touched the small of my back as if I might need the support. Their home had hints of both Anna's and Henry's personalities. I noted the understated, plain furniture, which would match Henry, but there was no doubt it was fine furniture, which spoke of Anna. Before we could reach their enclosed patio, I paused in the hall, which was graced by several pictures of the most beautiful girl I'd ever seen. My free hand went to my mouth as I took her in from the time she was a bouncing baby with rosy cheeks to the ones where her happy smile showed that she had lost a few teeth, to one that had to be recent. She had beautiful, long dark red hair, the same color as mine. And she had my eyes. Her smile though, it was all her own.

"She's gorgeous." I touched the glass in the frame.

"That she is." Henry was obviously proud of her. "Come now. She's even prettier in person."

Peter whispered in my ear as we walked. "She looks exactly like you."

Not exactly. She had a more beautiful soul. I could already tell.

My heart pounded as we neared. I could hear her giggle. It was the most glorious sound in all the world. Before I knew it, we were on the porch. She stood in front of Anna, who had her arms around her. There was no doubt they were mother and daughter. I thought my heart might break over facing that reality but no, it made it soar. This is what I wanted for her—what I couldn't give her at the time and wasn't sure I would have ever been able to give her.

Anna was as lovely as ever, with bobbed blonde hair that would probably never gray. Her blue eyes twinkled. "Oh, dear Delanie, here you are. I have someone I would like you to meet." She adoringly looked down on her daughter. "This is Xaria."

I held my heart. Baby X. I let go of Henry's hand and walked toward the first person I ever truly loved. I knelt in front of her and stared into her beautiful porcelain face. Tears streamed down my cheeks. "It is so nice to meet you, Xaria."

She instinctively touched my face with her delicate hands painted with pink nail polish. Not a shade I would have ever worn, but it fit her so perfectly. "My name means gift of love."

I looked up into Anna's wet eyes.

"We thought it was appropriate."

My eyes went right back to my daughter's. "It is the most beautiful name I've ever heard." I couldn't help but hug her. I was so happy when her thin arms wrapped around my neck. I held my baby tight, soaking in what I could of her.

"I have something for you." I reached into my pocket, not knowing how perfect the small gift would be. It was a choker chain I had worn long ago for months after she was born. I pulled out the silver chain with the dangling X and put it in her small hand. "This is for you."

She immediately held it up. "It has my initial on it." She handed it to Anna. "Will you put it on me, Mommy?"

"Why don't you ask Delanie?"

Xaria turned back toward me and handed me the necklace. "Will you please put it on me?"

She was the politest sounding child ever. That must have come from Henry and Anna. There was no way I had passed that down, and I refused to think it had been a trait of Blair's.

"I would love to." I took the chain and clasped it around her slender neck that she got from me. "There you go."

She took ahold of the X one more time, pleased. "I made you cookies."

I smiled, though I wasn't sure how I would get them down, but I would do whatever it took. "I love cookies." Normally that was true. I stood up and Peter came to my side. "Xaria, this is my…husband, Peter." It was painful to say because I loved it so much yet wasn't sure it would always be so.

Peter noticed the hesitation and raised his brow at me, but quickly turned his attention to Xaria. "We've both been very excited to meet you." He sounded nothing but sincere. He took her little hand and bent down and kissed it. She giggled, and I wanted to kiss him for it.

"Why don't we all sit down," Henry suggested. "We know you don't have a lot of time and we are anxious to catch up with you."

Peter helped me with my seat next to my little girl at the round, white table. I hoped Anna and Henry didn't mind me thinking of her that way. It was apparent where she belonged, but there was a piece of her that would always live in me, and I hoped some of me grew in her. Maybe not the foul mouth part. She was too lovely to be vulgar.

Anna and Henry were anxious to hear about my life, but all I wanted to hear about was Xaria's. To talk to her. To touch her hair and hold her hand.

"What grade are you in now?"

"Fifth." She blushed.

"Fifth?"

"She skipped a grade." Anna smiled.

Of course she did. I knew she would be intelligent. In the womb, I could feel it as she tried to communicate with me.

"What are your favorite subjects?" I wanted to know everything about her.

Her pretty brown eyes lit up. "I love to read, but my mommy won't let me read your books yet." So she knew I was a writer.

Everyone around the table laughed.

I beamed down at Xaria. "That's a good idea."

"Would you like to see some photo albums of her?" Anna asked me.

"More than anything."

Anna jumped up to fetch my daughter's past in pictures. Meanwhile, I couldn't get over staring at her and she seemed to be just as interested in me. She reached up and touched my diamond nose stud. "Did that hurt when you got it?"

"A little bit."

Then she touched my tattoo. I was so happy she felt so comfortable around me. "That's pretty. Green is my favorite color."

"Mine too." The shade of Peter's eyes.

Anna came back carrying a few photo albums. She handed them to me but stayed standing above me so as I took in each page she could tell me the story of Xaria. The most beautiful story I'd ever heard. The one I started but let someone who could do a better job finish.

I touched her newborn photos and felt the ache of remembering her tiny body against me.

"The only way we could get her to sleep," Anna fondly remembered, "was to play her Eminem."

I looked up to Anna and smiled. "I told you."

"What?" Peter wanted to be clued in.

I turned toward him. "At night, Xaria loved to kick and turn, but when I put my headphones on my belly, she calmed down."

"We only played her the non-explicit versions." Henry wanted to make that clear.

"Who is Eminem?" Xaria asked.

Anna stroked her hair. "I think one day when you're older, Delanie will want to tell you all about him."

Did I ever, but nine was a little young to expose her to my favorite musical artist. But the thought that I could tell her made my heart sing.

I flipped through picture after picture of first steps, first days of school, first lost tooth, birthdays. I laughed and cried at all her cuteness and personality that came through—from the way she posed with her hands on her hips to the way she smiled and lit up the world.

"She reminds us a lot of her tenacious, determined birth mother." Anna gently touched my hair.

"Never met a young woman as brave as your wife," Henry said to Peter. "She took charge of her life and faced some pretty tough obstacles with courage."

Peter rested his hand on my leg. "That sounds like my wife."

"She was and is our hero," Anna added in.

The person they were talking about sounded nothing like how I felt. I felt like a coward for giving Xaria away and I was far from a hero. Heroes saved other people, and I felt at the time that maybe I was only doing it to save myself.

Henry must have read my mind. He reached across the table and took my hand. "The hardest thing I ever had to do was take Xaria out of your arms. There was no doubt what a sacrifice it was for you. You loved enough to let go. That is the greatest love of all."

My eyes swelled with tears. Is that what I was supposed to do now? Show how much I loved Peter by letting him go? Would he be happier without me, like my daughter?

Anna placed her hands on my shoulders. "You don't know the guilt we felt, but now to see you, successful and married. It does our hearts good."

Little did they know the success was ruining my marriage.

Peter applied more pressure to my leg as if he knew what I was thinking.

I turned back to Xaria. She was my focus for now. What a lovely sight she was. "Tell me about your ballet classes."

Before I knew it, we had to leave. I didn't get to hear near enough of her, but this time I knew it wasn't a forever goodbye. I would work out how to see her in the future, though my celebrity status was going to make that difficult. I privately discussed with Anna what it might mean for them if the press found out about her. It was a risk they were willing to take, but for now, while Xaria and all of us got used to this new arrangement, we would do what we could to keep it quiet. Xaria and I would video chat once a week until I could see her again.

I knelt by the door to say goodbye to her, though I had no wish to leave her. I held her tight and whispered, "I have always loved you," in her ear.

She didn't return it. I didn't expect her to. But she squeezed tighter. "Thank you for my necklace and for giving me my mommy and daddy."

Those words both lifted and broke my heart. I leaned back and peered into her eyes. "I'm so, so happy you are happy and so loved."

It's all I ever wanted for her.

Chapter Thirty-Seven

WITH HEADPHONES SECURELY in place so I didn't burn Peter's ears off, I tried to write after my emotionally and physically exhausting day of meeting my daughter and hundreds of fans. I couldn't sleep, so I didn't know what else to do. Except all I could do was stare at the box of Cocoa Pebbles and half eaten bowl of cereal on the coffee table in front of me. All reminders of Peter. He wanted to take care of me and had Fiona send someone for my favorite cereal. My go-to cereal that had seen me through six books.

I thought of how he held my hand the entire drive back as I cried and cried, both happy and sad tears. I'd hardly said a word, but he kept apologizing for denying me the opportunity to tell him about Xaria last week when I tried. He repeated some of the same sentiments as Anna and Henry, that I was a hero and giving her up for adoption was the brave thing to do. I don't think I would ever feel that way about it. Would he feel the same way about me giving him up? Maybe in the future he would look back and thank me.

I watched Peter tonight as he stood in the background and observed me interacting with my crazed fans. I wasn't sure what he was thinking, but this couldn't be the life he wanted. I hated seeing what it had done to him. To us.

My eyes focused back on my screen, frustrated I couldn't write the story. Hunter's voice was completely gone. I couldn't even make anything up. I shook my laptop. "WHY WON'T YOU TALK TO ME!"

Peter came rushing out of the bedroom, showered and in pajama bottoms. I had told him to just go to bed. It would be another late night for me. Or maybe not. I was about ready to chuck my laptop across the room.

Peter landed by my side and saved the laptop by removing it and setting it on the coffee table. He ran the back of his hand down my cheek. "Hey, there, what's wrong?"

I rubbed my hands over my face. "I can't do it. I can't finish the story. I don't think Hunter wants Laine."

Peter shook his head in disbelief. He knew better than anyone my plans for Hunter and Laine. "I think you're tired."

"I'm not tired." Anger threaded my words. Well, I was exhausted, but that had nothing to do with this.

He stood and reached down to pick me up. "It's been a long day and you need to get some rest."

"I'm fine on the couch."

He didn't listen to me and scooped me up.

Where I used to melt in his arms, I was as stiff as I could be. "I said I was fine on the couch."

Peter stood still, refusing my request but gazing intently at me. "Delanie, you are my *wife* and the mother of my child. You get the bed."

What if I didn't want to be in it alone?

He didn't give me the chance to protest. He walked me straight back and laid me on the king-sized bed covered in a paisley bedspread. His eyes took a moment to linger on me before kissing my head. "I love you." He walked right back out, turning off the lights and shutting the double doors, leaving me to stare after him in the dark.

I sank into the pillows and tried to settle myself into the comfortable bed. It was nicer than the couch, but it felt so empty. I reached over to where Peter would have...should have been? I didn't know. I didn't know anything.

I pulled the covers up only to have Peter burst through the door. "Dammit, Delanie, I can't take this anymore."

I sat up, startled. Peter had never once sworn in my presence and he looked ominous with the light shining behind him as he marched toward me. He landed on the bed so forcefully we both bounced slightly. His green eyes focused in on mine.

"You're doing that thing where you keep it all in, but I can see you, almost hear you thinking about us. Please just yell at me or tell me to go to hell; just say something."

"I can't," I cried.

"Why not?"

"Because neither of us wants to admit it or hear the truth."

He brushed my hair back. "Baby, what are you talking about?"

He was going to force my hand, but maybe it was better to say it now before it killed me inside. I looked up to the trey ceilings and that stupid crystal chandelier. "We aren't meant to be together." I let out a heavy breath along with some tears.

"Of course we aren't."

What? He agreed? I stared at him stunned.

He smiled at me as if he hadn't just crushed my soul. "Delanie, I don't know that anyone is *meant* to be together, especially not a priest and a beautiful, agnostic redhead with a mouth that would give a sailor a run for his money."

I couldn't help but give him a small smile.

He moved in closer, taking my hand and holding it against his bare chest where I could feel his strong heartbeat pounding harder than normal. "But that doesn't matter. What does, is that we chose to be together."

"Maybe we shouldn't have."

"I don't believe that for a second."

"Peter, you're miserable and you had no idea what you were getting into when you married me. I feel like I broke you and the best thing for you would be to let you go."

"Did you know what you were getting into when you married me?" he asked.

I shook my head.

"Do you know how many times I've felt guilty for bringing you into my crazy family after everything they've done to you? If it wasn't for my mom, we wouldn't be here right now. Yet you chose to stay with me."

That gave me some pause.

"You're right though—I'm miserable without you. And I'm broken, but not because of you. Because we all are in some shape or form. These last few weeks, I know I screwed up. I've reacted poorly, and I've hurt you. All things I deeply regret."

"I've hurt you too," I whispered.

"Only because I realized you didn't feel like our relationship was strong enough where you could confide in me."

"You don't know how bad I wanted to, but I was afraid you would realize sooner rather than later that we were all wrong for each other. That maybe you had made a mistake choosing me over God."

He shook his head as if I'd struck him. "Have you always felt like this?"

I nodded. "More so now." I inhaled and exhaled. "Peter, I can't live in fear thinking some story is going to come out that finally drives home to you how different we are. And I can't stand the thought that my life is killing who you are."

He took both my hands in his and kissed them. "Baby, I don't know what to say." He sat dazed for a moment. He leaned in and rested his forehead against mine. "You listen to me, Delanie Decker, I didn't choose you over God. I chose you *because* of Him. You make my life worth living. Being without you is killing me, not the other way around. Maybe we weren't meant to be, but we do belong together. You are part of me, the best part. If anyone is undeserving in this relationship, it's me."

I desperately wanted to believe him. "I don't know about that."

"I do." He gently brushed my lips. "Please forgive me. Give me time to catch up to you. Let me be the man you can tell your secrets to."

I fixed my hands on his cheeks, pressed my lips to his, and held them steady. Our mix of tears dripped down my fingers.

"I love you." He kissed me once. "I choose you." He parted my lips. "Every day." He groaned deeply, tasting me. "For the rest of my life."

I rested my head on his strong shoulder. "I love you, Peter. So much."

He held me until I melted into him. "I should let you get some rest."

"Don't go."

He didn't need me to ask him twice. He crawled under the covers with me and I found myself where I longed to be—in his arms, my head resting in its proper place, listening to the sound of his heart.

He rubbed my arms. "Let's talk about the flannel."

"What about it?"

"You look great in it, but there's a lot of it."

My fingers danced across his smooth chest. "What are you saying?"

"Only that I miss you and I brought plenty of T-shirts with me that I'm willing to share."

"How very kind of you."

"That's the kind of guy I am."

I laughed against his chest. "I'll ditch the flannel tomorrow night. This baby has me exhausted."

Peter's hand found its way past the flannel where it rested on my bare abdomen. "We're having a baby." He couldn't hide the excitement in his voice.

"I know. What are we going to do?" I had no idea how to take care of a baby.

"We'll figure it out. *Together.*"

"I like the sound of that."

"Me too." He kissed my head. "I've been thinking."

"What about?"

"If you don't want to go back to Chicago, we won't. We can move wherever you want. And I've been thinking a lot about what you said about running Sweet Feet. I think I'd like that, and I can do that from anywhere."

I snuggled in closer to him. "I think you could do a lot of good with it. As for Chicago, I'll think about it. There are some people there I really love. I want our baby to have the family I never had growing up."

"Our baby is already the luckiest kid in the world to have you as their mom."

"I don't know, Peter. Look at what I did the first time around."

He pulled me closer, making me feel safe. "Honey, Xaria is every bit as lucky as this baby." His hand caressed my abdomen. "You gave her the best you had to give at the time by loving her unselfishly. And look at her. You can take credit for that."

I wasn't sure how much credit I could take. Anna and Henry, from all that I could tell, were amazing parents, as I knew they would be. "I just don't want her to think that because I gave her up for adoption that I loved her less than our baby."

"When the time is right to tell her, we will help her see that isn't true."

My head popped up so I could see his beautiful eyes that had just become more attractive to me. "We?"

His finger glided down my cheek. "You don't mind, do you?"

"I would love nothing more." I flashed him a seductive smile. "You know, I'm suddenly not that tired and this flannel is a little too warm for my taste."

He returned my smile with a sultry one of his own. "I think I could help you out there."

"I had a feeling you could."

His lips tenderly came down on mine. He took his time, teasing them, making the anticipation of what was to come grow, but neither of us were in any hurry to get there. We knew we were in it for the long haul, so we could take our time, knowing if we did how much sweeter the reward would be.

"Delanie," Peter whispered against my lips.

"Yes," I breathed out, aching for his kiss.

"Hunter will always choose Laine."

Chapter Thirty-Eight

"I SEE THAT YOU and lover boy made up." Joan took a long sip of her Red Bull, like she needed more caffeine.

I sipped on lemon water, enjoying the reprieve of fans and cameras. Joan and I were sitting on the floor in a corner, hiding out in the room where my panel about self-publishing versus traditional publishing was going to be held in a couple of hours. Only the panelists and organizers were allowed in until thirty minutes before it began.

"How can you tell?" I asked.

She waved her hand up and down me. "Are you kidding me? You have that makeup-sex glow and there's nothing fake about your smile."

I neither confirmed nor denied but gave her a smile that said it all.

She laughed and nudged me. "It's about time. You two are good for each other."

"Yeah, we are."

"Just tell me you got some inspiration for some sexy material last night to finish your book." She wagged her brows.

I rolled my eyes at her.

"Don't think I don't know who you've based Hunter and Laine on. Their chemistry is hot, hot, hot, like some other couple I know."

"I don't know what you're talking about." I gave her a deceitful grin. "But I know how the book is supposed to end now."

"I'm assuming it will be a happy one."

"You'll just have to wait and see," I teased her.

She took another swig of her liquid caffeine. "By the way, where is lover boy this morning?"

"That's a good question. He said he had to run an errand."

"What kind?"

I shrugged my shoulders. "He wouldn't say."

"He's probably out buying a baby boutique."

"He's really cute about it all, but I don't think so. We both want to keep it to ourselves for a while." Not to say he wasn't already obsessing over it. That's all he wanted to talk about last night, well, when we weren't *making up*. He was ready to talk about names. No surprise his list came from the bible since his family had some weird obsession with choosing "Christian" names. I wasn't against it, but I told him the name had to really speak to me, so he was going to have his work cut out for him. He looked forward to the challenge.

"Good luck with that, kid."

"Keeping secrets isn't really an option anymore, is it?"

She patted my cheek. "I'm afraid not."

"Speaking of secrets, are you ever going to tell me what's going on with you and Lucas?"

She turned from me and set her drink down. "No."

"Okay. But I don't know how I can sign that contract now, not knowing if things might get ugly between my lawyer and publisher."

She whipped her head toward me. "My, my, my, Del, you are devious. I like it. Hell, I'm even proud of you, but it doesn't work on me. I'm the queen and will not be dethroned."

"That's too bad. I know how much those Upper East Side townhomes go for."

Her eyes narrowed. "You aren't my only client, kid."

"But I'm your favorite."

Her face softened uncharacteristically. "You're more than a client to me, Del."

I wasn't expecting that from her at all. I took her hand. "I'm here for you."

She squeezed my hand with her razor-sharp red nails. "You're a good kid. You make me wish I'd had one."

"With Lucas?"

She let out a heavy sigh while staring out into the empty rows of chairs. "Yes."

"So why didn't you?"

She thought for a moment. "He had his life all mapped out and I was a detour he didn't expect. And every time I thought I would be his final destination, he had one more career achievement he had to reach before he wanted to settle down. First it was partner, then he made partner and the ring I expected never came. Next it was starting his own firm. The list continued, and each time he gave me the excuse that he was only doing it for our future. But the future always became the past and I always took a backseat. And as you know, I like to do the driving, so I left him in the dust."

"And now?"

She shook herself out of her melancholy. "And now what?"

"He obviously wishes things were different."

"It's too late. He had his chance."

I pulled down her turtleneck to see Lucas's handiwork. "Are you sure about that?"

She batted away my hand. "I'm not going down the same road with him again only to be left on the curbside."

"So why don't you drive this time and take the fast lane on the highway?"

"That's a good line, kid; you can use it in a book. But this is real life."

I took her hand back. "Yes, it is, so why waste it being apart from the person you...love?"

She leaned back. "I didn't say I was in love with him."

"You didn't have to."

"You know, you're a brat, kid."

I rested my head on her shoulder and laughed.

She kissed the top of my head. "You better sign that damn contract now."

"We'll see." Peter and I had yet to discuss it in detail.

My Peter was gone for quite a while and refused to tell me where he'd been. Not like I was worried. He was the kind of guy that felt uncomfortable walking into a bar. He was also being overly attentive, but I knew that was because we were still in the making-up phase, which we had never really had to do, but we were finding out how much fun it was. That, and he really dug my vampy ballgown. As in, he couldn't keep his hands off me and I finally had to wear my hair down because his fingers were very busy. Not that I didn't want to accost him in his dark suit and tie, but I had to make my appearance to keep more articles from being written speculating why I fainted. No, I wasn't in rehab for my nonexistent alcohol addiction, thank you very much.

He settled for making out in the elevator on our way down to the Sweet and Sexy Ball, until other people decided they needed to get on. It was still weird to see how happy people were when they were in my presence, like it was an honor. I gave them their money's worth by smiling and making sure my hand landed on Peter's butt when we exited the elevator. Peter blushed, but all our fellow elevator patrons laughed. It's how I had to cope with fame. I had to be myself. And I really liked my husband's butt, especially in his suit.

Peter and I walked hand in hand into the over-the-top ball complete with a balloon archway, disco lights, and a million rhinestones. Someone apparently was bedazzler happy. I imagined this was what prom looked like. I wouldn't know, as I protested it due to the dress code for girls while there was none for boys.

Upon entering, I was immediately swooped up by the publicist. "Oh great, you're here. We need you to come have your picture taken with Hunter Black."

His name wasn't Hunter, it was Ralph, which for some reason always made me laugh in my head. Probably because the model looked nothing like a Ralph. He looked more like a Jax or a Nick. No matter his name, there was already a crowd of women pawing and purring at him. They could have the model. The real Hunter was with me.

Ralph wasn't the only cover model there. At least he wasn't a Fabio wannabe like some of the other ones. Not like the women there cared—each of the models were being fawned over. It was embarrassing. You would have thought this was a Chippendales event. There was actual money being shoved down these men's pants. The models didn't seem to mind.

Poor Peter stood by with his eyes wide and glazed over like he'd entered Satan's realm.

I did my part by taking picture after picture with Ralph. Then it was time for me to sit at LH Ink's large booth—with my picture in the sexy sweater taken by Simon displayed prominently—and sign books until my hand cramped, and take pictures with fans until my face permanently froze. Did I mention I was still nauseous and sucking on ginger drops? Though I did feel better now with Peter by my side. He was relatively happy, or at least dealing with all the attention. For most of the night, he stood behind me in the background, diligently watching over me and making sure I had lemon water to drink and bathroom breaks. For something the size of a pea, the baby sure put some pressure on my bladder.

Toward the end of the evening, Peter surprised me. He had gotten in the book signing line. When he showed up in front of me I tilted my head, confused. "Do you want a signed copy?" I teased.

He shook his head no in this slow, alluring way. It was enough to make some butterflies take flight.

"What do you want, then?"

He held out his hand just as our ridiculous song began to play. We really needed to come up with something besides "Rock With You."

"Dance with me."

"Here?"

He nodded.

"In front of everyone?" We had never danced in public. There was a reason for that. Peter didn't dance well, and I mainly didn't as a matter of principle.

He wasn't taking no for answer. "Dance with me, Delanie."

All the fans in line cheered him on by their oohing and aahing.

I didn't need the cheering section; my hand went right into his, almost of its own accord. He helped me around the table in front of hundreds of onlookers. I wasn't sure why Peter was purposely drawing all this attention to us, but his only focus was me. He led us right out to the middle of the dance floor. Everyone on it parted and made way for us, snapping pictures and doing more of that annoying oohing and aahing. All things Peter wouldn't be comfortable with, but he acted like it didn't affect him. I caught a glimpse of Joan and Lucas, who were holding hands and smiling at us on the edge of the dance floor. They had been MIA for the night.

Once Peter took me in his arms and held me close, swaying off beat per his usual, everyone around us faded out of the picture. My arms fell around his neck while my eyes questioned what we were doing. What he was doing.

"The Queen of Romance has found her King," the DJ announced before turning up the music.

I refrained from rolling my eyes.

Peter slid his hand down my back and whispered in my ear, "I love you."

"I love you, too." I smiled. "What has gotten into you tonight?"

His picturesque eyes burned as they gazed into mine. "You. Always you."

My pulse and senses quickened. "Keep talking like that and I'm going to give everyone a bigger show."

"I've already taken care of that."

What? I was both extremely turned on and perhaps a tad worried what he meant by that.

Peter let me go only to drop to one knee in front of me. The music stopped playing and everyone around us crowded in. More flashes went off than a disco ball. This was not in the script.

I stared down at him, feeling self-conscious. "What are you doing?"

He took my left hand while he adoringly looked up at me. "I wanted to do something to show you that this life with you is what I want."

"I think you made your point."

"Not yet."

There was more?

He reached into his pocket with his free hand and pulled out a red velvet box.

"Peter?"

"I've always regretted that I didn't propose to you in some romantic way. I know you don't care about those sorts of gestures, but I do. You deserved at least that." He opened the red box that held a unique yet stunning filigree gold band with leaves that reminded me of my tattoo. The perfect ring for me.

He took the ring out and placed it on my left ring finger. He held my hand after, still holding my gaze. "I choose you, Delanie Decker. Wherever you are, that's where I belong. Please choose me."

My family didn't wait for me on the moon. My family was right in front of me. Peter was where I belonged.

"Forever."

Chapter Thirty-Nine

ITH HER TRUCK in his view, the knot in his chest loosened. It had only taken him begging her sister for information about where she'd run off to and driving hundreds of miles all night long into the heart of Idaho to find her, but he couldn't rest until he begged her to forgive him and told her how he felt. This time while she was conscious. After twenty years and all that had passed between them, he wasn't sure there was a chance in hell she would ever be his now, but the stubborn woman was like air to him and he was suffocating without her. He'd been a damned fool and he was kicking himself for all the lost time.

He pulled his truck next to hers in the cemetery parking lot nestled into the hills of Sun Valley. The sun was barely a glimmer over the horizon. Not another soul stirred around him, but he could feel Laine's in the vicinity. It called to him, but it came with a warning to approach at his own risk. He would risk whatever it took to be with her.

He walked on the grass between gravestones, hoping not to alert her by the stomp of his boots on the asphalt paths. Why had she kept the baby a secret from him, he kept asking himself as he put one deliberate foot in front of *another, trying not to crunch the leaves that had barely begun to fall beneath his feet. His breath played in the cool autumn air.*

In the distance, she came into view. There she knelt in front of a head-stone. Her head was down and that beautiful dark mane of hers fell around her. He stopped for a moment to take her in. How he had resisted her this long, he had no idea. Not even their friendship seemed like a good excuse now. He would gamble it all to have her, even if it meant losing every part of her.

A leaf crunched underneath his boots.

Laine reached back under her jacket for the weapon she always con-cealed there.

"Don't shoot," Hunter called out.

Her beautiful mane shook before she released her gun. "You should know better than to sneak up on me, Hunter."

Cautiously, he approached. "My life is in your hands."

"I don't want it." In the crack of her voice, he heard the lie. "How did you find me?"

He knelt next to her instead of answering. His eyes fell first on the head-stone of her grandmother, Sharon McCleary. In the shadow of the large stone stood an obscure, tiny one with a name that made his heart stop. Hunter Cavanaugh.

"You named him after me," he stuttered, hardly able to say it.

"Yes." The tears poured down her face.

"Why?"

"Because all I could do was give his lifeless body a name, and I wanted him to have the best."

He rested his strong hand on her delicate yet muscular shoulder. "Why didn't you tell me about him?"

She shrugged off his touch. "Why don't you ask your mother since she seems to know so much about it?"

"To hell with my mother. I want to hear the truth from you."

"You want the truth?" She shook where she knelt, fixed on her son's name. "You didn't seem to be so keen on the truth when your mother was feeding you lies about me. You ate them up like a starving man."

Hunter sank farther to the ground. "Laine, I'm sorry. I didn't want to believe that the man I'd wanted to be like for all my life was the worst sort of scoundrel."

"What about me? After everything we'd been through, you so easily believed the worst."

He hung his head in shame. "Laine, you've kept your secrets and I've let you, even though I wanted nothing more than for you to let me in. Those secrets planted seeds of doubt. I'm sorry."

She squared her shoulders. "Fine, you want to know my secrets? Well, get ready, because they're not pretty."

For a second, Hunter wasn't sure he wanted to know, but he'd waited so long for her to open up to him that he'd hear whatever she was willing to say.

Her breath swirled in the cool air around them as she built up the courage to say what she'd been keeping in for the last eighteen years. "My entire life I've been defined by the side of the tracks I grew up on and for my looks. Not even my parents could see past my face. I wasn't anything but an object to anyone until you saw me for who I really was and who I wanted to be. But even you knew our circumstances made it impossible for us to be anything but friends. Even that was difficult. We tried though, didn't we?"

Hunter nodded.

"Even when you went off to get your fancy Ivy League degree and I stayed home trying to save up money just to attend the community college. But while you were gone, someone else took notice of me. Clayson Giles."

Hunter's fists clenched thinking about the man old enough to be her father. The wealthy cattleman who had a penchant for young women and skirting the law.

"I did my best to put him off, but my parents were in favor of the connection and all but hand delivered me to him."

A sudden violent illness washed over him. He didn't want her to say another word for fear he would find Clayson and kill him with his bare hands. He couldn't stand the thought that he hadn't protected her.

"He took what wasn't his."

"Damn him." Hunter jumped up, ready to act on his previous fear. He paced around before falling right back next to her. "Laine," he cried while attempting to hold her hand.

She brushed him away. "Don't feel sorry for me."

"Why didn't you go to the police?"

"How could I?" Her laugh bordered on maniacal. "He had most of them in his back pocket. Even today, most of them turn a blind eye to him. It's why I joined the force. I vowed to take him down, but his pockets and influence run deep."

"Was the baby his?"

Laine swallowed and nodded. "When I found out I was pregnant, I swore I wouldn't let him have my child or me ever again. I ran here to my grandmother's. She was the only person I could trust. She helped me save up to move to Colorado. I got a scholarship there at a junior college, but then the baby came early." The tears poured out of her. "He was stillborn, but perfect."

He took her hand and this time she didn't brush him away. "Why didn't you tell me? I would have helped you."

"Hunter, you were happy living your life. You were on your way and dating Aspen. Your mom had plans for the both of you. I didn't want to get in the way. And for a long time, I was ashamed. I thought maybe it had been my fault."

"Don't you dare think that."

"I don't anymore, but I also didn't want to give your mother any more ammo against me." She let the rising sun shine on her face. She soaked up its energy. "Now you know my secret. Go back to your life, Hunter. You won't find me there anymore." She wiped her eyes and stood, ready to run away from him as she always did.

This time, though, he wasn't going to let her get away. He was up and holding onto her before she knew what happened.

"Let go of me, Hunter."

"Not this time. Not ever"

He had forgotten how strong she was when she elbowed him in the ribs. The pain she inflicted about dropped him to his knees, but despite that he desperately held onto her.

"Laine," he groaned. "Please listen to me."

"Give me one good reason to."

He turned her toward him. His blue-as-the-sky eyes watered from the pain and the thought that he might lose her. It was enough to make her pause and listen.

He brushed back her hair, longing to do so much more. "I love you, Laine."

"Don't do this to me now." She made a half-hearted attempt to pull away from his grasp.

He drew her closer like he had on the one night they'd had together in his cabin, stranded in a storm. Her body melded into his perfectly as if she'd been molded there. "Laine, listen to me. I've loved you since the moment you bested me running the mile in gym our junior year."

He earned a smirk.

"I know I've been a fool and I've hurt you, but I don't want to live my life without you. And I don't want to only be your friend." He tipped her chin up and pressed his cold lips to hers. His lips instantly seared when she didn't pull away. He'd only had a taste of her once before; this time, he would make sure it wasn't his last. "Marry me, Laine. Have babies with me. Lots and lots and lots of them."

She faltered, as if she couldn't believe what she was hearing.

He held her steady, vowing to never let her fall. "I'm not complete without you, Laine."

She fell against him, wetting his flannel shirt with her tears.

"Is that a yes?"

"Yes."

Phew. I set my laptop down next to me on the couch and took my headphones out, shedding my own tears. I couldn't believe they were finally together. I could hear Laine and Hunter thanking me and telling me it was about time.

Peter peeked around the corner. "Did you finish?"

I'd banished him to the upstairs of the house. I couldn't concentrate while he hovered over me like a mother hen. I loved that he wanted to take care of me, but the first draft was due tomorrow and I was down to the wire. Chad and Joan had been assaulting me with texts reminding me.

I wiped my tears through my smile. "Pretty much. I just have the hot and heavy honeymoon scene on the lake to write. Thank you for the inspiration for that, by the way."

He landed next to me on the couch. "My pleasure. Do you need a refresher, maybe some pointers?" He nuzzled my neck, his hand already under my shirt.

"I thought your dad was dropping by soon." He wanted to bring us a baby gift. I hadn't even been to my first doctor appointment yet. Dad was ecstatic when we told him by phone in Atlanta. There was no use trying to keep it from him. Sam, of course, knew, and she had told Avery, so we figured we might as well tell Dad. We were still trying to keep it from the press, but we knew it would be a losing battle.

"He is." He groaned, disappointed. His hand fell away from my warm skin. "Rain check?"

"Definitely." I propped my legs up on his lap. "It feels so good to finally have them together. I thought it was never going to happen. But I'm sad it's over. Laine and Hunter are riding off into the sunset without me."

Peter rubbed my legs, clad in his favorite flannel. I should have gotten some flannel pajama pants a long time ago. They weren't ideal for sleeping or other nighttime activities, but for writing, they were perfect.

"Hunter and Laine will always be a part of you. A part of us." He grinned.

"True."

"Have you decided what book you're going to write next?"

I leaned my head to the side and rested it on the couch cushion. "Not yet. I still can't believe I signed that contract. What was I thinking?"

"That it buys a lot of shoes and clean water. And you know you were never going to be satisfied walking away right now."

"You're right." I yawned. This baby zapped the energy out of me.

The doorbell rang before I could close my eyes.

"I'll get it." Peter gently removed my legs from him.

I sat up, eager to receive our guest. We hadn't had the chance to see him since we'd gotten home a few days ago from the whirlwind book tour. It felt good to be home, and for the first time, it truly felt like home. There was nothing between Peter and me, and it made all the difference.

I heard Peter open the door, then I heard, "Dad, Mom."

Mom? No. No. No. She wasn't welcome in this house.

"What are you doing here?" Peter asked coolly.

"Please," she begged. "I need to talk to you and Delanie."

She most certainly did not.

"I don't think that's a good idea." I heard Peter's heart break in there.

Oh, crap. I reluctantly got up to the sounds of his mother's pleas. When they came into my view, I could see Joseph behind her, not saying a word. It was as if he was saying, I got you this far, you're on your own to get in.

Joseph caught my eye and immediately barged past his wife and Peter to get to me. In his hands he held a brand-new football. He swore the baby would be a boy. The Decker men for the last five generations had a boy first.

Dad put his arms around me and gave me a gentle squeeze. "How are you feeling, honey?"

"Tired, a little pukey, but good."

We had an audience. Sarah stood outside the door with tears welling in her eyes and a downtrodden expression. With defeat, she turned to go. I could tell Peter ached to reach out to her, but he couldn't and wouldn't. I loved him for it because I knew it was because of me. But because I loved him, I couldn't let him.

"Sarah."

Everyone looked at me, waiting to see what would happen as if I was lulling her into a trap. Which wasn't a bad idea, but I was too tired to clean up the mess. And I didn't feel right asking Peter to clean up the metaphorical blood that I would like to shed.

"Come in." That left a bad taste in my mouth.

"Delanie, honey?" Peter was confused.

So was I. Love does weird things to you. "Let's hear what she has to say." I dared Sarah with my eyes. I thought that might scare her away, but she sniffled a few times and crossed the threshold with trepidation. She seemed to have aged ten years since I'd seen her back in August. Her pale blue eyes were almost translucent now, and she'd lost weight, making her skin sag more and wrinkle. Even her hair hung limp.

Peter shut the door behind her. "We can all sit in the family room." He came right to my side and put his arm around me. "Are you sure about this?" he whispered in my ear.

"Not at all." But it was too late now.

Peter sat on our comfy chair and pulled me on his lap. His parents took the couch but kept a person's distance between them.

At first it was a staring contest. Or more like look anywhere but at each other. While we waited for his mom to speak, Peter played with my wedding ring by twisting it. He now wore one too. I'd found this great flea market while we were in Seattle that had a vintage silver ring that was made to look like tree branches, and since Peter was still against tattooing my name around his finger and wearing rings meant so much to him, I got it for him.

Sarah took so long to speak that Joseph started tossing the football in the air and catching it. We were taking uncomfortable silence to new heights. Finally, Sarah shifted and grabbed some tissues from her purse. She blew her nose and sniffled a few more times before she could speak.

"I know you hate me." Sarah's eyes pleaded for us to contradict her.

Neither Peter nor I spoke, but he squeezed my hand. I hated that this was killing him more.

When the contradiction didn't come, she nodded. "I deserve it. I know you won't believe this, but I'm sorry. I never meant for those pictures to go online."

I wasn't sure I believed her. "The problem is that you felt the need to have them taken in the first place. Why is that?"

She met my eyes, and for the first time, I could see remorse in hers, not her usual I-don't-care-what-you-think look she had always given me in the past. Her entire body seemed to fall in defeat.

"Delanie, I'm jealous of you. You took my son away from me. Ever since you came into the picture, he no longer cares what I think." She looked at Peter. "You didn't even call me to tell me that you were thinking about leaving the priesthood or that you wanted to get married. You used to tell me everything. Then you showed up one day with a wife and suddenly I didn't exist anymore for you." A flood of tears streamed down her face.

Peter sat up and placed his arms around me. "Ma, that's not true. I didn't discuss my decisions with you because I knew you would disapprove, and I was confused enough at the time. I knew it had to be between me and God. You're right, I should have told you I was getting married, but I wanted Delanie to myself. I'd never been in love before. Never thought I would be. It overwhelmed me in the best way possible and I'm sorry if you took that as I didn't care about you. I was only in love." He kissed my cheek. "And it was apparent from the very first meeting you were determined to not like her. You didn't even try to get to know her; instead, you made every visit uncomfortable for us. After that, why would you think I would want to tell you anything?"

She closed her eyes and sighed. "I know."

"Do you really, Ma?" Peter asked. Pleaded.

She opened her eyes and stared directly into Peter's. "I do, son. I'm sorry. I want to be better. I want to be part of," she looked between the two us, "both your lives. Of my grandbaby's life."

Joseph scooted closer to his wife and slowly put his arm around her. At first it was stiff, but as soon as it relaxed, she turned into him and wailed. Joseph pulled her closer and held her. Between her sobs, all she kept saying was, "I'm sorry. I'm sorry."

I wasn't sure if I believed her, having been fooled by her before, but I found that even if it wasn't true, I didn't mind all that much because I knew where my place was now. I sank back into my husband, right where I belonged.

Epilogue

Nine Months Later

"Jonah." Sarah bounced him in her arms and cooed at our son during Sunday dinner. He was all she had eyes for.

Jonah. I smiled to myself thinking about his name and Peter's chart of all the bible names and their meanings. He campaigned hard for Jonah, which meant dove and represented peace. Looking at Sarah holding our son made me think we had chosen well. Jonah had not only brought peace to our family, but to me personally. I no longer wondered what kind of mother I would be. I knew now I was a fierce one. My every thought had him in it. My love for him was amazing and overwhelming all at the same time. It was like loving his father. And to watch Peter love him only made my love grow for both.

Jonah stretched his tiny six-week-old body and everyone at the table reacted as if it was the most adorable thing they had ever seen, even my nephews. He was the cutest baby boy to grace the planet with his red hair that had a life its own, sticking up in random places on his head, and Peter's green eyes.

"He's gained some weight since last week," Sarah commented without taking her eyes off him.

I would think so. I felt like I constantly nursed him. That wasn't a complaint, but I had no idea something so little could eat so much.

"Let me hold him, Ma." Sam held her arms out waiting, while Reed took the opportunity to rub his own baby—due in two months, right in the heart of football season. Sam wasn't thrilled about the timing, but she was more than excited to be having a little girl, even if she thought she was too old to have a baby. Her posts about being pregnant in her forties were hilarious as she delighted her readers with tales of hemorrhoids, heartburn, swollen boobs, and her desire for more sex.

Sarah reluctantly gave him up, but not before smothering him in kisses. I hated to admit it sometimes, but she was all I hoped a grand-mother would be for our baby. I had to remind myself often that she was trying, and she had changed. No longer did she scowl at me, instead she smiled. She even offered to help teach me to cook. I hadn't taken her up on it yet, but I had feeling I should, for the sake of Jonah, at least.

Avery looked longingly at Jonah, and as happy as she was for us, I think the new additions acutely reminded her that Hannah wasn't here. James too had become more melancholy the last few months; his phone now was more of a focus than the people around him. Peter and I wished we knew what to do to help, but neither were willing to talk.

Avery put on a brave front and smiled. "When is Xaria coming again?"

I smiled, thinking of my daughter and son finally meeting. "She'll arrive next week with Henry and Anna."

"She must be excited." Avery was keeping up her act.

"She is. She plans to teach him how to read when she gets here."

Everyone laughed. But she was so smart, I wouldn't put it past her abilities. I just wanted her in my arms once more. I hadn't seen her since spring break when we finally told the world about her. On my own terms, I posted about her with her parents' permission. It was a one-time deal with no other comment from me. The press had been relentlessly trying to find out who her birth father was, but the records were sealed, and Blair had never come forward. It was the only decent thing he had ever done for me, for her.

"They are all invited here for dinner next week," Joseph added in.

Peter put his arm around me. "That would be great, Dad."

Mimsy, in her usual fashion, started handing out money to the grandsons, including ours. She handed a ten-dollar bill to me. "This is for Jonah; don't you go spending it."

Instead of rolling my eyes, I took the money graciously. "Thank you. I'll put it in his account." I called it the Mimsy account. I felt bad taking her money, but she would never take it back. At least she wasn't giving it to felons anymore. Her *boyfriend* was now serving time, though to Dad's dismay, she was still living with them.

"How's your new book coming?" Sam asked while gazing at my son with a huge smile.

"I've hardly had a moment to work on it since he's been born. Night-time is party time for him."

"Are you keeping your mommy up?" Sam asked Jonah in a sing-song voice. "I need to know what happens to Jules and Maxwell. I can't believe you left them stranded at the Cape of Good Hope in the last book."

"Speaking of your book." Peter pulled out his phone with a mischievous grin. "Let's check to see where *Belonging* ended up this week."

I covered my eyes. "I can't look."

"Why? It was so good. Maybe even better than *Black Confessions*," Avery reluctantly admitted.

"Honestly," Sam chimed in. "My ice maker is broken again, thanks to you. Maxwell's English accent and manners are hot."

"Mom. Disgusting." Cody jumped up and fled, along with Jimmy and Matt.

I peeked at Peter, who was staring at his phone with a solemn expression. He stood up without saying a word, making me more nervous. He put his phone in his pocket and picked up our son. I was honestly surprised he hadn't taken him back earlier. Peter, like me, was addicted to holding him. He kissed our baby's head. "I think you better give your mommy the news."

I knew it. I knew it wouldn't live up to Hunter Black even though the words seemed to flow right out of me. Like the love that was growing inside me somehow manifested itself on the pages. Joan and Chad had even thought it was my best work, but I guess it didn't translate to my fans. I was a little surprised, since pre-sale numbers were good, and it had received some amazing reviews from the big names in the industry. No reviews from Grace, though, who had oddly disappeared. I evil-laughed in my head thinking about it. Joan had even mentioned how pleased her *fiancé* was over the projected sales this week.

Peter was back by my side as we all waited on bated breath. He placed our son in my arms and suddenly I didn't care if *Belongings* was the worst selling book in the history of books. I knew where we all belonged, and that's all that mattered.

Peter rested his phone on Jonah and I swore my son smiled, and not from gas. Peter stroked Jonah's baby soft head. "Tell her, son. Tell your mommy she's number one again."

I looked up and met Peter's eyes. "Are you serious?"

He pressed his lips against mine. "Congratulations, baby."

Before I could comprehend it all, the strangest thing happened.

"I'm proud of you, Delanie," rang through the table from the most unexpected voice.

Every head turned toward Sarah, but only she and I connected.

"I loved the book," she said simply.

"Thank you."

Sarah said not another word on that subject but stood. "Who wants dessert?"

I'm not sure how everyone around me answered that question; I was in shock.

Peter kissed my head and whispered, "See, I told you she would love you."

"You never mentioned it would take five years."

He gave me a heart-melting smile. "I never said it wouldn't."

SNEAK PEEK

THE DEAR WIFE

More Than a Wife Series — Book Three
Coming Soon(ish)

DEAR AVERY,
I LOVE YOU.
JAMES

About the Author

JENNIFER PEEL IS the award-winning, bestselling author of the Dating by Design and Women of Merryton series, as well as several other contemporary romances. Though she lives and breathes writing, her first love is her family. She is the mother of three amazing kiddos and has recently added the title of mother-in-law, with the addition of two terrific sons-in-law. She's been married to her best friend and partner in crime for a lot longer than seems possible. Some of her favorite things are late-night talks, beach vacations, the mountains, pink bubble gum ice cream, tours of model homes, and Southern living. She can frequently be found with her laptop on, fingers typing away, indulging in chocolate milk, and writing out the stories that are constantly swirling through her head.

If you enjoyed this book, please rate and review it on
Amazon & Goodreads

You can also connect with Jennifer on
Facebook & Twitter (@jpeel_author)

Other books by Jennifer Peel:

Other Side of the Wall

The Girl in Seat 24B

Professional Boundaries

House Divided

Trouble in Loveland

More Trouble in Loveland

How to Get Over Your Ex in Ninety Days

Paige's Turn

Hit and Run Love: A Magnolia and Moonshine Novella

Sweet Regrets

Honeymoon for One in Christmas Falls

The Women of Merryton Series:

Jessie Belle — Book One

Taylor Lynne — Book Two

Rachel Laine — Book Three

Cheyenne — Book Four

The Dating by Design Series:

His Personal Relationship Manager — Book One

Statistically Improbable — Book Two

Narcissistic Tendencies —Book Three

The Piano and Promises Series:
Christopher and Jaime—Book One
Beck and Call—Book Two
Cole and Jillian—Book Three

More Than a Wife Series
The Sidelined Wife — Book One
The Secretive Wife — Book Two
The Dear Wife — Book Three (Coming Soon)

A Clairborne Family Novel Series
Second Chance in Paradise
New Beginnings in Paradise — Coming Soon
First Love in Paradise — Coming Soon
Return to Paradise — coming Soon

To learn more about Jennifer and her books, visit her website at
www.jenniferpeel.com.

Made in the USA
Columbia, SC
24 February 2021